"THE JURY IS IN AND THE VERDICT IS UNANIMOUS—*SHOW NO FEAR* IS THE HOTTEST LEGAL THRILLER OF THE YEAR."
—Brad Thor, #1 *New York Times* bestselling author

"O'Shaughnessy knows how to spin a diverting tale."
—*San Diego Union-Tribune*

"O'Shaughnessy treats fans to the backstory of a popular character, which acts as a good starting point for those new to the series, too. Nina's balancing act and independent streak make her an admirable heroine."
—*Library Journal*

"Engaging characters, intriguing plot."
—*Booklist*

"The novel shows a remarkable uniqueness . . . interweaving a believable plot and providing a surprise ending. Highly recommended."
—*I Love A Mystery*

"O'Shaughnessy is in fine form."
—*Lansing State Journal*

"Fascinating. . . . Nina Reilly fans will enjoy meeting her younger self."
—*Freshfiction.com*

Also available from Simon & Schuster Audio and as an eBook.

OBSTRUCTION OF JUSTICE

"Nina Reilly is one of the most interesting heroines in legal thrillers today."

—*San Jose Mercury News*

BREACH OF PROMISE

"Lots of unexpected twists and turns. . . . A savvy legal thriller."

—*The Orlando Sentinel*

MOTION TO SUPRESS

"Fascinating, compelling."

—*The Hartford Courant*

Also by Perri O'Shaughnessy

PERRI
O'SHAUGHNESSY

SHOW
NO FEAR

POCKET STAR BOOKS
New York   London   Toronto   Sydney

Pocket Star Books
A Division of Simon & Schuster, Inc.
1230 Avenue of the Americas
New York, NY 10020

This book is a work of fiction. Names, characters, places, and incidents either are products of the author's imagination or are used fictitiously. Any resemblance to actual events or locales or persons, living or dead, is entirely coincidental.

First Pocket Star Books paperback edition November 2009

POCKET STAR and colophon are registered trademarks of Simon & Schuster, Inc.

For information about special discounts for bulk purchases, please contact Simon & Schuster Special Sales at 1-866-506-1949 or business@simonandschuster.com

The Simon & Schuster Speakers Bureau can bring authors to your live event. For more information or to book an event, contact the Simon & Schuster Speakers Bureau at 1-866-248-3049 or visit our website at www.simonspeakers.com

Cover design by Lisa Litwack. Photograph © Getty Images/ David Epperson. Stepback photo © Getty Images/Christoph Martin.

Manufactured in the United States of America

10 9 8 7 6 5 4 3 2 1

ISBN 978-1-4165-4867-6

Dedicated to Nancy Yost and Maggie Crawford,
with our deep appreciation

SHOW NO FEAR

PROLOGUE

Monday, November 26, 1990, 3:45 p.m.

I NEEDED TO TAKE CONTROL OF A DANGEROUS, TUM-
bling situation. She presented the worst threat I have
ever experienced.

I waited for her to return to the run-down little cottage where she lived. Her old car struggled up the hill.
While she parked, awkwardly, too far from the curb, I
assumed a bland expression, getting out of the big white
rental car to approach her. She turned around, arms full
of groceries, her strangely impassive face pale.

"Why are you here?" Her voice sounded interested,
although I heard an underlying suspicion.

I couldn't answer, naturally. All hell would certainly
break loose on this quiet street, so I lied, trying to keep
that exterior calm of hers going long enough for me to
get her into the car. Ideally, I could somehow convince

her to come along with me, but she was too smart, onto me somehow, spooked but not sure.

She jabbed her key in the lock with her right hand. "I'll just drop my groceries inside." And drop them she did. Glass shattered, and some clear liquid pooled on the worn wooden floor. She tried to close the door in my face, but she's relatively feeble and I'm not. I shoved my way in behind her.

I showed her the gun. "We're going for a ride. There are things we need to discuss. No need to get worked up."

She eyed the phone, asked to make a phone call. I felt the urge to laugh.

"I'm a mother," she said. Her otherwise clear eyes clouded.

But I knew for a fact nobody needed her at home that afternoon. "Out the door," I said. "Now."

She had guts. She definitely caught me off guard, taking off like a young and nimble runner, dashing for the kitchen. By the time I overcame my surprise at her ability to move so fast and followed her, she held a big butcher knife. "Get out of my house!"

I could shoot her right then and there, but I had a better plan. If she was going to make things harder for me, I'd make things harder for her. I stepped straight toward her, slapped the knife away with the butt of my gun, slapped her face, not too hard, just letting her know where we stood, and watched her wince at the pain.

She locked up carefully. We walked down the steps, me following her, gun hidden but present. She climbed into the car without another word.

We drove in silence past Carmel on Highway 1. I

kept one hand on the wheel, the other on my gun. The only sign of her fear was the way her hand gripped the dash as we took the curves. I glanced sideways at her, watching her look out the car window to her right. Carmel Highlands lay behind us now, and she scanned the gray sea off Garrapata Beach.

"I didn't think my life could get any worse. Just goes to show."

"Keep quiet."

"Are you going to shoot me?"

I didn't bother to answer.

"Where are you taking me? At least tell me that."

"To a beautiful place."

Just then we swung around a sharp curve. Bixby Creek Bridge lay ahead of us. I saw the scenic turnoff on the cliffside where tourists stop and admire the view of the old Depression-era bridge between two cliffs. It's steep by the turnoff, several hundred feet, a vertiginous drop to a confluence of Bixby Creek and the Pacific Ocean.

I pulled over and stopped the car.

A stiff wind harassed the low brush on the hillside on the other side of the road. The ocean glittered far out and I could see cloud shadows racing down from the north. The hairs on my skin stood up like tiny needles, irritated by the weather. I waited for a good long break in the occasional line of cars.

"Get out."

"No." She stared straight ahead.

"Get the fuck out!"

Slowly, laboriously, she took her seat belt off, adjusted the strap of her bag on her shoulder, and buttoned her jacket. She emerged too slowly, blinking in the cold breeze. I took her arm and led her the few feet to the edge.

We both looked out into the radiation from the horizon and down across the solid ocean flecked with whitecaps. She opened her mouth to shout something into the wind.

A wayward sports car passed, swerving along the curve. I ducked behind the car so that anyone in that car would see only one person. She had no chance against me. She stood about three feet in front of me, right at the edge. I found her back insulting. She had no right to hide the mortal fear she must be feeling.

I rushed at her, hitting her with my shoulder like a linebacker, with a whump, hard. She toppled away while I caught myself, fell to my knees.

She disappeared.

Her last shriek, animalistic, harsh, and loud, startled me. But she had time only for that one final sound, heard only by the two of us, muffled by the sound of distant surf. I jumped back into the car and turned around and headed north again. A semi roared south as I rounded a turn and I almost sideswiped him in my excitement. For the rest of the way, I made an effort to drive extremely carefully, hugging the mountain side of the road.

Yes, first, this fast breathing, this feeling that I had been very close to the edge myself.

Then—I don't know. Some glee. Ruefulness. Regret, I guess.

And finally—relief. The worst was over.

CHAPTER
1

September 20, 1990

THE LAW OFFICES OF POHLMANN, MCINTYRE, Sorensen and Frost surrounded a courtyard in a low, white-painted adobe building in the town of Carmel-by-the-Sea, California. Lush flower bushes, pines, and succulents bedecked the hilly front yard where steps led to the main door. In the bright sun of mid-September the building looked overexposed, bleached like the sand on the beach at the foot of Ocean Avenue. Now, at ten in the morning, streams of Lexuses and Infinitis already cruised this side street, hungry for parking spaces.

Nina Reilly grabbed a pile of mail on the receptionist's desk. She had worked as a paralegal at the law firm for the past year, having snagged this coveted job simply by submitting a résumé. Her mother called it Irish luck, but Nina suspected it had more to do with another Irish character trait. Her father, Harlan, knew Klaus Pohlmann because he hobnobbed with everyone, but he would never confess to having pulled strings with Klaus.

Nearing eighty, Klaus was a legend in the community, the most daring and successful lefty lawyer south of San Francisco. He only hired the best, and that included Jack McIntyre, Nina's latest crush. Jack was over at the Monterey County Superior Court at a settlement conference.

Nina called out to the receptionist, "Back in an hour, Astrid. I promise."

Hurrying down the walk, she caught her sandal on the edge of the stone steps and stopped herself from falling by dropping the mail and raising her arms for balance. She dusted the letters as she picked them up, then tossed them through the car window to the seat, counting to keep track in case one fell between the seat and gearshift.

Could mean the difference between a future and no future at all, getting every one of those envelopes to the post office. If she was going to be sloppy about details, she might as well slit her throat today and skip the stomachaches and nights of worry altogether, because in the legal profession, as in medicine and architecture, a minor oversight could be lethal.

Nina had finished college a few years before with a degree in psychology, studying film, art, and people in the luxurious fashion of a girl-child awaiting her prince. She wished now that she'd had better guidance from the adults in her life, who should have known—what? The future, what real life held for a single mother in her late twenties entering a slow economy? Her psych degree had not even prepared her for service positions in the restaurant business.

But she was making up for that now, between law classes, paralegal work, and Bob, not in that order. Fog murked its way in front of her. She scrutinized the hazy road for patrol cars, then executed a swooping, illegal U-turn, arriving at the post office in downtown Pacific Grove, heart pounding. She shoved the letters into the metered-mail slot.

Relieved to be rid of her latest emergency, she fired up the MG along with the radio. Moving out into the street, she narrowly missed a waiting Acura. She swung onto Pine Avenue, drifting toward the middle line as she rummaged in her bag for the address for Dr. Lindberg. She located his card, swerved to avoid a jaywalking tourist family, and turned left onto Highway 1. The pines loomed on either side as the fog drizzled over the Pebble Beach road. She drove swiftly the few blocks to her mother's cottage, parking in front of the huge Norfolk pine in the front yard.

Honking, she reminded herself about the miserable people she saw every day at work, injured on the job, alone and poor. She conjured these images to steel herself for the sight of her mother carefully locking up, pausing every few steps, looking down as if she weren't sure where the sidewalk was. Her mother had ordered her not to come to the door. She didn't like being reminded of the changes in her health.

In the one minute she had to herself Nina leaned back and closed her eyes. Breathe deep. In. Out.

Let's see, Wills and Estates tonight. Professor Cerruti made it her favorite class, but she also liked what lawyers called the "settled" law of that ancient and noble subject. Unlike environmental law, for instance, which fluxed through revolutions every time a new president came in, with Wills one could learn rules that had stuck for centuries. How nice if she could apply a few firm rules to the tatty loose ends of her own life.

I'll read the cases while I eat dinner, she decided. So much for school. As for work, she had all afternoon to obsess about how much she was falling behind there. Deal with it when she got back to the office.

As for friends, ha ha, they must think she had moved to Tajikistan, for all they ever heard from her; a boyfriend was not an option, she didn't have time, though she had fallen into some casual overnighters a while back that had left her feeling worse than lonely. But she did feel warm whenever McIntyre came into her office. Her mind began bathing in a certain bubble bath—but right now here came her mother, struggling down the concrete walk.

Today, the skin on her mother's face looked tighter than usual. Nina opened the passenger-side door from the inside. Ginny paused to remove her right glove, uncovering a hand scrimshawed in pale blue lines. She leaned in and touched her daughter's hand. "Honey, why not let me take a cab? You're a busy woman."

"God, Mom. You're like ice."

Nina's mother had changed so much. Always a handsome woman with sparkling eyes and a daunting energy, she had gradually seemed to lose all color and character. Her skin stretched as tight as a stocking mask over her cheekbones, even pulling her lips back as if they were shrinking. Her once mobile face now looked somehow both flat and puffy, due to both the illness and the steroids used to treat it. Still she tried to smile.

"You always look so cheerful," Nina said, giving her a brief hug after she had maneuvered into the low-slung car. "How do you do it?"

"The right attitude makes me feel stronger. You know how much you hate it when people condescend to you, 'Oh, poor Nina, raising a boy on her own, working so hard'?"

"Oh, come on. I don't pity you."

"Sure you do. Anyone with half a brain would." Ginny patted her shoulder. "Let's just admire how delightful the leaves are at this time of year, okay?"

Maybe it had been better, those days of not knowing what was wrong, because of the hope they'd had then. Did her mother still hope?

Nina drove quickly to Dr. Lindberg's Monterey office on Cass Street. Would she have time later to run by the school library for that book on reserve? She had a mock trial coming up in a week in her Advanced Civil Procedure class and a paper due for Gas and Oil Law that demanded lengthy research. If she hurried, she could pick up Bob at nursery school, drop him with the babysitter at home, stop by the library, and be back at the office by two. Would Remy notice she had been gone longer than her lunch break allowed?

Gritting her teeth, she thought, Remy would notice.

She parked at a meter and ran around to the side of the car. "Need help, Mom? Those stairs are pretty steep. Let me help you up them at least."

Her mother let her help her out of the car, then shook her off. "I rise to all occasions. That will never change. Please don't fuss so much, Nina."

"If Matt doesn't show up to pick you up, promise me you'll leave a message for me with Astrid. I'll come get you."

"You're a worrywart."

Her mother trusted Nina's brother, Matt. Nina hoped she would call if Matt didn't show up. Again.

A few blocks north of Dr. Lindberg's office, Bob attended a preschool chosen after Nina had looked at a dozen of them and settled on this one as the least of all evils. The playroom walls were covered with outsider art Picasso would have envied, committed by three- and four-year-olds who were never given fill-in-the-blanks coloring books. Children were making collages at each table, and she spotted Bob, dark hair fallen over his round, delicious cheeks, smearing a magazine tearout onto gluey paper à la André Breton or Max Ernst.

Seeing her, he called out, "Mom, look!" Resisting an impulse to check her watch, she pulled up a tiny preschooler plastic chair and sat next to him, nodding at the collage.

"Finish up, honey, we have to go." Thank God he loved the place and was reluctant to leave. "What's this?" she asked, pointing at a tray of wooden puzzle pieces alongside the collage.

"My job." He reached over and with startling dexterity stuck the pieces into their slots to complete a duck puzzle.

"Oh. A duck! Cool!"

"But now watch this." He dumped the pieces onto the table, then stuck them across the middle in a snaggletooth row. "My keyboard," he said with a grin. "Like at home."

"But this one you can't play."

"Huh?" He ran his fingers up and down the wood pieces, humming. He was playing a sea chantey CD at home these days. "'Way haul away, we'll haul away home—'"

"But you ruined your puzzle."

"We can go now."

Taking her son's backpack and his hand, Nina ushered him to the door. Bob currently loved the cheap battery-operated keyboard she had found at a discount store. He didn't want to learn real songs yet, just loved making noise, but sometimes she caught him fingering the same notes over and over with a thoughtful expression on his face. She would have to find a way to pay for piano lessons when he was older. Never squelch potential talent, Ginny always said.

As they pulled the door open, an aide handed Nina a paper bag full of dirty pants. "He had two accidents today," she remarked, carefully noncommittal. Nina took the bag. Bob looked up at her with a worried expression. "Mommy, don't break my heart," he said, watching her face. She smiled and patted his hot cheek, hustling him outside, chastising herself for her impatience.

On the way to the parking lot, she ran into an old friend she hadn't seen for ages.

"Well, look at you," Diana said.

Nina hugged her, remembering how much Diana favored flowery perfumes. "When I told you I was pregnant, you never said a thing about being pregnant yourself."

"I was scared," Diana said. "I'd already had two miscarriages and began to think I'd never have a child. Her name's Cori." They stopped to watch Diana's curly-haired daughter gather up her backpack.

"So you settled down," Nina said.

Her old friend waved a set of flashy rings. "He just wouldn't let me alone. Good thing. He teaches chemistry at the community college."

"You always said you'd never marry."

Diana corralled her daughter and nudged her toward a red minivan. "Yeah, surprise! I turned out normal. How about you?"

"No surprise. I didn't."

Diana tilted her head. "So what if you never go about things the way other people do. You're exceptional. Not abnormal."

"I decided to get everything out of the way at once, be a single mother, go to school, work like a cur. That way, I'll have earned the right to a long commitment to some quiet loony-bin spa by the time I'm thirty."

"I gotta scoot." Diana started the battle to get her daughter strapped in. "Let's gossip soon."

"You back at work?"

"Part-time until the little gal's ready to launch. Two

more years. I couldn't find full-time child care I can trust that would have her." Diana latched the seat belt across her daughter's car seat with a sigh.

"It's like getting them into a good college, applications, interviews."

"And then they reject you or your child, or your private financial status." Diana shrugged, slamming the door against her cranky child. "I discovered passable child care involved dark rooms with peed-upon plastic mattresses, watery peanut butter, and drunken college students. I realized, hey, I can do that and pay nothing."

How nice for her, Nina thought. Diana had a partner to help and an option to stay home with her daughter. How might that feel? No doubt good, no doubt fortunate.

"Take care," Nina said, strapping Bob into his own car seat. He had a new book to study, so he let the process happen peacefully for a change. Suddenly starving, she climbed inside her car, rustling around in the MG's glove compartment for a snack. She found nothing to eat there, only an old brochure for a restaurant she could never afford. Disgruntled, she raised her head to another unwelcome vision.

Richard Filsen leaned against the brick wall of the church that bordered the parking lot, smoking a cigarette.

CHAPTER 2

STANDING NEXT TO RICHARD WAS HIS PERENNIAL associate and right-hand boy. At first she couldn't remember his name. Oh, right, Perry something. Perry Tompkins. He had been a couple of years ahead of her in high school.

She considered ignoring them, pulling away, going home.

No point. Richard, now having dragged himself out of whatever pit he lived in, was back.

She got out of the car.

"Must be something real pressing to get you to church," Richard said. "What, no kiss?"

Richard Filsen. What a day for meeting up with old friends. Although he lived in the area, somehow she had managed to avoid any run-ins for the past several years. He obviously hadn't given up his fanatical bicycling. He looked as lean as ever, and she had heard he was as mean as ever, too. His eyes looked more deep set than she recalled, and his cheekbones stood out like rocky crags. His hair was shorter than she remembered; it could pass for stubble. Maybe it gave him some aerodynamic advantage on the road? Otherwise, he looked like an important man who had spent the morning in front of a jury, in a well-cut wool suit with a perfectly matched red Hermès tie.

"I hear you won that class-action suit against the oil company up in Hayward. You must be really pleased about that. Lots of buzz. Congratulations."

"How good it is that you remember how to be civil."

"Let's start there, okay? Meantime, I'm in a rush. What—"

"Working hard, eh? And you were always gonna be a lawyer someday, I hear. Meantime, you look like you could use some sleep. You'll need cosmetic surgery in a few years if you keep digging at that frown line on your forehead."

Nina ignored the insult. "Hello, Perry. You still slaving away on behalf of Richard's greater glory?"

"Hi, Nina. How goes it?" Perry held his attaché and didn't look happy, but then again Nina had never known him to look happy. Working for Richard for years must have something to do with that. One of those short, smooth-faced men who never age, Perry was a good detail lawyer who kept the interrogatories flowing and the calendar current for Richard, who did all the court work. Perry had married a court clerk and had four kids early in life. His nose hadn't left Richard's grindstone ever since.

Perry's relationship with Richard had that quality of the antisocial husband finding a sweet, sociable wife—together they created the semblance of one well-adjusted human being. You could talk to Perry; he was reasonable and prompt. Richard didn't talk. He acted. Often badly.

Nina couldn't imagine why Perry still worked for Richard. He might make one whole person on his own. Didn't he know that?

She had met Richard on the Fourth of July several years before on the beach at Seaside, watching the fireworks. Returning from a barbecue in Palo Alto, she had passed the beach just as the show started, and a car pulled out right in front of her, leaving a parking space that was too good to pass up. So she stood at the fringes of the crowd, all alone in her tank top and blue jeans, shivering and looking up at the display, excited as a deprived child.

"Pretty, huh?" he'd said, walking his bike, an Italian racer that must have cost thousands, up to her. "It's why war movies are so entertaining. What a world." Over six feet tall, he looked incredibly fit in his black biker shorts and red racing shirt.

"Yeah, it's pretty," she said. "I mean, not war. Fireworks."

"You come here often?" he teased after several moments passed in silence and the bombardment continued.

"I love the ocean." Beyond them, high-tide waves swept up the beach, catching some of the gawkers off guard.

"Swimmer?"

"Surfer."

"I always wanted to learn."

"That's what people say who find the thought intimidating."

He laughed. "I'd trust you to teach me. I'm a cyclist."

"I see that. Nice bike."

They talked. Absorbed by the spectacle, but also uncomfortably aware of the proximity of a good-looking male, Nina warmed up even more when he provided her with a wool blanket for cover. As they walked back to the parking lot, he invited her to dinner the following night at Casanova's in Carmel.

She should have recognized the name of the place as a warning. Inside, the hostess led her to a patio area that appeared to be entirely peopled by lovers. Couples drank, snuggled, and whispered over candlelight.

Neither of them finished the food they'd ordered. Instead, they talked and talked over glasses of the wine he had picked. He raised his glass in a toast, touching her hand fleetingly. He knew the moves, and she was lonely. The chemistry between them increased exponentially with each glass—Clos du Bois, a sauvignon blanc, she remembered, and remembered her private vow at the time that someday she'd make more than minimum wage and drink this wine all night long.

Richard, a criminal defense attorney with his office in Seaside, got his name into the local paper on a regular basis. He regaled her with tales of the hookers and drug pushers and petty thieves who made up his practice then, and it was fascinating, all of it, especially his attitude.

"Somebody's got to do it," he said with a shrug. "Protect their rights and keep them from being stomped on in the great purple-stained wine barrel of the law. I'm practical. They pay me, I do my best for them. They don't pay me, they can fuck themselves." He leaned over and said conspiratorially, "Besides, I like messing with the system."

"What do you get out of it, though? Besides getting paid? I mean, it's a stressful way to make a living, isn't it?"

"It's fun, sweetheart. I don't do anything unless it's fun."

"Fun how?"

"Beating the bastards."

A few weeks after they'd started sleeping together, Richard began disappearing, telling her he was entering various cycle races around California. They met only at night because after work he needed to put in fifty miles on the bike.

At first he couldn't keep his hands off her, but soon she noticed he seemed to be feeling her flesh in a funny way in bed, as if he were a doctor or something. "You ought to work out in the gym," he told her. "Any more than fifteen percent body fat is bad for your health." His kitchen was filled with nutritional supplements and the best Osterizer money could buy. She gagged on the stuff and found herself secretly heading for the nearby Burger King for lunch after one of Richard's breakfasts.

Aside from his bicycle and his protein and that first blowout dinner during which he had romanced her, Richard didn't like to spend money, and they began to have arguments over it. He was so frugal he reused his paper napkins. The heat never came on in his apartment, and he expected Nina to buy most of the dinners.

Full of brutal insights he seemed obliged to share, he often told her she was deluded or in denial about her life. Maybe she was, but his criticisms brought up her own stubbornness and she stopped listening. She still lived with her mother. He didn't like her mother. After a few excruciating meetings he pegged Ginny as a manipulator. "She's gonna keep you at home forever if she has her way."

"Not true," Nina said. "She loves me. She supports me. She worries but she never pressures me to behave in a certain way."

"I see what you don't," he said flatly. "Apron strings flapping in the wind. Get some distance."

He put down her brother, Matt, as an unregenerate troublemaker. "I've seen his type before."

"His type?"

"He's fucking lazy. He doesn't want anybody setting him straight."

The trouble was, Richard was right about Matt, who was smoking a lot of pot and drifting and had dropped out of college. "Matt's got a good heart, Richard."

"I love how much you love your family, Nina."

What did that mean? she wondered. That she was an idiot? Since he didn't like her family, she tried to make the best of it, especially since he was such an expert and reliable lover.

Soon enough, for her, the relationship was entirely built around sex. It made for a special, narrow, intense attachment between them that Richard seemed to appreciate. And that was enough for almost three months.

"We can make a life together in spite of your family," Richard said one night as they lay in bed, her head on his shoulder, his hand on her thigh. "You're gonna do great things. We can go to Christmas dinner and make nice if we have to. You can rise above your family. Everyone's family's a big mess."

After that, Nina cried a few times and made a cyborgian pros-and-cons list when she felt strong. Then she invited Richard to dinner at the local Chinese joint. They ate dim sum and drank tea. Richard had just gotten back from a long bike ride and talked about getting to bed early.

"Richard, you've been wonderful to me," Nina said, thinking, you've also been not wonderful and that's why we're here tonight. Her heart cracked, but fortunately her voice did not. "But—it's not working out. We have to move on."

He set his tea down hard. "You're dumping me?" he said, after an outraged silence.

"We don't have anything in common outside of bed. You don't like my family. You disapprove of my politics, my clothes, my haircut. I see no future for us. Do you?"

"I feel blindsided." He tapped a finger against the table, distracting them both momentarily with its hypnotic rhythm, allowing him time to think. "You and I," he said finally, "we're the same: ambitious, driven, athletic, sex-obsessed." He raised an eyebrow. "True?"

"In some ways we are the same. In other essential ways, no."

"Oh, sweetheart. You invent obstacles! You like the chase, the dramatics."

Shaking her head, Nina said, "My mind's made up."

"Don't be ridiculous. You need me."

When she stood up to leave, he surprised her, pulling her back into her chair.

"Let me go, Richard."

"You just listen—"

"Let go or I'll scream," she said calmly.

"You won't."

"Help!" she shouted. "Help me!"

The other diners turned to stare. They frowned at Richard.

"Shut up! They're looking!"

"Then get your hands off me."

He let go. "Show them it's okay."

She smiled.

Her fellow diners relaxed. Knives, forks, and spoons clattered again, tentatively.

"You have no right to treat me this way!" Richard said, his whispering voice crackling, hot as a forest fire. "I deserve your respect. I deserve your love!"

"You have no right to treat *me* this way," Nina whispered back, giving a nod to her nervous fellow diners.

A few of the more sensitive ones swerved toward her, watching.

Nina stood up.

"This is not over." Richard had collected himself and looked as smooth and together as usual.

"Oh, yes, it is." Nina left the restaurant shaken, pulled out of her parking space, and headed toward Pacific Grove. She drove several blocks listening to the radio before tuning in to her surroundings. In her rearview mirror she spotted Richard, face grimly set, in his car following her.

She sped away.

He caught up and lingered two car lengths behind, as if she wouldn't notice.

Nina took side streets only locals knew.

Richard wound up the side streets behind her. He edged up behind her car, flirting with it, too close for safety.

She slowed down. He slowed down.

He knew the only places she might go. He knew where she lived with her mother. She could drive to the sheriff's office or her house. Unsure, she drove to the house.

He pulled up right in front. She jumped out of her car and ran into the house. Then she turned off the porch light and peeked through the window at him.

He was out there, staring as if he could x-ray the curtains.

Her mother and her brother, Matt, had turned in. Nina turned off all the lights.

Richard remained in the car, his face obscure in the darkness. She wondered what he might be thinking and realized she didn't know.

She didn't know the guy at all.

All night, every hour she got up to peek through the curtains and saw him sitting, watching, resenting her.

She smelled the salt air, thinking about how much she loved her life, wondering how she had hooked up with such a frightening person.

At four o'clock in the morning, exhausted, unable to keep up her vigil, she fell asleep.

Only to awaken to a tapping at her window.

After pulling on a robe and putting her feet into slippers, she pulled the curtain aside just far enough to see Richard's mad face staring back at her.

"Bitch," he mouthed.

She let the curtain flap into place.

He tapped again.

Harder.

Scared, unwilling to show her weakness, she ignored the next three rappings, each successively louder. When she had her emotions controlled, she hurled open the window suddenly. "Richard, you want to go to jail? This could ruin you."

He said nothing. She heard him breathe.

"I'm calling the police."

After that, she heard nothing outside. She didn't feel an urgent need to call, although she felt afraid. She watched for a sign, unable to see anything in the darkness. Only when the California sun finally began its yellow, relentless march across the landscape did she hear Richard's car fire up.

She peered through the curtains, watching him head away toward the ocean.

Finally, she slept.

But that night did not signal the end of Richard's pursuit. He called Nina's mother, Ginny, to gripe when Nina didn't answer her phone. He turned up on his bicycle at Matt's new job in a fast-food joint to quiz him about Nina. When Matt gave him nothing, he told Matt he'd get him fired. Nina's phone rang constantly. She answered. Richard hung up.

"Time to leave town, Nina," her mother advised. "Give him time to get weaned and find somebody else to pester." Nina jumped at a friend's offer of a family cabin at Fallen Leaf Lake, near Lake Tahoe. Up there for a few precious summer weeks, where the squirrels scrabbled and she could take an old rowboat out on the calm waters, she unwound, quit crying, and started living again.

She moved back to P.G. and applied to the Monterey College of Law. Richard's stories had engaged her, and she knew she wanted to go into some kind of law, though the idea of criminal defense seemed too intimidating.

Soon after, she discovered she was pregnant.

She went to a counselor and decided abortion was not for her.

And now, more than four years later, here came Richard, smiling at Bob with a vulpine look she hadn't noticed before, something she had seen on other extreme athletes. She couldn't now imagine what in the world she had found sexy about him.

Richard stubbed out the cigarette butt against the building and dropped it, then, to her horror, walked swiftly around to Bob's side of the car, peering inside. "Good-looking little guy, isn't he? Handsome, like his daddy. C'mon, hey, roll down the window. Hi, there, Bob."

Richard was tall. She, at five feet three inches, felt physically intimidated by his size, his big voice and hands. She shook her head at Bob, who shrugged and continued watching the scene through the window with that fixed look that meant he would stow away this memory.

Her mother always said, never let fear stop you and never show them you're afraid. Nina would not think about the gritty mix presently turning her stomach acids into toxic waste. "What do you want?" She kept her voice steady. "I told you I'm in a hurry."

"Always in a hurry, huh, Nina? Some things never change." The vague sexual innuendo of his words sent a chill through her. He raised his hand to touch her cheek. She stepped away.

He said, "Listen up. I had a bout with cancer last year. Prostate. Doesn't look like I'll be having any more kids, so I want a relationship with my only child, okay? Don't worry, I'm over you. But I want to start hanging out with my little boy. I have a legal right, Nina."

"He doesn't know you."

"He needs a father's influence."

"So I'll date more," Nina snapped back.

"Ha-ha." Richard didn't move.

Then he started walking back and forth in a semi-circle, as if guarding her but, in fact, hemming her in. "Are you willing to sit down with me and work out a shared-custody agreement?"

"What's his middle name?" Nina said, looking Richard in the eye. "Bob's? You know, the child you're so interested in so suddenly? What's his middle name?"

"I don't know. So fucking what?"

She watched him flinch a little. "You're not even on the birth certificate."

"A DNA test will remedy that. You lied. It's common."

"You abandoned him!"

"With good reason."

"And then? What about the last four—"

"Good reason. But here I am, ready to make up for everything."

She looked inside the car, where Bob seemed utterly absorbed in their argument. Would he be traumatized his whole life by this conversation? "Talk to my lawyers," she said shortly, handing him the Pohlmann business card. He squinted at it and put it away.

"Let me talk to him, Nina. What's the harm?"

"He doesn't know you. He doesn't know about you. I prefer it that way."

"I'm his father."

"So get a court order."

"You weren't always so hard-assed. No wonder you can't find a husband."

Nina's vision went red. Was there a pay phone nearby? She needed a cop. But then Perry appeared at her side.

"Er," he said to Nina, coming closer, "sorry to interrupt."

He stuck a heavy manila envelope toward her and her idiot hand took it.

"Sorry, Nina. I'm Mr. Filsen's attorney in the matter of an action for paternity and child custody, and I hereby personally serve you with a Summons, Complaint, and other pleadings—"

"Child custody? Why you—!" She threw the envelope to the ground and kicked it.

Richard smirked.

"—you are no doubt familiar with." Perry picked up the envelope and dusted it off, then set it on the hood of her car. "Please," Perry said, "call me. I'm sure we can work something out. Richard, I believe our work is done."

"Go, then."

"We should really, you know, go together."

"Beat it," Richard said without looking at Perry, and the junior associate said, "Take care, Nina," turned his back, and walked away leaving Richard, Bob, and Nina alone in the parking lot.

Richard now apparently felt free to express his true feelings, unfettered by a potential witness. "How many men this year, Nina?" he asked her, rough-voiced, angry. "How many summertime flings? You keep a list? With stars rating how hot they were?"

"Go, Richard," she said calmly, while fright cascaded down her body. If she understood one thing about sex, she understood its power to incite violence in the most passive people, and Richard was certainly not that. She did not want him to fixate on sex. "We're not together, okay? I have my business. You have yours."

"You were okay in bed. I didn't realize you were gonna make a career out of it." He waited for her to react.

She didn't.

"I hear things."

"Touch either one of us and you'll regret it."

Suddenly Bob tried to open the door to the MG. Richard stepped between her and the car. Her heart pounding louder than the airplane roaring overhead, Nina pushed against him, attempting to dislodge him.

"What will you do, little girl?"

"Mince you," she said in a low voice, "with the sharpest knife I can find."

Big, strong, and unafraid, Richard laughed.

Adrenaline blasted through Nina. Her balled fist hit his square jaw. His head snapped back. He let out a grunt. He stepped away as she stood next to Bob's door, now holding her heavy bag by its strap, ready to swing it and hit him with it as hard as she could.

A long moment passed. She prepared for retaliation, stepping back, trying to protect herself from direct attack. Let him try. She could feel her chin sticking out, her breath quickening, her body bending a little for better balance. She had never struck another human being before, but she seemed to be ready to do it again, no problem.

Richard shook his head slightly and then cocked it, smiling a mean smile. Rubbing his jaw, he said, "You have a lousy, juvenile temper. Want me to beat the hell out of you now? Maybe you'd enjoy that? Or maybe you just thought it would help you in a custody fight." Nina ran around to the driver's-side door, and as she tried to open it, he snatched her hand away so hard she could feel the bruises forming. Then just as suddenly he let go.

"Not me," he said, opening the door for her. "I'm a perfect gentleman in front of our boy."

The hem of her jacket caught in the door as she slammed it, then turned the key in the ignition. She pulled hard and her jacket ripped. The tearing sound was the other thing she heard as the rough engine coughed, moving Nina and Bob back onto the calm Methodist streets of Pacific Grove.

CHAPTER 3

G INNY REILLY HAD NOT WANTED TO MAKE THIS
medical appointment, but Nina had insisted,
making all the arrangements. Useless, all of it,
Ginny thought, sitting in the familiar waiting room, each
spot on the rug already memorized.

At only fifty-two, she felt too young to be so sick.
For a long time, almost two years now, she had felt
weak or anemic or something. Her joints hurt and she
began to worry about arthritis.

At first, she suspected the problems between her and
her husband, Harlan, were making her sick. She had read
about that phenomenon in a magazine she'd found at the
organic-food store in downtown Pacific Grove. More
correctly, she believed their marriage, grown from fresh
joy into a moldy thing, might be making her sick; the
conflicts, always repressed by her, between his extrava-
gance and her frugality, his lies and her secrets, his crude-

ness and her sensitivities, his betrayals and her coldness, his shouting and her silences. Harlan never held back an emotion. He thrived on drama while she preserved her dignity and calm for her children and the world.

Had she become sick right after he said, "I'm leaving you, Ginny," one night in their bed? He had refused to explain, turning over, snoring within five minutes. The next morning he had packed up while she watched, stony with scorn on the surface, trembling with seismic emotions she hid from him. He moved into a condo by the Del Monte Golf Course. Within a month a much younger woman who apparently had some money moved in with him.

Harlan bloomed.

Ginny took aspirin and stayed home. She had put her extreme fatigue down to the fallout from the end of a long marriage, experiencing a numbing grief similar to what she had felt when her folks died. She decided she was simply exhausted from drama, loss of love, intrigue, desperation. Making a choice to settle gracefully into solitary middle age, she took up pottery making and tried a jazz dancing class. Vague aches and pains came and went. She tried not to pay attention.

Then her fingers and toes, which had always been sensitive to cold, bothered her too much to ignore. She wore socks to bed. Some of her fingertips began to actually look bluish at times. One morning she saw herself in the mirror and got a shock: the skin on her face, once mobile, alert, smiling, felt tight and looked stiff. Over a few months the joint pains intensified and her skin continued to pull over her bones. She looked different. Trying to compensate for the grimace that naturally appeared, she adopted a small smile at all times.

She told her kids, "Well, at least my wrinkles are disappearing." The frozen mask was a metaphor for what she felt like inside.

Nina made her go to the general practitioner in Pacific Grove who had always treated her. He told Ginny the not-fresh news that she was depressed and needed to get out more. "Take a vacation," he suggested. "Find somebody to laugh with." Ginny sure laughed when she told Nina about that encounter.

But then her joints really started to ache, sores on her legs didn't heal, a brown, painless rash spread across her face over her nose and cheeks. She needed better help. Her physician got serious and recommended Dr. Lindberg, a rheumatologist.

On her first visit, while waiting to meet her new doctor, she was wearing mittens, having one of these strange attacks of coldness in the tips of her fingers.

She trusted Dr. Lindberg immediately. He examined her thoroughly, telling her stories about his children in college the whole time. Later, he sent her next door to the lab he used.

Three days later, Dr. Lindberg put his head through the inner door, then ushered her into his office. He looked at her, expelling a brief sigh, then pulled X-rays and papers from the manila folder the nurse had left.

"I think you have something called mixed connective tissue disease, Mrs. Reilly, several different syndromes that appear together now and then." He listed them, using his well-manicured fingers.

"Raynaud's phenomenon. It's a vascular—a blood-circulation problem that means your fingertips and toes get cold and painful sometimes. Rheumatoid arthritis. Polymyositis, quite possibly. Lupus, judging from the butterfly rash on your face and some of the test results. Scleroderma that seems to be quite progressive."

She felt overwhelmed and for once could not control herself. Dr. Lindberg motioned to his nurse, who came back in with a box of tissues.

"I'm very sorry, Ginny. It's a lot to hit you with."

Ginny squared her jaw. "Thank God. Just what I was hoping to hear. I'm gonna walk out of here and dance like a pretty young girl again."

He looked up from his clipboard, frowning. "Um, Ginny—"

"Am I going to die? I mean, I know I'm going to die, we're all going to do that, but what I mean is," Ginny said, leaning forward and letting the tears start to flow, "am I going to die now?"

"I didn't say—no, I don't think you're going to die now. I'm going to give you a lot of information about this, but let me say this right now: you may have years yet."

"All right. All right," Ginny said, turning her head away. They sat in silence for a moment. Finally Ginny blew her nose and said, "What exactly is scleroderma?"

"A thickening, a hardening and tightening of the skin and internal organs."

"Hardening?" She touched her face, which had once been so soft. Harlan used to love her skin, called it baby silk. "I've never heard of these things."

"They aren't well-known or even well understood." The doctor shuffled through the lab tests.

"Will I be crippled?"

Dr. Lindberg sighed. "To be honest, I don't know how this illness will progress. Think of it as chronic, something to manage. But there may be remissions, sometimes. And we can give you medicine that will slow down the—the sequence."

"What sequence?"

"Your internal organs will likely become more involved over time. You may suffer kidney or liver failure much later in the game. Steroids are the treatment of choice at present. The medicine you'll be taking will slow things down."

Ginny sat back in her chair. The office became a bathysphere, silent in its descent into some terror she had never dreamed of. "Are you telling me there's no cure? My poor kids. I'll be disabled. I'll get steadily worse over time."

"We'll take the best care of you we can."

"But what causes this? Did I catch it somewhere?"

"We don't know. It's called an autoimmune disorder because the theory is that some of your protecting cells have begun to attack your other cells, mistaking them for invaders. We don't know why this happens sometimes. Women who are aged forty to sixty are most likely to develop it, we do know that. I can put you in touch with some groups that you might find helpful, other people with chronic or progressive ailments, who don't let it stop them from living."

"What else can I do to slow it down? I mean aside from the traditional treatment? Yoga? Meditation?"

He shrugged his shoulders. "Biofeedback helps some people." He took out a pen and wrote down a name and phone number on his prescription pad.

His nurse came in and whispered loudly enough for Ginny to hear, "You have another appointment waiting. She's in pain, or I wouldn't interrupt."

"Would acupuncture help?" Ginny asked him on her way out. She had seen something intriguing in the newspaper that very morning. Strange how at the time she had dismissed it without much thought, but now she clung to the image from the advertisement: "Live long. Live healthy. Be well."

"Good idea." He ripped a sheet off his prescription pad and handed it to her. "It can't hurt."

Ginny began taking the prednisone. At first, she was unbothered by side effects, though she did feel angrier, but who knew if it was the drug. She tried biofeedback, but disliked the damp hands of the practitioner and didn't go back.

Eventually, she dug up the old newspaper and called on Dr. Wu, or, as she called him in her mind due to his advertisement, Dr. Be Well.

Then came the pain, the surgery, the mutilation.

More than a year had passed since the incident with Dr. Wu, and here she was back in Dr. Lindberg's office, sicker than ever.

"There's continued degradation of the system," Dr. Lindberg began, and went on like that. She listened, her heart hurting, trying hard to show nothing.

He added little to what she already sensed after a

year of living with this diagnosis. Degradation. Yes, the word that rankled above all others, the word that expressed what her husband had done to her. She, proud and dignified, reduced to a life of doctors and deformation, while he—

Then Dr. Wu had taken advantage of her, hurting her when she was so far down she couldn't imagine anything worse. As she sat with Dr. Lindberg now, she began to experience unfair feelings she had never known before: envy at his smiling, lined face and healthy, hairy-knuckled hands, jealousy at the thought of Harlan and his new wife, hopelessness, rage—so many things.

She had always thought of herself as a nice person, and these ungovernable emotions challenged that image. Some mornings she woke up hating herself for what she felt. However, what kind of example would she set for her children if she couldn't stand up for herself this one final time?

She picked up her prescriptions at the downstairs pharmacy, paying with the health-insurance card from Harlan's plan that she had made him keep for her, went outside, and checked her watch. Matt must be running late. He must have gotten tied up, and of course he was always so hard to reach. Or maybe Zinnia had him laughing too hard to remember her.

Several minutes later, she gave up waiting and climbed back upstairs to the doctor's office to use the phone, remembering the first time Matt had introduced them, briefly. Good for him, she had thought, because the girl was pretty and he rarely brought his girlfriends around. Almost instantly, she had changed her opinion.

She didn't like the sly looks and giggling, as if Zinnia and Matt shared a hilarious secret and everyone else be damned.

Oh, she felt so frazzled by all these unresolved problems, and as a result, after making her call, negotiating the steps down, not paying enough attention, she stumbled.

And then she fell.

She fell forward and, in that instant, saw herself tumbling to her death on the hard concrete below, visible to those crows up on the telephone wire, and casual gawkers, and who knew who else.

Splayed like a dead squirrel on the street. Pecked by those big black birds.

This graphically unpleasant image helped her. Her good arm flew up to grab the railing and stop her from going down all the way.

She sat down three steps up from the street, gasping with pain, feeling bruises forming on her legs. Nobody came out of the silent offices. Nobody passed by on the street.

Her children were busy. The love of her life had remarried. She was on her own. She thought of Nina and Bob. She hardly ever knew what was going on with her daughter anymore, although to be fair, she held tightly to her own secrets, and one in particular that made her cringe, that would certainly make Nina hate her.

Ginny only wanted for Nina what any mother wanted—for her daughter to have a comfortable home and a loving partner. But Nina had shown no talent so far in making a home or marrying a good person.

At least Richard Filsen was out of the picture. Ginny had done what she could to drive a wedge between Nina and that man. She knew Filsen hated her for it, but so what?

She checked her watch and looked up the street. No Matt, no cab. No rescue. Then she buttoned her sweater against a growing afternoon sea wind that held just a hint of mist. Another idea began to grow within her about how to right the injustices that had been done to her.

A lightbulb went on. Or maybe what she experienced was more on the level of a bomb exploding.

Someone should pay for her dying.

Why hadn't she thought of it before? Provide for Matt and Nina and her beloved grandson and extract some justice out of the darkening world from which she was being cut off a little more each day.

CHAPTER
4

NINA STOPPED OFF THE NEXT DAY AT FISHER-man's Wharf for a fish-and-chips lunch wrapped in newspaper. She dribbled malt vinegar over the steaming fried food and ate it while leaning over the pier, head down in the breeze, worrying about Bob's bedtime questions last night. "Who was that man you hit, Mom? You told me never, ever, ever—"

Had he witnessed something indelible, something that would haunt him later, if Richard proved his fatherhood and got visitation? She looked north, where balmy Santa Cruz glittered like Xanadu thirty miles across Monterey Bay. Nothing calmed her like the ocean, and she could use soothing. She hadn't slept the night before. She really needed to talk to someone about Richard. She tossed leftovers to the noisy sea lions and headed back to work.

On the way in, she passed Jack. No court today, and he wore a green polo shirt and beige khakis. Not tall, he made up for it with a muscular build and a blaze of reddish hair. He fixed his eyes on her and said, "Whoa, you've got a load of books. Need some help? Don't tell me that's all for my stuff?"

"No, these are for Lou. Tax research. He dreams he can talk me into going into tax law."

"Steady money."

"Too much arithmetic, I think," Nina said. "Maybe I'd rather make real estate deals and settle personal-injury cases over the phone. Like you, McIntyre."

"I make it look too easy, obviously."

Nina laughed. "Can I talk to you for a second?"

"Follow me."

She walked into his office, dumped her books on a chair, and waited for him to sit down.

She told him about Richard, the bare facts, and asked his advice.

"You refused the papers?"

"I know. I was served in spite of having to kick the idea around a little first."

"Hmm. Let me make some calls, okay? Find out what's cooking. I'll call Perry for you, too."

"I appreciate it."

"You know I'll—we'll do anything to help you, Nina. If it comes down to a custody fight, I'll take it to court for you. I did family-law cases now and then at my first job. It'll be good practice."

She thanked him and left, remembering a remark she had once overheard when Jack was complaining about that first job to Lou: "I hated family law. Too many people crying."

Feeling more cheerful than she had since her run-in with Richard, Nina said hello to Astrid, who had a phone nesting on her shoulder, picked up her messages, hustled down the hall to her cubby, opened the next house-on-fire file, and drew the phone to her ear.

She dealt with Lou's case in an hour, then turned to one of Jack's that interested her more.

Jack's client's daughter had been hit by an ice cream vending van in front of her house, an event his client had not witnessed. Nevertheless, the mother felt entitled to damages for negligent infliction of emotional distress, since her son ran inside screaming, and she then ran outside to observe with horror her daughter's bloodied body. The little girl survived without permanent injury. The mother didn't really have a good shot at winning— Nina had done some preliminary research and found a recent First District Court of Appeals decision confirming that the plantiff had to be a percipient witness, had to have seen the accident with her own eyes.

"Did you hear a thump? Did your daughter cry out? What exactly did you see?" Opposing counsel had sensibly asked these questions at the deposition. Not good.

The one-year statute of limitations for filing a lawsuit was coming up, and Jack had told Nina this was a poor case to litigate. He wanted badly to settle for something better than nuisance value, because he didn't want to have to file the lawsuit, but if he didn't settle, he'd have to file it to protect the mother's right to take it to court.

But the L.A. lawyer didn't know how badly Jack wanted to settle.

Nina's phone buzzed and Jack said, "Have you got a minute? The lawyer for the insurance company in the ice cream case is calling me back in five. Good training for you to hear this call."

She gathered up the files, feeling psychic, and by the time she went into Jack's office, he was already on the phone trying to settle the case, the speakerphone blaring out the guy in Los Angeles. Jack waved her to a chair and continued his spiel.

"Look, let's consider this from a strictly cost-effective point of view." While Jack talked, he watched a video of MC Hammer on the VCR he kept in the office. "U Can't Touch This"—sex in the air, a fuck-it-all mood that was so right for this conversation.

"My client will not settle for nuisance value. She was absolutely convinced her daughter was killed and she had to go through months of counseling—you have the bills. True, the daughter's better now, but that also took months. . . . C'mon, she's not about to drop this. She was made aware of the accident almost instantly. Though she didn't have a contemporaneous observation, she was notified immediately and saw the results within a very short time. If you lose this, you'll lose big, you know that. Why not take this one off your plate?"

They had heard it a million times, but Nina knew this sort of talk always made insurance lawyers nervous. "It's going to cost you fifty thousand dollars at a minimum just to try the case. If you win, it's worth zero. My client has authorized me to accept one hundred thousand dollars as a full settlement, but if you can give me a hard offer of seventy-five thousand dollars I will talk to her about it." His client wanted $75,000 if Jack couldn't do better. The offer should tempt the insurer to get off so cheap.

Nina thought hard about the ramifications of the case. Who was right? She felt as jerked around as a juror as she listened.

Now Jack turned away from his VCR to give her one of those great big shit-eating smiles she liked so much, but she tried not to take it personally. She had seen the way he'd looked at Remy Sorensen just yesterday, when he probably had no idea he was being observed.

Today must be a day of psychic connections, because Remy chose that moment to walk past the doorway to Jack's office, and Nina had the full view as his eyes lit up and he breathed deeply to see if he could get a whiff of her. Remy moved like a flag in the wind, sleek and undulating, down the hall, her calves sharp-cut under the pencil skirt. His eyes followed the calves like small green heat missiles.

Nina felt an unwelcome jab of envy. She considered Remy a mentor. Along with her physical attributes, the ones that made Jack's eyes burn in his head, Remy had the professional brawn of a woman who has it all figured out. She knew her law and she held most of the important locals in her charismatic thrall. A Klaus Pohlmann recruit and protégé, Remy had impressed everyone in the Carmel legal community. She steamrolled any opposition so dexterously nobody felt hurt. She brought in a surprising amount of new business and old money. People in Carmel liked her. She had a level head and didn't push the sex angle. Nina didn't hope to become someone like Remy—she herself was too short, too edgy, too . . . much, and on top of that, not the pack animal the pols loved, but she wanted to suck up every bit of insight she could from this ultrasuccessful woman.

She could learn a lot from Remy. How to make a man pant. How to get her way. And, most urgently, how to beat every professional enemy senseless.

"You think you can get summary judgment on the lack of contemporaneous observation on this, you file your motion," Jack continued, but now he looked impatient to be finished.

Nina tried to imagine the other lawyer's state of mind right about now. He hated giving out his company's money, and Jack was wringing him for every dollar. He felt squeezed in his tight tie, scratchy in his starched shirt, and pissed to be stuck inside his high-rise office building on Wilshire Boulevard and not outside in the sunny Southland, frolicking at the beach.

"I'm sure you'll like our judges up here," Jack said in his most genial fashion. "I like them. They like me. Maybe they'll like you, too."

He dug at the faraway voice. "And of course if we do lose, we will appeal and make it perfectly clear for the next generation of claims against you guys."

"Forty thousand," said the L.A. lawyer on the speakerphone.

"Sixty-five," Jack allowed, controlling his enthusiasm. "She won't take less."

"Fifty. That's all we've got on reserve. That's how we assess it. Take it or leave it."

"I'll talk to her, but I don't think my client will go for it." But Jack gave Nina a thumbs-up. The client would.

Remy came through his door, nodded at Nina, and stood by Jack's chair. Jack looked as though he was resisting an impulse to put his arm around her waist and pull her down onto his lap. He disconnected the call and favored Remy with a dopey grin.

"Sorry to interrupt," Remy said.

Besides the narrow skirt, she wore a dark orange silk blouse that brought out the gold in her pulled-back hair and her pale eyes. Tall, slender, and cool, she made Nina think of Cybill Shepherd.

They had both forgotten Nina's existence. "Before you say anything," Jack said, "remind me we're still having dinner at the Pine Inn tonight. Eight o'clock."

"Of course," Remy said, her voice light, "our usual table." They exchanged a look and Jack relaxed. "I just came in to tell you Klaus had a doctor's appointment. He has a few things he wants you to deal with." She handed him a list, then stood for a moment as if relishing his attention.

"See you tonight," Remy said, looking back over her shoulder at Jack as she walked out. "Wear that aftershave you're wearing right now. Oh, and, Nina, could you please stop in my office when you are finished here?"

Just before five, when the secretaries were starting to pack up and he was signing his letters, Jack discovered a phone message from Paul van Wagoner. He punched the number.

"Van Wagoner? What the hell are you doing in San Francisco in weather like this, man? Fall's a great time of year at Pinnacles. I could meet you there. I could return your camera. Then you could take pictures of me beating your ass up the rock face."

Jack had met Paul in Cambridge when they were both going to Harvard and they had remained friends ever since. When Paul switched from Harvard Law, moving over the bridge to Marlborough Street in Boston to attend Northeastern and take a master's in criminology, and Jack had continued in law, they saw less of each other, but always made time for climbing trips to the White Mountains in New Hampshire.

"Thanks for calling back, McIntyre. I was just about to call you again. Yeah, you want to go up one of those crumblers, I'll race you. Might happen sooner than later."

"What's up, Paul?"

"Laura and I are splitting up."

"Ooh. You okay?"

"Sure."

Jack knew bullshit when he heard it. He knew Paul was angry, felt betrayed, and couldn't believe he had failed yet again.

"But the really big news is that I'm moving down to Monterey."

"What a shame," Jack said. Like Paul, Laura was a detective for the San Francisco Police Department. Jack didn't much like her, but that wasn't relevant. "So what happened?"

"Monterey County sheriff's department offered me

a job in the Coastal Investigations Division down there. I took it—I needed the change. I'll be working out of the courthouse down there. A little less money but—"

"Cut the shit. You know what I'm talking about when I say what a shame. You were so wild about her—"

"I tried to be faithful. For three years I was faithful, but we were both gone so much and there's so much crazy-making in my line of work—you know what I'm talking about—I got mixed up with someone. A witness in one of my homicide cases. My mistake. It was over in two weeks. Anyway, Laura found out, and, God, Jack, she's fucking adamantine, done with me. Won't talk."

So Laura had finally gotten tired of forgiving. "Stay with me until you find a place. That shouldn't be a problem, although I just have the one lumpy, dog-scarred couch. Let's see. It was that Swiss chard and anchovy on semolina you liked so much, right?"

"Spaghetti and a shitload of garlic bread."

"Name your day," Jack said.

"A few weeks from now. The fourteenth. I'll bring a case of Anchor Steam."

"That'll get us through dinner."

"Two cases," Paul said. "And, Jack? How about giving me a break from your latest girlfriend, whoever she might be, okay? I want to fish, hunt, climb, and forget about women."

"I can do that. You're really moving down here?"

"I am."

"That's sensational, man."

When he hung up, Jack pulled Paul's broken camera out of the bottom drawer of his desk and set it in front of him. He would get Astrid to drop it off tomorrow. Two weeks ought to be plenty of time to get it fixed.

He left the office by 5:30 p.m. Everybody else had already left. Great working conditions, exquisite scenery, low pay, he thought, locking the front door. He had just enough time to drive down the coast to the cabin in the Highlands, shower, get ready to drive back up to Carmel for dinner with Remy. He'd change the sheets just in case she chose to get all hot and reckless and go back down there with him, and God how he hoped she would.

He was excited. This could be the night. Jack's mother had recently given him a book of local poet Robinson Jeffers's works for his thirty-fifth birthday, and a phrase sprang to mind: *A woman from nowhere comes and burns you like wax.*

Jeffers must have met Remy Sorensen in a previous life.

CHAPTER 5

NINA PLUNGED INTO THE OCEAN ONE LAST TIME, struggling for air as a shallow, foam-topped wave smashed into her. This Saturday morning the sets were small, but she paddled out and floated on her board for a few minutes more, rolling on soft swells. Her chin was frozen—she had felt so macho she hadn't bothered to wear her hood—but the Billabong 4/3 neoprene wet suit kept her torso warm and the bootees saved her feet from the water. A few other surfers, some of whom she recognized from a long way off, sat removed and timeless farther down the break.

In idle moments of floating, waiting for a good one, she tried to predict which kind of wave would come next: one that rose like a mountain, then tumbled in a swift, long slide; the promising but short ride that petered out halfway along; or a bomb that might catch hold of her and drag her under.

She paddled fast into a six-footer, stood up, heart racing, breathing in the spray, balancing madly, rode it in without taking a single breath, then instead of kicking out, fell onto the board and let the swell carry her in. Shaking water off her wet suit, she walked quickly back to her car, clasping her board to her side, examining the hills of sand and the boardwalk overlook for signs of Richard. She saw none.

Stripping off the suit, she wrapped a yellow towel over her bikini, twisted a frayed cotton scarf over her wet hair, rolled down the top to her MG, and inclined her board in the seat next to her. Heart still pumping with excitement, she toggled the heat to high and drove the few blocks to her house.

Swinging up her own street, she thought, I do not want to leave this town. But someday, necessity might demand it. Many people here were highly educated, competitive, and determined to stay, and success in law might be iffy for a young person like her without dazzling credentials. Maybe she'd end up in San Fran, or even Lake Tahoe. She had such complicated and somewhat painful memories of that place, but the mountains definitely pulled at her.

She couldn't decide what kind of law she would practice, and she needed to focus her studies better and make that decision soon. After that, things would fall into place. She would have grass instead of concrete in her front yard, and a house with paint that didn't peel. She would wear foot-mutilating shoes in court, the better to kick hell out of her opponents. She and her brilliant, devoted lover would buy a second home at Lake

Tahoe, where she would learn windsurfing and read psychology books.

She would be in love, and she would be loved equally. Or loved even more!

She laughed, remembering a cartoon that had tickled her. Charlie Brown wished for friends. No, by gosh, he wished he had even just one friend. Lucy asked the round-headed boy, "While you're at it, Charlie Brown, why not wish for a million dollars?"

She pulled up to the curb in front of her house. Straight ahead where the sidewalks converged, downhill, she could see the familiar line of blue. From the house, she could only see the sliver of ocean from her kitchen window.

She parked and ran next door to pick up Bob.

Bob had a cheese sandwich and celery for lunch. He ran for his bedroom, where he plunked a plastic keyboard, humming along, mouth full. While he ate, she watched his pudgy fingers and listened to him chatter, then finally went around to the little table where he sat, stroked his hair and gave him a hug.

"You need a shower, Mommy. We're going to a party."

"I promise to dress up if you do."

"Oh, shoot."

Her present concerns crystallized around Bob's birth certificate, the one she might be compelled to produce in court.

She had been all alone with her baby at Community Hospital when the volunteer came by to collect the information for the birth certificate. After her breakup with Richard she had decided to raise Bob entirely on her own, to make enough money so that she wouldn't need child support. Richard had always told her he wasn't ready for a child; he wanted a Romeo and Juliet relationship. That relationship hadn't ended well either, but in the haze of her lust for him, she had thought only of the romantic comparison.

The day the hospital insisted she fill out the forms, out of anger at Richard, out of wishful thinking, out of exhaustion and foolishness and pain, she wrote another name for the birth certificate, someone else she could not put out of her mind.

The decision had seemed harmless at the time. When Bob asked her about it when he was older, she would say—oh, hell, she hadn't thought anything through while she sat nursing him in that hospital bed, her nipples sore, feeling completely unready.

When the DNA results came in, she'd look like a vindictive liar. Great.

Showered and changed into dry clothes, she picked up little-boy litter as she moved from room to room. Aunt Helen's place was a physical wreck inside. She had no time or money to embark on renovations, however, and only at night when she was too tired to think did staring at the blots on the walls bring on dreams of home improvement.

"What should I bring to Grandma's?"

"Put your shoes on and wash that orange gook off your face. Then pack some toys. Oh, and grab Uncle Matt's birthday present, okay? I think I left it on the kitchen table. Don't forget to sign the card."

In her bedroom, she took a look at herself in the mirror. The black T with the peace symbol made her look younger than twenty-eight. Maybe makeup would help. She got out the magic mascara wand and went at her lashes one by one, put on some lipstick, then changed the shirt for a red sweater. Better. She tried smiling into the mirror.

Reality flooded back like a stinker wave.

Richard had left three messages the night before. He wanted to talk to Bob. Nina listened to them anxiously. She might have to get a restraining order or something, and that might be hard because Richard, a smart attorney, knew better than to get overtly violent. His intimidation was the menacing, underlying kind you had a hard time proving. How could she have loved him, even for one second? She felt unnerved and divided.

She could imagine the hearing, the judge saying, "So all he wanted was to talk for a minute to the little boy? And you are opposing all visitation, I see, in the related custody matter."

If she wasn't careful, Richard would outsnake her. She would look vindictive. Somehow it would be her fault that he had ignored Bob his whole life. Richard's illness, his change of heart—she didn't believe a word of it. He couldn't have grown a heart from the wizened pea-sized object lodged in his chest.

She should change her phone number on Monday, too. She had already written a note urgently instructing Bob's school never to allow him to go home with anyone but her, Matt, or her mother.

She had gone to see Jack right before leaving work

the night before. He had spoken with Perry and told him she would cooperate with the orders.

"Richard may have rights, Nina," Jack had gently said. "But there's a bright side. He'll have to pitch in with child support."

"No!"

"You can use the help, can't you?" Jack asked mildly.

"If I take money from him—" He would own her. He would be in her and Bob's lives forever.

Afterward, she went in to tell Klaus what was going on in more humiliating detail than she had offered to Jack. The old man sat behind his immense desk in the dusky office with its warm lamp, reading from a *Supreme Court Reporter*. Sensing her distress, he sat her down on the leather sofa.

"This man accuses you? Of what?"

Embarrassed, she told Klaus of the bad time after Bob's birth, when she had felt so desperately needy she had gone home with strangers. Her boss had stood beside his window looking at her as if from a great and compassionate distance, though he was shorter than her now that advancing age was stooping him. He had picked up the intercom, buzzing the secretary. "Astrid, please screen Ms. Reilly's phone calls. Don't put through any calls from a person called Filsen, or anyone who refuses to give a name."

Klaus had told her not to worry about the legal fee, but she had insisted, and finally he let her promise to pay $50 a month for Jack to represent her in the custody matter. "Not to worry," he told her. "If Jack gets too busy, I will take the case myself."

• • •

Nina collected her books for an afternoon stop at the library after Matt's party and tossed them onto the floorboard of the MG with all the other papers and books she'd filed there, while Bob talked to his stuffy.

Placing Matt's present in the small space behind the car's two seats, she tried to fluff the bow. Matt, her little brother, turned twenty-one today. Their mother had suggested—no, insisted upon—a party. Next to the present, in a cardboard box, sat Matt's cake. BIG 21! said the cake in script. Delicately wrought blue flowers decked out the edges.

When she arrived at her mother's, she found Matt sitting at the dining table wearing a cowboy hat. He had propped his grungy boots right over the pristine white Nottingham-lace tablecloth. Ginny sat across from him on an antique love seat. A long sleeve hung loose about six inches below the elbow of her left arm, which was the first thing Nina saw as she walked into the room.

Nina kissed her mother on the cheek, then took a chair and sat down. "Hi, Matt."

"Yo."

"Hi, Uncle Matt!" Bob said, running toward him, giving his uncle a hug.

"Hey, big boy." Matt hugged him back, then Bob ran off to play with his cars.

Matt put his feet on the floor. "I haven't been feeling that great lately," he complained. Nina watched his hands twitching in his lap, like an infant's, out of control. She guessed he was doing crack again and sighed heavily. She didn't allow Matt around Bob when he was high. He knew that. Was he high?

Ginny noticed Nina's distress and frowned.

"I'm sick of my stupid job." Matt worked out in Carmel Valley at Barney's, a store for locals. "I never pictured myself as some dumb flunky working in a convenience store that caters to winos. But on the plus side the boss puts up with me, no matter how late I show up." Behind a new and straggly spray of whiskers, his face still looked angelic. Even when he'd been toddling behind Nina on her treasure hunts or following her on tree-climbing expeditions, he had charmed people with that look.

"Can you believe this? He says I'm getting too scary with the customers." Matt's expression hardened. "That guy acts like he's giving me my big fucking break."

"Watch your language, Matt," Nina said.

Bob, running cars across the rug, seemed not to notice any of them.

"Honey, you'll get back on track soon. It's been hard for you since Harlan and I—you can get back to school now. Work on your writing." Ginny spoke quickly as if that would somehow etch a real truth onto his shifty skin.

Looking at Nina, Matt said conversationally, "I've been wondering if someone's been screwing around with my food. Nothing tastes right. Or injecting me with AIDS while I sleep."

The spooky words hung in the air for a moment. Ginny leaned over to pat Matt's knee with her right hand. "I remember the day you were born. How happy we were. We loved having a girl first," she said, turning wet eyes on Nina, "but I think all parents want a boy, too."

Matt patted her hand distractedly and said to Bob, "Hey, Bob-o. Wreck 'em!"

Bob slammed two cars together. "Yeah!" he cried as they flew into the air.

"Mom, how are you feeling?" Nina asked. Her mother looked so frail. Bony limbs protruded from a silky, mint-green dress that was now at least two sizes too large. Ginny wore a white cotton glove on her remaining right hand and moved with evident pain.

"Better," she replied. "But you know sometimes I think about animals. How careful we are to save them from suffering. Why's it wrong to end people's suffering?"

"Mom, not this again. You were raised Catholic. You can't think—"

"We understand when our time has come. God's on our side. He doesn't condone needless suffering. The universe is infinite. We aren't. Why not accept that?"

"Oh, for Pete's sake! Don't talk like that. We need you."

Ginny patted Nina's hand. "I'm not jumping off any balconies today, okay?"

Matt looked at his mother, frowned, and got up to clump around the hardwood floor, whispering to himself, sputtering curses. "I ought to kill those goddamned bunglers, those doctors of yours," he finally shouted.

CHAPTER
6

"MATT. SIT DOWN AT THE TABLE," HIS MOTHER said sternly. "Eat your cake."

Matt sat. He was trying hard, but he was barely holding it together. Bob scrambled onto a chair beside his uncle. They sang the birthday song. Nina cut the cake. She handed each one of them a piece on a paper plate.

Ginny always used to cut the cake.

"Nina," Matt said. "White cake? You know I hate this shit."

"Don't eat it then."

"I picked the cake, Uncle Matt. The flowers are your favorite color, blue. That's what boys like, blue." Bob's serious face studied his uncle's. "But I'll eat your piece if you really don't want it."

"Oh, Bob-o. I'm just teasing your mom. See?" Matt

shoved in a huge mouthful, nearly choking while Bob laughed.

"Have another piece, Bob," said Ginny, putting another small piece on Bob's plate.

Bob begged for television and, when everyone said no, returned to his other toys, a garageful of cars and trucks Nina had brought.

Matt stood up and brushed cake from his T-shirt. "I should've driven you up to see another specialist. It's getting worse all the time, isn't it? There's gotta be someone out there who can help you—"

"Sweetie, it makes no sense for me to run off and see a new specialist every time I have questions," replied his mother. "Don't worry so much."

"Maybe Dad can do more," Nina suggested. "He knows everyone. He should help."

"You're an independent young lady, Nina, so I know you'll understand why I don't ask your father for anything more at the moment, okay?"

"What's going on with you and Dad?" Matt asked.

Nina could hardly believe they were talking about this. Her mother did not discuss their father with them.

"Things aren't perfect. That's natural. You know, we were married for thirty-one years."

"You've been divorced for a year now. Isn't that right?" Matt said. "I figured the two of you had things settled."

"Not exactly," Ginny said. "It's ongoing. Even though we had an agreement, spousal support can always be modified. Maybe I should modify it more to my benefit, do more to help you kids."

"Mom, do not squander one single thought on us. Matt and I are fine."

Matt slouched, looking far from fine.

"You need to concentrate on your health," Nina said.

Ginny smiled. "That's so boring. I like thinking about how to help you all have better lives. That makes me happy. What do you think, Nina? Should I go back to court?"

Nina pulled a card out of her wallet. "You know my number at work. You need to talk to Remy Sorensen for an unbiased legal opinion. She's good."

"Thank you, Nina. Advice from experts is good. I know I should stand up for my rights, if not for myself, for you all, to show you what fair looks like. Yes, I was already thinking about seeing Miss Sorensen."

"I'm glad to hear that." Nina studied her mother. She had come to think of her as something of a push-over when it came to Harlan.

"But not about your father. I think I need to do something about the acupuncturist." Ginny moved into the kitchen. "Would you get me a glass of water, Matt? I have to take my pills."

Nina sat back in her chair. She had been trying to get her mother to do something about the acupuncturist for ages. Another lawsuit? Now? What was happening? What was precipitating these lightning-swift changes everyone was going through in the family? She felt sucked down into a wave that wouldn't quit, that just kept pulling her, her brother, her son, her mother, down deeper.

Fear gnawed at her insides. She cupped her hand over her mouth, her throat tight. Get hold of yourself, Nina, she told herself. One thing at a—

"That's just what she needs right now, Nina. First the quacks, then bring on the shysters. More vultures to fight over the carcass," Matt said as he got up.

"Shut up, Matt!"

Ginny Reilly put a pill on her tongue and accepted the glass. She drank, spilling a little. Matt returned, handing her a paper towel. "Thanks, sweetie," Ginny said.

"I need to say this, okay? Nobody fucks with my family and gets away with it."

"Control yourself, Matt. Set a good example for your nephew. You can do that, can't you?" Ginny chided.

"Oops. Sorry, Bob-o." Matt's voice sounded mocking to Nina. Heartsick, she felt certain now that Matt was high on something. Even in this cool house, he sweated.

"Let's pack up that nice cake your sister brought for you. And thank God for your good health, and the day he gave you to us." Matt relaxed when Ginny hugged him, all the tics momentarily gone.

"I need to rest." Ginny leaned close to Nina and murmured, "Take the cake with you for Bob if Matt won't. Just leave me a little piece for tomorrow. It's so good!"

Nina kissed her mother on the cheek. Ginny went to Bob and put her arms around him. With a final long hug and many secret whispered words, Ginny let go of him and went to her room.

"Give me a ride home?" Matt asked.

"How'd you get here?"

"I hitched. People are so naive. I could be a psycho killer. They ought to be more careful."

"Sorry, Matt, I can't give you a ride. I have to go to the library." She gathered up Bob's things, which filled most of a large backpack.

"Okay. No problemo." Matt used a wall phone, murmured a few words, and said, "See you in five."

"You lined up a ride?" Nina asked.

"Yep."

"Go ahead, open your present. I'll be right back."

Her mother was lying down, fully clothed, on top of the bedspread.

"Let me tuck you in," Nina said.

"I'm fine. Sit down a second. Are you all right, honey?"

"Please don't worry about me, Mom."

"That's the problem. We all worry about each other but don't talk enough. Is something special going on with you right now?"

"I don't want to add my problems to your problems."

"Tell me," her mother commanded, still able to pack a wallop.

"Richard Filsen turned up."

"Well, he lives in Seaside, doesn't he? You must see him now and then."

"Actually no, I don't. But he's back and he wants back in our lives. He filed a suit for joint legal custody of Bob and for visitation. They'll be taking Bob's DNA to compare it to Richard's."

"But this is—sickening." Her mother did look sick. "What the hell is he up to?"

Trying not to react to the rare profanity, Nina said, "He claims he's been sick."

"Oh, he's sick all right." Her mother frowned so deeply even her rigid face registered severe alarm. "I knew you couldn't trust him. I told you not to trust him."

"You did. But he left us alone, and I really thought I was off the hook. Now all I can think about is that he wants some kind of relationship with Bob and that means one with me. Oh, Mom."

Her mother's bright eyes caught and held hers. "Don't you dare let him scare you. He's nothing. Nobody. He can't get custody, you know that."

"Even so, I can't believe I allowed this to happen. That man could be in our lives forever."

"That will not happen."

"It's just—it all starts to feel like—"

"Too much. I know the feeling." Her mother tidied her sheet. "Tell me everything he said, okay? Matt can wait a couple more minutes."

When Nina returned to the living room, Matt grabbed her around the waist with his strong arms and picked her up, laughing hysterically. "Smoked almonds, my favorite food from my favorite sister."

"I picked them," Bob said. Matt picked him up and tickled him, while Bob laughed.

Nina watched them. Matt was getting worse. She would have to talk to somebody about him. If she called county services, would they help him or put him in a cell to rot? She dreaded involving Matt in the legal system.

If she did nothing, he'd involve himself soon enough. He was as sick as her mother in his own way.

Had the divorce done all this to them? How could she take the lead for them, get some control of this careening descent?

The doorbell rang. "Um," Matt said, "talk to you for a second, Nina? Can you get the door, Bob?"

Bob went for it.

"Got a few bucks you can spare till I get paid, Nina?" Matt whispered.

"Define 'few.'"

"Twenty?"

She pulled her folded wad of cash out of her jeans pocket and counted it. "Eighteen big extras until my next payday. Will three help?"

He pushed the money back at her, gently. "Forget it, Nina. Buy Bob a Happy Meal. Buy yourself one, for that matter. You look like you could use it more." He smiled his sweet smile at her and went to the door.

Zinnia, a friend of Matt's Nina had never met and had only heard some unsettling stories about, stood in the open doorway, one hand in the pocket of her ragged khakis, gazing vacantly at Bob, a finger wound through her long black hair.

"Bye, all," Matt said.

"Yeah, and, hi, all." Zinnia waved an unenthusiastic hand at them, turning to leave. "You get the money?" she asked Matt before she got out of earshot.

"Birthday bucks from my mom. I'm good."

Nina and Bob left a few minutes later. Ginny closed the door behind them, locked the latch, and picked up the hall phone.

Dust on the table, she noticed, pulling her index finger over its surface. She used to take much better care.

He answered after three rings.

"It's me, Ginny Reilly."

"Hey, Mama, or should I say Grandma?"

"We had a deal."

She almost heard the shrug. "That was then. This is now."

CHAPTER
7

"**I** KNOW I HAVE IT HERE SOMEWHERE," JACK REPLIED.

"You lie, McIntyre," Paul said, smiling. "Took the camera to the shop yesterday after I called, didn't you?"

"Damn the world's detectives."

"The light meter always has been a problem."

Paul took a seat at the table. Jack brought him a plate piled with steaming scrambled eggs. They were at Jack's place, a ramshackle cottage with a sunny deck amid a flourishing forest of poison oak, off Fern Way in the Carmel Highlands.

Paul had arrived the night before, unexpectedly early. While Jack pulled out sheets and blankets for the couch, Paul explained that his boss in San Francisco had told him his replacement, a transfer from Fresno, would be in the next morning. "I hate being redundant," he explained. "Besides. When you're done, you're done. I wasn't going to limp around the place like a duck for two weeks when somebody was available to take over. So I kissed the women and slapped the guys on the back and went home and packed my duffel. I'll finish moving when I find a place down here."

"Stay as long as you like," Jack said. "I know about moving on."

They'd stayed up late watching a replay of last week's 49ers game, drinking a forty-ounce bottle of malt liquor Jack had found in the fridge.

In the late-morning light Paul's eyes had a blasted, staring quality. Unshaven and crusty, he looked to Jack like a hostage stumbling out of a Colombian jungle. He would need some serious rehabilitation.

Such is love, Jack reminded himself, and resolved to try, even if he couldn't possibly succeed, to protect himself slightly from its depredations this time around with Remy.

"So who is it?" Paul asked, tucking in.

"We are not going to discuss my absolutely fantastic love life over eggs."

"You have a new lady. I knew it when you dropped out of touch. Mmm." Paul ate more.

"You said you didn't want to obsess about women. Let's talk about boar hunting. Season will be starting up soon in the Los Padres Forest."

"Have I said how much I love fresh pig meat with my eggs? I'm up for it, but right now it's all I can do to stuff myself with food and pretend I am a fully viable human."

Jack laughed. He picked up the *Monterey Herald*

and read the sports section. While Paul finished up, Jack took a final cup of coffee outside. A couple of early pumpkins decorated the teetering deck that extended out the front door of the wooden cottage. On stilts, the deck hung as sturdily as a leaf in winter.

He lived up the hill from the Carmel Highlands Inn, a venerable hotel that still entertained its cocktail crowds with piano music. Jack preferred to go down the coast to Esalen for hot baths or to eat an expensive hamburger at Nepenthe in his off-hours. He finished his coffee and considered a drive by the ocean, thinking of Remy, her pale skin, her soft cries while he worked her, worked it, felt it happening—she had said she would be tied up today.

He should hang out with his old buddy Paul, who no doubt was feeling lonesome as hell and ready to put a six-shooter to his head. But Paul disappeared up the road, promising to meet up later. Jack went back into the house and, not allowing himself to think, called Remy's place in Carmel. She answered the phone as if she had been waiting.

"I hoped it was you. You made it home all right?"

"In one piece. Yesterday: amazing. You're amazing."

"Careful. I cast spells."

"Too late."

A silence ensued, during which some increasingly heavy breathing came on from one or both of them. Jack imagined her holding the phone—what did she wear to bed? He hadn't found out yet.

Finally she said, "See you in a half hour? Your place."

Stricken with joy, Jack said nothing.

"Put your ear close to the phone."

"It's melded to it."

"I need you," she whispered. "Okay?"

A happy welcoming feeling warmed his scrotum.

Jack lit a fire in the big stone fireplace, shaved, and changed. Outside, fog drifted through the redwoods.

He heard Remy's car crunching leaves in the driveway. He walked out onto the deck as she turned off the motor and stuck her head out the window, blinking up at him through the filtered sun of the forest.

"Hey, what are you driving?" he said, leaning dangerously over the railing. "Where's that ugly Acura you love better than any man?"

Remy laughed. "In the garage. The heater's out again. It hasn't worked well since the day I bought it. Klaus likes me to take his out for a spin now and then anyway." She stepped out of Klaus's mint-condition, white Jaguar convertible, a sixties relic with soft curves and the glow of hand wax. "He likes taking care of me."

Remy climbed lightly up the stairs. At the top, Jack captured her, hugging her long, lissome body for a long time. She smelled like all the spices of China. Leaning her head back, she closed her eyes and went limp. He caught her warm lips. The kiss deepened, turned into open-mouth explorations. Neither of them broke away, until it felt to Jack that he had entered a dream during which they had melted into each other, holding tight.

She rubbed against him, whispering, "We're alone?"

He nodded.

They walked with their arms around each other into the house, stopping to close the curtains and lock the door, getting as far as the pool of warmth in front of the fire, where Jack kicked the chair away and lowered her to the Swedish rug.

He took her cold hands between his own and held them until she took them away and pulled down her jeans. Her silk camisole was cut low over soft breasts. Her shoulders were so white they seemed to shine in the light filtering through the curtains. Jack slipped the thin straps down and bent his head, kissing her. Her panties were gratuitous, evanescent; easy to push aside whenever. He liked the feel of them and decided to keep them on her. Stroking his hair, she raised his head up and kissed him harder on the mouth, electrocuting him with her lips.

This sort of mad love doesn't last, Jack thought, so I'd better enjoy this as hard as I can.

She unzipped him, slipping her hands inside to touch him, first tentatively, finally with frantic strokes. When she began to strike his chest and push him, he grabbed her hands and took over. Raising them over her head, he pulled the rest of her clothes off while she writhed, eyes closed. He fucked her in several ways with a royal roughness not in his usual style, but Remy wanted it, she wanted him, and every moment felt perfect. If that was her thing, rough was their thing. Whatever she wanted.

Afterward they faced each other, Jack back in his jeans and Remy nude as a white birch, her light hair shining red in the firelight. She wore a mild expression, a satisfied expression, the kind that makes a man feel as if he's done his job.

"You know Botticelli's Venus? That's you."

"He was gay and never used live models," she said.

"You're too damn smart." He tried to take her into his arms again, but she murmured protests and wriggled away, heading laughing for the shower.

Outside, the sky slipped into gray the way it does as the year grows late. The redwood-paneled room with its fireplace now seemed to be drifting into a January night instead of a September afternoon. Right then, in a swift, definitive energy shift, Jack felt the season change from summer to autumn. He smelled winter ahead, feeling the comfort that comes from being part of the rolling parade of life and time.

Peace overcame him, the peace of balance, when all comes together: Remy's beauty, their heated lovemaking, that it was still only Saturday and he had almost two free days. He congratulated himself on his luck.

Used up, replete, simple, he lay on the couch with his hands parked behind his head, awaiting her return.

Another shift occurred, though, when Remy came back into the living room fully dressed. She had slicked her wet hair tightly against her head, and for a moment her face in the shadows had the highlighted look of a skull. She's too thin, Jack thought.

"I have to go," she said.

He sat up fast.

"I'm the defense in that real-estate-swindle trial. You remember me describing it at the last partners' meeting? Trial is next Monday. I have a lot of prep work." She moved toward him.

He smelled the soap on her skin and reached up to pull her to him. "Sit down here," he ordered.

Sighing, she sat down next to him. Jack slid down onto his knees and knelt in front of her. He took her hand and kissed it.

"You are my Queen of Sheba."

She smiled. "A legend."

"Cleopatra. Nefertiti. I will worship you all day in various specific ways we can discuss henceforth if you stay with me."

"Oh, Jack."

"All of me will need all of you in a few minutes. Keep looking at me like that and we're talking a few seconds."

"You're so different from the man I practice law with at work. So—ardent."

"You're different, too."

"No."

"Glorious in the sack. I need say no more."

"We're well matched. I like your body, how you are compact but strong. I like to be the one to lie back and take it, and I know you like to be the one who gives it." She gave him a sideways look. Her eyelashes swept across her eyes.

Jack grabbed her, saying, "That does it. Now we'll go to the bedroom."

"No, no. Back to work." She stood up, straightened her clothes, and left.

Jack finished dressing, had a beer, collected the

pumpkins on the deck, and began carving them into salacious, leering faces.

They would be rotten long before Halloween. The moment of bliss had passed and he felt lonely for Remy already. Oh, shit, he was falling in love. He saw it coming on like a disaster that cost lives, a freight-train flu.

When he finished with the pumpkins, he set them on a chair by the door to greet Paul and drove down to Nepenthe. He drank more Coors as the Big Sur sky clouded and unclouded and watched the waves hundreds of feet below, water to the edge of the world as far as he could see, water too cold to touch.

CHAPTER
8

THE NEXT DAY, BOB STOOD AT THE WINDOW OF THE
kelp forest, his nose pressed to the glass. "Look!
That fish has sharp teeth." Nina hauled him back
behind the railing. "They put this here so little boys will
stay safe behind it," she said as he took off for the next
exhibit. She pushed through the crowds, straining to
keep him in sight.

The Monterey Bay Aquarium overwhelmed what
was left of Cannery Row. The building was designed to
recall the old canneries that had sat on this site for many
years, in the early part of this century busy and produc-
tive, and since then abandoned and derelict. Now a
huge attraction, it extracted local sea life from the bay
to amuse the masses. Bob loved everything about it, especially the jellyfish tank. Nina tolerated the crowds for
a glimpse of the sharks in the central tank.

They didn't have time this foggy afternoon for a

grand tour. Sundays, she usually studied while Bob played with a neighborhood friend. She hadn't slept long enough, but this morning was important.

"Hi, Dad," she said in the big, busy lobby.

"Hello, Nina-pinto." Harlan Reilly kissed her cheek and looked her over. "You look tired, sweetheart." At least he had refrained from commenting on her unhemmed jeans, which he could not usually resist doing. "Where's our boy?" he asked, locating Bob a few feet away. Her father wore a casual golf shirt and slacks, perfectly pressed. He placed the grubby boy on his shoulders and began trotting in a circle. "Whew! You're one hefty muscleman!"

Other mothers watched and nodded approvingly. Had he done those things with Matt when he was little? Nina was sure he had never put her on his shoulders, yet it appeared so natural. She remembered the lulling charm, that social glow that made him such a pleasure to be around. She recalled the verbal gymnastics at the dinner table. Harlan loved to argue. He always won, too.

As she grew older, Nina realized her father's talent lay in making the most incredible story entirely plausible. He made up facts to support his arguments that she could not trace and therefore refute. He was a master confabulator, a perfect preparation for the blusterers in law school.

"Our young man has a technical mind," Harlan pronounced, watching as Bob fingered his current favorite toy, a plastic sub from their latest fast-food meal. Harlan himself was solid corporate management for a media firm, but he had never finished college. He had worked his way up and told who would ever know what lies to land a lucrative, respectable position. He had waited in vain for Nina, then Matt, to exhibit an interest in business. He reveled in the political connections he had gained through local social clubs and personal magnetism.

Nina steered them to an outside deck that hung over the water. Bob circled the perimeter, settling on the ground near a concrete bench, pulling out his sub, making noises.

"You said you had something important to talk about, Dad, and I do want to hear why. But I need to get back to study."

Her father looked at her, his face serious, then a corner of his mouth turned up. "How was the party yesterday?"

"Party?"

"Your mom wouldn't miss Matt's birthday, would she? She loves a party."

"Fine."

"How's Matt?"

"Don't you talk?"

"I sent him a present. A fancy shirt."

"If you care about Matt, I guess you would have called and found out."

"That's not fair. I love you and Matt. You know that much. You're a smart girl, for God's sake!"

Nina sighed. "You know I have to study on Sunday, Dad. I'm glad to see you, but you said we had to talk. Why?"

"This isn't easy."

Nina didn't say, *Poor you*. She didn't want to hurt

her father. When she drove near bicyclists, she had the same thought. Don't hit that poor guy on his bike, even though he's in your lane, acting arrogant. His headgear looks weird and he reminds you of a certain unpleasant person.

"I hope you can understand," he said, timid and persuasive at the same time. "It's about Angela."

Nina remembered her mother's pain about Angie, oh, yeah.

He cleared his throat. "Oh, God, it's probably been six months since you met. You remember her from the night we had dinner? At Casa Maria's." He trilled the Spanish *r*.

Angie, a divorcée in her thirties, only a few years older than Nina, had laughed, smoked, and acted entirely awkward with Nina and Matt. Nina reddened at the memory of how Angie had kissed her father, long, red fingernails scratching his neck.

"Yeah, at your wedding celebration."

"Right!" Harlan said with the false enthusiasm of a teacher encouraging a dumb student. They had flown off to Vegas several months before the dinner party. Nina had first learned the news from her mother, who relayed it matter-of-factly.

"So here's the thing."

"Spit it out, Dad."

"Well, looks like I'm going to be a father again."

Nina blinked. Her father was fifty-eight years old. She didn't like to think he had sex, and even less did she like thinking he contained live sperm.

Oh. A second wave of realization almost drowned

her. This meant a tiny baby sister for Nina or, worse, another brother. No, no, no.

He beamed. "I've got twenty years on her. Not bad for an old man like me, eh?"

More like twenty-five years, but Nina didn't correct him. "What do you want me to say?" She wanted not to care, to wish him the best, but she couldn't say it; she could only think badly of him and wish that life had some objective gauges.

"Try, 'I'm glad for you. I want you to be happy.'" He poked her on the arm. "I don't expect you to dance a jig, babe, but I sure as hell don't want you dancing on my grave yet either."

"Don't call me babe."

He laughed. "You know what you want, Nina? Because I do."

"Really. What?"

"You want us to be perfect. Sorry. Wish I was for your sake."

"What about Mom?"

"Naturally, you worry about her."

"I just asked a question."

"Your mother is stronger than you imagine. You baby her."

"She's sick, Dad!"

"You think I've failed her, don't you, Nina? I didn't know she was sick when we broke up. I swear I didn't."

"Matt and I just want Mom treated fairly. You should know I told her about a lawyer from my firm. She was thinking about getting further advice about your financial agreement." Not true exactly, but she couldn't resist hurting him a little.

Harlan lifted his chin and Nina looked into icy blue eyes. "She wants more money. That's natural." He squeezed Nina's shoulder. "And of course you want the best for her. From my point of view, this is not just about money, though I admit alimony has become a hell of a burden. I want a fresh start. I deserve it. I can't have her hanging over my life forever—"

He scrutinized Nina's face. "I've always done what's right for your mother, but can't you see my changed situation affects things? Please talk to her for me. Feel her out. She called me, you know. She's pressing hard on the support issue."

"Let me remind you about spousal support in California, Dad. After such a long marriage, you are obliged to take care of Mom for life."

"I don't necessarily object. The question is whether she's going to make it impossible for me to take care of the rest of my own life. I think of myself as more than just the man bringing home the money. That's all I ever was to her. Someone to complain to. Someone to gripe about, who tracked mud in, who dirtied up the place. I'm going to be a lot happier now, Nina-pinto, and I hope my happiness means something to you. You're my daughter, too."

"Does Angie meet you at the door with a 'Hi, darling'? Bring you your newspaper in the evenings?" Nina felt she should be crying but her eyes were dry and her voice rock hard. "Will you buy her a new couch when she wants one?" Old stories, old wounds. They marched out and erected a wall.

"Take a look at it again, Nina, when you recover from the shock. Get used to the idea. Everyone better just get used to the idea. A new life. A child. A new family. This is a good thing."

She tried to wrap her mind around people in the world without food, water, and bare necessities, but her mother's face overrode every single thought. After decades, the family she and Matt had known was dissolving.

So she thought, shit. Repeated three times.

Then she looked around. "Dad? Where's Bob?"

They split up. Harlan took the touchy-feely area where kids could hold urchins and sea cucumbers. Nina ran back toward the shark tank.

They met up in front of the lobby gift shop. By now Nina was crying.

"We'll find him, honey," Harlan said, seeming surprised at her sudden complete disintegration. "Kids get lost, and then you find them."

"You check the otters outside. I'll check the upper deck, then the theater, okay?"

"Okay." They split up again.

Nina rushed up to the deck at the top of the otter exhibit, one of Bob's favorite places. No Bob.

She looked down at the layer of people below. Again, no son.

He was wearing a bright red shirt and carrying his favorite stuffy, a white seal he called Harp.

She caved in to fear so severe she felt earthquaked, firestormed, hit by an asteroid. "Bob!" she shouted. "Bob! Oh my God! Bob!"

People looked up at her from below, curious.

A security guard, female, looking concerned, materialized beside her almost immediately. "You lost someone?"

"My son! His name is Bob. He's four years old, wearing a red shirt. Poppy-colored. Some orange mixed—he's four years old."

"Ma'am, we'll find him. He's here at the aquarium, okay? I promise we'll find him. He got stuck staring at the sharks or the jellies or the undersea camera." She took Nina's arm, trying to steer her down the stairs.

"You don't know he's okay! Don't you lie to me."

"Kids get lost here every hour of every day," the guard said as they continued down. "Chances are, he's okay. Please don't panic."

"I need to meet my dad. Maybe he found Bob. Maybe he did."

The guard nodded and rushed with her toward the huge kelp tank. Dozens of people stared, riveted at the sight of huge fish circling, nowhere to go.

Harlan huffed up beside her. "No luck." He put his arm around her shoulders. "Nina, honey, we'll find him. Please don't cry like that."

"Let me check with our people, okay?" The security guard, with a badge reading AUGUSTA, began speaking into a walkie-talkie.

"Lost and found," Harlan said, holding Nina tightly. "Like a lost wallet. Some honest person found it and will return it. Him. This isn't New York City, for God's sake."

She didn't answer.

"You are such a stressed-out mom. He's a kid, okay? He wandered away. Strangers who abduct children are so rare, honey. Just people in the media make it into big news."

"You don't get it!" Nina pulled away from him, shouting.

Harlan looked bewildered. Even the security guard stepped back nervously.

"Richard has been coming around. He wants custody. He wants visitation. He wants to ruin our lives!"

"Richard Filsen?" All the ruddy Irish blood in her father's face drained.

"Oh, Dad. What if he kidnapped Bob?" Here in stark relief, her fears had an outlet and a power she could not control. She wanted to die. She wanted to live. To see Richard Filsen dead and gone and her son by her side unsullied, untroubled, perfect as always.

"That's impossible. Richard Filsen is out of the picture."

She didn't have time to register the strange parallel response he and Ginny shared at the thought of Richard's reappearance because at that exact moment, a young woman with a stroller approached them, Bob's hand in hers.

"I couldn't find you, Mommy, and I needed to go."

"Don't worry." The young woman smiled. "I had an extra Huggie for him."

CHAPTER
9

REMY LIKED JACK. SHE LIKED HIM SO MUCH THAT she had suspended her better judgment by getting involved with him. But just barely into the relationship she was seeing her worst fears realized. He was possessive, even critical. Why was it that once a man got to know you, he wanted nothing more than to change you? Bad timing on Jack's part.

She felt self-confident these days, stronger, taller, slimmer. She liked how close to the bone she had become. She had an exciting prospect ahead of her. Rick Halpern, current president of the county Bar Association, had passed on rumors that one of the Superior Court judges was about to retire. "Gonna go for it, Remy? You know you've got my support," he had said, giving her a little squeeze on the arm. The casualness of his comment thrilled her. Apparently, others viewed her as a realistic candidate.

She wanted it. She would channel all her energies into getting it. She would make whatever sacrifices were necessary, and she would be the best and brightest judge Monterey County had ever seen.

She had a court appearance scheduled this morning. Bending her head down so that her hair fell forward and brushing from her neck up, she luxuriated for a moment in the sheer pleasure of her life. The coffee was hot; her house was in excellent order. Even this tension with Jack excited her. She had wanted him for a long time. He was such a temptation. He had no idea how tempting, even though he wasn't very tall. She saw the looks other women gave him when the two of them were together.

Just like Jack to be oblivious to his own charms. The world was gracious to Jack. Life was easy. She on the other hand worked hard for everything. Only lately could she relax like this and enjoy the richness she had earned with her efforts, including this house on the beach.

Ten minutes later, she pulled the Acura off the highway onto Aguajito right by Monterey Peninsula College, gliding up the hill to the three-story courthouse and jail. She found a parking space quickly. She always found a parking space here, a far cry from the main Chicago Circuit Court.

In Chicago, nobody would have recommended her for a judgeship. That was why she'd left. No matter how many times she proved herself there, she couldn't shake the initial image that had formed because of that one stupid mistake. Well, it was natural to want to gentle the raw bones in adulthood. It never paid to hang around where the kids remembered your big, awkward elbows.

As she walked into the courtroom, heads turned. A judge looked over his glasses at her before looking back to the files in front of him. The criminal defendants in orange jumpsuits waited patiently to be led back to jail until their next hearing. She walked past mostly empty pews reserved for witnesses and spectators, through the low gate, to the nearest empty chair in the lawyers' section. Derek Agee leaned over and whispered in her ear, "You're up next. He didn't notice you weren't here for roll call."

"Thanks," she whispered. She sat back in her chair waiting for the court to come back around to her case, which involved a union grocery-store clerk who had been fired for having a couple of garnishments against his paycheck. Barry Tzanck, opposing counsel, represented the insurance company for the grocery chain. He studied his notes. She opened her briefcase and removed three stapled pages. She passed them down to Tzanck, who took them, looked at them, and began to shake his head as he read.

Judge Sturdy called her case. She and Tzanck stood before the bar. Tzanck started to talk, but the judge brushed his arguments off with a wave of his hand.

"I am inclined to find that Mr. Tzanck's motion to dismiss this case is well-taken, Ms. Sorensen," the judge said. "Do you have anything you wish to add?"

Lying awake in bed the night before, Remy had rehearsed this moment. How had it begun? "Yes, Your

Honor," she said slowly. "I stand before the Court today ready to concede many points because the concessions no longer matter. That is because, Your Honor, the argument Mr. Tzanck and I were going to have today has just been decided by the United States Supreme Court in its decision in *Rosetta v. Happy Valley Grocery Stores*." That case had been pending for two years. Nobody expected the decision would be out this term because of the large volume of death-penalty appeals.

She walked over to the clerk and handed her a copy of the case opinion, which was then handed on to the judge. She looked at Tzanck, who was devastated, although he was trying not to show it. He had to answer to a senior claims adjuster, who was not going to be happy. "I regret I could not get a copy of this dispositive case to Mr. Tzanck earlier. But of course he has several research associates whom I must assume brought the case to his attention." She observed the other attorney out of the corner of her eye, deflated as a busted balloon, and rightly so. He had been absolutely confident of a win. He'd had all the case law on his side until four days before, but had failed to check the newest decisions.

Remy had asked Nina to check the most recent cases yesterday. Nina had come through.

"The Court will take a fifteen-minute recess to read this case. Then we'll see the two of you in chambers," Judge Sturdy said mildly. He had already skimmed the headnotes. He knew she had Tzanck.

"How many rabbits do you keep in that invisible hat, Remy?" Derek said with admiration when she left the courtroom a little later.

* * *

Surrounded by a flurry of papers that needed filing or action, Nina sat at her desk unable to work. She couldn't get her latest bout with Richard out of her mind. She saw that a DNA test loomed, and that once his paternity was established, he would have a permanent place in her life. She had hands on both cheeks, although they weren't working so well to hold her head together.

How had it come to this? Was Richard dying or something? Was there no way out of this mess?

"Hey, play tennis with me this afternoon?" Jack said.

"Tennis? Huh?"

"I'm thinking you'll lose and I'll look good."

"Further confirming you're a smart man."

"What's the matter?"

Sighing, even reduced to wringing hands, Nina told him. "Is it possible Richard could get custody?"

"No."

"No?"

"We won't let that happen. We'll do whatever it takes to help you."

His confidence bolstered her. She felt a tear roll down her cheek. "I can't lose Bob, Jack."

"I know." He put a hand on her shoulder.

And it sizzled like a house on fire.

Matt arrived a few minutes after Jack left, again needing money.

"No," Nina said shortly.

"You'd let me starve?"

"Come to dinner with me and Bob. I'll make meat loaf with ketchup just the way you like it, okay? No need to starve. Mom likes to cook for you, too, and her food's way better."

"Nina, c'mon. You can spare fifty." He gestured around her office, taking it in. "Or how about twenty?"

"She's out there waiting for you, isn't she?" Nina nodded toward the window.

"Huh? Who?"

"Your drug-dealing pal, Zinnia."

He did not flinch. "No."

"Matt, you lie to me. You lie to yourself. I'm onto you, okay? Don't ask me for any more money. I won't give you any."

"You're my sister. You should help me when I need help."

"I won't help you buy drugs."

"I need money for rent!"

"Move home. Mom would love the company, and she has an empty bedroom just waiting for you."

Suddenly, he looked like her little brother again, angelic and mischievous. "Nina, you know I'd drive her as crazy as I've driven myself."

"I didn't suggest it was a good idea, did I?"

They parted on good terms, as they usually did, him shrugging off her refusal, her admiring her sweet brother, and so sad, watching him slink away, defeated and nervous.

She loved him so helplessly.

On her way up the courthouse hallway, Remy was stopped by a gaunt-looking woman with a cane. "Excuse me for bothering you."

"No problem," said Remy. "What can I do for you?"

"Well, first of all, my name is Virginia Reilly. You know my daughter, Nina. She works for your firm." This bent-over person looked old enough to be Nina's grandmother. "Nina mentioned you might be here and told me what you looked like. Cute jacket, by the way."

"Thanks," said Remy automatically. "Please go on." She felt a wave of sympathy for this woman who looked so fragile, Nina's mother.

"I need a lawyer," said Mrs. Reilly.

"For?"

"An acupuncturist stuck needles in my fingers. An infection developed, a very bad infection, and they had to take—"

"What did they take, Mrs. Reilly?"

At the same moment Virginia Reilly raised her arm and pulled up a loose sleeve. "My left hand. You see. It's gone. Gangrene. Such a horrible word. Sorry, it's hard to say and must be even harder to hear. Nina has been urging me—she says we should make some sort of claim."

"*I'm* so sorry," said Remy, shocked. She moved her eyes with an effort back up to the woman's face. "Here's my card. I'll be happy to discuss this with you more, tomorrow in my office. I'll ask Nina to set it up. Would you like her there?"

Mrs. Reilly shook her head. "Leave her out of this, but I do thank you, Miss Sorensen."

"Call me Remy." She gave Mrs. Reilly a pat on the shoulder and walked down the stairs. She had places to go. She put the poor lady out of her mind.

CHAPTER
10

WHEN NINA ARRIVED AT THE OFFICE THE next morning, Astrid cornered her on the way in and asked her to verify a pile of petty-cash slips.

The usual motley crew of clients sat draped around the reception area, their faces expressing discomfort or desperation.

Down the hall Nina passed Jack's office, then turned into her own tiny office, which seemed smaller than it was because of the bookshelves from floor to ceiling on three walls. Before she could pick up the phone, Jack walked in and plopped down in a chair. His hair nudged his collar. He needed a shave. Fidgeting, he said, "Hot in here. I'd suggest you open the window if you had one."

"Good morning to you, too," said Nina. "You sure have been dragging around here lately. You okay?"

"The usual. I'm too old for this shit." Jack's eyes drooped but on the whole he looked pleased with himself.

"Oh, yes, happy belated birthday. Just keep those gray hairs sprinkling around the temple. Makes you look very distingué." She wondered if he had had a party.

"Such language," Jack murmured. "How're you doing?"

She thought about the appalling fear she had barely survived on Sunday, thinking of Bob lost forever. Gone. But these were not thoughts to share with a handsome attorney who made her shiver sometimes, just walking past. "Well, Halloween is weeks away, and Bob keeps coming up with new concepts for his costume, and they keep getting more complicated. He's so excited about going trick-or-treating for the first time."

"I remember those days. Magic in the air."

"Main reason never to grow up."

"Then you'd miss out on the X-rated stuff."

Nina smiled and indulged in a fantasy. She and Jack would go out to dinner, do some kissing after, maybe even go back to her place, where magic would indeed fill the air.

"You need some fun," Jack said as if reading her mind.

Oh, we could sure have some fun, but you're all tangled up with Remy, Nina thought. "You have something in mind?"

"I do. I want you to meet an old friend of mine. His name is Paul van Wagoner. He moved down here from

San Francisco. I knew him in college and we were both in the Peace Corps together. Went to law school together for a while. He and Remy and I are having dinner tonight at Club XIX. Will you come?"

"Blind date. Uh-oh." She lifted her hair off one shoulder of her sweater, leaving a damp mark behind.

Jack stood up and walked behind her, lifting a few strands of her hair. "Still wet from the shower. All that long hair's impractical for someone who loves to surf and swim, isn't it?"

"So tell me about this guy who needs a messy-haired blind date like me?" She moved away.

He leaned against a bookcase. "He's a detective with Monterey County. A serious-crimes investigator. He's working out of the Coastal Division of the sheriff's office."

"Hmm."

"You don't have to marry him. And the food at Club XIX is not frozen or from cans. And he'll pay. He admits you're taking a risk. He said to tell you he's got a good Irish joke for you."

She laughed. "Sold."

"By the way, I ran into Richard Filsen. He continues to nurture an unhealthy interest in you. He bent my ear wanting to know all about you."

"What did he ask, Jack?"

"Everything. He hinted a lot, you know? Before I could shut him up."

"Assume the DNA proves he's my son's father."

"Okay."

"When the results come, do they mean I will have

to allow Richard rights like visitation? He hasn't shown any interest in Bob until now. I've raised him entirely on my own."

"The judge will consider that, yes."

"And the judge will consider Richard's paternity."

"Yes."

"I feel like I made a fatal life mistake. Isn't that awful?"

"You have your son."

"Thank you for the reminder. Yes, I have my sonny boy. What about a restraining order that would stop Richard from hanging around me or Bob?"

"Has he hurt you or threatened you or your son?"

"He's too smart to do anything obvious. He followed me home once. He parks in front of the house sometimes and sits there, staring. He follows me in my car and shows up in places I go. I feel intimidated, although I'm not sure that's what he intends. I don't know what's going on with him."

"You could try for an order, although it doesn't sound like a sure bet, and you might just antagonize him into hardening his resolve."

Klaus passed by her door and looked in at them.

"Time for me to look busy," Nina said.

"We'll pick you up in P.G. around seven, okay?"

For the next hour, Nina talked on the phone, answering at least ten calls and initiating another dozen. She had Astrid's temp trying to get the State Department of Corporations. She needed to reach a lawyer who had written a brief on another tax issue she was researching for

Louis. She also lined up some witnesses for Jack's prelim in a drug case set for tomorrow.

About eleven, the temp, a round-faced, young fellow named Griffin, came to Nina's door to announce that Virginia Reilly had arrived. She met her mother in the reception area, noticing the carefully applied makeup and sprayed hair.

Nina gave her a hug. "You look nice today, Mom."

"I swear the older you get, the more time you have to invest in your looks, and this while your looks along with your derriere are both in steady decline. It's one of those futile acts, like pushing a boulder up a mountain only to have it roll down and knock you over." Ginny studied her daughter, lifted a hand, and pushed Nina's hair back from her forehead. "You should get that hair out of your eyes. Show off those fresh pink cheeks of yours."

Nina laughed. "You're right. I should put the whip to it. My hair, I mean."

But nothing would happen that day. Astrid handed her mother some forms to fill out and told her she would have to come back the next day to go over details of the case with Remy, because Remy had an unexpected court appearance. Nina felt the familiar catching at the back of her throat, so she hurried her mother along, dropping her off at home.

Nina put in a heavy afternoon, then picked up Bob at the sitter's and rushed home to fix him something to eat while he took in the evening cartoons. She called Bob's regular sitter to remind her she needed her tonight.

"Shoot! I'm sorry, Nina. I forgot! I have a rehearsal.

I'm playing Viola in the school play. I get to dress like a man. Isn't that great?"

Nina took down numbers for two other friends, both of whom said roughly the same thing, although they were playing at something else, then sat staring at the phone for a minute before calling her next-door neighbor, Kanani Cherry, an empty nester from Oahu. Kanani had come to live in California because her sister had a hot job as a divorce lawyer in San Francisco and her kids had settled on the peninsula.

"Oh, goodie," Kanani said. "I'll make Bob *lilikoi* cake."

Nina dashed around, putting on her only pair of real gold earrings, a low-cut black sweater and short skirt, fluffed her hair, and dabbed jasmine oil all around because it smelled like what she imagined of the tropics. Kanani arrived, brushing off Nina's apologies and abject thanks.

"Don't answer the door to anyone, Kanani, okay?"

Oh, you paranoid mom, Kanani's calm face said. "Go and have a good time," she said kindly. "I promise to keep Bob safe, okay?"

"I mean it," Nina felt compelled to add.

"I mean it, too." Kanani pushed Nina out the door.

The first thing Nina did when she got into the backseat of Jack's car was to take a long look at Paul van Wagoner. After taking a similarly long look at her legs as she entered the car, he smiled back at her in approval, and she noted hazel eyes in a strong, tan face, blond hair like Remy's. "Those are some hot shoes."

Everyone peeked at her heels, Jack and Remy leaning over their seats.

"Heels make useful weapons when the arguments aren't going well."

They all laughed. "Glad you could make it tonight. You have an adventurous spirit, I'm thinking," Paul said with interest and warmth, and Nina felt herself heating up fast in response. She had made mistakes in the past, okay, but she sure missed male companionship, and Paul seemed eager to offer it. Within five minutes, he was pressing his leg against hers accidentally on purpose, squeezing her in the small space.

Jack and Remy must have picked up some of the mood in the backseat. Remy's hand slid over and rested on Jack's thigh. "Here we go," she said. She wore a buttery leather jacket that smelled like the interior of a new car along with long, wide-ankled silk pants. She bent toward Jack and kissed his cheek. The back of his neck turned red.

Jack said, "I'll cruise past Asilomar Beach on the way to Seventeen Mile Drive. Paul hasn't been down here in a long time."

The evening was unusually warm, an Indian-summer night, mellow and clear.

In spite of the fine evening and fine company, Nina couldn't help thinking about the letter she had received just a day before requiring a DNA test. Then she imagined Bob's upcoming appointment. He hated being poked by needles. He might cry. She hated to see her little boy cry.

She could fight it, but Jack had assured her, on this

point Richard would win. She should allow it, then duke it out with Richard. He had no rights when it came to Bob. None. The law should agree, or what good was it?

A sudden thought assailed her—Bob would want his father. He would miss him all his life.

She couldn't fix that. She couldn't fix everything.

She couldn't help her mother, either.

But now was not the time to indulge in these daily worries. She needed to concentrate on what was happening right now.

A terrifyingly attractive man sat next to her, concentrating. On her.

CHAPTER
11

NINA LEANED BACK AGAINST THE SEAT, CLOSED her eyes for a moment, and took in the atmosphere. She had almost forgotten how female they could make her feel, these attractive fellows with their jokes, hairy bodies, and bigness.

She opened her eyes again, willing herself into the moment. Her skirt felt suddenly shorter. She pulled on it, trying to get comfortable. Paul was so close that when they turned to talk to each other, their noses almost touched. Jack played tour guide, but they were all too busy bathing themselves in the glow of sunset and each other to look at the scenery.

At the Pebble Beach golf course, a few late golfers were turning in their carts next to the restaurant. Inside, the dining room was full of people, mostly older men wearing blazers, the women in flowery dresses though summer was long gone. The four of them had a reservation, but the place was running late, so they retired to the bar. Remy took off her jacket to reveal a satin blouse cut close to her lean body. She looked tall and confident, leaning into Jack as she talked.

Perched on a bar stool beside Remy, listening to the low murmurs of the bar-and-restaurant crowd, Nina felt young and slapdash. She couldn't even reach the bar stool's foothold. Did she belong here, among all these confident, accomplished people? Why were they all so tall? She bet not a one of them was worrying too much about what junior would be wearing to his first real Halloween. Why, that woman's blue-and-gold scarf would buy a whole haunted house.

Remy, Jack, and Paul caught up on each other while Nina studied the room, wondering what it was about this world that had attracted her. In fact, she had never much considered that much of an attorney's job involved networking, listening to gossip, and hanging out with other attorneys wearing suits. She and Remy had worked together for two years, but this was the first time they had done something together socially. She had no idea what Remy thought of her.

This sudden feeling of not fitting in made her shy. Nina's first rush of enthusiasm tempered as she realized that Paul was interested in her but not thunderstruck. Still, as the four chatted and the cocktails took effect, she realized she was feeling good, pleased to meet a man who seemed intelligent, and amazed at herself for liking him so swiftly; also wary, since that had gotten her in trouble before. She also loved watching Jack. He could be so cute, telling jokes and then laughing like a barking seal at himself, louder than anyone else.

Remy was in her element. More expansive than Nina had ever seen her, she ordered a second round of drinks, was sarcastic and funny about the canned music, and laughed at Paul's lawyer jokes, all the time looking like someone famous. "You and Jack knew each other at Harvard?" she asked Paul, teasing Jack with her stockinged foot.

"For undergrad and a few months of law school," Paul responded, smiling. "I decided for a guy like me the streets would be better than the courtroom. I switched to grad school at Northeastern, but we saw each other almost every weekend. We went rock climbing in New Hampshire."

"There aren't any really big mountains there. The White Mountains aren't high," added Jack. "But the weather can change in a second. Mount Washington has the highest wind speed ever recorded in the Western Hemisphere."

"What about that one rock face near North Conway?" Paul reminded him.

"Oh, yeah. We climbed that one dreaming of the Himalaya."

Paul took a sip of his drink. "Jack's a competitive sucker when it involves something he really cares about. And very sleazy. If he decides to be first up the mountain, let him. Hold on to your dignity if you can."

"That's dubious, van Wagoner. When was the last time I got up there first? Huh? You're a goddamned inspiration to me!" Jack punched Paul's arm. "Then we joined the Peace Corps. We both got posted to Nepal, and there we were as the plane descended into the Kathmandu valley, this long line of snowy peaks farther up in the sky than any mountains have a right to be. We wanted to summit a big mountain together. Machupuchare or Thamserku—"

"Why?" Nina asked.

Paul answered, "To impress the ladies with stories of courage and manliness, of course."

"Would that impress you, Nina?" asked Remy.

"If they came back alive."

Jack continued, "We were assigned to teaching English in schools on opposite sides of the country. We figured—Nepal, it's just a dot on the map. We'd get together and climb on weekends. But the whole country turned out to be cut by transverse mountain gorges with furious rivers running down the middle. And the main way of getting around was walking.

"We weren't on opposite sides exactly, but I was in the eastern Terai, at sea level down toward India. Paul was a couple of hundred miles away and twelve thousand feet higher at Namche Bazar. There was a small plane that flew into Lukla, a couple days' trek from Namche, but who had money in those days?"

"The result being that I did almost all the climbing while Jack consoled himself with ganja," Paul said.

"And working hard to make a better life for the locals," Nina said lightly.

"We worked our fool heads off," Paul said, "definitely."

"In totally different ways," Jack added.

"Did you pick investigation of serious crimes as your career? Or did it pick you?" Nina asked Paul.

"It picked me."

"Okay. Care to elaborate?"

"I'll pass on that. That reminds me of this Irishman who was on a quiz show not too long ago. Something you might relate to, Nina."

"Oh?" Nina said. Jack and Remy leaned forward.

"Yes, he was a dyed-in-the-wool county Galway sort of guy. Smart guy on an English TV show. He picked as his area of expertise modern Irish history. So the MC asks his first question: 'Who was the first president of Ireland?'"

"'Pass,' says the Irish guy. The audience is appalled. Not know Eamon de Valera? How stupid is this guy?"

Paul took a long drink of water. "So the MC says, 'Here's your second question. What's the year Eire became an independent country?'

"'Pass,' says the Irishman.

"Now the audience is staggered. What an idiot! These aren't exactly hard questions. So the MC says, 'Here's your last question, then. What was the crop whose failure led to the great Irish famine of the nineteenth century?' What do you think the Irishman says, Nina?"

"What?"

"'Pass.' The audience starts to boo, but then, from way back in the audience, a loud Irish voice calls, 'That's right, me boy, don't tell those bastard English a thing!'"

Nina laughed with the others and thought, true enough. You don't volunteer information to the enemy. Her dad had taught her that rule long ago.

The waiter arrived to tell them their table was ready. As they followed his white jacket toward the dining room, Paul held Nina back for a moment, whispering, "Any chance I can see you again?"

"Well, sure."

"Great. In addition to your obvious charms, Jack says you have a cottage behind your house for rent. And that you'd make an excellent landlord. Now that I've met you, I think he made a mistake." Paul laughed at the look on her face. "You'd make a spectacular land-lady."

She didn't approve of this turn of events, but would never admit it. "Jack never mentioned you needed a place."

"I thought we should meet first."

"To see if we hit it off?" Nina leaned against the brick wall just outside the dining room. Paul had a good eight inches on her in spite of her heels.

"Well, didn't we?" He put his head close to hers and instead of kissing her, which she expected, rubbed his cheek against her cheek. Neither of them seemed to breathe. Then they both laughed and he took her hand.

At dinner, Nina and Remy were called upon to provide brief sketches of their histories. Jack drank too much and Remy made an appointment with Paul to talk about a wrongful-death case she had. After starting with a bite-sized basil soup, and duck foie-gras ravioli, Nina ate a sublime rock lobster paired with a Sancerre. When the beef dish arrived, she made a valiant try, and she sampled the potato puree with a lobster béarnaise. "I'm hereby spoiled for real life," she finally admitted, putting down her fork and allowing the waiter to clear her mostly uneaten plate.

Jack touched her on the inside of her elbow. "Soft," he said, "on the outside, but hard when you need to be."

Remy ignored the interaction, but Nina understood she had heard. Paul said, "Nina plays a good game but she does not play hardball."

Elected most sober, Paul drove them back. They dropped Nina just after midnight. Paul walked her to the door. He rubbed his cheek against hers again, then turned to face her, bent down, and gave her a tender kiss. "I love the curves of your body, your hips," he said.

"Uh," she said, listening for the distant waves, right there on her own porch, enjoying his touch.

"You're so fine." He squeezed her hips.

"Stop that." Nina pulled away from him, feeling his fingers continuing to explore.

His other hand joined in the fun. "So nice."

Nina stepped away. "Stop again."

He looked at her calmly, only the hint of an eyebrow raised. "Don't blame me for hoping. You're a catch."

Nina waited with the door ajar while they drove away, then stood on the porch to wait for the tingle to wear off for a few moments before going into the house.

"How was it?" Kanani looked up from her book.

"Very nice," Nina said, thinking, outstanding. "Did anyone come here while I was out?"

"Nobody."

"Any calls?"

"Not a one."

Bob had fallen asleep sideways in his bed. After profuse thanks to Kanani and good-byes, Nina woke him up a little, straightening him out. He smelled so good, like toast and butter. She had to smooth his hair a few times and kiss his plump cheek before she pulled his covers back over him.

"Zorro, Mommy," he said drowsily. "In a big, black cape."

"We'll talk costumes tomorrow. Back to sleep."

She caught herself thinking happily, Bob doesn't remind me of Richard, not in any way, but by the time she had her clothes off and was sliding into bed, her thoughts had switched to a review of the evening. Yes, she could fit into that world of Club XIX, the drinkers, hopers, losers, aspirers. She would think of them all naked whenever she felt daunted. Remy had been so friendly tonight, closer than her usual cool distance, and especially nice to Jack, who wore a smug look by evening's end.

Nina really liked Jack but recognized that Jack really liked Remy.

And Paul, well, she suspected she understood him. He was a man on the make, not serious, reeling from some emotional kick, but handsome, single, and maybe even interested, she thought groggily. She pulled the covers tightly around her, curling into a dream where he kissed her, and she loved it, and Richard watched them kissing through a window, menacing, dangerous.

CHAPTER
12

ON OCTOBER 2, TUESDAY, ASTRID ESCORTED Virginia Reilly into Remy Sorensen's office. Remy helped her to sit down in a gray leather armchair, watching the new client trying to get a handle on her by looking at the decor: spare, neat, heavy sets of books carefully organized. No vase of flowers, no photo of the loving hubby and gap-toothed kids chasing the Irish setter across a suburban lawn.

"We don't read them for fun," Remy explained, smiling, attempting to ease some of the tension. "I'm sorry I had to miss our appointment. I've freed all the time we need this morning."

"I thought about this for a long time before I decided I just had to come here."

"You don't want Nina to join us?"

"No."

"I'm sure she'd like to be here . . ." Remy gestured toward the phone.

"She's got more to face than I do in the long run. I'm not going to be around very much longer. I remember how much I mourned my mother." Mrs. Reilly's lips tightened. "The thought of my kids having to suffer makes me so upset—"

"You're sure?" Remy said as gently as she could.

Mrs. Reilly nodded her head. Several minutes passed in chitchat. Remy looked her over—graying brown hair cut neatly over a ravaged face that seemed oddest when she tried to smile—hard to look at—frozen like a bad face-lift. Here sat a very sick lady, judging from that and the painful way she moved. And one arm, her left—Remy looked away, not wanting to stare. Nina had already told her some of the story.

Might be some good money for the firm here.

"Mrs. Reilly, Nina told me a little about your circumstances. How can I help you?"

"Call me Ginny. My nickname has such a youthful air, even if I don't anymore." A deep breath, a few blinks, and Ginny said, "My husband left me for a much younger woman. We're divorced now and he pays me support, but I know he's going to ask the court to reexamine it.

"But that's not why I came today. Not that I forgive my cheating erstwhile life companion. I just got to thinking, if I die soon, I can't leave my children with nothing." Ginny stopped, smoothing her hair with her remaining, shaky hand. "You see how hard Nina works. Our son, Matt—he's got problems and his father's attention will naturally lie with his new family, even though Matt needs him very much. My kids need me. When I'm gone, money will help, although neither one of them would admit to giving a damn about it."

"You use a cane," Remy prodded gently. "Is that connected somehow with your injury?" In her mind, she added, what price could you put on a hand?

Answer: a lot, when it came to the law.

"I've been diagnosed for a year or so, although I was sick before that and didn't know. I didn't see a doctor until some time after Harlan—we separated."

Remy jotted everything down in her neat notebook. She knew Lindberg as a competent physician and an occasional expert witness for the plaintiff in insurance cases. He was a good man, on the right side. But even good men made mistakes.

"Did you seek further medical advice?"

"When biofeedback didn't work, two weeks later, at the end of last September, I found Dr. Wu. His offices were close to Lindberg's, and I had seen his advertisements in the local newspaper. By then nothing I did could keep my hands warm. So freezing and painful—it was like I spent my time soaking them in the ocean out there." Ginny tilted her head west.

"Dr. Wu is an acupuncturist?"

"On Cass Street in Monterey, just like Dr. Lindberg."

"Did Dr. Lindberg give you Dr. Wu's name? Did he recommend him specifically?"

"No."

Too bad, Remy thought, but she underlined Lindberg's advice, knowing it might present some opportunities. "But you say he told you, 'Sure. It can't hurt.'"

"That's right. That's what he said. I believed him."

"Did you check Dr. Wu's credentials as carefully as you did Lindberg's?"

"No, but he had a license number printed on his cards, and an extravagant office."

"Go on."

"I went in there on a Thursday. September twenty-eighth, last year," Ginny said, consulting a daybook she pulled out of a pocket. "His receptionist was out to lunch, or else he didn't have one because there was no one else in the office. That made me nervous. Are doctors allowed to treat women without nurses present?" Ginny didn't wait for Remy to reply. "Are they even doctors?"

Ginny described the day vividly. She had been asked to lie down on a table. Dr. Wu, efficient, smooth, professional, pulled out a set of long, thin needles.

Ginny had felt scared. She also felt committed, like a person getting a tattoo. She told Remy that she had decided on this course and couldn't see any easy way out that wouldn't humiliate both of them.

Dr. Wu, a small Chinese man, squeezed her hand, enough to make her cry out. He apologized but was encouraging, saying, "I can help you." Then he inserted a needle into each of her fingers. She experienced excruciating pain almost immediately. However, warmth flooded into her hands, the first warmth she had experienced in a long time. The color of her fingertips began to change from pale to pink.

"My God, this hurts!" Ginny had cried.

"Very natural," Dr. Wu had said. "Please understand, healing takes courage."

"He hurt you badly?" Remy asked after a moment.

"A lot, not a little."

"What else did he say?"

"He said he had stimulated a meridian flowing through my fingertips which would benefit my entire system. He told me how acupuncture was an ancient healing art, more than two thousand years old, based on the idea that our bodies have a system of channels—meridians. These kind of steal energy from one part of the body to propel another. He showed me ancient charts that outlined which channel affects a given part of the body. His theory was that an obstruction in energy flow produces physical and emotional issues. The needles unblock the obstruction, restoring health."

"Hmm."

Ginny shook her head. "I must have been demented to believe such horseshit."

"Many people claim healing effects due to acupuncture. How long did he leave the needles in?"

"He bandaged my hands—with needles in place—and told me to call the next day. He said it was a severe case and it wouldn't do any good to leave them in for a half hour or something." She stopped talking and her right hand crept over to guard her left arm.

"Did you call him the next day?"

"I got an answering service saying he would be out of the state at a conference in New Mexico until Tuesday." Ginny paused. Her eyes darkened. "That was the worst four days of my life."

"You continued to experience pain?"

"Shooting pains that went all the way up my left arm. I was walking the floor all night. I was afraid to rip the needles out. He had said not to touch them. When I couldn't get through to Dr. Wu, I tried Dr. Lindberg. He was also out of town. He had left another doctor for referral. I called Dr. Chase's office—he used to be my neighbor's GP. I explained to the receptionist what was going on, and she said to come on in. I did. Dr. Chase saw the bandages but he wouldn't touch or unwrap them. He said he knew nothing about acupuncture and couldn't risk harming me out of ignorance."

Remy was surprised. "You told him you were hurting?"

"He recommended ibuprofen. Said to go to the emergency room at Community Hospital if I had to."

Doctors were usually good about helping patients in pain, but Remy appreciated the difficulty. One lawsuit might ruin a medical career. She wouldn't take that kind of risk either, however abstractly she abhorred the thought.

"It's easy now to see I should have gone right to Wu's office or even taken the needles out myself. But I was in his power, you see? He was supposed to take care of me, and I believed he knew what he was doing. I might have made things worse, plucking them out.

"As I said, I couldn't sleep for the first two nights, so I started taking prescription painkillers I had left over from gum surgery the year before." Ginny reached awkwardly into her bag to find a fresh tissue and blew her nose.

"I took them until Dr. Wu returned. He took the needles out without saying much. What could he say? My fingertips on my left hand looked like I'd slammed them with a hammer. The right hand wasn't so bad. I didn't have the energy to complain. My left hand seemed to get worse, and by then I didn't trust Dr. Wu, but I couldn't get in to see Dr. Lindberg either. He had some sort of family crisis and I kept getting referred to Dr. Chase."

"When did you finally see him?"

"Not before the next big drama. A few weeks later, I reached into the refrigerator for some piecrust and the tip of my index finger fell off my left hand."

CHAPTER 13

REMY FELT HER JAW TIGHTEN BUT FORCED ALL expression from her face.

"Now, here's something strange. It didn't hurt. Remember when you were a kid, losing teeth? This felt like that." Ginny's brow knitted as she remembered. "By now all the fingers on my left hand were black. Angry-looking red streaks ran up my arm. I had fever. I guess I must have called Nina because she came and took me to the hospital. Guess I used my good right hand to punch in the numbers, huh?"

Remy refrained from imagining it. She made a note.

"They put me under. When I woke up, at first I thought all was well. But then I tried to touch myself. You can't imagine, Miss Sorensen. You just can't. At the hospital, I woke up maimed. The doctor said I had developed gangrene. They had to take my left hand to save my life."

"You need a minute?" Remy asked.

Ginny wiped a tear away with a handkerchief. "No. Let's finish this."

"All right. Were you wearing gloves when you reached into the refrigerator, as Dr. Lindberg had advised?"

"I couldn't wear gloves by then. The Raynaud's was driving me nuts—once in a while my other nails turned blue and my fingers froze, but by then, they burned. Rotting, we now know."

"What made you wait so long to come to me for legal help? I would think Nina must have urged you."

"She did. I should have done something right away."

"You're a patient under the care of doctors. It's a tough call."

"Anyway, I'm sicker lately. The pain's reminded me of those four awful days, and the thought of leaving my kids so exposed . . . I also remembered something that happened at the hospital after my surgery. A nurse was giving me pills and fooling with my IV, and the resident physician came in to examine me.

"I was half-asleep, not paying close attention. The resident hadn't seen me before, but she turned out to be so sympathetic. Her mother had the same illness as I had. When the nurse told her about my adventures with acupuncture, the resident almost hit the ceiling. 'That damn fool,' she said. 'You can bet this guy wasn't an MD. He clearly hadn't read up on Raynaud's. You never puncture their fingertips.'

"I made a mental note to ask her about it, but you

know how hospitals are these days, somebody new every day, strangers prodding you, trying to help. My thought got lost. I guess Dr. Lindberg should have known his advice was wrong, too, shouldn't he?" Ginny sighed heavily.

Remy stood up, walked over to Ginny, and took her good hand between hers. "Do you know the exact date you heard the resident physician at the hospital speak about not puncturing the fingers of Raynaud's patients?"

"Yes, I wrote it right here in my book: October twenty-ninth."

"Good. Ginny, do you have a receipt for that visit to Dr. Wu?"

"I paid cash. I'm sorry, I think I may have lost it."

Remy rose. "Let me get you some coffee."

When Remy returned, Ginny looked at her hopefully, expectantly, as if Remy could turn the clock back to some earlier, happier period in her life. Remy felt grounded when people looked at her that way.

"You've been victimized by a man who took your money and harmed you. You deserve recompense for the pain and suffering you have endured because of this treatment, which appears, at least from what I know right now, negligent in more than one respect."

"I'm so glad to hear you say that."

Remy ticked off the negligence on her fingers. "First, trying to treat someone with your illness at all. He delayed other, urgently needed medical care in order to submit you to an acupuncture treatment. I doubt anyone can prove acupuncture is helpful in your circumstances. Second, the resident's statement at the hospital might be useful. We may be able to find medical authority backing up her remark that Raynaud's patients should never have their fingertips punctured. Third, Dr. Wu left those needles in and left the state for several days, leaving no referral for patients like you who might experience complications. Even taking acupuncture at face value, as a medical treatment, Dr. Wu may have fallen below the standard of care for his profession."

"I never put it all together like that before."

"But there are potential problems. We'll address those as they come up. Meantime, in my opinion, I can protect your right to go after Dr. Wu. We'll send the required claim letter by October twenty-ninth of this year. Let me explain. The American Medical Association and the state medical associations are very effective lobbyists for health-care providers of all sorts. Several years ago they managed to pass a very special set of rules, of impediments, in fact, to filing a case against a doctor or any medical practitioner, like an acupuncturist. Unlike other negligence cases, in a medical malpractice case you have to first send the provider a letter saying certain specified things, in effect notifying him that you intend to sue him and why. And you have to do it ninety days before you can sue."

"So we do that," Ginny agreed. "Send that letter out."

Remy nodded. "That extends the time to sue for another three months beyond the one-year rule. But if you don't get the letter out within one year of the discovery of the medical malpractice and its negligent causation, the courts will not let you continue the suit. The deadline for this letter is a year from the date of injury or the date of discovery that malpractice occurred. We'll have to show that you had no idea that what happened to you constituted malpractice until the resident whose mother was ill raised it with you in the hospital on October twenty-ninth."

Remy's tone softened. "I think you will be all right on this, though we may have to fight a summary judgment motion on that basis." She gathered her thoughts, listening to the office crew slam doors and gun motors as they began leaving for lunch.

"The second requirement is that we cannot file a lawsuit without a Certificate of Merit from another acupuncturist or more probably an MD saying there is probable cause to believe medical malpractice occurred. I think we can get that. The third problem in a medical malpractice case is that, by law, there is an upper limit on how much a jury can award you for your pain and suffering. And the defendant can request to have it paid out in installments."

"A limit?" Ginny asked.

"Two hundred and fifty thousand dollars, plus your compensatory damages, your medical bills and so forth. The loss of a hand is a very expensive injury. As long as we can show causation, you should be awarded the maximum amount."

Ginny almost smiled. "Oh, that would really help my kids."

"Every case has problems we'll have to address:

whether we can find a witness to the needle insertion. That's important because Dr. Wu might not admit to anything. Whether he destroys or alters records of your treatment. Whether he carries liability insurance or has enough assets to satisfy a sizable judgment. Whether"— Remy hesitated—"you might have lost the hand anyway, somehow, due to underlying illness. No doubt they will argue that."

"I know my health situation is complicated."

"Don't worry too much about that right now," Remy said. "But you should know your legal position the way I view it, since you have consulted my professional opinion. We need to look into the medical aspects more, but, Ginny, I want your case. I don't like seeing people like you hurt by profit-seeking quacks. I hope the rest of the firm will agree. I have to consult them and obtain their approval before taking the case. I'll take care of the necessary legal and medical research. Do you have a problem with Nina doing some of the research on your case? She'll look at your medical treatment, look into finding witnesses, that sort of thing."

Ginny thought for a moment. "Yes. That's a good thing."

"I'll send your letter within the applicable time period to preserve your rights. I will ask you to sign a contingency-fee agreement in which our firm is paid one-third of your recovery prior to trial, or forty percent of your recovery if there is a trial. Is that acceptable to you?"

"Yes."

"If our research shows a major problem with your

case, you will have to agree to release the firm from its commitment at any time, and we will refer you to other counsel. We won't ask for a penny for our time. All right?"

"I don't pay if you can't continue?"

"Not a penny."

"Should we—should we sue Dr. Lindberg? He's a good doctor, he really did try to help—"

"He might be more useful testifying for our side somehow."

"I'll leave that decision to you." Ginny grabbed the edge of the chair with her right hand and stood up. "Thanks, Miss Sorensen. My daughter told me you are an outstanding attorney. I see why you have that reputation."

"I'll do the best I can for you," Remy said, smiling. Immediate work would be required. Ginny Reilly's situation was interesting and would present a new challenge, but Remy had two short trials likely to go in the next two weeks. She would simply have to squeeze the work in. If her judgeship came through, she would put this one into Jack's competent hands.

Nina came into the room. "All done?" she asked Remy.

Remy nodded.

"Hey, Mom," Nina said, touching her mother's shoulder.

Her mother stood up. "Time to go."

CHAPTER
14

"I HAVE A NEW CASE," REMY SAID ON FRIDAY morning, sitting between Lou Frost and Jack McIntyre on Pohlmann's leather chesterfield. Klaus was holding court on Friday instead of Monday because they had been painting his office. They all talked at once.

"Just a moment," Pohlmann said, smiling.

"Klaus, I know you want to tell Jack and Louis about the appeal. We got the Ninth Circuit to remand it back for further factual findings. The Army case," Remy reminded them.

"Oh, yeah. About the teachers at the Defense Language Institute getting laid off?" asked Lou.

"How old is that case now?" Jack asked. He didn't add, although they all thought it, is anyone ever going to pay us for any of this? Klaus was currently working on two appeals, both *pro bono* cases.

Klaus never cared whether a case would be profitable or not. The longer and more tortuous the appeal, the more doggedly he fought. He attracted the younger lawyers into the firm with his causes and political clout and kept them there by allowing them to take on the "conscience jobs," as Jack called them. These fiscally irresponsible cases came with the territory.

Sometimes it grated. Any of them could have made more money elsewhere. But they had respect for Klaus and earned it for themselves by bringing in paying cases. Jack concentrated on personal-injury, real estate, and criminal law. Remy did mostly civil trial work. Louis stuck with tax and probate. Although they didn't punch time clocks, Klaus kept a close eye on how they spent their time.

"Getting on," said Remy, "I'd like to take on a new personal-injury case, actually, a medical malpractice."

"We don't handle malpractice," Louis pronounced, looking more frazzled than usual to Jack today.

"We don't handle *legal* malpractice," Klaus corrected.

"Who's the unlucky doc?" asked Jack.

"An acupuncturist on Cass Street named Albert Wu. Our client would be Nina Reilly's mother." Remy explained the grounds for malpractice, the need for relatively quick action and all the potential problem areas. "You can imagine her pain and suffering," Remy said, then waited for Klaus.

"Has Miss Reilly asked us to take her mother's case?" he asked.

"Yes."

"Then we take it."

"What's the fee agreement?" asked Louis. "Does she get a break because we're handling Nina's custody issues?"

"Standard contingency-fee agreement. One-third of her recovery. Forty percent if it goes to trial." Remy looked directly at Lou. "If he's even moderately successful, he's loaded. He should be good for a couple of hundred thousand even if he doesn't carry insurance."

"Okay," said Louis, now sounding slightly interested.

Jack said, "Couldn't she have lost the hand due to a preexisting condition? It's her left hand, not her primary hand as I understand it. She can still drive."

"Oh, come on, Jack. She can't even open a can without acrobatics or engineering."

He nodded. "If she's as sick as you say, with all these problems I've never even heard of—"

"I'll get Nina to research that." Remy put up her hand to stem the protests. "She says she'd rather be working on this than stewing. She's really going to focus. She can go up to Stanford Medical Library in a day or two. We have to get the ninety-day letter out by October twenty-eighth. That's the deadline. If you approve, Astrid can type up the fee agreement and run it over to Mrs. Reilly for her signature right away."

"What's her recovery look like if the case goes all the way?" Louis asked.

"The surgery cost over thirty-four thousand, including everything. In spite of the prosthesis her husband's insurance already bought, there's value in the lost hand.

Deformity value, use value, oh, it could be bad. Certainly far better than worker's comp value for a lost arm."

"Plus up to two hundred fifty thousand for her pain and suffering," Louis added.

"Yes. She'll make a good witness talking about it, with a little coaching. She even kept a diary."

"Sounds promising," Lou said.

"We'll have to move to advance the trial date because of her illness. If she dies, this all dies with her," Remy said.

"What about converting it into a wrongful death action and substituting Nina in as the plaintiff if she dies?" Lou asked.

"Smart suggestion, but two problems I see with that, Lou," Remy said. "If Ginny dies, there's no way we'll be able to prove the malpractice, not the underlying illness, killed her. Also, remember the heirs can't get pain and suffering in a wrongful death. The case wouldn't be worth pursuing."

"How comfortable are you given the time frame?" Klaus asked. "We wouldn't want anything to get in the way of more urgent business."

"I can pick it up. I'm wrapping up the Salinas barfight case this week. If for some reason I can't keep it, I know it will be in Jack's competent hands."

"Remember, I may end up doing Nina's custody case," Jack said. "That could absorb any extra time I can pull out of my schedule."

"Duly noted." Klaus nodded. "Meantime, make any arrangements, Miss Sorensen, and allow me to offer assistance."

"Thanks, Klaus."

"I will see you all at the Bar Association dinner tonight."

"Ugh," Lou said. "Count me out."

"He's such a shy fella," Jack said.

"I hate schmoozing. You guys are better at it than I am."

CHAPTER
15

WHEN A LAWYER IN LOS ANGELES OR SAN Francisco thinks longingly of moving to a small, easygoing practice, leaving behind the traffic and crime, the Monterey Bay area comes to mind. By 1990, so many lawyers had moved in or stayed after graduation from the local law school, the competition for clients had turned fierce. Fees nose-dived. The charming offices with their fireplaces and Spanish courtyards saw their share of binge drinkers, plate-throwing divorces, and bad decisions.

So this Friday evening at the monthly meeting of the local Bar Association, the Crazy Horse Restaurant was mobbed, mostly around the bar. The ones drinking martinis, on stools or standing straight as soldiers, were the older, corporate-and-trust lawyers, mostly men, struggling to put their children through graduate school at Cal Berkeley or Stanford and secretly nervous about heart attacks, hence the calming martinis. The middle group, fit and tan in spite of heavy workloads, drank complicated mixed drinks, worrying about trials when they should have been worrying about their marriages. Finally, the newer admittees, including more women than in the other cliques, festooned the fringes of both groups, still tickled by the glitter of the profession, still fresh enough to hope their names would someday appear as counsel for the winning side in the U.S. *Supreme Court Reporter.*

Latecomers sat at the back tables. From his spot directly in front of the podium, Jack watched Remy arrive precisely as the meeting began. She found a vacant seat beside Barry Tzanck, her recently defeated adversary in the courtroom, who gave her a strictly civil nod. She wore her usual creamy silk blouse with pearl earrings, which emphasized her slenderness and pale skin, and her usual mysterious, slightly aloof smile.

Remy nodded back at Tzanck. Jack watched her then direct her attention to Rick Halpern, a rumpled man in glasses who sat across from her. A devout Catholic with four young children, Halpern was a partner in the county's biggest law firm. He never lost his temper and never sprang surprises, qualities that were greatly appreciated by his colleagues. As a result he had won overwhelmingly the most recent election for president of the Monterey County Bar Association.

"I can't wait to talk to you, Rick," said Remy in a voice Jack could barely hear. He couldn't catch her eye. She wasn't looking around for him either.

"Hang on a minute," Halpern replied, rising to

quell the roar, slapping the gavel on wood and beginning the business meeting. Tzanck threw them both a
sharp look.

A few minutes after the meeting was scheduled to end,
Nina followed a gaggle of young women from her car to
the Crazy Horse. Loud, having fun, they clacked confi-
dently along in shoes Nina could identify by maker and
only admire from afar. How did such young women afford
such luxuries? Nina wondered, upstaged but thankful she
would not have to walk into this particular scene alone.

Maybe they only had the one pair of killers, as
she did.

The last woman in the group held the restaurant
door open for Nina and smiled. "Another one of the
non-Bar crowd hoping to find a place at the bar?" she
joked. Nina nodded, smiling back, although she decided these weren't law students, they were spouses,
girlfriends, or aspiring girlfriends. Or else they were
born-rich students. She scanned for a familiar face, saw
Jack, and made her way toward where he stood by
himself, glaring at something. She had added a white
wool blazer to the shirt and slacks she had worn at the
office that day, trying to soften up her usual workday
severity.

Apparently, she had. He looked at her body, all of it,
but with a subtlety that suggested admiration, not lust,
then kissed her on the cheek, a first, and took a deep
breath. "You always smell—delicious." He held her close
for more than a moment.

Who was she fooling? She couldn't resist men, Nina

thought, feeling her own breath deepen as she pulled away from him.

Child, job, family—she had those figured out, if not under control. Now she only needed, simply, achievably, a good man to love and be loved by, in this kingdom by the sea.

But wait—didn't Annabel die in that poem and didn't Clint Eastwood grapple with a stalker named Annabel and barely survive in that atmospheric old movie set right in this very neighborhood?

And inadvertently embodying the true spirit of Poe, Jack's eyes darkened with pain, straying from Nina and lingering on Remy.

Was he checking to see if Remy had seen him kiss Nina?

He was.

Oh, Nina had been used. Still, nice kiss. She didn't get enough of those.

But Remy, embarked on her own agenda, had not noticed or not cared. Nina ordered wine and drank some. That helped. Jack had fallen silent. His teeth chewed through his jaw while Remy, bright-eyed, cheeks flushed, exchanged hellos with several people at the bar, joking with the nearby tables, Jack's eyes following after. Finding Klaus, Remy put her arm through his and together they worked the room.

Following Jack's second whiskey on the rocks, or at least the second one Nina had observed, Remy finally came over to them. He tried to kiss her. She held back. "Shoot, Remy. I have better luck with my cat."

"Sorry," Remy said, looking over the room. "Can I

have a sip while I wait for my drink?" She took his glass, sipped, and left blazing red lipstick on its rim.

Nina drank the rest of her wine, watching Jack look at the stain, narrowing his eyes. In lust if not in love, Nina decided.

Damn. But how classic, having a crush on a co-worker/boss-type guy who would cry on your shoulder but never think to lick it because he wanted someone else. Better Nina should focus on Paul, who had given her a few mighty sweet dreams already. He would be coming to check out the cottage behind her house tomorrow. A cop. Or was it ex-cop?

Never mind. She had lost her antipathy to cops when Richard Filsen had reappeared in her life. Danger had a way of compromising youthful philosophy. So what did Paul have to offer besides a sexy body, physical security for her and Bob, the appearance of sanity, and a steady income?

He made her body tingle. He made her laugh.

Describe the perfect man, Diana might say.

Meanwhile, Remy's face held the same pleasant smile she always wore at meetings. Jack's face got progressively redder as she worked the bar, smiling, laughing, joking with other friends.

Oh, they were sleeping together, Nina realized, observing him. And, wisely in Nina's opinion, Remy did not acknowledge it.

"Let's get out of here," Jack said to Remy after a few minutes.

"Let's stay. I need to wind down," she answered, and Nina heard tension in her voice.

They all sat down to dinner together. Remy drank a single glass of wine. Jack drank two on top of the whiskeys. When the food appeared, Remy moved the poached fish around on her plate, looking bored. Nina ate every bite of her fettuccine Alfredo. She loved anything someone else cooked.

As the neckties loosened and the drinks took hold, the mood of the room around them swelled beyond the initial controlled civility, giving way to an atmosphere as festive as an elementary-school recess. The men punched each other on the biceps and told golf stories, edging for position near the three judges in attendance. The women relaxed and tucked their painful shoes under the tables. Every few minutes, someone dug in a shirt pocket or purse for cigarettes and disappeared out the door.

Nina studied the dessert menu. She loved mousse but had eaten too much. Perhaps lemon sorbet?

At that moment, Richard Filsen appeared beside her.

"Not you," Nina said, putting down the dessert menu, folding her arms defensively. "Not here."

Filsen slammed his shot glass down on the table. "You have to talk to me. I want—"

"You don't know what you want." She saw it though, read it in his eyes. He wanted her back. He wanted her love and some fantasy family. "You want to talk, talk to me through my attorneys." She tried for a fierce look, but felt her lips quiver.

"Hide behind the bosses," Filsen said, squinting at them. "Hello, Jack, Remy. Hey, Remy, so we finally have a case together. And, man, are you gonna get your scrawny ass kicked. Don't look down you—your nose at me, honey, I'll blow your fucking—"

"We're on opposite sides of a case, you mean," Remy said coolly. "I look forward to winning."

"Ha-ha. Funniest thing I've heard all day. You have any idea how much I look forward to a nice private conversation with you in a few days?"

Remy appeared not to react, but Nina saw how her knuckles paled as they squeezed her napkin. "Don't you dare threaten me."

"Got a lotta friends." Filsen waved at the room. "Well, I thought I did, too. Don't imagine you can trust 'em."

Jack stood and took Filsen's arm. "Anyone ever warn you that if you drink too much, you say regrettable things?"

"What's that I smell on you, pal? Cheap aftershave? Or could it be expensive Scotch?"

"Look, my fellow attorney. Save your posturing for a more considered, sober time." Jack's muscular body propelled the taller man away from the table. Nina, compelled, followed a few safe steps behind.

Jack let go of Filsen right inside the door, as the man stumbled and held on to the handle. "Want to tell me your problem?"

"How about, I have a son nobody lets me see. And his mother—" Filsen spotted Nina, frowned. "Hey, I go around there when her mom's watching the boy and she acts like I'm some creepy kidnapper. She's got nerve. Hey, baby," he called to Nina. "I could tell you things—"

"What would you tell her?" Jack asked.

"Forget it." Filsen lowered his head. "I owe her nothing."

"I know your associate is representing you in the custody case. Why not let Perry do his job? If he were here, he'd tell you that bothering Nina won't help your case."

"Ha. No, Perry's busy at home with his big family, fucking his big wife, watching cartoons with his too many kids. Fuck Perry. I can handle this—I'm the man. I know the secrets. I know the secrets the men don't know that young girls understand. Or they will soon, all the little—" Filsen swayed on his feet.

"This can't be good for a guy who I hear rides his bicycle at six every morning," Jack said, steadying him.

Filsen attempted to focus his eyes. Failed. "What do you fucking know about it?"

"There's a pay phone around the corner. Call a taxi. Get home safe, okay?"

"What's your story, Angel Jack? You fucking Remy first, Nina as sloppy seconds?"

A collective gasp lit up the faces of nearby gawkers. Nina fell back, wishing for invisibility.

One second Filsen was completing that question, and the next second he was barreling backward out the door, arms spread, then he was lying on his back in the middle of the walkway into the restaurant.

Jack winced and massaged his right hand. They all watched Filsen pull himself into a sitting position, hair falling over his eyes, a little blood on his face. Twenty-five grand if Filsen sued him and won, and no doubt worth every penny for the satisfaction Jack must now feel, Nina thought.

"Watch those stairs. They're steep. Especially when you are blind drunk, as everyone here will attest," Jack said mildly.

"I'm gonna—I'm gonna sue you!"

"You'll be out of a profession soon after. Go home."

Filsen got up and turned to walk away, but not before he muttered something.

"Hey," Jack called. "Hey!"

But Filsen had turned the corner.

CHAPTER
16

RETURNING TO THE TABLE WHERE REMY AND NINA now sat, openmouthed, Jack said, "He's a lesson in the heart of darkness, isn't he?"

"Thanks, Jack," Nina said. What could she say. My hero? "How's the hand?"

He stretched it, flexing all fingers. "Survived a school-yard bully, something I never did so well in the school yard. So—that's Bob's father?"

"I'm so sorry, Jack. I had no idea he would—"

"You're not responsible."

"Oh, I am."

Remy put her hand on Nina's. "It can't be easy for you. You're in school, working. You've got your mom to worry about, and a son."

Nina felt tears gathering behind her eyes. She pulled her hand out from Remy's as soon as she could. "You do wonder, in the dead of night, why you make mistakes on such a grand scale."

"You thought you loved him," Remy said. She wasn't looking at Jack; she was wrinkling her napkin. "You convinced yourself you needed him. It's hard for women, you know? Hard to know if you might be better off alone."

Nina nodded, unable to speak. Without a partner, could she attain the strength she needed to become a success, raise her son to be a titan, and take proper care of her mom and Matt?

"He's out of control. This can't continue," Jack said. "There are better men. There's someone out there to love and need you properly, the way you deserve."

"He's *attractive*," Remy said playfully.

"He does have a good job," Jack said, picking up on the game.

Nina drank the last sip of her wine, trying to smile. In spite of her mood, she was amused by how much this resembled her earlier ruminations about Paul. "And it's a job he adores."

"And, of course," Remy said, also sipping at her glass of wine, "he's spanking hot in bed."

"A faithful fellow," Jack said. "I can see that."

"Better yet, rich," said Remy, ignoring Jack's look.

"No, no, no," Nina said. "Comfortable. That's rich without the Bentley. Although he could easily afford a Bentley if he was a despicable show-off."

"A CEO," Remy said.

"Who works part-time so you can go on long vacations to exotic places," Jack said.

"Who adores your ambition and supports your long hours," Remy said.

Jack's mouth took a downturn.

"Someone," Nina said, "who says things you don't expect him to say. Smart. Wise. Full of heart."

The table fell silent.

"And blah, blah, blah." Remy suddenly seemed to lose interest. "God, what weak hopes for the females of America. I'm proud of your lone stance, Nina. Do you know how many single mothers there are in America?"

Nina saw the look on Jack's face and jumped in to change the mood again. "Look, Richard showed up four years too late. He needs to get on his expensive bicycle with the painful little seat and ride out of Bob's life again."

Remy spilled some wine. Nina watched her dab at the damage with her napkin.

"I can imagine how hard it must be for you, Nina," Jack said.

Could he know? Did his mother raise him alone? Maybe. It happened as often as Remy had implied.

"I have some good news about my mother's acupuncture case, Remy," Nina said. "As you know, I spent today at Stanford's medical library. Found a very useful statement in an article about Raynaud's." Nina dug in her bag and pulled out some papers. "So here it is: 'Pricking of the fingers in cases of Raynaud's is contraindicated.'"

Remy sat forward. "Really? Why?"

"Blood circulation is compromised. I knew we needed confirmation that this was a perfectly logical caveat, so I called the lead author of the article, in Cincinnati. He's in private practice there, a rheumatologist like Doc Lindberg. He's got a great rep. His curriculum vitae is on your desk, Remy. He has been an expert witness for the plaintiff in several medical malpractice cases. I told him you'd be in touch."

Remy said, "That's fantastic. Where was the reference?"

"The *New England Journal of Medicine*. Doesn't get any more solid."

Remy smiled. "Good work." She looked at the wine bottle in the middle of the table, then poured herself another glassful of wine and drank deeply.

Jack said, "Now, wait, ladies. Don't celebrate yet. Believe me, Richard Filsen can't be discounted. He's done very well for himself on cases that had a lot less going for them."

Nina took in the implications of Jack's statement. "Exactly what does Richard have to do with my mom's case?"

Jack frowned. "You didn't know? He's sent us a letter of representation, hasn't he, Remy?"

Remy shook her head. "He called me yesterday. I have nothing official. We're still in the claim-letter stage. There's no attorney of record. And I had no idea about any personal connection between you and Richard Filsen."

Nina bit her lip, thinking, that's true. "He wants visitation."

"With your son?"

"Yes. And maybe even joint custody, although Jack and I consider that unlikely."

Remy thought about what that implied. "Wow."

Nina said, "I take it he's involving himself in my mother's malpractice claim."

"It seems he is," Remy said.

A waiter in a white, ironed shirt appeared. "Dessert?" he asked brightly.

When they said nothing, he said, "Coffee?"

"My treat," Jack said. "Anyone for anything?"

Nina and Remy shook their heads.

"Okay. Just the bill, please."

"What did he say, Jack?" Nina asked as the waiter left. "I heard Richard say something right around when you pushed him out the door."

"My fist hurt like fire ants biting." Jack flexed it. "I heard nothing."

"Liar. You heard him. I heard him. Many people heard him. We just need the exact threat."

"Okay, he said something disturbing. Nothing to take seriously. C'mon, the guy was bent, hammered, blitzed, clobbered, legless. Not to be believed."

"What did he say?" Nina asked again.

"I'm not sure," Jack waffled.

Nina remained silent, waiting, stubborn.

"I may have heard him say, 'I'll kill her.'"

That stopped Nina from her plan to leave immediately. She took tighter hold of her napkin instead.

"Who do you think he meant, Jack?" Remy asked.

He shrugged. "He meant nothing. That's a drunken bum talking, okay? An inebriate missing his balls, on a rampage to find them."

Nina got up to leave. "Thank you for the dinner,

Jack, and, well, for everything. I hope Richard Filsen gets his ass kicked from here to Juneau on any and all fronts, including my son's and my mother's. Good night, friends." She walked out, dozens of eyes crawling down her back.

"Should I go after her?" Jack asked Remy as they waited for the bill. "I mean, whoa."

"She needs to digest all this," Remy said. "What rotten luck, Filsen ending up on the other side. That guy is out of control. It'll make everything harder—missed depos, frivolous motions, outbursts, settlement-conference tantrums—I wish I could call up the acupuncturist and tell him what he just hired. But I do like and admire Nina. She's fearless."

"Like you?"

"What do you think?"

"I consider you sexy. Fear factor: unknown."

"Jesus, we're at a law dinner talking about law, and you come up with that?"

"Maybe you fear I'll get too close?"

"I'm not afraid of you or anyone."

To Jack, the evening already constituted a total loss. He tapped his fingers on the table impatiently. "So tell me, what was all the glad-handing with Klaus earlier. What was that whispering session with Halpern?"

"I'm networking, obviously. That's what we're here for tonight, isn't it? You think you don't need to network? Don't kid yourself."

Jack put a hand on her knee under the table. "What's going on, sweetheart?" he said gently. She melted at his touch.

"Klaus is promoting me hard for the judgeship."
Remy glanced at him with that cast of the eyes that always imprinted on Jack's heart. "I didn't want to say anything until it started looking like a lock. Judge Sturdy's going to retire and soon—don't tell anybody yet—"

So she was going for it. If anybody had asked, he would have said she was too young. But nobody had asked for his opinion. Klaus had put together her candidacy without even talking to Jack.

His hand stung from defending Nina's honor. He'd had a few. He didn't like this news. Bluntly he said, "That's why you're kissing up to Rick Halpern? Because it looked personal."

"Don't talk to me that way. Jealous men are so dreary."

"Wait a minute. You proved what you set out to prove. You were on the law review at the University of Chicago. You are highly respected in your work. You're young yet, so why get out of the practice and put on a black robe? Hasn't it struck you that where you are right now is where you can do the most good?"

"Stagnant is your style, Jack, not mine," Remy said, and, after delivering this verbal slap, looked away.

Jack had to repress the urge to take her chin in his fingers, turn it so she would have to face him. He realized, dammit to hell, she's gonna dump me. Dizziness made him blink and hold the table. He didn't want to be dumped. They were just getting started and he was burning for her.

After a moment, he said, "Look, I didn't mean to

offend you. You'd make a fine judge. But why push so hard and so fast? I want to get closer to you, that's all."

She sat very still. "What am I supposed to do, turn down an offer like that? For what? I want that judge-ship. It could be a launching point to a bigger career. I could end up doing something statewide, federal—this is my life."

"What, do you want to be president?"

"You sound like an exotic marsupial with a burr up its ass, Jack."

"Okay, okay. Listen, I'm in love with you." He tried to grab her hand, get her to face him, but she stood up, grabbed her bag, and said, "Good night."

She left without saying good-bye to anyone else, touching Halpern on the back lightly, familiarly, as she passed him a moment later. Halpern left soon after, Jack noted, then, looking at the empty wine bottle in front of him, wondered whom he would get to drive him home.

Go home, buddy, he told himself, and don't ever tell a woman you love her at a law dinner again.

CHAPTER
17

THE NEXT MORNING PAUL SHOWED UP AT NINA'S house in Pacific Grove over an hour early. A canopy of aqua sky hung over the old house, and Nina watched him look up at it, hands shading his eyes. Situated on a small lot surrounded by fencing, windswept, close to neighbors, Nina's house boasted an indirect view of the Pacific at the end of the street. The wild rosebushes and picket fence made it romantic looking, in Nina's view anyway.

She stood near a flower bed speckled with dead stalks, spraying a line of drooping flowers between her house and the next-door neighbor's. She wore frayed pants that stopped halfway down her calves and a grubby cotton sweater. Her brown hair had blown out of its clip and into spacey realms, so when Paul arrived, she felt unnerved. She reached into her pocket for something to tie her hair back and found nothing. She turned off the hose.

Bob rode a tiny bicycle with training wheels, the words HEAT STRUCK plastered in fluorescent paint all over the middle bar. He made repetitive engine noises and drove toward Paul, his drone getting louder.

"Hi!" he said.

"Hey there, little buddy," Paul said. "Hey, Nina, how's it going?"

"Well, you can see," said Nina. "This is their last watering for the season."

"The rains will come, you know," Paul said.

"Not before my plants die. The rainy season is so late this year. But you're early."

"Too early?"

"Depends on for what." They smiled at each other.

"Come on in and see the place. It's open." Nina led him around the side of the house to the cottage, which sat near the house at the back of the lot on an alley. Bob followed them in the door and ran for the bed, leapt up, and began to jump.

The cottage was uninsulated and bare-raftered, but clean, with a big window overlooking Nina's flower bed, where a few blooms rose helter-skelter even this late in the year. Paul looked the place over and said it was a little rustic for his taste but that he thought it would do as a month-to-month rental. Nina told him the rent, a reasonable amount, and offered to help him pile wood for the woodstove. He accepted her offer, explaining that he couldn't afford the Doubletree Inn, where he'd ended up after a week on Jack's couch. Nina said she had a rag rug he could use, too.

"Now all I need is a rocking chair," he said.

"My aunt Helen's. It's on the porch."

Their business concluded, they sat on the steps in the sunshine. Bob hopped back onto his bike and disappeared out the back gate into the alley.

"You let your four-year-old out of sight?"

She hated the insinuation and hated even more the sharp reminder of fear it brought. Perverts. Richard. Kidnappers. "He stays within calling distance. We know our neighbors. Working in San Francisco made you paranoid, didn't it?"

"I see dangers you're better off never thinking about. We lived in the Richmond district in San Francisco near the Presidio. Nice neighborhood. Ugly shit happened. Let's leave it at I don't trust anyone, nice neighborhood or no."

"I can't restrict my son's childhood because I'm too shaky to let him out of my sight for five minutes."

He shrugged. "You'll lose that attitude fast when you start practicing law or—"

"Or what?"

"Nothing."

"Or when something bad happens to my son?" The ominous suggestion hung between them.

"Being a single mom's hard. Being a good parent is hard."

"Hmm. You miss the big city?"

"No. Everything that excites me is here, too. Rocks and racquetball, pretty women—"

"Your new job?"

"Nothing worth talking about. Dead people. Bad people. Good people gone bad."

"You like being a homicide cop?"

"I like sitting next to a tempting girl on a porch in the fall, when the sun makes you crazy because you know it's playing with you."

"Even if that girl lets her kid run wild?"

He spread his hands. "Sorry. Hey, let's take a ride. Could we?"

Nina closed her eyes and enjoyed the sun skimming her skin. "I have to put in some time at work this afternoon."

"Just an hour."

"I guess I could spare an hour. You realize Bob comes along. And I guess we need to pack Bob's car seat into yours, since mine's so small."

"Will do." That day, Paul was driving a rented Dodge, which fit Bob's car seat perfectly in its wide, old-fashioned backseat.

Nina took them through Cannery Row, John Steinbeck's old hangout, past the old sardine factories filled now with T-shirts and collectibles, past the Aquarium, the Outrigger pier, and around the instep of the bay to Fisherman's Wharf.

"I know, I know, yours is bigger in San Fran, but we have more pelicans." Hundreds of the heavy, hollow-beaked brown birds roosted on the roofs of the restaurants built onto the pier. Tourists from France, Japan, and Ohio hung over the pier railings, sneaking stale bread to the noisy seagulls and a few loudmouthed sea lions. Otters cruised near the rocks at the base of the pier, but it was the pelicans that amused Bob. He sidled up to a big, grizzled bird sitting on the railing that seemed to look down its beak at all the hubbub. Like all wild animals, it looked wary and unfriendly up close, its silver topknot bristling.

"Not so close, Bob," Nina warned as the bird took a side step away from the boy. Bob held out a crust of bread. The bird snapped at it, knocking it out of his hand. Bob jumped back, hollering for Nina. Paul laughed but Nina ran to him. "Just look, okay?" she said, holding him by his thin shoulders. "You don't have to touch everything."

On the way back to the car, Bob dawdled behind. Nina took his hand to keep him close. He yanked his hand from hers and ran to climb a parking meter, and she hauled him off. From the backseat of the car, until he drifted off for a short nap, it seemed as if he spoke up every time Paul tried to talk.

"He's tough," Paul said.

"Whisper and we might get to talk for thirty seconds without interruption," Nina said.

"I'm glad I never had a kid," Paul said, lowering his voice.

"Really."

"My father made a poor role model."

"Don't they all?"

"Your dad, too?"

"Was your father a police officer?"

"Yes. He and my mother still live in San Francisco, getting older every minute, wondering why to live. It's not easy. He fell down a steep set of stairs back when I was in high school. Broke both legs."

"What happened?"

"They accused my mother of causing the accident but could never prove anything. Seriously, she might guilt-trip him, but I'm sure she'd never physically trip him. Dad was certainly capable of falling down the stairs all by himself. Still, the fall down the stairs ended the marriage, sort of. Both of them live in the same house, but have separate rooms, like two neighboring countries that both have nuclear-power capability.

"Anyway, my life changed fast. Enter Jack and rock climbing. He saved my butt more than once."

Nina listened, feeling bad for Paul, then said, "And now you work in law enforcement. Why do you like being a police officer?"

"The short story is I like kicking guilty butts. Excuse me, I mean, apprehending dangers to the community. There's a mythological element, too: I like bringing bad people to face justice like the Greeks did."

"You aren't Greek."

"Dutch, but we have a shared ancient history, I believe. Even you Irish fit in somewhere."

"It's great that you're still friends with Jack after all these years."

"He's like my brother. You have a brother, right?"

"I do."

"You know how charged that is. Are you and Remy friends?"

"Friends? No. She's my senior," Nina said. "She's more mentor than friend. I never met another woman who was so conscientious and good at her work. She's probably sitting at home working on her case files right now."

"The dedicated type."

"And—you're divorced?"

"As soon as my wife sends me the final papers to sign." Paul was quiet for a few moments. "The older I get, the more I see my parents in me. My face fissures into the same wrinkles my father has. The old house is the one in my dreams. Sometimes I catch myself during an arrest or just pissed at some bad driver and I'm fuming, practically foaming at the mouth, just like the old man."

"Hmm."

"I work hard. I don't drink very much. I don't make babies." Paul unclenched his jaw with effort. "And I find women who are as unlike my mother as possible."

It was a remarkably intimate and unguarded statement. His mother sounded abusive, possibly mentally ill. Awful for a kid. So this rock-solid, reassuring frame hung with male flesh sitting here with her right now had once been a terrified kid.

"How about your wife?"

"Yeah, she'd never remind anyone of my mother." Paul relaxed. "She wanted kids, but I wasn't ready. That was the sticking point. Not that your son isn't an exception."

"Stop!" called Bob from the backseat. He had awakened. Nina pulled over. They were parked on the road beside Asilomar Beach. Behind them stretched half a mile of sand dunes and ice plant. In front they could just make out the white golf carts of Spanish Bay. To their far right, across more than twenty miles of blue bay, floated the purple shoreline of Santa Cruz. And before them, buffed clean in the breeze, were the sandy beach, dogs and hikers, surf and the eternal sea.

They walked down the path, Bob skittering ahead. A speedboat left a white wake like a jet trail. The water, turquoise blue toward the shore, turned emerald as it approached the sandbars and translucent brown where the otters plied the kelp in search of abalone.

Bob jumped into an abandoned sand hole and began to dig. They sat down on the sand and watched him get dirty. Nina produced a bottle of cheap wine from her bag, deftly opened it with a bamboo corkscrew, and tilted it to her mouth. "Sorry, no delicate glassware, but then, we're talking four bucks." She handed him the bottle. "You were telling me about your wife."

He drank and wiped his mouth. "Like I said, I didn't want kids."

"How old are you?"

"Thirty-four. So someone else came along with a different agenda and we got involved. She didn't care that I was married. I cared, but not enough to resist." He paused. "I thought I treated my wife just the same, but one night I came home and most of the furniture was gone. The good stuff," he added with a wry smile, swallowing the thing stuck in his craw.

"Did you try to—you know, fix things?"

He twisted his mouth. "Neither of us missed a day of work over it. The one time she talked to me about it, she said it was the first time she ever felt like pulling her weapon down in cold blood. She had this strong urge to go kill this girl. Then she said she had stopped loving me and didn't care about the other girl anymore. Would you have pulled something like that?"

"What?"

"Killing your rival in love? Shooting the other woman?"

"I don't know."

They watched a pale-skinned man in a bikini Speedo wade out chest-high in the freezing surf.

"He must be from Latvia," Paul observed. "Or maybe Antarctica?"

"You know Robinson Jeffers? The poet? He was local. Jack quotes him all up and down the halls of justice. Anyway, he used to swim up and down Carmel Beach every day, winter and summer," Nina said, piling some sand behind her for a backrest. "I went in last May without my wet suit. The water was so cold it didn't feel like water. It felt like knives. Fifty-one, fifty-two degrees."

"But you surf here?"

"Over by Lovers Point. Not in the fog and hardly ever in the winter anymore. I do it for pleasure, not to prove something."

"What might you have to prove, if you had something to prove?" Paul took off his shoes and socks.

"I don't know." She moved closer and took another drink out of the bottle, then stretched out her legs and tickled Bob, now damp from the sand, with her toes. Leaning back so that the sun could shine on her face, she let Paul assess her.

CHAPTER
18

"SO THIS IS THE LIFE YOU WANT?" PAUL SAID slowly. "Have you got it all figured out?"

"My life's a wreck, Paul."

"How so?"

"Never mind. Anyway, I'm living for the future, really. I want to finish law school, get established."

"Why be a lawyer?"

She closed her eyes. "Because knowledge is power."

"So power is your thing?"

"So interrogation is your thing?"

Paul ignored her. "What about the macho posturing in court? The slam-dancing? You enjoy theatrics?"

"Most lawyers never go to court. Some, like Jack, are naturals but don't like doing it anyway. Some, like Remy, are terrific at it, but work at it way harder than I want to. I do like going to court and watching the lawyers. I did well on our moot court at school. I kind of like slam-dancing. But, you know, mostly in court you're just trying to be sincere, your manner is kind of formal and respectful."

"What kind of law do you want to practice?"

"Maybe corporate law?"

"Why?"

"Lots of options, some intriguing gray areas. Or maybe I'll do that impossible thing—go into a general practice in a small place. People in trouble will sniff me out."

"You do smell good, like the sun is releasing phero-mones."

"Like water bugs do. Like roaches."

"Your hair." Paul lifted it out of the sand. "Don't want a mess." He stroked it. "I like long hair."

"Hey! Look what I found!" Bob cried. He had wan-dered toward the surf and picked up a huge brown bub-ble of seaweed, its long sea tail dragging behind him.

"Pop it," Paul offered, "or lay it down and jump as hard as you can."

Bob chose to jump, making popping sounds, and ran down toward the shore to find more. Nina took off after him, then Paul ran, too, leaving his shoes behind. At the edge of the ocean the seaweed bubbles lay tan-gled where the tide had dropped them, and the three jumped and stomped on the piles, laughing and yelling. Nina ran out into the shining water up to her knees. Paul stood still, holding on to Bob, as the outgoing waves pulled the sand from around their feet and the new waves buried them up to their ankles.

After a while, they rinsed off as well as they could

and clambered back up to the car. "Where to?" Nina asked, aware of her wet clothing, sobering up.

"How about if you drive us to Carmel and I buy you lunch at the tourist trap of your choice?"

"Mickey D's," the little voice trapped in the backseat said. "Best fries on the planet."

They drove along Holman Highway in the wind and sun. They took the Carpenter Street turnoff and passed through the shady streets of upper Carmel. The overall effect was of a pricey English village mocked up for some movie set, each house uniquely charming. Carmel had been a den of bohemianism in the twenties and thirties. Jack London had spent a lot of time here. Clean, safe, and quaint, the police log must be a laugh. "The rest of the world should be so lucky," Paul said. "Where do these people work?"

"Often they don't. They made their money someplace else, in San Jose or San Francisco, lived in the nicer burbs, and saved for a romantic retirement. Now they paint, draw, write, sculpt. Throw pots. Have lunch. Play golf. Shop."

They parked in the Pohlmann office parking lot since there was no place else to park on Saturday, walked a block, sat down in the dark pub called the Bully III, and ordered stew and garlic bread for Paul and Bob and a chicken sandwich for Nina. Bob said politely to Paul that he was having a nice time and proceeded to spill his stew all over himself, muttering about the missing but hotly anticipated fast-food fries. Paul, looking at Nina, said he was having a nice time, too.

Back in the car after lunch, they all felt drowsy.

They turned back onto Ocean before Paul first noticed the BMW in his rearview mirror. The glossy car stuck close behind.

"Look behind you," he said to Nina. "Check out that Beemer a couple of cars back."

"Oh, no, no, no."

"You know this guy?"

"I guess I do. He's—harassing me." She felt scared, and she felt Paul sense her fear.

"That's the man," said Bob. "Mommy hit him."

"Please, let's ignore him," Nina said, wishing she could.

But Richard was not giving up.

"I'm going to stop the car," said Paul.

"What?"

"Let me deliver your message."

"No." Nina touched Paul's arm, alarmed. He drove up and down a few streets but the BMW stayed right behind them. Richard Filsen was smiling below his sunglasses.

"He's following us," Paul noted.

"He's waving at me!" Bob said.

"Okay, pull over," Nina said, just before they reached Highway 1. "Sorry, I'm going to handle this." She opened the door and marched toward Filsen, who had pulled up behind them.

He got out of his car and leaned on it.

"Time for you to get the hell out of my life, Richard."

"Just a reminder. Don't conveniently forget the DNA test appointment next week."

"You thought enough of me to love me once, Richard. You have to stop following us, okay? You're scaring Bob. You're scaring me."

"Your problem. I'm taking care of my problem."

Nina walked back to Paul's car wondering what his problem was, other than a sudden maniacal interest in a child who was a stranger to him.

Paul waited until Nina returned to the front passenger seat.

He got out, walked a bit, and put his face into Filsen's face. "I don't like you."

"Fair enough," Filsen said. Up close, Paul didn't smell alcohol, and a look around the car failed to establish any plain-sight weapons, bottles, or hypodermics. Filsen wore a fatuous smile on his face. Californians smile too much, Paul thought, not for the first time.

He looked toward his car, where Nina was moving her hands in frantic signals. He blocked her view of the driver's window with his body and took a handful of Filsen's hair, squeezing until Filsen emitted a pathetic little scream. Paul let go and Filsen raised his hand to his head. He didn't move.

Paul turned and walked back to his car.

Nobody spoke. Paul pulled out. Filsen dropped back and disappeared. Paul was thinking that lawyers are so used to carrying on their wars of words that they forget how to fight. He was also feeling as if he had overreacted, perhaps, slightly.

Finally he said, "I fixed it for you."

"You shouldn't have touched him."

"Oh?"

"We're in the middle of a custody—um—issue."

Paul looked at Bob. "Oh," he said again, although this time much more softly.

"Even threatening him without touching him can be an assault."

"I know what a fucking assault is," Paul whispered so that Bob wouldn't hear. "I'm a homicide detective."

"Big help. Great. You don't understand, Paul. Richard enjoys the attention. Like a neglected kid? He craves it."

"Not the kind of attention I give."

Paul drove silently back to her house.

"I'd like to stay this afternoon," Paul said. "You could work for a couple of hours. I could arrange for supper."

Nina thought, I should send him away. He's impulsive and rough. Then she remembered socking Richard in the preschool parking lot. "Supper would be great."

He lowered his hands to his legs while she climbed out of the car, helping Bob and all his gear get free. "Thai, Indian, Italian, strange?"

"Hot dogs," Bob said. "With spicy mustard."

"And garlic fries," Nina added.

"No garlic," Paul said.

"Oh, really?"

"I'll bring the hot dog, Bob, plus—something strange to please your mama."

He left for a while, then returned with food after Nina and Bob had time to clean up, settle in, and start Bob's preschool art project.

After Bob ate his hot dog with relish and finished

his project, Nina carted him upstairs, singing his favorite Burl Ives song, "Little White Duck."

"You're a good mother," Paul said.

"What delectable food did you bring me?" she asked, plopping down on the couch beside him.

"Escargot. Snails to the American."

She pulled her legs into a triangle on the couch, trying to figure out how to respond.

"Kidding. I brought homemade slow-cooked pork tacos with green sauce from Maria's."

Nina turned down the lights, lit candles, and found plates for the food. Both of them ate heartily.

Wiping sauce from her cheek, Nina said, "About the cottage . . ."

"When can I move in?"

Nina uncrossed her legs and crossed her arms. "The thing is—"

"Uh-oh."

"Yeah."

"You're nervous. Is that good?"

She smiled. "Maybe it is." She liked him too much. He scared her. She was not ready.

"That's a really soft bed you've got in there."

"Don't get ahead of yourself, buster. C'mon, it's the old wood floors. The lack of a dishwasher. The lack of electrical sockets, cheap rent and a landlady who can't afford repairs. I'm having second thoughts about taking advantage of you."

"So you don't want me."

"I never said that."

Paul put his hands around her neck, so gently it felt

soft as the breeze. "You don't want such close proximity, just in case? In case—"

"I have issues but I can't expect you to fix them. Sorry."

"No need to apologize. However, I think this means you owe me another date at the very least."

At this point, concentrating entirely on his touch loitering so suggestively on her skin, she couldn't speak, so she nodded.

He kissed her good night on her aunt Helen's porch, her feeling heat that began in her heels and moved up, him trying to hold on much longer than was polite.

"Night," he said, walking down the few stairs toward the sidewalk.

While he walked to his car, she waited for the tingling to subside, which took several minutes.

At three in the morning, when she habitually woke up perturbed about her mother, Bob, Matt, or Richard, she found herself, eyes open, imagining explicit and raunchy activities with Paul instead. She fell back against her pillows into the best night's sleep ever.

CHAPTER
19

REMY DRANK BLACK COFFEE IN HER IMMACULATE white living room, looking out at the strollers on Scenic Drive. Tourists cruised slowly past searching for parking or gaping at the ocean. Just across the street, a concrete stairway led down to the wide, white beach and a cold, seaweed-heavy Pacific. The morning overcast had not deterred a steady stream of families, leashed dogs, and power walkers.

She loved Sunday mornings. Her house was her refuge, and she spent a lot of money maintaining the place. Sipping the scalding-hot liquid, she thought about how to continue her lifestyle should she get the judgeship—judges didn't make big money, but there were opportunities there.

She had worked all her life toward this goal, she decided, not for the prestige, but for respect and admiration. In preparation, she kept herself fit, clean, and presentably dressed. Today she had already ridden the exercise bike, done fifty sit-ups, completed her yoga exercises, and soaked in a hot bath, then cloaked herself in a flowered satin kimono.

But right now, her most pressing, urgent question involved food. She was insistently, gnawingly hungry. However, she had noticed she was starting to put on water weight. Her stomach felt bloated. She feared that today's brew of hunger plus PMS would make her overeat. She decided to have another cup of coffee with nonfat milk and four strawberries. Klaus and Elise expected her for tea this afternoon. Tea, luckily, had no calories, no issues.

The phone rang. Her machine was off. She debated answering. She hadn't talked with Jack since the Bar dinner and she still wasn't ready, but it could be Klaus. She answered.

"This is the governor's office for Miss Sorensen," a woman said formally. "Will you hold for Mr. Alex Antioch?"

The governor's assistant for judicial affairs came on the line. "Remy. Sorry to call on a Sunday."

"It's always a pleasure to talk to you, Alex," Remy said. "How are you?"

"Fine, fine. I wonder if you know why I am calling?"

"You're such a tease, Alex. C'mon. What's up?"

"The governor wants me to get you up here to Sacramento for a breakfast meeting tomorrow. Is that possible?"

"Certainly," Remy said, murmuring to herself,

keep the breath even, that's it, you're composed, you expected this—

Alex's voice lowered. "He's down to two candidates for the judgeship. You're made for the position. I noticed that when you came up."

"Thank you, Alex." She allowed only a small drop of the ebullience she felt to leak into her voice. "What time?"

"Seven thirty. The governor's mansion." He paused. "I'll be there, too."

"I look forward to seeing him. And you, Alex."

"Ditto," he breathed.

Breakfast. Well, she would have all day to decide how much food she would have to choke down. Meanwhile, what should she wear? Even now, at the end of October, it could be warm in the Central Valley. She needed a new suit—maybe she could nab a Calvin Klein or even another Armani at Nordstrom at the Stanford Mall on the way. She needed to cancel Klaus, get a hair appointment, and call Jack and ask him to take over her cases just for a day.

And bring along a couple of condoms just in case something developed. She had an idea about that and it had nothing to do with blubbery Alex Antioch.

"I changed my mind," said Bob, crunching on his Lucky Charms. "I don't want to be a ghost tonight. Jason's going to be a ghost, and I hate Jason."

Nina's heart sank. Coming on the last day of the month, a day she needed to file important papers and study for a quiz, Halloween had galloped up and gobbled them whole. "We don't hate people, honey," she said automatically. Bob had missed school the day before, and she had missed half a workday, taking him over to a county-approved lab to have samples taken for a paternity test. Richard had received his court order. She hadn't been able to do anything about it but seethe.

"I want to be Captain Hook. Here. Look at this picture." He studied a big picture book he had laid out on the breakfast counter. "I already have a sword and hat."

He did, she realized with relief.

"What I don't have is the hook." She took the book from him. Not only did he not have the hook, he didn't have the red jacket, the lace necklet, or the black boots with the silver buckles, and tonight was Halloween. Her son ran out of the room, returning with items he felt might be relevant, including a nasty-looking plastic sword in a scabbard. "I don't need to wear it this morning. The parade is this afternoon," he announced.

Nina scavenged frantically in her closets while Bob brushed his teeth. Nothing that would make a good jacket. An old lace tablecloth. Two fake-silver napkin rings that might morph into buckles, if someone far cleverer than she did the work.

Bob tied his shoes laboriously. She looked at him, her heart aching with love and inability, as it always did. "Can I help you with that?"

"I can do it."

Nina watched with increasing anxiety as the clock ticked. "I thought you really loved Casper the Friendly Ghost. And then you could wear your costume to school this morning. I bet a lot of the other kids will be wearing their costumes."

"I changed my mind."

Nina bent to retie his shoes. "You liked Jason last week. Why don't you like him anymore?"

"That man in the car is my dad, right? The one that was behind us?"

"Oh, honey."

"Why doesn't he live here? Jason says his dad's at home. Dads live with their kids."

"Not always, honey."

"Will my daddy ever live with us?"

"I don't think so."

"Why not? That's what I wonder. How come you aren't married? That's what Jason asked me." Bob attempted to stuff his lunch bag into his backpack. "He's smart."

"Life's complicated. We will talk about these things when we have more time, but I want you to think about this for today, okay? We're happy, aren't we?"

"I guess so," he said, emphasizing *guess*.

On the way to preschool she said, "You know what's the best thing to do when somebody says something you don't like? Just walk away."

He looked at her as if she were crazy.

By habit, she scanned the parking lot for signs of Richard. When she saw no one, she walked Bob to the door. "Remember," he said, kissing her. The entryway was blocked by a fat, yellow bumblebee and what appeared to be a turtle in drag.

"I'll be there," she promised.

At noon, she stopped by Astrid's desk. "I need a huge favor."

Astrid whacked away at her keyboard. "Everybody needs something. Remy and Jack both loaded me up this morning. I've got depo summaries on Patel and Rasheedi to do. That letter for your mom's case. Plus Jack wrote a forty-page opening brief on his writ in that Coastal Commission case." Astrid inclined her head toward a cassette. "You'd think he'd get tired of the sound of his own voice." As she talked, her fingers kept up an energetic pecking on her computer keyboard.

"How is it that you manage to talk the same time as you type?"

"Autopilot. Over a hundred words a minute. It passes through my brain like white noise. God, the job would turn deadly if I read this garbage."

"Listen, Astrid. I know how busy you are. You're always busy. But this is important. Tell you what. Help me out for an hour right now, and I'll treat you to dinner afterwards."

"I should work late."

"I'll provide a delicious, mouthwatering meal, okay? Here at the office. At your home. At your lover's. Wherever."

Astrid said nothing. Her brow furrowed.

"On the beach! At the Carmel restaurant of your choice!"

She shuffled paperwork on her desk.

"I'll cook it myself!" Nina said, desperate.

Astrid finally raised her eyes from the shambles on

her desk to look hard at Nina. "This is just sad. Now I'm scared. Does this have to do with Richard Filsen?"

Startled, Nina asked, "What?"

"Did you forget I'm Jack's secretary? I type everything and am privy to everything. You've got big problems with that guy."

Nina didn't know what to say.

"And, ahem, girl talk. It's only fair to add that I know him," Astrid said, mouth turning down at the admission. "I met him at a party at Klaus's a couple of years ago, two maybe. He chatted me up, gave me his card. I didn't think much about it, because he's not my type."

"No?" Nina asked, fascinated.

"After three days of me not calling him, he called me every single day for a week. He sent bouquets of exotic flowers to the office, like saying, 'Hey, everyone in Astrid's workplace, a sleek guy wants her bad!' He sent me crush notes!" She laughed, but her eyes were chilly. "I wonder if he wrote them himself or if he had his assistant write them."

Nina tried to imagine Perry writing mash notes and couldn't.

"Really good stuff, not gooey, just the right balance between gracious and romantic."

"What did you do?"

"Look, he had expected me to fall down and kiss his shiny Bruno Magli shoes at the first invitation."

"You recognized his shoes?" Nina couldn't help her astonishment.

Astrid read her mind. "My boyfriend at the time wore the same style and never let an opportunity pass to mention how much those pointy leather babies set him back. Anyway, along comes Mr. Handsome, successful lawyer, lowering himself to woo a lowly assistant type. I surprised him by not falling for his shtick. He took me for a challenge." She shook her head. "Fool. He was on the make. I've seen and rejected an even dozen like him. I told him to go fish."

Astrid had seen through him, and Nina had not. Astrid, who kept the office running, who never faltered under fire, now held a new image in Nina's eyes, that of a sexual sophisticate.

"Now you know my sordid past. So tell me, does it relate to yours or have I revealed myself pointlessly, as usual?"

"My past has to do with Bob. Richard seems to want to worm his way into our lives, not in a good way."

Astrid nodded. "The dinner bribe shook me because I know you hate cooking. Now I'm getting the picture. It's all about Bob."

"I hate cooking for a four-year-old. For grown-ups, I come through. You like moussaka? Veal scaloppine? Name your dish."

"You'll bring it here this evening?"

"Yes. If you come to my house right now."

Astrid shrugged. "Everything important always comes in at the end of the day. I've put out the most raging fires." She pushed SAVE on her computer. "Let's get out of here."

On the way to Nina's, after stopping at the post office to mail urgent documents, Astrid studied a picture

of Captain Hook. They stopped at the department store
in Pacific Grove to pick up supplies. In another life, Astrid must have been a tailor, reflected Nina, admiring the
way she grabbed red felt, ribbons, and glitter and
whirled around the store.

Nina gave Astrid some of Bob's old clothes to go by
and made lunch. By the time Nina was finished, Astrid
had a tailored jacket cut, two side seams sewn, details in
the works. After they ate, she applied lace at the neck
and armholes, purple ribbon down the front, and glit-
tery decorations with a glue gun. "This ought to do it.
Now where's that hat?" She pulled a yellow plume out
of the bag. "Don't forget to take makeup so you can give
him a mustache."

"I can never repay you for this."

Astrid beamed.

"Come see the parade?" Nina asked. "Fifteen
minutes."

"Why the hell not?" asked Astrid, gulping down a
glass of milk at Nina's, leaving her supplies in brown
bags on the floor. "I'm late back to work anyway."

Most of the children were dressed up by the time
they arrived at the school. They located Bob waiting patiently near the door. Astrid helped him wriggle into the
felt jacket and purple tights while Nina painted his face.

After they were done, Bob looked at himself in the
mirror, face solemn. "My hook?"

Nina ground her teeth, her mind whirring through
possible mitigations, looking at Astrid. "Maybe if you
held your hand like this?" Nina curved her hand into a
hook shape.

Bob appeared ready to let loose and cry.

Astrid rummaged in her paper sack, pulling out a plastic thing with a hook on one end and a handle hidden on the other. Bob tried it out. The long sleeve on his right cuff just covered the handle. The music began, and he marched around the parking lot and up the block with the other children, waving his hook, while parents bumped into each other in their eagerness to position themselves for photos.

"Where on earth did you find that?" Nina asked Astrid.

"In the Halloween section of the store. Jeez, Nina. Open your eyes. There's a world out there."

At dinnertime, Nina brought Astrid a huge plate of her mom's favorite recipes, Southern-fried chicken and rice. Astrid, always on a diet, ate every bite and raved about it for days.

CHAPTER
20

JACK'S FOUR FINGERS GRIPPED A HOLD ALMOST OUT of reach, which made an ominous *chink* sound as he put weight on it, the only hold he could locate on that portion of the rock face. The small rocks inside the hold, loose but big, would probably make it safe enough, as they would be affixed like jigsaw-puzzle pieces to the walls and unlikely to pull out. He left his right hand there to hold him as he raised his foot to a two-inch ledge, moving slowly up the spire, legs light and strong. He spared a second to watch Paul, above him, sweating in the late October sun, glued as tightly as a swatted fly to the brown breccia, his head angled back as he scanned the rock, searching for his next move.

The Gabilan Range, east of Soledad and inland from Monterey in the Salinas Valley, was one of Jack's favorite places on earth. Pinnacles National Monument was a rock climber's paradise with spooky outcrop-pings, caves, and bluffs challenging enough to defeat the most careful planning.

Jack and Paul had met that Sunday morning at Jack's place in the Highlands. When they finally reached Pinnacles, their watches showed a little past noon. The place was deserted, probably because Jack's dog-eared guidebook described this particular climb as off-limits. "It doesn't have a grade," Jack commented when Paul pointed the way. "It's rotten in places."

"About a 5.7. We can take a good run at it. Look at that slab about halfway up."

"There's a trail to the bottom on the left side," Jack said, moving toward it. At the bottom of the rock they pulled on their rock shoes and rubbed chalk on their hands, gearing up for the climb.

Paul eyeballed a route marked with easily visible handholds along the way. The beginning was a chal-lenge—they had to back up and take a run at the thing and then just go on spit and energy for the first twelve feet.

No protection, chance of a harrowing fall—yeah!

They jumped up the first bit and climbed side by side, separated by several feet, increasingly quiet as the crumbly surface revealed itself. After another twenty feet Paul moved into the lead as they both moved into the climbing line.

Searching for the next crack, toeing minute knobs of rock, Jack fell into a way of thinking that was completely physical, a spacious refuge in his usually crowded and wordy mind, what he loved the most about climbing.

Then suddenly, when he was about halfway up, he couldn't see the next move. A tiny edge offered refuge for his fingers, just a crimp, just barely in reach, but gave him nothing to stand on. He wished for just one piton—a rope—a hammer—shit!—and hung on, looking across the valley toward another north-south range, trying to figure out what to do. He could try a traverse ten or so feet across the face to another area where the rock was more promising. Screw Paul and his invisible line.

"Uh, Paul," he called up, "the line?"

"Right there. The knob for your fingers."

"Not sure I can reach it. You have a few inches on me."

"Jump to it?"

"Can't find the toeholds."

"Hang on with your fingers. I put all my weight on that hold. It's okay. Just glue your toes to the rock there."

Paul seemed to be moving smoothly, inching over the hot, dusty stone, the spire outlined against the sky above him.

Jack tensed and made the little jump for the handhold. His fingers held like a grappling hook, but the freaking hold disintegrated. His body jolted down. Snaking his head smoothly inward, he pushed his face into the rock, hard, clinging to two bumps at about chest height. He stopped to breathe and to stuff his heart back into his chest.

"You okay?" Paul called.

When Jack could speak, he said he was.

Jack took his time, recapturing his inner rhythm. When he heaved himself to the top a few moments behind Paul, he paused at the edge, looking down the rock face. Paul was sitting on the edge, legs drawn up, taking in the sun, eyes closed, a slight smile on his mug.

"You look like the guru on his mountain," Jack puffed as he drew himself alongside. You could hardly call this thing a summit. Two horns of rock rose about six feet high on either side of them with a small saddle just big enough for the two of them to sit.

"Want to know the secret of life?" Paul asked.

"No."

"Even if it's your last chance?"

Jack tucked into his supplies, slurping water. Around them the spires cooled rapidly as the sun set. "Why not. What is it?"

"Keep your pants on."

"That's it? That's as helpful as the solution to the question about life's meaning in the *Hitchhiker's Guide to the Galaxy*. I feel cheated."

From a small knapsack, Paul pulled out a silver thermos. Jack accepted a cup of hot coffee. They looked down the shadowy range and across the plains toward Soledad Prison, then beyond toward Paraiso Springs, where they could just make out a few palm trees around the old resort. A hawk swooped down to look for dinner possibilities before heading into the evening. The quiet echoed the quiet Paul felt in his body, now that the work was done.

Jack drained his cup. "Okay, I no longer feel cheated. Not one bit." He spotted a man and a woman on a trail below, out of earshot and unaware of his scrutiny. "I was glad when you called last night. Had an argument with Remy and needed to blow off steam."

"You're still seeing her?"

"You sound surprised."

"She's not your type. Anything new on the judgeship?"

"Not that I know. Not that I would necessarily know. Certain topics are off-limits. I'm in love with her. That much I know."

"How?"

"You know that old black magic feeling?"

"I mean, how's it hit you?"

"I ache for her all day and all night. Everything I do without her, I wish she had seen. I look forward to going into the office because she'll be there. I fantasize about the next time I'll be with her. I'm not alive when I'm not with her. I have a constant desire to give her presents. I have no interest in other women. I want to fulfill all her wants, in bed and out. For her I bob my crest and do a little dance."

"That's not love; that's a haunting."

Jack laughed.

They continued to follow the progress of the hikers below, who had stopped and were huddling together in a crack between two boulders. Unaware they were being observed, the couple touched each other through their clothes.

Paul nudged Jack. "My, my," he whispered.

"We should move off, give 'em some privacy—"

"They don't know we're watching."

The couple were now pressed against a rock, the girl standing higher than the guy. Paul watched the man's back hunch and move. "Look at that. Goddamn."

The two below finished quickly, adjusted their clothing, and put packs back onto their backs, turning a corner out of sight. Their laughter faded away.

"There it is," Paul said, watching them disappear.

"What?"

"The only thing that beats climbing."

They prepared to leave. Paul pulled the rappelling rope from his day pack. "Shall we slide?"

"Exit Rosencrantz," said Jack. "We have earned another day."

On the way back to Monterey, Jack, who was driving, described Remy's acupuncture case to Paul. "Naturally I'm glad for Nina's sake. Remy's the best."

Paul said, "You say Richard Filsen's representing Wu?"

"So Remy tells me. I'm not directly involved, but I have a really bad feeling about this case."

"Something I should do something about?" Paul asked, turning toward Jack as he maneuvered the car past a car doing eighty miles an hour. The fields around them, brown with summer sun, awaited the rain.

"Just a feeling that maybe Nina or somebody could get hurt." Jack described the scene at the Bar Association meeting. Paul then took his turn, explaining how he had intervened on Nina's behalf the weekend before. "Oh, ho ho," Jack said. "I'll bet she loved you doing your *Sturmbahnführer* routine."

"No. Don't think I impressed Filsen much either. I think he's losing it."

Jack chuckled. "Nina's not a girl who appreciates being rescued."

"How long have you known her?"

"She's been working with us since she started law school. Guess there's a good chance she'll get asked to join once she finishes. Klaus loves to nurture new talent."

"Tell me about him."

"He came here before the war with his wife, Elise. She's a psychiatrist. One of them was in a concentration camp. Jewish. One's an Austrian Protestant."

"Which is which?"

"Doesn't matter. Since the day I met Klaus, he has set the standard for tenacity. He works a case to death. Every word he says carries gravitas, an accumulation of common sense and experience. And he is the most persistent lawyer in the cosmos."

"You wish he worked faster and richer though, I bet."

"The money goal remains a given. I expect to get paid well for this level of aggravation. Klaus is definitely an old-world idealist. Money's nothing to him. He's a symbol in our midst of what lawyers should be."

"Another way to say his days are numbered," said Paul.

"I suppose." Jack fell silent.

"What'll you do then?"

Jack shrugged. "I'll either drop out and get high a lot and play my Fender Strat, or I'll appraise properties. I love real estate, and I always wanted to work in the town you just left. Just finished a few courses. I'm prepared."

"San Francisco real estate, now that sounds like such a kick, so stress-free." Paul laughed for a long time. "I don't believe you, okay? You're totally hooked on taking care of the world's sad sacks."

"Paul, life's short. I'm getting gray hair on my chin and my favorite tunes are going on twenty years old. I miss Johnny Rotten. I'm single and always end up being the beta male while the alpha carries off the girl. Now that I'm trying to remedy. I've got myself such a fine woman and I sure would like to keep her."

"How long has Remy worked with you?"

"A couple of years. I hardly even noticed her the first year."

"Unbelievable," said Paul.

"You get busy and blind on this job." Jack pulled in front of the sheriff's station. "Shall we try for another climb next weekend? I enjoyed that."

"I'll let you know," answered Paul. "A couple of hot bodies might just cross my path between now and then."

"You're making a rapid recovery from your pending divorce."

"I'm in recovery, yeah. That's a good way to put it. I gave up on monkhood pretty fast. Female company makes me feel better for a short while. Nothing I like better than to chill on a comfortable couch with my arm around a honey who doesn't mind watching New York beat Dallas."

Paul took his pack out of the backseat and leaned his arm on the car door, looking thoughtfully at Jack. "As for you, be careful, buddy."

CHAPTER
21

ON MONDAY MORNING, THREE DAYS BEFORE Thanksgiving, Richard Filsen opened up his spacious law office in Seaside early. He liked how much he could afford in this neighborhood, and he liked that in this case his innate parsimony came off as a demonstration of a democratic nature to his snootier fellows. As usual, a couple of homeless types were propped against the sun-warmed wall. "Hey, Counselor, dollar for the poor," said the younger one.

He gave them a dollar apiece and a business card apiece, then said, "Now get away from my office."

"Fuck you."

"Not gonna happen."

He got the coffee going and opened the shades, then sat down at his desk the whole morning thinking about how royally, how imperially, pissed off he was, and how he would soon mete out punishment to all concerned.

Old, failing Ginny Reilly and the deal she thought gave her some kind of power over him. As if. He could mow her down with a feather. Tell Nina. Ruin their relationship forever. Leverage. Secrets. How he loved the game.

He had an important entry in his daybook: a junket to Reno the next weekend, an all-nighter at his favorite casino-hotel, the good old Nugget. He needed at least $10,000 in case he didn't hit a hot streak for a while at the poker tables, though he was sure this time would be different from the previous few times.

Nobody would pay him this week, unfortunately. They would be spending all their money on Thanksgiving turkey with all the trimmings.

He checked his voice mail. His part-time secretary wasn't in today.

Perry came in at ten, his jaw swollen from dental work and arms full of files. Richard could relate to the jaw. His own had been receiving too much attention lately. He sat impatiently while Perry ran through a list in his deliberate fashion, asking for Richard's approval on things and giving him letters and pleadings to sign. Perry was a fucking pain in the ass, but he was a detail-oriented pain in the ass, and indispensable for the dirty work.

Perry put his files away and said, "Could we talk about—about my employment again?"

"I'm pretty busy right now. Somebody's got to get out and bring in clients."

"Could we talk about it for five minutes?"

"Oh, if you insist."

Perry was obviously not feeling too well. He held his jaw and said, "I've been working for you for over four years."

"This is true."

"I've done a good job for you. Worked hard six days a week, done whatever the firm needed."

"I acknowledge that." Ugh.

"It was my work that brought in the big fee from the oil company case, but you didn't even give me a bonus. I handle the accounts and I see you've made several large payouts to yourself and we've almost spent the money."

"Okay, I'll give you a bonus."

"How much? When?" Perry's rabbity ears had turned red. "I need something more specific."

"Perry, I have to apologize. I have been insensitive and unjust to you. I'm going to make it up to you. I'll give you more than a bonus. Know what I'm gonna do? Make you a partner in this firm." Richard smiled widely, stood up, and shook Perry's hand. Perry's eyes widened and he stood up, too. His eyes were suspiciously bright.

"Do me a favor. Please don't weep."

"I can't thank you enough. It means a lot to me."

"You keep us going, my friend," Richard said. "You are the heart of our enterprise. It's true, I have had some special budgetary needs these past few months, and I did have to take the profits from the oil case, but next time we have a win like that, we're going to split the fee."

"Fifty-fifty?"

"Of course not fifty-fifty. I'm still the senior partner. How about"—Richard tapped his lips—"eighty-twenty. How about that?"

Perry shook his head. "I—that doesn't seem quite fair."

"Your name will be on the door in big silver letters. I know how long you have been imagining it. 'Law Offices of Filsen and Tompkins.' You can put an announcement in the paper."

"But eighty-twenty—"

Richard let out a small exasperated sound. He allowed a disapproving expression to cross his face. Perry looked away like the beta boy he was.

"Seventy-five–twenty-five. Because it's you, Perry. Because you're my right-hand man. You've shown your loyalty. You love this place as much as I do. Together we'll build this into the biggest and best law firm in Monterey County."

"When would this happen?"

"Well, there's no money to split right now, but rest assured it'll happen soon."

"I need a definite time."

Richard knew that stubborn expression. It seemed that the worm was developing a nascent spine. Perry might possibly have another job offer. Richard pursed his lips. "All right. January first."

Joy spread over Perry's features. "Really?"

"No question."

"I can't wait to tell my wife."

"Thought you two had broken up."

"This will help," Perry said. "She told me my career was going nowhere."

"Well, you tell her, you're gonna be rich and it won't be long. We've got some hot cases and you're gonna make them work for us. Right?"

"Right." Perry had forgotten about the bonus.

"Damn straight. Now I have to run. I gotta bring us in some bacon by the end of the week."

"From who?"

"Dr. Albert Wu."

Wu's offices on Cass Street were open. An Asian girl at the desk said the acupuncturist was with a patient, but she would tell Dr. Wu his lawyer had arrived.

Wouldn't she have seen Virginia Reilly? Filsen paced around the anteroom, looking at the delicate bird paintings on the wall. Old habit kept him from sitting down—it put you in too passive a position. Two more patients waited: an attractive athletic type leafing through a magazine, and a mother-daughter combo.

When the acupuncturist came out, wiping his hands on a towel, a young woman was with him. He escorted her out the door before he turned to Filsen.

"Counselor!" Wu said, smiling. "What a surprise!"

Filsen followed him back past an examining room to a big office with a Chinese rug and jade frogs with coins in their mouths, koi watercolors on the wall—the whole restful-decor thing. One wall was taken up by a massage table.

"You're doing well, Dr. Wu," Richard remarked, settling into a straight-backed, carved rosewood chair.

"Western people are finally accepting the virtues of acupuncture. Back problems, neck problems, knee problems, problems with bad habits." Wu leaned forward suddenly. "You perhaps could use a course of treatment yourself, Counselor. Please forgive my suggesting it."

"Nothing wrong with me. I do fifty miles a day on my bike."

Wu sat back. "What brings you here?"

"You called me, remember?"

"I didn't know lawyers made house calls."

"Attorneys do all kinds of things that might surprise you, Dr. Wu. I'm here because we have something to discuss."

Wu steepled his fingers. Long and graceful, they were weighed down by a ludicrously heavy gold ring. "I'm concerned about this woman. Mrs. Reilly. I'd like to know how all this is going. Ever since she called my office last month and said she had hired this law firm, that she was going to sue me—"

"I told you, I'll get you off this hook in a jiffy. But you have to trust me and let me handle it."

"Why not tell me the details?"

"It's my job to protect you."

"That's not an answer, Mr. Filsen."

Richard made his voice harder. "I guarantee this woman will go away by the end of the year. That's thirty-six days away. She will trouble you no more. Your only job is to be patient."

Wu bit his lip.

Richard stretched out his legs, looking Wu right in

the eye. "Remember the case with the girl? Didn't I dispose of that quietly and without any trouble? You want this taken care of just as quietly, don't you?"

Wu looked down, no doubt recalling the disagreeable nature of that case, which had cost Wu plenty. But he had been glad to pay.

And Richard had also, during the disposition of that case, discovered an exhilarating detail that should make Wu's stiff bow tie droop some, once he heard Richard knew.

"I would just like to know how—"

"There will never be a lawsuit, and it won't cost you a dime over your legal fees. Trust me."

"But how can you settle this? I can't compromise. I never touched this woman. Meantime, I can't sleep at night, Counselor."

Richard had to laugh. Wu, with his big, broad innocent Buddha smile, carried concealed weapons, knives to stick you in the back. Richard had seen him in action before, when the man had violated a patient too drugged up to testify about what had really happened when the time came. He would never forget that.

"Let me get this straight. This sick lady, Virginia Reilly, who has probably never done a thing wrong in her life, although I'm certainly going to check into that, made up a story about you for no reason and has no proof that you treated her? Was she stupid enough to pay you in cash?"

"Many of my patients pay in cash."

"Let me guess. Because you demand it?"

"I never treated her."

"What's your daily planner gonna say about that? No appointment notation?"

"She made an appointment, but she never came in."

Why oh why did all of his clients lie? Didn't they realize he was on their side?

"She won't have a canceled check cashed by you?"

"No."

"No receipt?"

"I often misplace my receipt book."

"What happened after her fucking finger fell off due to your treatment? Did she at least call to complain?"

"You offend me, Counselor."

"And no one, not that smart-looking girl you've got out there in your reception area, no other waiting clients, no chauffeur or cabbie, absolutely nobody saw her or spoke with her directly about her injury."

"Correct."

Richard nodded. "Good."

"You don't believe me?"

"Of course I believe you. I was only playing devil's advocate for a moment to keep you aware that this is indeed a serious situation, although I will have it resolved shortly. Now. Are we clear? You will not question my methods, and I will give you the result I have guaranteed?"

"I suppose I can wait another month to see if you can deliver," Wu said.

"I will need another twenty thousand dollars. Additional fees. In cash. By Friday."

That got Wu up on his feet. The genial smile turned

poker-faced. "What? Our arrangement was for an initial five thousand, which I have already paid."

"You're not licensed to practice acupuncture in the state of California. The opposition will be onto that in a second. I have to work fast and hard here. That's gonna blow your image, pal."

Wu's expression did not change.

"Why don't you have a license, anyway? You have plenty of money. You seem to be well educated, but I don't see an OMD among those certificates on your wall."

"I am well educated. I know what I'm doing."

"I always check on my clients' licenses." Perry had quickly turned up Wu's problem.

"You are a diligent man," said Wu, curling his lip at him as if at a stinking salmon. "Right. I passed the national exam but not the state one. I do not have much formal training in acupuncture. And there were some irregularities. But—I'm good at what I do. I've studied extensively, both here and in China. I view the lack of a license as an arbitrary decision made by ignorant bureaucrats. Unfortunately, I now have to deal with an unscrupulous character like you."

"Look. Twenty-five grand total and the case goes away. The alternative is far, far worse. You could lose everything, your business especially."

Wu dropped the calm Buddha face. "You are blackmailing me."

Richard said with just the right touch of injured incredulity, "What? Of course I'm not doing anything of the sort. I'm requesting a supplemental legal fee. I'm cheap at the price. Think about it. By Friday. Cash. Or—"

"Or what?"

"Why, I will not be able to prevent the unfortunate working out of your own karma."

Wu remained impassive. "I have also checked your reputation. Your record is"—he cleared his throat, English suddenly nonaccented and much less formal—"spotty, in spite of all your recent successes. You've had trouble with the state Bar. You lost a huge case a few years back that cost your original firm hundreds of thousands of dollars and got you fired. Now you work with one associate. You have a high profile, but few big cases. Do you carry malpractice insurance?"

"Of course I do," Richard lied. What? Pay those shysters for the privilege of fucking up? He never intended to fuck up again.

"I'll need to see the certificate of insurance, considering your gambling addiction," said Wu with that meditation-music calm of his.

"Sure, sure. I'll get around to that when I get around to it."

"What would your associate do if he realized you were frittering away all the firm profits playing high-stakes poker in Nevada?"

For one brief second, Richard thought he had met his match.

Nah. "Pay up or close up shop," Richard said. "Friday."

The poker face grew dark. Wu's face meridians must be in full flow. Richard got up, too, happy to make use of his few inches of extra height.

"Your guarantees are as slippery as your fee structure. You'll hear from me," Wu said after a minute. He pressed the intercom button. His sharp-eyed assistant came in. "Escort Mr. Filsen out."

On the way back to Seaside, Filsen continued to smile. This case alone would cover his junkets for a bit, and a few bills that needed paying. He'd give Perry a couple thousand, just because he really needed Perry right now on the custody thing with Bob.

Richard and Wu were like a married couple, knowing each other's secrets, a mutual protection society. And Wu knew Filsen delivered.

So many balls in the air, and he juggled so well. In his office, settling himself in his red chair, he called Remy Sorensen. A message claimed she was out of her office for two days, so he left a message for her to call him back first thing Wednesday morning. He could wait.

Reilly v. Wu et al. would never come to trial. Counsel for the defendant was on the case, and all because of an incredible stroke of good luck that had fallen like manna upon him. He was being watched over by angels, and he hoped they'd stick with him over the weekend at the poker tables.

At 5 p.m. he had just pulled the Jim Beam bottle out of his drawer when he heard the unlocked outer door open. Maybe it was a courier with a check from Wu.

But it was a false alarm. Nobody was there. Shrugging, he turned back, thinking about how everything comes together in the end.

CHAPTER
22

WEDNESDAY MORNING JACK CALLED REMY as soon as he woke up. He had expected her back on Tuesday night, but she hadn't answered the phone even though he had called until midnight.

"At last."

"What time is it?" Remy asked in a growly, sleepy voice that aroused him instantly.

"I haven't had a minute alone with you in weeks," Jack said, unhappy with the yearning he heard in his voice but unable to control it. Remy brought out the visceral in him. He had to tell her how he really felt or allow her to slip through his fingers once and for all. "You'll come to the cabin for Thanksgiving, won't you?"

"Hang on one second."

As he waited, his mind hinted that she might be

moving to another phone for privacy. When she returned, she sounded edgy.

"You know how busy I am. I spent the past two days in Sacramento and I wish you could see what's waiting on my desk. With these trials coming up and everything else—listen, why not meet me at the grocery store at Carmel Rancho Center in about an hour? Maybe we can take a quick walk around the Barnyard before I have to get to the office."

Contact! Lifting a detailed list from the refrigerator, Jack walked out to his dirt driveway. The price of living in the Highlands was having to drive miles to the nearest supermarket. And he had fancy plans for tomorrow's dinner with Paul and a few other friends: stuffed Cornish game hens and pecan pie. Might as well take care of that chore, along with meeting up with Remy.

Coming up from behind her in the produce department, where she was smelling a melon, he whispered, "Can't smell as sweet as you." She turned and kissed him briefly on the cheek.

"Hi." She had a few items in her cart already and quickly continued to cruise the aisles. Jack got a cart, steering it alongside hers, rubbing up against her, teasing her with bananas and tomatoes until she finally said imperiously, "Stop that right now." Leaning over stacked tomatoes, she weighed a pear. Jack attempted to kiss her again, and a few of the tomatoes rolled to the floor.

"Oh, shit, Jack!"

He bent down to retrieve the fallen fruit. "So good over spaghetti."

"I only eat them raw."

"They're juicy this way, make a hearty sauce."

"Jack, you told me you don't cook much."

"I lied. Come over after you go to the office and I'll show you. Spend the night."

"That would be nice. I'm sorry, I don't think I can."

He started to protest.

"Not those," she said, plucking brown-spotted bananas out of his basket and replacing them. "This bunch looks fresher." She moved efficiently through the store.

Jack's cart, piled high as they approached the checkout counter, held twice what Remy had selected. "You call this food?" he said, gesturing at her cart, loaded with fruit, lettuce, and yogurt.

"Don't nag, Jack." Remy loaded all her food onto the conveyor. She wouldn't look at him.

"Dammit. What happened in Sacramento," he said softly, "to turn things around like this?"

Remy pulled out a wad of cash to pay and turned away from him, pushing her cart angrily toward the exit.

"Wait for me, Remy. Wait just a second."

She kept going.

"Here," he said, waving his check, "finish ringing it up. I'll be right back."

He caught up with her at her car, putting her lightweight plastic bags into the trunk. He helped her, setting them neatly side by side. "So, you're determined to break some eggs today."

"I care about you, Jack. And I wish I could be who

you want me to be, but you can't really expect me to be laid-back and go hang out with you and your pot-smoking buddies whenever you feel like it."

"We're talking Thanksgiving dinner. Two hours max. Eating, not indulging in mad excess."

"I have work." Her voice shook a little. "There are so many things I need to wind up if—"

It's not about me, Jack thought, it's about that damn judgeship, and she won't talk about it. He took her hands in his and gave it one last try. "I really want you to come."

"Sorry."

A college-aged boy in an orange bib touched Jack's arm. "Sir? We can't check anybody else out till you've paid." He sounded annoyed.

"Be right there." Jack turned his back. The boy shrugged and trudged back up to the store.

"Don't leave now, Remy. How about a walk? Wait for me?"

Shutting the trunk firmly, she said, "Okay."

Jack disappeared into the store for a few minutes but found her again just where he'd left her, leaning against her car. He unloaded his groceries into his car and took her hand. They walked across Carmel Valley Road. All the shops grouped around a garden at the Barnyard were open. Woodsmoke perfumed the air. He dipped into a souvenir shop, returning with a neck-lace made of shells. "Not your usual style, I know, but I'm sure you get the intention."

She put it on over her sweater and put her arm through his. They walked over and sat on a bench surrounded by jasmine bushes. The blossoms seemed to be yearning up toward the weak fall sun.

Remy leaned forward and put her head in her hands. "I'm so tired, Jack. The interviews were grueling. I imagined knowing Rick and Klaus would ease my way, but that wasn't the case. I talked to at least six political types besides the governor trying to convince them that I could do the job, which I know I can, and two committees. But they doubt me, and at a certain point, I doubt myself." She pulled sunglasses off her head and put them over her nose. "I—I'm worried."

"They loved you. Are you kidding? They'll be lucky to have you."

"If I don't get the judgeship—the political tides will turn back to the other party. I'll quit law and leave. I'll feel humiliated, because let me tell you, I refuse to become some perennial candidate." They began to walk back.

"There's something between us," Jack said. "Please don't deny it."

She sighed. "You just turned thirty-five, didn't you?"

"You missed my birthday."

"Naturally, you want to settle down. You won't say, you'll never admit, that you want me to drop out, cook suppers, entertain your friends, and raise your children. You can't imagine how impossible this is to contemplate for someone who worked to put herself through seven years of higher education, then spent eleven hard years becoming a master in this field."

"We've never discussed marriage. Aren't you leaping ahead?"

"You've thought about it. So have I." Her smile looked sad. "Your way of letting me know what you want is subtle. You talk to me as an equal about the long hours, the lack of sleep, the lousy love lives of our fellow attorneys. You flatter me by assuming I've experienced the best the business has to offer—prestige, money, and power—and tell me how hollow it all is for someone with an empty personal life, meaning, I am sure, me. You make me look at myself in ten or twenty years, burned-out, sexless, cynical, and bitter. Maybe an alcoholic."

"You need to relax and enjoy life, not drive yourself so hard. I do see us together: two lawyers who work a little less and have a lot more fun." Why was it this, his credo really, sounded suddenly so uninspired?

"Marriage." She looked at him and sighed. "Everybody's fooled by it. Remember once we talked about romance? Marriage is the opposite. It's work. It's gritty detail. A fine home, and somehow I'm the one who maintains it. Then, a baby because you love kids and what's life without children? We plan ahead about how to split up the work, engage a nanny. I go to work. The phone calls come about the baby. Somehow I'm the one who feels most responsible, the one who gives our baby top priority." She shook her head as she spoke.

"I compensate by working harder. But you don't like me all tired out in bed. I know, you don't take work home very often, so why should I? You don't like the house being a mess. When you complain, I tell you to do it yourself and you do some of it, for a while, and with constant reminders. I'm not comfortable leaving the baby, and skip some important trips and meetings. If I do make judge, I can't follow the cases as closely as I should.

"Pretty soon my work and my reputation suffer. I feel so frantic trying to keep up with everything that I might even stop struggling altogether and think about limiting myself to the baby for a year or two. A couple of years later, without the hard edge, I go back, but I'm not as good. I'm never this good again."

"That's not us. That's some worst-case scenario."

They reached her car. Jack felt frustrated, hopeless.

"This is my chance," she continued as if she had not heard him. "I'm going to be a judge, and all those assholes out there who have caused me so much trouble, made passes, refused to take me seriously, tried to browbeat and insult me, are going to see the governor made the right choice." Opening her door and jumping inside, Remy looked at him standing stricken by the car and seemed to finally see through to his pain. But it didn't move her. "Don't count on me for dinner, okay?" She strapped on her seat belt. The electric windows whirred as they rolled up. She drove away.

Watching the Acura disappear, Jack thought, well, I'll take that as a no, honey.

After Remy dropped off the groceries at home, she stopped in at the office hoping to get as much work done as possible in the morning before things fell apart in the afternoon, as they always did on the day before a holiday. A half hour was all any case warranted. She was carrying seventy cases, so one run-through each week was thirty-five hours. Add another thirty-five hours for the ones she was trying each week. She returned Richard Filsen's call in the Reilly matter. His message left her unsettled, but she didn't leave a message when she couldn't reach him. She would call again later. Something about the case was nagging her. Sighing, she poured herself some coffee, made a few calls, then opened up the Reilly folder.

CHAPTER
23

"BOB, YOU BE GOOD NOW," NINA SAID. BOB HAD a lot of energy tonight, and as anyone who has ever been around a four-year-old boy knows, that means A Lot of Energy. Her mother didn't seem to mind, though; she seemed to delight in his clambering across the couch to reach her and pull at her. He was hungry for supper and knew Ginny would make him mac 'n' cheese right out of the box, all chemicals intact and plenty of milk and butter, a dinner Nina didn't approve of, but so what? He and Ginny could do whatever made them happy tonight.

"You're going to be late for class, honey. Better get going," Ginny said.

"It's good to see you smiling," Nina said, shoving her textbook and notebooks into her backpack. She had just enough time to make it to her Advanced Civil Procedure class, where the 1930s Erie-Tompkins case had played a prominent part for a month now. The instructor, Mr. Patel, was doggedly walking them along every step of this swampy trail, and Nina's boots had long since soaked through.

Regretfully, she took another look at the scene—the homey, warm living room, the stack of library books on Ginny's table, the impressionist prints on the walls. "I don't even feel like going," she said.

Ginny managed to catch Bob as he caromed past and sat him on her lap. "Are you worried about leaving him with me?"

"Of course not."

"Go make me proud. I want to be around when you graduate. Time's a-wastin'."

"Jeez, Mom, do you have to talk that way? Of course you'll be around!"

Her mother said tartly, "Not at this rate." Then she laughed. She looked younger suddenly, not as ill. "You know, honey, although I get down sometimes, and upset sometimes, I'm really not the gloom-and-doom type. The knocks always come with some kind of reward, I've noticed. Look how well you're doing. Look at this silly fellow—Bob, leave the lamp cord alone. And Matt's going to move right on out of this stage soon. Look at my life tonight. What more do I need for happiness?"

Nina grabbed her purse and swung that over her shoulder. Between the pack and the purse and wool coat, she felt like a heavily laden burro, but she managed to get over to the couch and bend down and give her mother a hug. "Thanks. You're the best."

"Go, go, go. In case Bob and I are asleep when you come to get him later, don't forget to bring some veggies tomorrow. I'll do my standard turkey, your aunt Helen's recipe, slathered in butter and cooked in a brown-paper bag. So Southern."

"You make it sound prosaic when you make the best turkey on earth."

"Thanks, honey. But you know, all kids think their mothers are world-class cooks."

Nina's smile lasted until Lighthouse Avenue. She still had ten minutes to get to class. She could sneak in late even, her head down, and slip into a chair in the back.

Some massive emotion began rolling in like a tide, and she pulled over in front of Patrick's used-furniture store, thinking it would roll on by. But it didn't. It just grew and grew, got overwhelming.

That class—so boring! She would definitely get drowsy and fight the nods the whole time. She'd never practice before the Supreme Court either, and she didn't need to know this intricate stuff. Besides, she was hungry.

Deciding to ditch class, she drove around the Fisherman's Wharf curve and pulled into the McDonald's parking lot. One Big Mac with fries later, she was back in the car, feeling better, lips greasy and belt pulled out a notch.

But she wasn't good yet. She had three hours to play on a Wednesday night, because she was going to shine that class and for once she didn't have the slightest worry about Bob. Too dark to surf. Too foggy and cool to enjoy a walk on the beach. Visit a friend? Her friends were sacked out in front of their TVs, exhausted, kids finally in bed, and besides, who exactly were these friends?

She felt a sudden urge to drive to Mortimer's in Seaside to gamble away her life savings. But she had no life savings. She had $22 and change in her purse and couldn't afford to lose money for absolutely no reason. That would be insane.

If only she had somebody, somebody like Jack, or Paul, somebody to hold her—phooey, this loneliness again—Jack pining away in Carmel Highlands for someone else, Paul not returning her phone call—

I could sure use a glass of wine, she thought suddenly. She looked down at a self that was reasonably presentable under the short coat in her black sweater and jeans, gold hoops in her ears, the purse a gift from her mother, fancy leather with a gold buckle. Confidence, or maybe recklessness, filled her.

She drove over the hill to Carmel, headlights warming the fog, radio playing Motörhead. Paul had talked about the Hog's Breath. He might even be there. What an amazing coincidence that would be.

She parked right in front, not a good sign. Where were the cheery hordes of summer? True, November was not a big cheery-hordes month. Disappointment struck her, though, when she walked through the half-empty restaurant to the heat-lamp-strewn courtyard with its early Christmas lights to find it almost empty.

With its thatched roof, the bar looked like a better choice than sitting alone at a table in the midst of her

vast existential emptiness. She walked in, hoping a male
or two would experience a flare of lust when they saw
her. Oops, the coat. She stopped and took it off, grati-
fied that now every guy in the place was staring at her.
Of course, besides the bartender, only two men were in
there, an ancient man in a baseball cap and—

Oh, no! Perry Tompkins, eyebrows raised, specs
slightly askew, beckoned from the corner.

"What are you doing here?" he asked as she reluctantly went over and said hello. "Sit down, sit down."
He patted the padded stool next to his.

"What do you think, Perry? I'm having a drink at a
bar." She ordered a glass of sauvignon blanc, noting to
herself that she could at most afford three glasses, if she
scrimped on the tip.

"Shouldn't you be somewhere?"

"Your tact, Perry. That's what got you so far in high
school." Perry picked up his drink, drained it, and motioned for another. Nina didn't bother snuffing at the
fumes of her wine like a pig for truffles, didn't bother
swirling it or looking at its color. She took a long drink
and swallowed it down, while Perry grinned at his luck
in finding some company.

"I'm not him, you know," Perry said, obviously referring to Richard.

"Well, last time I looked, you were shoving papers
at me on his behalf. You work for him. You do his bid-
ding at midnight in graveyards, bring him fresh corpses.
Don't you?"

"No need to be so belligerent. No, don't get up. I'll
tell you a secret if you'll stick around."

Nina slowly sat back down.

"I didn't want to handle the case about your son. Of course I didn't. I still like you."

"Then tell Richard to stick it and find somebody else to work for."

"I can't do that. He's gonna make me a partner."

"Sure he is. He sold me a lot of bull, too."

"Oh, yes, he's an asshole. I should know. I see him day in, day out." Perry stared into his glass.

Nina felt a brief pang of pity for him. "What does he really want from me?"

"You know I can't talk about the case. You're represented by counsel."

"You can talk. My counsel is my boss and I'm a lawyer, practically. All I want to know is what it will take to make him back off."

"It's always about him," Perry said. "Here we are. We could talk about so many things, but you want to talk about him. Why can't we talk about something nice? Like Mexico? Or—I don't know—something else that's fun."

His kids and his wife, for example? She noticed now that his speech was slurred. Excellent. She put her fingers on his arm. "I don't mind doing that, but, first, just give me some clues about the situation. I'm really having a hard time with this."

"I know." Perry hung his head for a moment and looked truly ashamed. Then he rallied, drank up. Maybe he would spill Richard's garbanzos. It was worth a try. Another motioning gesture to the bartender. "Another for you? I'm buying."

"Sure."

They sat with their drinks. Perry said, "You think he'll cheat me."

"I just know him. What I can't understand is why he's jumping out of the bushes after all this time claiming to want to know Bob."

"His girlfriend tells him it's immoral of him not to take responsibility. He's got this twisted conservatism in him. He doesn't want to look bad in front of her. She's Hispanic, I think, Catholic. Very traditional. She doesn't like it that he has a son out there he doesn't know."

Nina let this sink in. Richard, in love? Trying to impress his lover by destroying her, Nina's, life?

"Wow," she said.

"It's the self-righteousness that gets me. He's seen the light. He's absolutely sure this is the right course. Better watch out, Nina."

"You, too."

"I appreciate the advice," Perry said, morose.

"Who is this girlfriend?"

"I don't know her name. She never comes by the office. He talks to her sometimes on the phone, but he's discreet."

"You really think he's doing this to look better for her?"

"That, and—he didn't like how you ended it with him. He prefers to leave people, not the other way around."

"That's what I thought." The wine was hitting her. She asked for a glass of water, thinking about the drive back over the hill. Was there more to learn from Perry? "How can I get Richard off our backs?"

"My kids and family mean everything to me," Perry said, off-point. "I'd do anything for them."

"If that's so, why aren't you home?"

"Money problems. Communication problems. Problems that will be resolved when I make partner. But to return to your problems instead of mine, don't you want your son to have a father?" Perry turned slightly unfocused eyes on her. "It's not right, all you women raising children without fathers."

"Of course I want my son to know his father. Even Richard, I suppose. Maybe when Bob's older and can handle it, in a few years, with supervised visitation. That sort of thing. Tell Richard to get lost and maybe come back when Bob's twelve or so."

"One thing I've learned. You can't control everything. You can't control the results of a paternity test. He'll assert his rights."

"Unless and until the court makes some orders, he and his mystery girlfriend have no rights as far as I'm concerned."

"You can't fight the truth."

"I have to go, Perry." She stood and scootched her stool back under the bar.

"Wait. I haven't told you the secret."

"So tell me now."

"Can't you stick around awhile? How about dinner?"

"You're married, Perry. Remember how much you love your wife and kids?"

Blearily he nodded. "Okay, just lean your head down. I'll tell you. Come on. Don't be that way. Come closer." She exhaled in exasperation, then leaned her ear toward his mouth.

Before she could spring away, he planted a big, wet kiss on her lips.

"I'm sorry," he said. "You have no idea how dreary my life is."

Following an unpleasant visit from an unwelcome visitor, Richard said, "Fuck it," out loud, even though no one was there to hear him, pried his Bianchi track bicycle out of a crowded closet, slipped into some spandex and better shoes, stuffed his work clothes into a backpack, and locked up his office.

Out on the street, feeling the holiday spirit, magnanimous for a change, he tossed a couple of bucks at an unconscious street guy, then clamped his helmet tightly below his chin and took off, pushing hard through the evening traffic, sweating and happy. The cycle took his mind off things. He concentrated on working his legs and heart, and how the blood felt pounding through his veins.

He planned to enjoy Thanksgiving in his own way, with a long bike ride through Monterey's empty streets, maybe swing past Nina's mom's house in Pacific Grove to see what was cookin'.

That used up a few hours. Not that he was lonely; he expected company that night.

At home, showered and changed, he slammed down a few beers on the balcony, enjoying how the big seagulls circled and scraped with each other, a civilization up there in the sky, almost unnoticed by the civilization down here in the dirt, but very likely just as complicated.

He watched sports on television until bedtime, crawled into bed nude, and fell into a dark sleep.

She materialized in the bedroom and climbed into bed without fanfare. He loved the curve of her hip, and the soft skin of her thighs, and he showed her how much he loved them.

She didn't stay long, but slipped away after the usual murmuring and the silly promises women enjoyed so much postsex.

Calm, happy, sated, he fell promptly asleep.

Somewhere around dawn, when the dull gray light of the ocean eased toward golden, someone knocked on his door insistently.

She had a key. She never knocked.

This early morning, Thanksgiving, he put on his silk boxers and a robe and peered through the peephole. "What the fuck are you doing here?"

He opened the door.

CHAPTER
24

PAUL HAD DRAWN THANKSGIVING DAY DUTY AT THE sheriff's office. He got to his desk at six thirty in the morning, not too bleary considering the quantity of Olde English malt liquor he had imbibed the night before. Around him, telephones rang sporadically and a marching band of people passed loudly by his cubicle. The noise level here was manageable for now, though later the raucous after-dinner crowd would be ushered in for alcohol-related arrests. Encircling him were cardboard boxes full of paperwork he needed to organize, mostly research materials on law and evidence he consulted often and tried to keep up-to-date. On the desk's surface sat a telephone, a green leather blotter he'd salvaged from his home in San Francisco, and a gold pen. Through some strange miracle, his tiny space overlooked the forested area south of the courthouse. He enjoyed the luxury of seeing some sky from the office. This was nothing like his place in San Francisco, in a mosh pit of desks and people.

Had it really been months since he had arrived? Today, and at other times like this, smothered in paperwork, he felt vaguely irritated at the relative quiet of the job. He had too much time on his hands, too much time to think. Too much time to get into mischief. This was his first day back after a four-day hiatus, during which time he had done things he now deeply regretted, but that was nothing new.

Detective Armano Hernandez poked his head through the cubicle opening. "The chief wants to see you." His voice held no emotion, but his face betrayed his curiosity.

Paul's boss sat in a huge, new green leather chair. Sheriff Carsey was in his sixties but not even close to retiring. He was first in and last out and made sure everyone knew it. "A gift from the department for twenty years of damned good work," he began, in reply to Paul's stare. "Which by the way, doesn't seem a likely outcome for you."

Paul said nothing.

"You know," Carsey continued, "we checked your references pretty thoroughly before we hired you for this job. You've got a fine record: solved two serial murders practically single-handed. Plain old drug executions, wife killers, all the normal shit you did damn well. Now I'd like to know, what the hell's it take to get you interested here? Sex crimes? What's your fancy?"

"I'm not sure I understand the question."

"From your coworkers' and from your general attitude since you got here, I've had the feeling you've been a little busier with your personal life than with your work. A few days off here and there is one thing. But disappearing without notice?"

"It was an urgent personal matter. I made sure I was covered. I left the request on your desk."

"A request is not an approval, Detective!"

"It'll never happen again. It was very urgent. A family thing. Armano was all set to—"

"Armano?" roared the chief. "Armano's no substitute, you understand? We hired you and him both. You go out in pairs. It's a long-standing policy. I have two detectives here. It's a small division. I. Need. Reliability. You ever want to take a leave again, you follow the procedures and clear it with me in advance. Next time you'll be looking for opportunity elsewhere."

"Yessir," said Paul, leaving the sheriff snorting.

Returning to his desk, Paul passed Armano in the hall.

"He loves you, in spite of how he talks," Armano said. "Simple cure? Bring him homemade tamales. He becomes Platero the gentle burro."

"I had no choice." Paul's soon-to-be ex, Laura, had come down the previous weekend, ostensibly to discuss their pending divorce. They had driven east on a country road. They met two farm trucks going in the opposite direction; otherwise, no one. There in the filmy gray-greens of beginning winter they observed the cows and climbed a muddy hill from which they could see clear to the ocean on one side, all the way along the hilly ridges to the south.

Laura wore a sleeveless T-shirt and got cold in the breeze. "Put your arm around me," she demanded. When he did, he steered her to an oak tree and pushed her up against it. "Once more won't hurt anybody," she said softly, and he was kissing her eyes and her mass of curls. She smelled like lavender. He began to feel the old lust. Then she pushed him back, both hands on his chest.

"Last kiss," she said. "Don't touch me. Don't sweet-talk me. Don't try to seduce me. We talk through my attorney from now on. That's what I came here to tell you."

Just like many other times they had interacted during their marriage, Laura's brief visitation left him feeling crazed. Steinbeck had called those hills and valleys the "pastures of heaven." Paul wondered about that proximity now, the way he wondered about everything in his life lately. He had really needed the couple of days that had followed, when he had recovered, regrouped, and felt like a man again.

A couple of hours later, the sheriff appeared at the entrance of his office. He beckoned to Paul and Armano, and they went in. He shut the door.

"Don't sit down," he said. "There's been a shooting in Seaside. Seaside police chief was just on the line. He's short of detectives and I'm sending you over."

Paul and Armano looked at each other. "Gang stuff?" Armano said.

"No. A prominent attorney. The guy's name is Richard Filsen. Shot twice in the abdomen just after six a.m. this morning in his apartment. Bled out probably in a few minutes. Happy holiday. Now get moving."

CHAPTER 25

GINNY REILLY AWOKE FOR THE SECOND TIME Thanksgiving morning, this time to streaming sunlight. She checked her bedside clock. Almost eight thirty! She probably shouldn't have tried to clear the leaves off the sidewalk last night, but sometimes she found it difficult to remember, much less to accept, these new physical limitations. In her mind, she remained the girl who could dance on after everyone else had gone to bed.

She pulled herself up. She had better put something nice on. Nina, Bob, and Matt would be coming over later for turkey. But before she put the bird in the oven, she had an important errand to run.

As she was only going a short distance, she drove slowly to the Pohlmann firm. The reception area was empty so she called out a hello.

"Hello, Ginny," Remy replied. She led her back to

her office and nodded toward a client chair. "I hate interrupting your holiday, but this shouldn't take long."

"It's my fault. You've been great, checking on me so often. But I had to wait for a good day." Relieved not to have to face an awkward handshake, Ginny eased herself into a hard chair with arms. She thought about her turkey, her kids, her grandson. How sad to be sitting in this office today, trying to deal with business.

Maybe Remy just considered this another workday. Most of the world probably didn't celebrate Thanksgiving. Maybe Remy was born in New Zealand or some faraway place like that.

"People resort to the law to remedy their suffering, to extract justice from an unjust situation," Remy said after a moment. "But—you know Clarence Darrow? He's a hero of mine."

"He defended Leopold and Loeb. Lawyer in the Scopes trial—in the, um, twenties?"

"Right. Well, he once said there's no such thing as justice in or out of court. Sometimes that is true." Remy was looking down, pressing the thumbs of her hands together.

"Why be a lawyer if you consider your work futile?"

"I don't. It's just not automatic, a just outcome. I like to think when justice is possible, I can make it happen."

They both sat quietly for a moment.

"A problem has come up," Remy said. "Did you know that Nina was working on medical research for your case, by the way?"

"She told me. What problem?"

"You remember we had to rush our investigation because the time to send the claim letter was running out? We didn't get to do the full investigation we normally would in a case like this." Something like pity clouded her eyes.

Ginny waited.

"According to a specialist I consulted several weeks ago, your Raynaud's—the blood-circulation problem—leads in a very substantial percentage of cases to infarction in the extremities and consequent gangrene," said Remy slowly, with care, making sure Ginny heard every syllable. "He said we will not be able to separate out the medical cause of the amputation."

"What?"

Remy leaned in slightly. "The problems that sent you to the acupuncturist—those were most likely the earliest signs of the infarctions. An infarction is a death of tissue caused by an inadequate blood supply. Do you understand? What happened to you probably would have happened to you regardless of the acupuncture."

Ginny shook her head. "The pain was different, much worse after Dr. Wu left those needles in my fingers. Dr. Wu caused me harm. That I know."

"I spoke with Richard Filsen after I got back from Sacramento yesterday. He has a declaration signed under penalty of perjury from Dr. Wu and from his assistant that you canceled your appointment."

"Lies!" Ginny felt tears of fury, frustration, and weakness roll down her face. She wiped them with a sleeve. "Nobody was there the day I went. That lawyer, Richard Filsen? He and my daughter—you know about the custody issue?"

Remy rubbed her forehead. "I do. I've been very careful dealing with him, I promise you. I talked to Dr. Wu and his assistant myself on the telephone. He's smooth, and she was quite convincing. She says she was on duty at the time of your appointment and you did not appear for it."

Ginny racked her brain. The receptionist's desk had been empty. She had paid cash. She had no memory of a receipt. Had Wu given her a receipt? She didn't think so. Damn.

"Based on her account and on the medical research, I don't believe we can help you with your case," Remy went on. "I wanted to let you know personally."

"You're dumping me?"

"Not at all. You and I need to make a joint decision regarding ongoing legal representation based on this new information."

"You think it's hopeless."

"There's no chance of a settlement, Ginny. If we continue this fight and lose at a trial, you could be liable for Dr. Wu's legal fees. He could even cross-sue for—"

"I know that. But I wanted to—obviously that witness is lying!"

Remy shook her head. "I am truly sorry."

"Do you just not have time for me? I've heard you have a lot going on right now."

Remy shook her head. "No. We would never decide not to move forward based on our own convenience. We have several competent attorneys on staff who could take over for me, if needed."

"Nina said that she had turned up some medical

information that might clinch the case. 'Pricking the fingertips in cases of Raynaud's is contraindicated.' She found that in a medical journal, just like what I heard that doctor say in the hospital. Oh, Nina's going to be disappointed. She knew this was a hard thing for me in the first place."

"I'll speak with Nina about this, with your permission. Of course, I needed to talk to you first, as soon as the decision was made at our most recent partnership meeting."

"Wait—what about that doctor I went to while Dr. Wu was gone? Dr. Chase?"

"He saw bandages, nothing more. Of course, there's a record of the surgery you had later. But Dr. Chase only heard your report of needles. The hospital noted that you complained of pain in your fingers. They diagnosed the gangrene and recommended surgery. They did write down what you said, but we have no verification."

"I was in pain. I told Dr. Chase everything."

"He can't verify your story, Ginny."

Her story. Better than any she had ever read. "Everything I've told you is true. You believe me, don't you?"

"I believe you. But the underlying question remains, will a jury? After assessing the medical evidence and the witness's testimony, I'm compelled to advise you to drop this claim. If you have further questions, that's what I'm here for."

"What happens if I drop my claim?"

"No financial consequences at all. All you have to

do is sign this letter indicating the Pohlmann firm has withdrawn in this matter." She gave Ginny a short letter and a pen. Ginny read the letter, then signed her name.

"If you have any doubts or want to seek advice from another attorney, please call me. We have a lot of background on this case, and of course, I'll refer you to someone reputable. It's dangerous to pick someone out of the blue." Remy stood up. She looked warm, her cheeks colored a bright pink, matching Ginny's blouse.

"I'd like to keep my options open."

"I'll make sure Astrid calls you with referrals tomorrow. Ginny, I'm so sorry. I really hoped we could help you."

As soon as Ginny unlocked the door to her house and entered, the phone rang.

"Hey there."

Harlan. Trust him to catch her off-balance.

"Happy Thanksgiving, cutie. How are you? Nina and Bob coming over? Matt?"

He sounded slightly forlorn, which gave her pleasure and made her dislike herself. "What do you want?" Why tell him about the malpractice case? He would write it off as just another loss for her. Loss of pride, loss of family, loss of her good health; chalk up another one in the series. What more was there to lose, except her life?

"Just wanted to hear how you are doing."

"I'm getting along. Why are you really calling?"

"I did have another reason for calling. Did Nina talk to you about my new circumstances?"

"You mean that your baby-doll wife's pregnant? She mentioned it."

"Whatever you think, I don't want to hurt you—"

"Really?"

"Aw, Ginny."

Now he called her Ginny, not babe, not honey pie or sweet cheeks. His happiness sliced through her. She sat down.

"Ginny?" His voice seemed remote. "I can't keep up the current level of support. We'll have to renegotiate. How's two hundred a month sound? I could swing that."

"You were everything to me. You broke my heart."

"Oh, Ginny. Honey. We have to move on. Life's full of twists and turns. We can make the best of them, can't we?"

He still hurt a little. Good. She felt less humiliated about having loved him. "You promised to take care of me. I need you to live up to that promise." She hung up.

Frustration compressed in her chest, lodging like a jagged rock, and she thought again of the acupuncturist. He should not get off scot-free for what he had done to her. The world would be too unjust to live in if people like that got away with that kind of behavior. She pulled out the phone book, feeling angrier than she had ever been before.

CHAPTER
26

T HE TOWN OF SEASIDE LAY NORTH OF MONTEREY in a parallel universe. Highway 1 ran along the ocean here, physically separating the town from the sand and the frigid sea, depriving it of resort status. Fort Ord had once been its lifeblood, but the base was due to close and a new university campus was planned, so the town was undergoing a lot of transition.

Seaside had none of the romantic pretensions of Monterey and Carmel. Military families bought cheap furniture and crammed it into the single-story wooden houses, and would eventually move on, leaving behind metal bookshelves to gather dust in one of the thrift stores lining Del Monte Boulevard. Farmworkers, service workers, people new to the United States, all might temporarily settle here until they could find a way out, work their way across the money abyss one day to settle in one of the peninsula's famous tourist towns.

Noting the efficient police cordon at the entrance to Richard Filsen's apartment building, Paul parked right on the busy street. "Gimme two minutes," he said to Armano. He drank the last of his coffee and took in the early-morning scene, the market right in front of him, doors wide-open, a couple of kids on skateboards, some neighbors gossiping in clumps. The building wasn't what he would have pictured Filsen living in. Didn't even have a pool. Filsen had strutted around as if he had plenty.

Paul made a note to himself to look into money problems.

He had a concern here, and he didn't want the sheriff to have to find out about it if it wasn't entirely necessary. He had technically assaulted Filsen that day with Nina and Bob. Had Filsen made notes, left a memo in his desk or something? Probably had, he was a lawyer, wasn't he?

Not to mention Jack had decked him at the Bar dinner.

And Nina. She had evidently had some sort of physical altercation with the guy, too.

Paul might not be able to investigate this thing at all. He resolved to look around and think about it and tell Carsey if he had to.

As they got out of the sheriff's vehicle, Paul said, "I talk, you keep the record today?" Armano took out a tattered spiral notebook and the stub of a pencil. Paul reached into his pocket, handing him his gold pen. "Use this. We might need to read it."

The building's street entrance, a door opening directly onto a flight of wooden stairs, was beside a busy delicatessen.

"¿*Qué pasa?* Hey, Armano! How you doing?" A skinny young man came out of the apartment next to Filsen's.

"Hey, Helio," said Armano with a slight nod. "So this is where you live. All right. This is Detective van Wagoner. Somebody's gonna come over and get a statement from you soon, so don't go anywhere."

"Okay, but I work the graveyard shift in Marina at the Shell station now, man, so I have to try to get some sleep."

"You do that, Helio."

"I got home an hour after the neighbors heard a shot. Gotta be careful here, man. Lotta thieves." Helio pointed at the scratches around the keyhole of his own door. He watched as they nodded to the patrol officer waiting for them at the door to Richard Filsen's apartment and stepped inside.

"How do you know that kid?" Paul asked.

Armano said, "My sister's oldest son. Has a few problems."

"Don't we all." Seaside police had sent over a forensics team, two women criminal-investigations specialists and a photographer named Gabe, who was setting up for another shot. They all nodded at each other as Paul and Armano drew on their gloves. The senior forensics technician filled in the details concisely.

"What's the sheriff's office doing here?" she asked. "This happened within Seaside city limits."

"Your boss called my boss. He's tired of waiting

around for your investigators, who are still tied up with the triple shooting on Broadway, so here we are. Happy to help." Paul had heard gossip about Filsen, about his many successes. Why did he live in such a crappy neighborhood?

Looking around, Paul decided it was because Filsen was a phony. He could afford a large place here, but couldn't in Carmel or Monterey.

Richard Filsen lay with his arms straight out from his body, legs curled to the side, knees together. Blood covered his torso and the rug beneath him. He wore black silk underwear and a white cotton robe with the logo of the Pebble Beach Hotel on it, open now so his long body was displayed.

"Fancy," said Armano, pulling on his gloves and squatting down and fingering the fabric of the robe. "Not the norm in this building."

"He was a lawyer," said the Seaside patrol cop who had just come in, as if to say, they are all such poseurs. He told Paul and Armano how the call had come in at 6:11 a.m., a woman reporting two shots in or near apartment 2A. This person had refused to give her name and hung up, and the team on dispatch arrived at a sleepy apartment house, woke the manager, and went in. They had searched the area and the car parked down below on the street, where they found the lawyer's attaché.

A snazzy racing bike stood in its support stand against the wall behind Filsen. No blood on it.

"Shot twice at close range, not more than six feet," said the senior technician. About forty, businesslike, she wore goggles and gloves. "Both bullets are still in him."

"Weapon?"

"None found. We already did a preliminary inventory."

"Too bad."

They searched the apartment. Paul checked the usual hiding places, under the toilet lid, behind pictures tacked and curling on the walls. In the desk, he reviewed the papers, mostly bills—but then, oh, Jesus—he found an old photo of Nina Reilly at some beach.

He fought against an impulse to slip the picture into his pocket. The idea that Nina could have anything to do with this was nonsensical. She'd be all right, and besides, it was a crime to obstruct justice and tamper with evidence. He stuffed what he had found into one of the evidence bags he had brought in his pack and labeled it, fumbling in the latex gloves.

The attaché from the car was not locked. Inside they found several business files and utility bills, also unpaid, along with a round-trip ticket for a flight to Reno.

Were there other files?

They moved around the place in accordance with protocol. Filsen's car keys lay on a table by the door. He had lived alone with his bicycle, his big TV, and his bottles of Jim Beam.

Selecting handholds away from the bloodstains, Paul pulled down the yellowed shades for prints.

"Already checked 'em," Armano said, grinning.

Time to check out the neighbors and Filsen's office. The county coroner, Susan Misumi, a young physician with improbably shiny black bangs, had arrived but had little to report other than the probable caliber of the bullet: ".357 Magnum. Dead about two and a half hours now." They all followed her gaze to the body, with one of its eyes half-closed. It made Filsen look half-asleep, as though he were no longer interested in this business of the body he had left behind. In death, he looked uncertain, his mouth askew.

The photographer and the coroner finished their work, saying little. The morgue crew loaded the body on a gurney and filed out ahead of them. Dr. Misumi gave Paul a wink. Armano locked Filsen's door, taping it off.

They went into the hall. Paul tapped on the door across the way.

A young Latina woman answered. A baby with a little pink bow gathering a wisp of cowlick clutched her blouse. As her mother spoke, the baby grabbed a wad of her hair, yanking and twisting. Mom patiently un-curled the baby's fingers, only to have her move in for another attack.

"I'm Detective Paul van Wagoner and this is Lieutenant Hernandez. The man across the hall from you, Richard Filsen, you knew him?"

Her face collapsed. "He's really dead? The police wouldn't tell us anything."

"Yes."

"God rest his soul. I suppose you already guessed that I'm the one that called the police. I'm Barbara Santiago." She caressed her baby's head. "I have a lot to tell. I was Richard's best friend and I heard the shots." Paul slid a sideways glance at Armano. She would be protecting herself, but she might know something useful.

While she composed herself, Armano poked around the room. Paul watched her stroke the baby and whisper to her. The husband came in. His name was Carlos Santiago and he was off work for Thanksgiving.

The smell of turkey wafted through the room. They tackled the young wife first. "How well did you know Richard Filsen?"

"We're neighbors. I'm a college student, full-time till I had Lucinda, so I'm at home a lot, studying. Carlos works at Carmel Valley Ranch. Richard was our friend, a good friend." She sounded sad. For the first time, Paul noticed the darkness around her eyes. She didn't apologize for the lean-tos of paper and books jamming the small living room. "Let's sit down." Using a hand to clear the couch, she set the baby down before a pile of rubber blocks.

Her husband picked up the infant, then said, "My wife and I first met Richard at a free legal clinic when we were having trouble with our landlord. He helped us resolve our problem. Then we referred a bunch of our friends who needed legal advice. We got to know him."

Paul said to Mrs. Santiago, "Living across the way from him, you probably saw more of his private life than anyone else in the past few months. With your husband gone all day, you're obviously here alone a lot. You were close friends?"

She was already bridling. Interesting. "Not as close as you seem to imply."

"Okay." Paul scribbled *Barbara loves Richard* in

his notebook, trying it out. It rang vaguely true. "But you observed him coming and going?"

Barbara visibly winced, while her husband joggled the baby.

"What I can't figure out," Paul said, "is why a guy who obviously cared a lot about appearances and drives a BMW, who seemed to be financially successful, lived here and had an office in Seaside."

"Not to insult our town or our lives or anything," Carlos Santiago muttered, rocking his arms while the baby got sleepy. He looked like a guy who worked out, ex-military, beefy but open-faced, not the angry type.

Mrs. Santiago took a few moments to work herself up to her next statement. "Richard gambles."

"Uh-huh."

"Mm-hmm, a cardplayer, always in money trouble. I know he was ashamed, but he broke down practically every month, went somewhere, and lost a lot of money. We couldn't help him with that. When he was with us, he talked about Bob, especially after he got that big scare."

"What scare?"

"Thought he was dying," Carlos said. "Pancreatic cancer." He snorted. "Turns out after the tests came in, he only had an infection."

"But it affected him," Barbara said. "There are moments in life that stop you cold and make you look hard at what you might leave behind. He thought of Bob."

"Are you talking about Bob Reilly?"

"Right. His son by that girl. Nina Reilly, her name is. Have you talked to her?"

"I will be talking to her for sure."

"But you know her, don't you? Richard mentioned she was dating a tall cop with blond hair."

Filsen gave a damn about Paul's blond hair? Paul felt strangely flattered. Armano's eyebrows had flown to his hairline.

"He meant you, didn't he?"

"Richard took quite an interest in this ex-girlfriend, didn't he?"

"He wasn't in love with her anymore, if that's what you're suggesting."

"And you know that how?"

"The way he talked about her." She blushed. "He said she didn't satisfy him. She was needy, an intellectual. He wanted someone warmer."

Oh, Paul thought, I am so onto something with this woman. He held back slightly due to the presence of her husband and baby. He would catch her alone later. Nail her feet to the floor. "What else did he tell you about Nina Reilly?"

"She's a student at the Monterey College of Law. Her whole family, including her mother, has conspired to keep him away from his son. It hurt him so much."

"It's my understanding he had no interest in Bob Reilly until very recently. The boy is four years old."

She nodded. "So you do know them."

"What did he specifically tell you about the kid?" Paul asked.

"That he didn't go see his little boy at first because they weren't getting along, and when they split up, he had sort of given up." Mrs. Santiago shook her head.

"Even though Richard made that mistake at first, that is so wrong. To let a little boy grow up without knowing his father—

"So we talked a lot about it, and I explained how important fatherhood is, how he needed to involve himself and how I felt he had a right—"

"He decided to see the boy because you talked him into it?" asked Armano.

"No. Mortality shook him up. My arguments amounted to nothing beside that."

"Did you and he discuss going to court to change the child's custodial parent?"

"We all agreed Bob needed to be reunited with his father."

"You and Mr. Filsen did quite a bit of talking," Armano observed.

"Pretty much every day. He needed a friend. Oh, poor guy. Poor, poor guy." She choked up. The baby, maybe sensing her mother was upset, began to wail. Her husband took the squalling baby out into the hall.

"Forgive me for having to ask," Paul said, taking advantage of the moment, "but were you intimate with Richard Filsen?"

"I'm married." She held a hand over her eyes like a visor.

CHAPTER
27

CARLOS SANTIAGO HAD TAKEN UP A POSITION IN the gloom of the doorway, holding Lucinda in his arms, his expression dire. From her vantage, Barbara Santiago could not see her husband. Her husband on the other hand, observed her with single-minded intensity.

Her words tumbled out. "Richard felt bad about neglecting his only child. He saw an opportunity to make a connection. I saw a picture of Nina Reilly once when he was burning papers in the wastebasket. He said, 'Why can't she let me see him? What's so bad about me?' He seemed so injured. Tell me, Detective, do you think Nina Reilly killed him to keep him away from her family?"

Maybe you killed him, Paul thought. Maybe he didn't want to be saddled with a married woman with an infant that wasn't his own. Maybe he was afraid of

Carlos. Maybe he found someone new. Maybe he wanted to mend things with Nina. Damn, no, he didn't want to think that kind of thought. "To return to today. What did you hear?"

"A shot, then a short pause, then another shot, blasting through the place. Everyone in the building heard them."

"Anybody cry out?"

She shook her head. "No, no sounds like that."

"At what time?"

"Well, I was up nursing the baby. It was just after six this morning, I think."

"Did you look at a watch? Notice a clock?"

"No, but I was going to put the turkey in the oven at seven, so I was up good and early."

"Where were you, Mr. Santiago?"

"At the gym."

"Carlos goes to the gym on Thursdays at five a.m. most mornings. He already left," Mrs. Santiago said.

"Which gym?"

"Gold's, not too far up the road." They took down the details. They would check.

"And you, Mrs. Santiago? What did you do after you heard the shots?"

"I was freaked. I mean, gunshots in our building? It seemed impossible. Here's a strange thing. You hear something like that, you automatically want to know what's going on. I stepped toward the front door, then realized that was an insane thing to do. I had the baby! I made sure the door was locked. I just got on the phone then and called the police."

"Smart choice," Armano said.

"Lucinda screamed and screamed. I've heard about stray bullets so I got in the bathtub then in case more shots might come our way. I could see out the bathroom window. I have a view of the entrance if I lean out a little, and that's what I did. It was only a couple of minutes after the shooting. I saw someone leave."

"You had time to check the door, call the police, get in your bathtub, and look out the window, all in two minutes?" Paul asked. He was getting excited. A witness!

"I don't know. Not long. But, see, whoever shot Richard had to get downstairs and out the door. It would have taken some time. Honestly, I'm starting to feel kind of sick right now. It's all so awful."

She shook her head, wiped a tear away. Mr. Santiago was putting the baby in her crib, judging from the sounds in the next room.

Paul said, "Okay. Describe who you saw leaving, in the best detail you can." Armano was taking it down.

"I assumed it was the same woman I had seen knocking on Richard's door last night, which surprised me."

"Back up. Who did you see knocking on his door the night before?"

She shrugged. "A woman. She wore pants, a peacoat. A cap over her hair. I was coming home from the store a couple of blocks away, unlocking my door, and he was letting her in. Last time I ever saw him. I can't believe it." Her eyes welled again with what seemed to Paul to be genuine emotion.

"What time did this happen?"

"Maybe seven o'clock last night?"

"Did Richard Filsen do drugs?"

Shocked, she clutched her hands to her chest.

"Well?"

"He had issues, but he was no low-life addict, if that's what you're implying."

"Ah," Paul said. "So what did the woman you saw this morning look like?"

"She was far away and her head was covered with a scarf maybe, or a hat. Or a hood."

Armano looked out the window and gave Paul a look. His look said, *True statement.*

Paul felt deflated, but the game wasn't over yet.

"So you thought the person you saw leaving the building this morning was that woman?"

She nodded. "I thought it was the same woman leaving the apartment after I heard the shots or maybe I just assumed it. I can't swear to it. I saw someone moving away, a quick glimpse. I'm sorry. I'm not helping you, am I?"

"Think hard, ma'am. Why did you think it was the same person?"

"An impression of body size, maybe?"

"Anything else?"

"The sun wasn't even over the horizon. Just let me think."

Paul waited. Armano drew out a stick of gum and started chewing.

"I don't know. I can't say it was the same person. Somebody else must have seen this person! I mean, we all must have heard the shots!"

Paul let it lie for now. She would be asked these same questions many more times.

"Did you hear knocking on his door, or his door opening and closing any other time last night?" he asked.

"No."

"But you claim you saw a woman? Definitely not a man?"

"A small man dressed as a woman?" She almost smiled. "That only happens in movies."

Not true, Paul knew. Small men dressed as women all the time. So did tall ones. What a protected life this woman must lead, or else she might be lying like a rug. "Know anybody in the building with a gun?"

"No."

"Anybody who might have a grudge against Mr. Filsen?"

Aha! She had glanced toward her husband as he came back into the room.

"You could talk with his associate, Perry Tompkins. Oh, but I think Richard told me Perry would be out of town this weekend."

"Tompkins had issues with Filsen?"

"I just think—I think Richard was a little insensitive about Perry. I don't think he took Perry seriously enough."

"If you think of anything else that might be relevant to this investigation, please call me right away." Paul handed her a card. Armano, planted near the door, tucked his notebook into his jacket pocket and reached for the doorknob.

"Wait. Before you leave, here's his last batch of mail," Mrs. Santiago said. "I collected it for him sometimes. Find out who killed him. Please? We'll miss him every day."

Before they left, the detectives checked out Armano's nephew Helio down the hall. "I work out when I finish my shift," said Helio. "In my bedroom. I had these headphones on and I was listening to Rubén Blades—you like his music? I play it real loud through headphones. That way I don't disturb anybody. But right now, I gotta get some sleep. Rain check?" He closed and locked the door.

"I'm backing Carlos," Armano said. "She was poking Filsen. He's the jealous husband, crazy in love with a no-good mama. I'll get him to myself this afternoon."

"My money's on Barbara. That's who I'll be looking at. Bet Helio has a lead on her and Filsen."

"He's no rat."

"I have my ways."

"Hombre, she loved the dude! You see how she teared up every five minutes thinking about him dead?"

"But he done her wrong. Happens all the time, Armano."

Other people at home in the building swore they hadn't seen or heard anything. Paul and Armano walked down the stairs of the building rather than trust the elevator they heard groaning through the walls of the apartment house.

"So you know this Nina Reilly she mentioned?" Armano asked Paul. "I mean, you have blond hair and all. I think you're the only one in our department—"

"Yeah, I know her."

"Sounds like she had major problems with Richard Filsen."

"I'll talk to her," Paul promised, trying to include in his voice a warning not to pursue the topic further.

"I can leave at six? That was the deal, right? Big family dinner at seven." Armano fingered the key in his hand. "What do you think the chances are that Barbie saw the killer and it was a woman?"

"We can't rule out a little guy."

"You think Carlos is innocent?" Armano asked.

"Well, forensics tested the hands of everybody in the building at the time, and him, too, because he lives here. They gave me a quick heads-up. Nobody flunked the silver nitrite test."

"So, an outsider. Still I feel the need to have a look at Carlos. Check his alibi, the gym, at the very least."

"Go for it. Hey, buddy," Paul said.

"Yeah?"

"You seen the new coroner? Susan Misumi. She's hot."

"She's married and, plus, think about where those hands have been," said Armano. "Now that you mention it, she does look a little like Barbie Santiago."

"I don't see it."

"Whatever you say, hombre."

Paul dropped Armano at home to pick up another car. From the station, he called Nina at her house, then swung by, but the place was closed up, the day in full swing for her.

He would have to reach her soon.

CHAPTER
28

O N THE COAST, MORNING HOVERS OVERHEAD like a damp gray hat.

Nina sat on her porch the day after Thanksgiving, book propped on a scratched wooden table beside her chair, waiting for sun but prepared against the cool, with a wool blanket over her jeans. Determined to study and spend some more time with Bob, she had taken the day off. Now she found her mind drifting away from the words on the page like the fog drifting up the street from the ocean. Inside the house, Bob sang loudly along to a tape, *Wee Sing Silly Songs*. The tune was from the stately and dignified "Battle Hymn of the Republic" but the words were nonsensical, and naturally Bob loved that.

She felt, oddly, happy. Again she focused her eyes on the page and watched the words fade. Again she looked down the street. This time, she saw Paul's car approaching.

She assessed herself quickly, wishing she had paid a little more attention to her mirror earlier, then shrugged. She had decided against Paul. Something about him scared her and she had had enough of that with Richard. Maybe at another time in her life she would welcome the pull she felt in his direction, but for now, she had achieved a welcome measure of stability. She wasn't willing to let him rock that.

He pulled up to the curb and slammed the car door behind him. She removed the blanket from her legs and stood up.

"Hey, you," Nina said as he walked up the steps to the porch.

"Hello, Nina." He put out a hand and touched her arm, then listened for a moment, head tipped slightly. "He sings really well, doesn't he?"

"He does, dang it. Just what the world needs, another boy who grows up wanting to be a rock star." She smiled but Paul didn't smile back at her.

"Nina, sit down, okay? I'm here on official business."

"What? Is something wrong?"

He took her arm again, and sat her down gently. "It's Richard Filsen. He's been killed."

The news surged through her like a bullet, ripping and tearing everything in its path, and for a moment, the shock stopped her from breathing. While Paul went on, giving her some details about what they knew so far, she hardly heard him. Richard, dead. Murdered!

He was not old enough to die, was her first thought. Then she pictured him as she first saw him, confident, vibrating with energy, so attractive she couldn't resist.

"We've talked with neighbors and have a few leads . . . the body will be autopsied . . ." Paul droned on.

Every word stung. Such things did not happen to people you knew. Such things happened to others, distant people. Who would kill Richard?

Reason resumed. Many people might want to kill Richard.

"We'll need to talk with your mother," she suddenly heard emerge out of the buzzing.

"What? Why?"

"We have a few questions."

"Don't be ridiculous!"

"Just a few things we need to clarify . . ."

"My mother is sick. She has plenty to worry about without a bunch of cops coming around to intimidate and scare her. You know her condition. This is outrageous!" She knew how she sounded, how disparaging. At that moment, she didn't care.

"Me, Nina," he said. "One cop coming around, and I promise I will do my level best not to intimidate or scare her, okay? Look, I know this has been very hard news to hear but . . ."

"She's the last person on earth you should talk to. Many people had what they thought were good reasons to hate Richard, including me. You saw what he was like."

He nodded, and she saw impassivity mixed with curiosity in his hazel eyes, which jarred her. She had been right to fear him. He had the rock-hard soul of a cop.

"Did you know the firm declined to take my mother's malpractice case?"

"I didn't know."

"That really upset her. Please don't bother her, Paul." Her mother would be horrified to hear of such a thing happening so close to home. And of course, knowing Richard's relationship to Bob—

"Oh, my God," she said. "Bob."

"Does he know?"

"He doesn't know Richard was trying to get custody, of course not. He doesn't even know—" she gulped, and could not speak.

She put her face in her hands. She felt for the man she had once loved, however briefly, for his terrible end, and she wept out of pure guilt at the vastness of her relief.

Richard was out of their lives for good.

Paul waited until she finished wiping her nose on a handkerchief he handed her.

"Nina, I have to ask you a few questions . . ."

The acupuncturist, Dr. Albert Wu, came into the station the next day, on Friday, November 23, after a summons from Armano. He sat serenely on the bench outside Paul's cubicle for half an hour while Paul reviewed Susan Misumi's autopsy report and preliminary lab results. No surprises there. Nothing to do with long, thin needles, anyway.

Wu agreed to be taped and to sign a statement when it was typed up. He expressed regret and polite dismay at Mr. Filsen's death. He explained that Mr. Filsen had been representing him in a professional matter. He had seen him on Monday. Mr. Filsen looked all right, if a little tired. He just wanted to clear up some facts and had nothing new on the case. No, Wu didn't have any record of the conversation. Yes, they had been alone. Mr. Filsen bragged about keeping everything in his head and so did Wu.

Paul didn't believe much of it.

"Why did you hire Mr. Filsen?"

Wu launched into his own version of the events involving Virginia Reilly that Jack had already told Paul about at Pinnacles.

"I'm curious about why you chose him specifically."

"He helped me several years ago on an unrelated matter. I did try Henton Jones Horvath, but the attorney there was not interested when I told him I don't carry malpractice insurance."

"Acupuncturists don't carry such insurance?"

"It's not required. Mr. van Wagoner, my profession has an honorable history in Asia and we are considered health providers here. But I could find no company willing to provide malpractice insurance at a reasonable rate."

"Well, you stick needles in people."

"Very fine, thin needles. Superficial. Almost entirely painless. This treatment is not dangerous."

Armano laughed. "That's why this lady, Virginia Reilly, went after you? You didn't stick 'em in far enough?"

Dr. Wu stared at him, his face giving nothing away.

"Did you have any social contact with this woman, Mrs. Reilly?"

"None whatsoever."

"Did you ever talk to her after you removed the needles from her hands?" Paul asked.

"I never met with that woman in person. She did leave several messages at my office. The last one came on Thanksgiving. I can't say what time, the machine picked up. She seemed furious. Delusional. She threatened me. She said some very sad things, for instance that I wouldn't get away with"—Wu blew out air—"'maiming' her. That poor woman. She needs psychological help."

The way Wu said it, with a comma punctuating both sides of his mouth, reminded Paul of those two-faced drama masks, one happy, one miserable.

"Do you have the tape of that call?" Paul asked.

"Yes." Wu dug into the inside pocket of his suit jacket, then handed Paul a microcassette. "It should be here. I erased all other messages, so you need to listen for it to come up about midway through the recording."

"Did Mr. Filsen do a good job for you?"

"As far as I know." Wu glanced down at a solid-gold watch. He smoothed his tie, a muted dark blue silk print.

"Do you know how Ginny Reilly or any member of her family reacted when Mr. Filsen became your attorney in this matter?"

Wu looked interested in the question but said only, "I have no idea."

"Where were you yesterday morning at six a.m.?"

"At home. Asleep with my wife. She's right outside. You can check with her."

"Thank you."

"That's all?"

"That's all," Paul said. "Unless you decide to tell me how your conversations with Richard Filsen really went."

Wu smiled slightly and turned to go.

"Oh, one more thing," Paul said. "Did you or did you not treat Virginia Reilly by inserting acupuncture needles into her fingertips?"

"Detective, you surprise me."

"Just tell me," Paul said quietly.

"She broke her appointment. I never treated her."

"So Ginny Reilly is insane. Why else would she lie about such a thing?"

"Not insane, ill. She could not make peace with her ailments. She looked for someone to blame. She picked me as her persecutor. In your business, you see how people lie, not just to you, but to themselves? Delusions, Detective. Delusions."

As Wu walked away, Armano murmured, "Easy for you to say, ya fuckin' liar."

"He's ashamed he hurt her, and now he's defending himself," Paul said. "Add that to the idea that he's not happy she could ruin him."

Paul tried to reach Perry Tompkins, but got only a message machine. Then he tried Remy. Armano hadn't arrived at the firm yet, presumably held up by Rubén Blades.

"Ooh," Remy said. "Hello, Paul."

He hated the way she said that, so seductively. He

wondered if her law clients heard the things in her voice he heard. He knew Jack did, and the thought made blood rush into his cheeks.

"You hear about Richard Filsen?"

"Yes."

She revealed no emotion at the news. Well, Filsen was her adversary, and almost no one who knew him well seemed to like him. "Does this mean the end of any legal issues regarding Dr. Wu?"

"There's something else going on here, Paul, a coincidence. I had just informed Mrs. Reilly our firm could not go forward with her case."

"I heard. Why not go forward?"

"Problems of proof. I can't go into details. Attorney-client privilege. I very much doubt Filsen's murder had anything to do with Mrs. Reilly."

"Mrs. Reilly had some good reasons to hate him."

"Jesus, Paul! She's sick and has only one hand!"

"And she's angry." He had listened to Wu's tape, heard the bitter mixture of rage and fear. He told Remy about Ginny's phone message.

"She shouldn't have done that. She must have called him right after we talked. She wasn't happy about our withdrawal. I felt terrible about it myself."

"What's your take on what happened to Richard Filsen?"

"I barely knew him," Remy said. "We attorneys make so many enemies. An ex-client, maybe."

"You have enemies?"

"If you don't make enemies, you don't make it at all."

• • •

Paul tried Perry Tompkins again and got the machine. He left a message.

They put a new tape into the remote recording system and asked Matthew Reilly to come in. Ginny Reilly's twenty-one-year-old son seemed to have been sleeping in his clothes for the better part of a week. He had been picked up out in Cachagua, a remote valley in the hills where drugs devastated many a family.

The thing about crack—different from crank, which dissipated quickly—you could smell it on a user's clothes, if you knew what to smell for.

"Crack?" Paul began conversationally.

The boy jerked as though Paul had pushed a cue stick at his solar plexus. "I stand on the Fifth. You're supposed to be a friend of my sister."

"That makes you a friend of mine? I've seen the counter where you work. Chore Boy metal-mesh scouring pads and those little single roses in those handy glass vials right at hand. You do it at work?"

"I don't do anything."

Underneath the grungy clothing was a blond kid with a narrow, suspicious, good-looking countenance. When he smiled, the face looked more elfin than evil. The kid looked all tired out. The legs of his jeans hung so low he was walking on them. Every once in a while Paul took in the acrid whiff from the clothing.

Paul looked down at his notebook. "Where were you Wednesday night, the twenty-first? And Thursday morning? Thanksgiving?"

"By the way, I'm taping this," mocked Matt.

"I am taping this. Where were you?"

"Out and about," Matt answered, scratching his head.

"Take him into the next room and let him think awhile," Paul told Armano.

"Oh, no, Officer! Not the third degree!" Matt laughed.

Paul got up and stood over him saying calmly, "Talk to me now or you can sit around for a long time without any drugs before I get to you again."

"Okay, okay. Whatever. Let's make it snappy, though. I got to get to work."

"You were where on Wednesday night?"

"I worked at the liquor store until nine thirty. Closed up about ten. Then I went home."

"Spent the night alone?"

"No, I was hanging with my friend Zinnia until pretty late."

"Zinnia who?"

"Zinnia—uh—Farr?"

Paul made a note. "Where does she live?"

"Salinas. With her mom and a bunch of other people near Hartnell College. Excellent old house. Big yard. Hot tub in back and lemon trees."

"Address?"

"Marion Avenue. Sorry, I forget the number."

"So how late did she 'hang' with you?"

"Don't know. I was sleeping but I don't remember her being around when I got up."

"So how about Thanksgiving? What happened that morning?"

"Slept late. Watched the tube. Did an errand. Went over to Mom's that afternoon. Mom, Nina, me, and Bob had a classic American family dinner. Mom made the best turkey ever. Did you know the cooked bird needs a rest before carving? Keeps the juices inside, Mom swears."

"Can you swear Zinnia was still around that morning at, say, six?"

"Nope. Nina called me about seven, wanting to make sure I remembered to pick up this hairy, totally fattening pumpkin pie she had ordered. I promised I would. We talked a little, then I went back to sleep for another hour." Looking more closely at the boy's features, Paul could see that in spite of the greasy hair, torn jeans, and general air of disarray, the kid resembled Nina. They both had a kind of bravado but Paul sensed that it masked vulnerability.

"Where was Zinnia?"

"Still sleeping on my couch? Home in Salinas, setting the table for her huge extended family? I can't say for sure. Sorry."

"What else did you and Nina talk about?"

"You."

"Me?"

"Joke. We talked about me making sure I wore clean clothes, making sure I went to the laundromat. That I should bring a speeding ticket she was going to help me with."

"Did she tell you about seeing the victim last weekend?" Paul asked, feeling his initial sympathy for the boy fading.

"Richard Filsen?"

"Right."

"The victim. That's rich. My sister and my mother, now *they* are victims. His victims."

"How so?"

Matt gave Paul a hard look. "Scaring the hell out of Nina. Threatening to take my nephew away. Worrying my mom, who has enough to worry about. Those kinds of things. Nothing much."

"Did you ever have any contact with Richard Filsen at any time?"

"I met him when he was dating my sister. And I spotted him once with her, trying to push her around."

Turned out, Matt had seen Perry Tompkins serve papers to Nina one day in September outside of Bob's preschool.

"How did you feel about him?"

"I wasn't happy about how after four freaking years he suddenly felt he had some say in Bob's life. I mean, here's our mom, so sick she's talking about offing herself—"

"Your mom is suicidal?"

"She's—strong. That's all. She talks sometimes about controlling her final moments, going along with what God wants, just kinda tweaking his decision, that kind of shit."

"What's your reaction to that?"

"I hate it! I don't want her dead, okay? Not when she chooses, or God or anyone else. Jeez. You people."

"What did you do about this threat to your family, Richard Filsen?"

"Nothing." Matt's otherwise handsome face turned ugly. "Nina hates interference. You ought to know that about her. Plus, that's not my style, you know, going around threatening people with guns or shit like that."

"You ever play drums in a rock band, man?" Armano said suddenly.

"Huh?"

"You keep that beat, don't you?" Matt's fingers stopped tapping as all three men watched. Then they started up again, seemingly by themselves.

"We'll be seeing you again," Paul said.

Matt jumped up. "Later."

"He's as high as a model's ass. We should—"

"We wait awhile," Paul cut in.

"Wait till you get to know the sister better," Armano said. "Your predicament." He grinned. At the door he asked, "What if the sister admits she did call him?"

"I'll talk to Nina again, pin down the time she called. But I have to say, he lives a good forty minutes from Seaside. I'm not sure he could get back by seven. Maybe. Hard to believe he could talk with her about laundry after gunning down a man. He's not a big guy. He might look good in a flowered headscarf."

"Reminds me of a case down in Watsonville I was assigned to. Farmworker comes home, wife has a hot dinner cooked for him. They get into a big argument before supper. He knocks her against the wall and she conks."

"Yeah?"

"And then he sits down with the corpse, eats his

chiles rellenos, watches *Wheel of Fortune*. Then he calls to report it. I asked him what took him so long? Says he was hungry. His wife was a great cook."

"Matt could have done it," Paul said. "But it looks to me like Richard Filsen had a lot of people feeling unfriendly toward him. We need to get some more statements from his clients, too."

"I never had a case where the guy had so many people wanting to shut him up for good. Let's pick up some food first," Armano said. "All of a sudden I've got this urge for—"

"Don't say it."

CHAPTER

29

ALTHOUGH IT WAS ONLY ELEVEN O'CLOCK ON THE Monday after Richard Filsen's murder, his associate, Perry Tompkins, had already gone to lunch, according to the young woman sitting at the front desk of the law office in Seaside. She thought maybe he had gone over to the restaurant around the corner.

For some reason, Tompkins hadn't found the time to call Paul back.

Window-box flowers and brilliant winter light gave way to a deep gloom as Paul and Armano entered. *Restaurant* aggrandized the place. This bar sold sandwiches somebody probably delivered from elsewhere.

Tompkins stopped talking as Paul and Armano approached and introduced themselves. Then he introduced his lunchmate. Ralph Soto didn't look like his name. A big, rangy, out-of-shape lawyer sporting a bushy blond mustache, he had settled into his third or fourth beer. Perry Tompkins was much more fit, with a trim waist and good shave, but also much shorter.

"Sorry I didn't call you back. I got your message just this morning," Tompkins said. "My family and I were out of town for Thanksgiving."

"Where out of town?" Paul asked.

"At my in-laws' second home, down in Big Sur."

"When did you leave for Big Sur?"

"We drove down Wednesday night."

Which did not preclude the possibility that he had driven back up to Seaside early Thursday morning, killed his boss, and made it back down in time for a delicious turkey feast.

"I assume you didn't leave at any point, go out for cigarettes—"

"I don't smoke. No, I didn't leave. My wife will back me up."

Paul expected she would.

Miffed at being left out, Soto took the lead, asserting that he represented Tompkins. This turned out to be a rather informal representation, though, since he let his client talk freely and mostly nodded and drank. "You guys want a beer?" Soto caught the waitress's arm as she passed the booth and ordered another one for himself.

"You drivin', Ralph?" she said, looking warily at the two detectives. Paul could feel the disreputableness of the place—practically smell the garbage rotting out back. He had the nose, that was why he had become a detective, the nose and the nosiness.

But his quarry was a killer, not a dubious restaurant license. He let the restaurant drop away and turned back to the associate he had come to smell. Tompkins had been closer to Filsen than just about anybody else.

Ralph Soto laughed. "Everybody practices law these days." To the waitress he said, "Thanks for your concern. As per usual, I'll stagger on foot to my office, which is three doors down. Now bring me another beer, dear." She brought one, which he held up.

"To absent friends," he said. Tompkins looked away.

Paul established the basic facts of the working relationship fairly quickly. Perry was Filsen's bitch.

"He had a complicated personality," Tompkins offered. "But we had a good professional relationship. He brought in the clients, and I did a lot of the work. I was going to become a partner as of January first."

"I hear he took advantage of you."

"Really? Who said that?"

"I hear he used you and didn't respect you," Paul lied.

"I wouldn't say that."

"Everyone else would," Ralph muttered. "Shit. Forget I said that."

When Tompkins had nothing further to offer on the respect issue, Paul asked, "Did you consider Richard Filsen a good lawyer?"

"I don't want to speak ill of him, but he made mistakes. He could get reckless."

"Give me an example."

"Well, we had a big personal-injury case. Richard insisted on demanding a million bucks when the kid wanted to take the sixty-five grand the insurance company offered. There was a big problem with liability.

Richard—the firm—didn't have the money to buy the same quality of expert testimony they had. The kid lost. Naturally, he and his parents sued us. We barely squeaked by." Tompkins shrugged. "That's the way he played things. He thrived on risk."

"How long ago was this?" asked Paul.

"About three years ago. The kid and his parents haven't forgiven us."

"You didn't like the way he handled things."

"He promised Perry a partnership but he treated him like scum," Soto said.

"Is that right?" Paul asked.

Tompkins chewed patiently, then said, "He would have come through for me. As I said, I was just about to make partner. He depended on me, okay?"

"What's the upshot, now that he's gone?" Armano asked, impatient. "What happens to you?"

"According to our oral agreement, the firm is mine. That is my position. He has a ninety-one-year-old grandmother. She's his only heir. I'm sure I can work something out with her."

"Good deal for you," Armano said.

"If you think seeing your colleague murdered is good deal," Tompkins said.

"C'mon. The guy had problems. I'm sure working with him wasn't completely easy."

The lawyers looked at each other.

"Okay. I'm going to let you in on something. Vegas was his problem," Ralph Soto said. "Reno. South Lake Tahoe. Atlantic City. The Bahamas. Know what I mean? Where he went depended on how much he had. What money he made, he blew. He favored seven-card stud. Big pots."

"You could tell on Monday mornings," Tompkins agreed.

"He was tired? Or mad? What?" Paul prompted.

"He'd go out cycling before dawn and come in half-dead. He'd be at the office at seven and hector me for coming in at nine. Talk to clients he'd been ignoring. Worked like a madman to catch up on everything, drove the secretary crazy. By afternoon he would have plane reservations for the next weekend. He had it bad. Still, I'll miss him," Tompkins said suddenly.

"What I see is if you killed Filsen, you thought you would get more than the partnership. You'd get the whole business."

"Hey, now. Are you accusing my client of murder?" Soto suddenly tuned in.

"I didn't kill Richard," Tompkins said firmly. "I didn't kill him so that I could take over. Richard's death causes the firm all sorts of problems. I'm just hoping I can carry on."

"You made out good," Armano said.

"Not the way I see it," Perry said.

Back at the car, Armano turned to Paul. "Walrus and the Carpenter," he said.

"Crocodile tears."

"Hope I die before I develop a legal problem," said Armano, dusting the seat with his hand. They got into the car. "How's that guy ever get any work done with a load on like that every afternoon?"

"You mean Soto?"

"Yeah."

"Ralph's the equivalent of Richard Filsen for his firm. He socializes and brings in the new cases, even at AA meetings. He's a phony and a hypocrite, but that never stopped anyone from becoming a lawyer."

"What about that uptight associate of Filsen's?"

"He's reserved and awkward, isn't he? He probably actually did do most of the work."

"Think there's any more to him than meets the eye?"

"Perry's scared. He gets the potentially lucrative practice to himself. He hasn't got a definite alibi. He's a person of interest. So he says, 'I don't know much,'" Paul continued, parodying Ebenezer Scrooge's associates. "'I only know he's dead.' He has Ralph sit in just in case he's got a problem with us."

"At least Filsen's granny cares. Maybe. Should we interview her? She lives in Los Angeles," Armano said.

"Why don't you give her a call in case she's in the mood to blurt out some family secret. Ask her if she packs a .357 Magnum."

"And then there's the charming Mrs. Santiago, so sweet and kind and sad for Richard, she can hardly even hide it from her husband."

"Thank God for sympathetic women," Paul said. "Men wouldn't last a year on this earth without them."

Back at the office, Paul dug out the letters from Filsen's attaché case. They were both from Filsen's creditors in South Lake Tahoe. Harvey's Club wanted more than $40,000. Paul picked up the telephone to call the lab. "Anything new?"

"Yeah. We've got something for you. A lot of prints

from all over the apartment, including the bedroom." The technician gave Paul a name he did not bother to write down.

Barbara Santiago's fingerprints. No surprise, just a verification of his suspicion. They were sleeping together.

Did Carlos know?

Paul spent that afternoon tracking down Matt's friend Zinnia Farr. Her two dozen or more relatives swore she had come home by midnight the night before Thanksgiving and slept on the couch in the living room of the house on Marion Avenue.

He did enjoy the father's sincere alibi: "We were partying all night. For sure, Zinny was there, keeping up, snort for snort."

Paul tracked her down. She came into the station and spoke to him, dressed conservatively in a long skirt and ironed blouse, courteous and deferential. She could not provide Matt with an alibi, she said politely, because she had left before midnight after Matt hit the hay during a movie they had been watching, *Alien*. "You ever seen it? That is some awesomely creepy shit," she said.

Paul didn't like her, although he did like her hair. He liked women with long hair.

The afternoon wore on. He'd be off-duty soon. Paul rubbed his face slowly. He had been so late he hadn't shaved that day. Picking up the phone to order pizza, he jumped as Armano burst in. "Here comes another death under suspicious circumstances down the coast near Big Sur. This is our jurisdiction all the way. Carsey says we hit the road."

CHAPTER
30

THEY HAD NO DIFFICULTY LOCATING THE SCENE.
Four police cars, bright lights flashing and spinning, were parked at crazy angles along a narrow patch of Highway 1 just north of Bixby Creek
Bridge, at various precarious pullouts. An ambulance
stood ready, attendants lounging on its bumper. There
were no other cars. The police had cordoned off the
pullout closest to the bridge, stretching a yellow plastic
strip from stakes in the ground. Gawkers parked ille-
gally alongside the road beyond and stood on the narrow walkway on the bridge, pointing down toward the
beach and muttering to each other. A CHP was just
starting to clear them out.

"The vultures have landed," Armano said as they
pulled their unmarked beige car alongside a police van
on the wrong side of the road. They crossed Highway 1
and walked around the stakes.

"Detective van Wagoner?" a deputy sheriff said, scratching himself furiously on the arm. "Poison oak," he apologized when he noticed Armano's expression. "Everywhere."

The deputy led them to the edge of the overlook. "Look out. The cliffs are unstable. You never know when a chunk might break loose."

Down below, in light that was beginning to fade, Paul saw the body of a woman through his binoculars. He had expected a fall like that would produce an ugly sprawl, so he was surprised to spot the body curled up, as if sleeping, several hundred feet down on the rocks below the pullout. On the side of the woman's head he couldn't see, a head wound had caused blood to pool around the gray hair. A trickle of water in this season, Bixby Creek flowed out to the ocean. As fast as the police cleared people from the bridge on the cliffs above, more came to peer over the side at the scene below.

"Anybody been down there yet?"

"The coroner and her henchwomen."

"Anyone thinking suicide?"

The deputy shook his head and scratched his leg. "Who knows?"

There was no place where they could easily get down to the body, so they hiked up the road and found a path etched by water runoff and climbed gingerly down. By the time they reached the bottom, Armano was puffing.

"What kind of Californian are you, buddy?" Paul asked, skipping onto the beach.

Shivering and wet with mud, Armano answered, breathing hard, "The fat kind."

As they approached, two more officers nodded. Susan Misumi was delving into an aluminum case in the sand beside her. Seeing Paul and Armano, she dusted her gloved hands off, waving her hands at them without one touching the other.

They introduced themselves. "We meet again," Paul said. "How's it going?"

"Hiya, Paul. I've just been here a few minutes but there are a couple of things. The woman, in her late forties, early fifties, died of severe head injuries sustained in a fall. Looks like she died instantly. One huge gash cracked open her skull on the right side. The trauma from that alone would have wiped her out."

Paul and Armano crossed the small slice of sand and approached the body, which lay a few feet up from the beach among the rocks.

The woman's eyes were open in a twisted face, a face already so removed from humanity Paul thought for a jolting moment he was looking at a theatrical mask. A mask of malice. A mask intended to frighten. The mouth gaped widely exposing teeth on the top and bottom, as if interrupted midhowl.

Susan took a deep breath. "Yes, the expression isn't the usual. I'm thinking that this woman suffered from a medical condition which caused facial disfigurement. In death, the muscles normally relax. She looks older than she is. Was."

"She moved," Paul noted, responding to a small

disturbance in the sandy patches around her that explained the body's position.

Susan nodded. "Amazing what the human body will take. She couldn't have lived more than a few moments after that fall. Shouldn't have lived even that long."

Quietly, they examined the sand and rocks.

"Have we got photos?" Paul asked. The tide or wind would make short work of this patch of beach soon.

The attending deputy nodded.

Paul rolled the body over with gloved hands to examine the skull wound, pulling the right arm out from underneath.

She was missing her left hand.

Warning bells rang in his head. It couldn't be! Picking up the black leather purse he found still dangling from a strap attached to her right hand, he opened it and pulled out the wallet.

Virginia Reilly of Pacific Grove.

First Filsen, Nina's ex-lover. Now Nina's mother.

"Maybe she stopped to look at the view and jumped on impulse," Armano said, sounding sad. He looked toward the ocean. "Looks like she had reasons to die."

"Who called this in?" Paul asked Susan, who had straightened up. She had a round, intelligent face, not a whole lot of humor in it, not that he'd expect a comedian to go into her line of work.

"Exactly. There's a witness. He says it wasn't a suicide, Detective. A passing motorist, who did not leave a name, called it in. It was a male voice. He said he just saw somebody pushed off the cliff near Bixby Creek Bridge. The 911 dispatcher asked for a description, but he said the people were hidden when he approached the overlook, and he just glanced behind in his rear-view mirror long enough to see her fall. He said, 'I had the definite impression she was pushed. Somebody else was there with the old lady.' He didn't stop, just rushed to the nearest phone, which is a few miles further down the road."

So much for suicide. The witness might not be able to describe the people standing at the cliff's edge, but he should be able to describe their car. The witness had to be found. Paul looked up at the faces of onlookers leaning over the cliffs like small white moons against the darkening hills. The body would not be visible from a passing vehicle, so they were lucky someone had spotted her. The murderer probably waited for one of those unpredictable pauses in the afternoon traffic, pushed the woman, then hightailed it out of there.

"When did the call come in?"

"About four thirty in the afternoon. Jibes with my rough estimate of time of death."

A team of paramedics came up to them, carrying the portable gurney, and Susan fell into conversation with them. Paul and Armano took another long look around.

They clambered back up the steep hillside by flashlight. A harsh evening wind had begun to blow. Dr. Misumi, finding handholds in the rocky mud, complained all the way up about the dirt on her good suit. "People die in the most inconvenient places at the worst times. I'm supposed to be at a wedding reception."

Armano tumbled down a few feet and let loose a sharp Spanish profanity, which he translated with relish.

The ground at the crime-taped overlook was gravelly dirt, too hard to show signs of a scuffle, trampled besides by thousands of tourist feet. It was impossible to see if one or two people had stood at the cliffside, but from the position of the body, they could fix fairly closely where Virginia Reilly had been standing. Convenient for the killer that they had been hidden from view by the car. Or just plain resourceful.

They got back into the car as the ambulance drivers reached the top with their burden and began putting the body bag into the truck. Watching them, Paul was struck as he always was by their gentle handling of the body. Mrs. Reilly had been an important person, a living person, a mother. She deserved their respect, even at the end.

Filsen. Reilly.

Filsen had represented the acupuncturist Mrs. Reilly was going to sue—or had sued, Paul remained slightly murky on the details. The key to the murder had to lie in that situation. He couldn't put it together in his mind, though he was looking forward to talking again with Dr. Wu.

Minutes later, heading south on Highway 1, they stopped at the first store they came to, a small redwood cabin that serviced campers. Two outdoor phones on the porch stood idle.

"Anyone use those phones lately?" Paul asked, showing the woman at the counter his identification.

The woman was more of a girl, with brown braids she had looped and pinned to her head. Her tone was not friendly. "You're here about the woman who fell off the cliff at Bixby?"

"You can hear the phone from in here, can't you?"

"Sometimes. It gets busy." She sounded defensive in the empty store. Pulling out a stack of newspapers, she neatened them.

"We don't have all night."

"Okay, okay. A guy came in about a couple of hours ago, at about two thirty, three. Maybe close to four. It was getting on in the afternoon. He called the police. Saw something awful at the bridge. I heard that. That's all I know."

Paul luxuriated in a small itch of excitement. Maybe this cashier had seen the witness and his car. Maybe Paul had a real lead. "What did he look like?"

"Like half the people that come here: three-day growth of beard, short, stocky, wearing a plaid flannel shirt. All the city guys wear those when they come down here, it seems like. Let's see. Levi's. The shirt—black-and-white. A red watch, waterproof plastic. He looked vaguely familiar, but it wasn't anyone I know from around here. You know the type, always on the make for girls about the age of his youngest daughter."

"What did he do after he made the call?"

"Took off." She brightened. "And what a car. Red Ferrari, an older one, vintage. That thing was smooth, and so quiet I never even heard him pull away. I heard cars like that were supposed to be mechanical disasters."

That probably explained why the killer had moved

when a witness was approaching. The road curved before and after the bridge, without a lot of visible road-
way, but he or she should have been able to hear a
standard car approaching from some distance on a
quiet Monday afternoon.

"You won't have much trouble finding that Ferrari,
I bet," the girl said.

"Did you notice which way it went?"

"Took a right. Went south. Probably on the way to
the Ventana Inn for dinner or maybe on to Esalen for
some soothing meditation? That guy had money falling
out of his pockets."

A family of campers in parkas and boots stomped
in. Paul thanked the clerk and took down her contact
information, then he and Armano left.

They took the winding road slowly in the dark.
Several times they missed a driveway and had to reverse
direction. Cabins and campgrounds lined the river that
ran parallel to the highway. News of the killing had already spread, probably thanks to the girl at the store.
Some families were packing up to leave. Nobody had
seen the red sports car or its driver.

By seven o'clock their hunger had become insup-
portable. They pulled in to park at Nepenthe, a local
landmark. The building, made of redwood shingles,
loomed up from the lot in the moonlight, and the lines
of windows surrounding the top-level restaurant
glowed with tiny Christmas lights.

Armano took two steps at a time up from the parking lot, eager to procure a table at the restaurant or,
failing that, perhaps a spot at the café below, while Paul

toured quickly through the parking lot, which extended onto two levels.

Not too many cars were parked there now, although Paul imagined that earlier plenty of armchair adventurers had been leaping from their sheepskin seat covers toward the upstairs deck with its welcoming margaritas. The lower lot remained almost empty. He was ready to make the hike back up to the building when instinct suggested he go just a little farther up the road.

There, in an alcove of bushes just beyond the lot, a red Ferrari sat, empty.

He thumbed his nose, smiling. He approached and found it locked.

CHAPTER
31

ARMANO PUSHED A MAN OUT THE DOORS OF THE restaurant onto the deck with its fire pit. "Here's our proud Ferrari owner. The bartender knew him. Talks about his hot-shit car. We're going down to find a sandwich." The man shook him off and walked on ahead, pulling a leather jacket over his flannel shirt. He was middle-aged and pissed off. "We have to get some food," Armano whispered urgently to Paul as he approached. "Or else I'll have to eat him."

The middle-level café was on an outdoor patio that sat high above the ocean and in the daytime offered spectacular vistas. A young guy with his hair in a top-knot and a right arm covered with black-ink tattoos wiggled a dishcloth at them. "Who left the gate open?" he called. "We're closed."

"No, you're not," Armano said firmly.

"Just a quick order," Paul said, flashing his ID.

"A Reuben," Armano specified as the cowed waiter began to scurry. "Extra cheese. Extra sauerkraut. Extra hot."

They sat down on chairs across from a wooden plank. On the bench, they placed their witness. The sandwiches came quickly, huge and steaming. Armano bit and chewed. "That's one fine vehicle you got," he said with a full mouth.

"Correct." The witness lifted one nicely pressed jeans-clad leg over the other. He was about fifty, mostly bald, and would rather have been anywhere else. He grimaced, exhibiting the whitest teeth Paul had ever seen on a human. Another problem with Californian smiles, this uniform white they all worked so hard to maintain.

"Guy in the restaurant says you come in often, always with a different woman. Braggin' on your car," Armano said.

Paul took over, introducing himself and Armano, apologizing for Armano's rough handling. "We have reason to believe you were a witness—"

Recognition flitted across Armano's face. "Hey, you were the guy in that old movie—ah, what was it called? The one about—at the Dream? Last week? A retrospective."

"I'm Dan Fordham."

"That woman you were with upstairs?"

"On her way back to L.A. by now. She'll find a ride." Fordham turned his attention to Paul. "You're here about that 911 call. I guess this means you found something. Bad luck for me."

"Much worse luck for the dead lady."

Fordham acted as if he hadn't heard. "I can't add to what I said on the phone. We're all better off leaving me out of the picture."

"You're an eyewitness to a possible homicide," said Paul. "We want the whole thing, with details, please."

"On the cliffs?"

"Yeah."

"The lady's dead?"

"Yep."

"Whew." Fordham worked his jaw. "I was late for my date, speeding some. What a stunning drive."

"How fast?"

"Fifty-five. Okay, eighty. Slower on the curves. But there was hardly any traffic. I was heading south on Highway One, coming down from Carmel. Left there about three thirty."

"It's a dangerous road for speeding."

"This car's built to demolish that road. So I rolled around this tight curve. There at one of those scenic pullouts before Bixby Creek Bridge sat one of those blah American cars. White, maybe. A Monte Carlo, maybe. Not a classic car, you understand. Just far enough past banal to rate ugly. I spotted two heads above the car, then whizzed by." Fordham shook his head. "The wind was blowing. I guess they didn't hear me coming. Anyway, I saw an old woman standing there, I thought with another person, for just a second, then she went flying." He sat back.

The waiter hovered. "You done? I'm due home an hour ago."

"Soon, *hermano*," Armano promised.

The waiter scowled and cleared a couple of plates.

"At first it just didn't register," Fordham continued. "I guess I assumed car trouble or people stopping to look at the view there, which is pretty stupendous. I had my stereo on right in the middle of a song we—I really like. Maybe it's being in the movies—I didn't believe what I saw. Then I thought, 'Oh hell, that woman just got—unbelievable,' I thought, 'I have just witnessed a murder!' I looked back in the rearview mirror, as I said before. I couldn't see anyone else anymore."

"You passed very close by when you drove by. I can't believe that someone would push another person off a cliff right in front of you. It's stupid."

"It happened, though. Must've started pushing her before I rounded the bend is all I can figure out. And like I said, when I looked back, there was no one at all by the car. They ducked down."

Paul said, "So, tell us. Who was in the car with you? The woman who's now on her way to L.A.? We need her name and number."

Fordham reddened slightly. "I'll be glad to provide whatever information you need. She wasn't with me, though. It was a girl I picked up hitching. Nobody ever hitches anymore, do they? It's rare. Dangerous. But I'm a sucker for a young, pretty girl. Her name's Becky, but that's all I can tell you about her, except that I picked her up a little south of Carmel, near the Highlands Inn, and dropped her at the store where I stopped to call. She's a carrottop. Young. I think she was staying at one of those cabins down by the river."

"You'll have to go back up to Monterey to give a statement," Paul said.

"God dammit," said Fordham.

Five minutes later a deputy arrived to make sure he didn't head back to Hollywood.

Armano, sliding into the driver's seat beside Paul, said, "He was showing off for the hitchhiker. Speeding, showing he still had balls. His movie? Did you see it?"

Paul shook his head.

"Vampire movie. The guy's a terrible actor. Still riding on history." Armano pulled a hunk of chocolate out of the glove compartment and waved it at Paul, who shook his head.

"He looks just like Malcolm McDowell," Paul said. "A little less hair. Can't be all bad."

"Should have asked him to autograph a napkin."

By the time they got back to the River Inn cabins, hidden in the tall pines that sloped down to the Big Sur River, it was nearly ten o'clock. They parked near a trailer that said OFFICE but looked deserted and began knocking on doors.

At the third cabin, a yellow bulb lit a porch decorated with forlorn laundry, and a young girl in a tight tank top answered the door. She pulled a sweater off a peg, stepped outside, and pulled the door shut behind her, first looking anxiously back into the room.

"Who are you?"

They explained.

"Don't mention the hitching, okay? My mother will kill me. She thinks I was with someone I knew.

Well, I guess everybody knows Mr. Fordham, don't they? Awesome, wasn't it, that he stopped?"

Paul assured her that they would only tell if necessary, and that was all she needed before her story began pouring out.

Her name was Rebecca Barjaktarovich. Becky was sixteen. She and her mother were living temporarily in the cabin, while her mother applied for jobs as an attendant for an elderly, handicapped person. They had lived in Castroville for several years with Becky's father, but following a nasty breakup ended up broke and without a home. A long time ago Becky's mom used to come down to Big Sur to hang around and still had some good friends here, one of whom was loaning them the cabin during the off-season, till they were able to get back on their feet again.

"See, I was applying for a waitress job in Carmel for after school, which I got by the way. All you have to do to get a job is to lie and say you're eighteen. It's something to do with insurance. They want you to lie; they beg you to lie. So I did. I start tomorrow." Becky sat on a rusty, pink metal chair, twisting her red hair between her fingers. "I hope you're not here to put me in jail for that, because then for sure the world's totally pathetic."

"There's a bus you can take," Paul said. "No more hitching. You'll get hurt eventually."

"How'm I supposed to pay for the bus?"

Paul opened his wallet and handed her a $10 bill. She gaped at it.

"Bus fare," Paul said. "After that, use tip money. I

don't want to find your body by the side of the road one day. Okay?"

"Okay."

"We need to know what you saw at Bixby Creek Bridge."

"You mean the car? Hmm. White. One of the big, plush kinds old ladies love. And what I thought were just a couple of people admiring the view."

"What did they look like?"

"Oh, jeez. It went by so fast." She pursed her lips, looking down. "I wasn't paying much attention. I was singing along with the radio, then Dan—Mr. Fordham—got all excited and told me to look back, which I did. I didn't see anything, but he went on and on about how there were two of them and where'd everybody go. Stuff like that."

That was all she had, and it wasn't enough. They thanked Becky, got the inn's telephone number and the name of her new employer, and headed back north toward Pacific Grove.

"You hear anything more about the Filsen thing?" Paul asked Armano.

"Helio and the Santiagos are the only ones on that second floor, and we already know their stories. That gun must've sounded like explosions. Here's what I've heard. There's a grocer on the ground floor, Mr. Gomez. He said he was opening the store. He opens at seven in the morning to cater to the local winos. He heard the shots. I went around yesterday to check it out. He says he just ducked until the shots stopped. Then he hung around at the back of the store for a few minutes. Didn't want to see anything, you know? Then he closed up shop, pronto. I also checked the neighborhood. Nobody else admits to seeing anything."

After dropping Armano off, Paul arrived in front of Nina's house at about quarter to eleven. He took a couple of breaths in the car, dreading what was to come. Here he came again with more bad news, the worst kind. The lights were on in the living room. She answered the doorbell immediately. She wore cutoffs and a tight little T and was barefoot. The kid must be in bed. Why, she's just a girl, Paul thought with surprise, sadly. She wasn't very tall, but she stood tall.

"What are you—"

"I have more bad news, Nina."

She had already taken note of his expression and her eyes widened. "Not Matt?"

"No. Not your brother." Paul drew her inside and made her sit down on the couch. "I'm so sorry but . . ." He told her quickly and simply, and didn't say anything about the possibility that her mother had been pushed.

Again, Nina wept, this time for a very long time and Paul didn't rush things. He didn't try to hold her hand either. This was business.

After a few minutes and many questions, Nina's face began to harden. "My mother did not—she never would—commit suicide!"

"I didn't say she did."

"She wouldn't have gone there alone, stood on the edge of a cliff like that. It's impossible."

"She might not have been alone." He told her the

rest of it, and watching strong emotions cross her face as he spoke, he had two thoughts about Nina Reilly: that she hadn't had anything to do with it herself, and that she'd make a good lawyer someday, the way she was holding herself together now.

Nina marched mechanically to the closet. "Bob's not home tonight. He's at a friend's, sleeping over."

"I need you to come with me."

She nodded. "I need to see her."

After that, she sat stony-faced in his car, hugging a leather jacket. She had changed into jeans and hiking boots. "Could you turn the heat on?" she asked once, then lapsed back into silence.

She lost it as they drove along a winter field, bare earth now. They had left the shoreline and were driving inland. Paul looked over to check out the silence. She cried soundlessly.

The morgue in Salinas served the entire county. Susan Misumi had checked out hours before. An attendant pulled out a slab and lifted the sheet, and Nina, as gray as the cold aluminum drawers, nodded and cried out, "Mom! Oh, no, no." She put her hands on her mother's face as if to warm it, then began stroking it.

"I'm so sorry, Nina," Paul said.

"Mom."

He held her while she puddled against him.

"Mom."

CHAPTER 32

B Y THE TIME NINA FINISHED AT THE SHERIFF'S OF-
fice, early morning fog had fingered its gray way
all the way to Salinas. She wouldn't let Paul take
her home even though he insisted on someone escorting
her there.

Once home, she had a talk with herself and decided
not to collapse, which turned out to be easier said than
done. She sat down at the kitchen table with a cup of
coffee and didn't move for a long time.

She saw her mother falling into an unruly wind,
into the sands below, the ocean waves pounding, eternal and eternally indifferent.

She saw her mom's sweet face from before she got sick
and thought about how her mother loved to argue, laugh,
dance. Mopping herself up with a napkin, she made a list.
She called Matt. Nobody answered. She called the mother
of Bob's friend and asked her if she could keep Bob for one

more day, not saying why. She called the Monterey College of Law and said she had a family emergency and would not be able to make her Wills and Estates exam. She called the Pohlmann office and told them she couldn't work today. She called her father and heard his sleepy voice on the line.

"You and Bob want to come over here?" Harlan asked.

"No, thanks, Dad."

"How could this happen?" he kept asking. "This doesn't sound like Ginny. Throw herself over a cliff? Never. She loved you all too much."

"I need to reach Matt, Dad. If you hear from him, tell him to call me, okay?"

He became all business. "You haven't told me everything, Nina. You said you spent the evening with the police. Tell me the rest."

Harlan badgered her for a few minutes for details until she finally said, "I'm sure you'll get a chance yourself to have a nice long talk with the police. Ask them then."

"You sound so angry."

"I'm not angry at you."

"Nina. In spite of the money pressures on us, things that made me say things, do things I regret now, I never meant to hurt your mother. You know that, don't you?"

How absurd, she thought. Everything you did hurt her. She said nothing.

"Makes me wish—" He broke off.

"What?" When he didn't answer, she prodded, "What does it make you wish?"

"I'd loved her better. I'm ashamed of myself. I can't

believe she's gone and I'll never see her again. I miss her, too, just so you know." His voice broke.

"I'm going, Dad," Nina managed to say. "I'll let you know if I hear anything."

"What about the arrangements?"

"An autopsy. Then I'll call a mortuary."

"An autopsy? Aw, hell." A long pause followed. "Call me if you need me, honey." Then he gave her four different phone numbers.

She tried calling Matt again and again, but there was no answer. She didn't have his number at the store where he worked and couldn't remember the name. She went into the bedroom, crying again, cleaned her eyes up with water from the bathroom, and cried some more on her way out to the car.

Once in the car, driving, her tears dried up. She began thinking about Paul, wondering how he managed to be both cop and human—it had been a relief to have his solid, heavy-shouldered presence there with her at the morgue. Once she had officially identified her mother's body, he had filled her in on the rest, though he wouldn't let her ask questions, just arranged for her ride home.

He had made her feel like a kid in the middle of a tantrum whose parent says, "When you stop crying, we'll talk about it." He had an old-fashioned streak to him that frustrated and even angered her. Then, before saying good-bye, back in cop mode, he had asked for keys to her mother's house so that the police could inspect it for signs of forced entry.

She provided them, unable to decide if it was wise, only thinking about her mom.

She stopped in at the office first.

"Oh, Nina," Astrid said, standing up, face stricken. "We're all so sorry!"

"Is Remy in?"

Astrid paused. "Yes. Yes, she is." She buzzed Remy's office. "She's ready for you."

Nina opened the door to Remy's office. Remy, immaculately clad as always, spoke into the phone. "Don't worry. It's taken care of. We've got it handled." Et cetera.

She hung up, stood up, and reached out to hug Nina. "I'm so sorry, honey. So sorry."

All Nina's strength fell by the wayside. She fell into the hug and allowed her tears to flow. Finally, she composed herself, stepping back. "Can I sit?"

"Of course."

She sat in one of the plush leather client chairs, leaning her head against the headrest. She closed her eyes.

"Nina?" Remy finally spoke. "Can I get you anything?"

"You really upset my mother the last time you saw her. Can you tell me exactly why you decided not to pursue her case against Dr. Wu?"

"Yes, of course." Remy's brow creased. "Nina, in spite of the fine work you did researching Raynaud's, we had some rock-bottom, insoluble problems with your mother's claim." Remy went into a long, involved explanation that Nina barely heard. The collapse was beginning inside her. She wasn't going to be able to hold it back now, and she didn't want it to happen at the office. She held a hand up.

"Okay. Okay."

Remy nodded. "I want you to know, I believed every word your mom said. I never believed Dr. Wu. But the question always comes down to, can we convince a jury?"

"You thought we couldn't."

"He's smart. No, let me correct that. He's canny. He had things to show and say that cast doubt on her story. And the medical side of it—I'm so sorry."

Nina finally found Matt at the counter at Barney's, ringing up a couple of six-packs for a man in expensive sunglasses and a torn T-shirt. Matt took one look at Nina and pulled her into the back room.

"What's wrong?"

"I have very bad news, Matt. Please sit down."

"Mom!" he breathed, and read confirmation in her face. He grabbed her by the shoulders. "Tell me."

"Sit."

He sat.

"Mom is gone."

"Gone? You mean she died?"

"She fell off a cliff by Bixby Creek Bridge."

"Fell? Huh? What?"

"I saw her. I saw her body. She's dead, Matt." Nina barely got the words out, then sobbed into her handkerchief.

"Holy shit!" Matt said. "What was she doing in Big Sur? How did she fall? Do you think she jumped?"

Nina couldn't stand to tell him. She didn't want to feed his paranoia. "Right now, what matters is she's gone."

Matt got up. This time, his arms around her were loving. "God, Neen. I'm so sorry. Really? This can't be! This can't be! She's dead?" He paused. "It's got to be that maniac who tried to kill her! You know, that quack? Believe me, she never said a word to me about those needles until after it was too late. You saw at the hospital. I didn't know till then or I would have found a way to stop her." He waited for Nina's nod.

"That fucking butcher, Dr. Wu. He hurt her, and when she fought back, he killed her. They better arrest him before he gets away." His face screwed up in agitation and his voice rose. "Do you remember her in that red dress at Christmas? Before Bob was born? God, Mom was beautiful! If he's still loose, I'll kill him myself!"

Matt let go of her. He stood staring at boxes stacked against a wall, speaking almost under his breath. She strained to hear. "It's my fault." He kicked the boxes. "Do you know what she'd say to me?" Now he was suddenly shouting.

"Matt, come home with me today, okay? I'll take care of you. Please, just come outside with me. Let's be together. Play with Bob, watch something stupid on television. We'll call your boss later." Nina tried to sound soothing as she took his arm and tried to wheedle him out of the store.

He shook her off. "I should be punished for what I've done," he said in an angry voice. Then, drawing himself up: "You go on, Neen. It's okay." When she didn't move, he said, "Go ahead now, I have to do something." Then he was pushing her out, putting her in the car, helping her with her seat belt, advising her to drive carefully.

She buckled up to please him, worrying about her brother. He needed help; he wasn't well, but it was all she could do to start up her car and pull away, crying helplessly.

"Go!" he shouted after her.

She dragged slowly along the road, accumulating a pile of angry tailgaters without noticing. When she arrived home, she thought at first she would go get Bob. Instead she called the office. She called Jack.

CHAPTER
33

JACK CAME OVER RIGHT AWAY. HE PUT HER IN BED and sat by her. She could never remember later what she said that evening. He stayed there, holding her, easing the loneliness of the night.

When she awoke at dawn, he was right next to her bed in the rattan dressing-table chair, sound asleep, tie loose, mouth open, stubbly, dead beat.

She felt empty, watching the steady rise and fall of his chest. The worst thing was knowing that from now on there would always be an empty place inside her.

They picked up Bob later and broke the news. Nina talked about the concept of heaven, how Grandma was safe somewhere like that. Bob had questions. Nina answered as well as she could, fabricating when faith failed her.

Back home, they dressed him in clean play clothes and took him to his preschool, where the teachers gave him a warm welcome and put him to work on a building project with some other kids in one corner of the room. Nina spoke with the teachers, explaining what had happened. He would only be staying for a few hours this morning. They lavished conventional expressions of sympathy. She realized the world had ways to deal with death, which she was learning fast.

Jack and Nina arrived at the sheriff's office in Monterey late in the morning.

Paul told them much of what he knew.

"C'mon, Paul," Jack said. "You have ideas. Who killed Richard Filsen? Who killed Mrs. Reilly? Are the deaths connected? Where are we on this?"

"We don't know. Nina, we think your mother was persuaded or forced into the car and driven to Big Sur. Neighbors mentioned a white car parked briefly in front of the house, but reported nothing else that appeared out of the ordinary. There were signs of disturbance inside, a dropped bag of groceries near the entryway and a knife was lying on the floor in the kitchen, but we found no signs of blood there. It doesn't appear she was wounded in that way."

"She tried to defend herself," Nina said dully.

"Maybe someone she knew showed up claiming an emergency, and she simply dropped those items and went without a peep. Maybe a weapon showed up, and she was forced to go. We don't know. We have to look at a lot of possibilities, among those, the possibility Jack mentioned, that there's a link between her death and the death of Richard Filsen."

"I told you they were enemies," said Nina.

"Antagonists. Adversaries," clarified Jack. "In the legal sense. Mrs. Reilly and Dr. Wu. Mrs. Reilly and Richard Filsen."

"Not only that, of course," said Paul. The two men looked at Nina.

"You think this has to do with me? With Bob?"

"Possibly." Paul shrugged. "Don't ask me how these deaths fit together, if they do. I won't press you now, Nina, but I need you back here tomorrow to give us another statement. Maybe you can enlighten us."

"If I knew anything, I'd have already told it to you. How did she end up at that bridge? That's what you want to know, isn't it?"

"Someone drove her there," Paul replied. "Persuasion. Force. Who knows? Does the description of the car match any that are familiar to you? Friends of your mother's? Friends of yours? Think."

"No. No. Have you looked into rentals?"

"Yes, we have. We couldn't connect anything."

"How about, um, the hundreds of people who might drive that kind of car?"

"Well, we have lists that spread fast as cockroaches. We haven't eliminated everyone, but we have nothing new to go on."

Jack stood up, blocking light from Paul's window. "Is Nina a suspect?"

"I gather information, Jack. That's my job. You know that."

"I'm going to figure this out, Paul," Nina said. "I'll let you know when I have. You know my mom was upset when my firm couldn't go ahead with her claim?"

"Yes, you told me. What was her decision after hearing that news?"

"I don't exactly know, except she couldn't let go. She told us on Thanksgiving she was considering carrying on."

"Did she have a routine on Mondays?" Paul asked.

"Wash the dishes?" Nina said. "Groceries?"

"Nothing someone might rely on."

"I don't think so," Nina said.

Paul looked at Jack.

"Nina, we should go," Jack said.

She rose from her chair, still looking at Paul. "You both see this stuff all the time. Dead bodies. Mothers, fathers, children, even little babies, murdered, tortured sometimes. I don't even let myself picture most of these things. But this is my mother. I can't stop imagining—"

Nina saw that neither of the men wanted to hear more, but neither could leave such a stupendous hint hanging.

"Imagining what?" Jack asked gently.

"What nightmares your dreams must be."

Jack tried to get her out the door before she could say more, but she pulled away.

"How can you do this terrible work?"

Paul got up from his desk and walked over to her. He stopped and bent his head to look into her face. "There's no justice for your mother, Nina, only for you and for her killer."

"Platitudes," Nina said. "I expect better from you. I expect an arrest."

"Call you later," Jack said as they left, Jack clutching her arm and dragging her away.

Nina and Jack collected Bob from his preschool. Clinging to Bob's hand on the porch, Nina stood in front of her door. "Go back to work, Jack," she said, but he was up the stairs holding her tightly. He stayed as long as she wanted him, then released her.

"Call me," he told her. She watched him drive away. Bob said he needed food right now, so she heated up soup from a can. She read to him and called Harlan again, telling him what Paul had told her. Harlan said little. Matt did not answer his phone. Bob watched cartoons. She sat with a torn hem in her lap, along with a needle and thread, watching the gray drear of afternoon darken.

After Bob's bath and bedtime—they said a little prayer for Grandma—Nina checked the locks on the windows and doors, then went into the living room and held a pillow lightly over her face so the sound of her crying wouldn't keep him up.

Paul went back to see Barbara Santiago the next morning, early. Carlos was at work. The baby was not around.

"You were sleeping with Richard Filsen," he said, after she let him in.

"Who do you think you are, coming at me like this?"

"A homicide detective with the Monterey County sheriff's office. Now. Let's get this over with. You were in love with him."

Tears bubbled in her eyes. "Get out." She pushed him toward the door. "Go, you asshole!"

Paul went outside, took a breath, and walked a few doors down to Helio's apartment.

Helio was watching a soap opera. "See this guy?" he said, letting Paul inside. "He's stealing from his mama. She knows but she doesn't say anything. She's superprotective. He can do no harm." Helio nodded. "That's good stuff. Loving mama. Friends who overlook his evil. Girlfriend who accepts his shit."

"Can I sit?"

Helio pointed to the couch. "Want a beer?"

"No thanks." For a few more seconds, they watched a guy with an unreal tan lie, steal, and kiss up to everyone left and right, and all of it in Spanish.

Helio slapped his leg when the show ended. "You have to admire the man! Don't we all want that kind of love!"

"Sometimes."

"My mama? She packed up and left when I was three. Daddy worked two jobs and was never home. Me and my brother, we played in an alley, and now it's a shock to me we're still alive and kicking butt."

"I have a sister," Paul said, "from planet Pluto. She drives me nuts."

Helio nodded sagely. "Family, man. Real life."

"Kinda like Barbara Santiago and Richard Filsen."

"You know about that?"

"Yeah."

Helio nodded, flicking off the television. "She loved that guy. She would do anything for him. Oh, boy, if you had seen her when she found out he already had a kid. She wanted his babies, for sure."

"She told you stuff about his son? About Bob?"

"Said she wanted the boy's mom dead and the grandma that kept Richard away from his son dead. Came over a few afternoons now and then after Richard left her. She got tough when she drank, okay? I get mellow. You get mellow?"

"I get mellow," Paul lied. "After Richard left?" he repeated.

"Right. He came on afternoons when Carlos was working and the baby was asleep. She said he gave her two, sometimes three orgasms a go. How about that? I don't think I can do that," Helio said, gloomily sucking at the dregs of his beer. "You ever do that?"

"Not to my knowledge," Paul said, feeling quite sullen at the thought.

CHAPTER
34

NINA WOUND UP THE HILLS TOWARD MATT'S current digs, a house-sitting situation off Esquiline in Carmel Valley, to see how he was doing. Their mother was due for burial the next day.

Earlier, she had stopped off at her mother's house, using her own key. The crime-scene tape was gone. This bothered her, as if it meant the police had given up, even though she knew that wasn't so. Inside she observed signs of fingerprint dust, and although the house looked freshly cleaned, she smelled it, too. The furniture, wallpaper, even the rugs also gave off the faint scent of her mother's cologne, Chanel No. 5.

The floor near the entryway held only the usual red wool carpet. She saw no sign of the groceries her mother had bought on her last day.

In the kitchen, all looked tidy except for a few dirty dishes. The police had apparently removed the groceries and the knife. She checked the wooden block holder. Only one knife was missing, the butcher knife, the one her mother always kept supersharp.

Ginny had dropped the groceries so that she could grab a knife, Nina decided. However desperate or afraid Ginny had been, she had not gone like a lamb. She had fought, as she always did. However weak she must have felt, she fought and stood up to her assailant.

Never show them you're afraid. Never let fear stop you.

Her mother's words haunted her. Wandering into Ginny's bedroom, her sanctum, she recalled skidding the length of the freshly waxed, long hallway with Matt in socks, screaming like crazy, and how her mother, sitting on her bed watching, had laughed and laughed at them.

Four pictures had been tucked into the frame around the mirror above the dressing table. One showed Matt, longer-haired, younger, lovingly polishing Harlan's sports car. One showed Nina, hair blowing out behind her like a fan, at the beach building a sand castle, aged about six. In another one, bigger and more brightly colored, Bob stuck out his tongue. The last one hurt the most. Ginny, maybe nineteen, and Harlan, only a little older, sat on a blanket at Carmel River Beach, holding hands, smiling and squinting into the sunshine.

She had thought she might find something the police missed. And maybe she had.

Love.

As she locked up, she decided the only image missing to complete the painful history of their family might just be one of Richard Filsen.

She parked in front of the house in Carmel Valley and knocked on the door. No reply. She rang the doorbell. No reply.

"Matt?" she called, peering into the dirty front window from the porch. She could see a light inside.

A curtain shifted.

The door opened and he let her in.

The house, a single-story, sprawling, low-slung ranch built in the seventies, showed nothing of Matt. Bookcases held books he would never read. Pictures reflected a four-person family, mom, dad, boy, and girl. The entryway was mauve. In the kitchen, Formica masqueraded as oak. In the living room, vinyl performed the same function.

What did he do in this place? Nina wondered, then spotted the huge stereo system, tapes and records strewn about, a plump set of headphones lying on the floor.

"How are you, Matt?"

The red webbing around his irises deepened as his eyes made the rounds. "Fucked up, Neen." He chuckled, and it made her cringe. "People came around and injected me with virus. Kept me from eating. And now I can't sleep either. I warned you! I warned you and Mom!"

"Oh, Matt."

"I'm sick now. Maybe dying."

She took his pathetically thin arm and sat him down on a couch. He put his face into his hands. "Mom," he said brokenly. "She kept me going. I ran out of stuff and I'm out of money, too. And I got fired yesterday."

"Wait, wait. Tell me about this so-called virus?"

"AIDS. I feel so bad I must be dying."

"Have you seen a doctor?" She sat down, stood up, and stared at him, shocked and almost ready to believe him, he kept saying it so much.

He got up, gesticulating. "A doctor? A doctor? Do you hear yourself? Do you know what so-called doctors did to our mother? How about they killed her, huh?"

"Matt, we'll get you tested, and then—the drugs are affecting your thinking. Matt, you need more help than I can give you."

"They want me dead, underground with Mom, worms going in, worms going out, in that cold, dirty place."

Nina went over to him and held him by the shoulders. "Jesus, Matt, what did you use today? Crank? Cocaine?"

"Drugs are bad, Nina. They make me sick. They don't work right anymore."

"Pack a bag, like for a vacation."

"Maybe I need to call Zinnia. Figure out what's going on first."

"You're not calling Zinnia. Not now. Not ever again."

He paced the living room while she packed him a bag.

"Sign here," said the kindly black woman covering the front desk at Community Hospital's psych ward. Located in the basement of the hospital, the low-ceilinged ward was a claustrophobe's nightmare. From the desk Nina could see various small rooms leading off the brightly lit reception area—patient quarters. All the doors were shut tight. She bet some of them were locked, even though they had just passed through a heavy, locked door to get this far.

"Sign right here, Matt," Nina said, pointing.

"What the hell's this!" He picked up the paper and examined it.

"A safe place."

"You agree to stay for seventy-two hours," the woman said. "We protect you, get you the help you need."

Matt looked around wildly. "A doctor's going to inject me?"

"You see anything dangerous here?" Nina asked, waving her hands into the white space. "You believe I would find you a place that's dangerous? Matt, I need you. Bob needs you. Dad wants you safe, too. Please, stay for a few days. I'll come see you, I promise. Please sign."

Matt gave her that younger-brother look, quizzical, trusting. "Is that what I should do? Really? Lock myself up?"

"Yes, Matt." Nina touched the pen to his hand.

He signed.

"Seventy-two hours, that's all we can hold him," said the woman at the desk. An aide searched through Matt's suitcase. Matt looked on, disoriented. He looked so defeated, so wasted, that Nina almost said, *Let's get out of here, baby bro*. But she kept her mouth shut.

"He needs help," she said finally.

"What about Mom?" Matt asked forlornly. "I'm going to miss going. They'll bury her without me, put dirt over her."

"I'll be there, okay? I'll tell her you meant to come. I'll give her a rose from you."

"A white rose. She liked white roses." He closed his eyes. "I hate all this feeling. Hate it. Hate it."

"This is a voluntary commitment. He'll be seen by the psychiatrist once a day," the nurse said after a respectful pause. "We'll call you about any meds."

"That gives us time to track down long-term treatment. Do you have suggestions?"

The receiving nurse handed Nina a list.

"We get this all the time, dear. Some come back repeatedly, okay? You have to hope your brother will come through this."

Leaning against the wall, feeling as tired as a marathoner, Nina tried to remember. Had she slept the previous night? She recalled an exhausting storm of weeping. Yes, eventually she must have slept. She remembered nightmares.

To get to Pebble Beach, California's premier golf resort, Paul had to follow the tourists down Seventeen Mile Drive, a winding toll road that connected Pacific Grove and Carmel. That meant he drove carefully, slowing as each breathtaking pullout snagged yet another smitten, swerving driver.

He parked in a lot near Spanish Cove and locked the car, as if here, in such exclusive company, with the cameras and the extensive security, a thief lurked.

Walking toward the course, he thought about Nina's younger brother. Impulsive kid, an addict, it appeared. Unstable. Hated Wu and Filsen.

In other words, a worthy suspect in Filsen's death. But what would that mean for Nina?

Harlan Reilly dragged his golf bag behind him, his arm heavy on the shoulders of a young blond woman with bright eyes and a wide smile. Nina had mentioned that Harlan's new wife was pregnant, but Paul wouldn't have known at first glance.

Paul introduced himself. Harlan introduced Angie.

"Mind if we go just a little longer?" Harlan asked, sorting through his irons. "Then we can go inside and sit down and talk."

"Sure." Nina's father didn't exactly appear prostrated. Of course he was divorced from Nina's mother. Still, Paul wondered about such a man, resorting to golf in the face of a family tragedy.

A tall, buff, handsome man in his late fifties, the kind who stays salt-and-peppery for a long time, Harlan had held on to his hair. His prominent chin and the mouth now set so firmly reminded Paul of Nina.

He stood at the tee, drawing the line between the distant flag and the tee with his eyes, back and forth, back and forth, readying himself. He pulled the club back, keeping his eye on the ball, and gave it a hell of a whack. The ball flew up, then bounced close to the distant green.

Harlan smiled.

"Good correction going into this breeze," Paul said.

"You a golfer?"

"Now and then. This is one of the best courses on earth. It's always a high, playing here."

Harlan and Angie both nodded. Angie waved an arm around, gesturing toward a sparkling ocean as deep as her blue eyes. The wind made her hair dance. She looked very young to be with Harlan, but from the way she rubbed his back as she passed him, Paul thought she didn't mind. The wind revealed her stomach bump. She was just a few months pregnant, Paul judged. "He comes for the golfing. I come for the rest of it."

"You're here, sweetie, because you're a competitive little monkey. I'm betting you'll be able to better my handicap in six months."

She touched a finger to her new husband's face, right where his lip curved. Paul could see the warmth from her passing into Harlan. Boy, these two had it so bad it looked good even to Paul.

"So—how to handle oceanside conditions?" Harlan said a moment later. "I do a low running shot to play the firm turf. That keeps the ball under the breezes."

Angie took a club from the bag. Pushing hair out of her eyes, she swung. Her ball rolled weakly off toward the woods. "You see how I fake it?"

"She hasn't got a rhythm yet, is all."

His new wife after several strokes finally hit her ball onto the green. They walked toward his ball. One more stroke and he made the green of the par-3 hole. She nudged her ball into the hole after several more strokes. Harlan tapped his in smoothly. "Better this time, Angel," he encouraged.

"Meet you at the clubhouse in a few minutes."

"You don't want to finish, Angie?"

"What, twenty over par? No, I do not. I'll cling to what's left of my dignity." Angie passed close to Paul, saying in a soft voice, "He needs this distraction. He's upset." Then she took off at a trot, her pregnancy no impediment.

"Soda, remember, Angie," Harlan shouted after her, his voice thin, breaking.

Paul and Harlan walked back toward the clubhouse together, squishing in the damp grass.

"I hate those goddamn carts," Harlan said. "They take all the sport out of it." Paul and Harlan walked lightly, the wind at their backs.

"Your ex-wife's burial is tomorrow," Paul said. "Closed casket."

"You're a subtle bastard, aren't you?"

Paul said nothing.

"I'll be there. Of course I will. I owe her that."

Ignoring the financial implications of that statement, Paul asked, "Where were you on Thursday morning, early, Mr. Reilly?"

"Driving back from Vegas. With Angie. Spent Wednesday night there. Got home Thursday about three."

"She'll verify that timeline?"

"Sure she will."

"What was the fight about?" Paul asked.

"Fight?" Harlan stared at him.

"When you beat up your wife four years ago?"

CHAPTER
35

"**D**AMN." HARLAN STOPPED. "WHY BRING THAT up? Trying to knock me off-balance?"

"You put her into the hospital," Paul said. "Broken jaw, wasn't it?"

"Look. That happened just before we separated. The end of a long road. Emotions running high. She—she—it doesn't matter anymore. It wasn't like it sounds. She ran into me."

"How'd you get the charges dropped?"

Harlan looked toward the clubhouse. "Ginny didn't press charges. I went to counseling. Got the judge to accept probation. I have been apologizing to Ginny and my kids for that ever since. Believe me, Detective, you're on the wrong track. I realize that because I'm the ex-husband you have to consider me. But I had nothing to do with her death."

"I'll be looking up the police report and talking to you again," Paul said mildly. "Matt was there, right?"

"Yeah," Harlan answered, looking thoughtful. "You got kids?" When Paul shook his head, Harlan went on, "It's the worst pain. They're little. Sweet. Hold your hand. They draw pictures of you with a giant head and stick legs all day long. They love you very much. Then one day you look at this hulking animal. An innocent in a grown-up body, but not so sweet anymore, you know what I'm saying?"

Paul waited.

"Matt has problems. He's not reliable."

"Drug addicts tend not to be."

Harlan frowned. "I went to see him today, around noon. Somehow, Nina got him to go to Community Hospital. He's detoxing, but sick. Not all there. He didn't say much. The expense is going to be a bear. How the hell did he get himself so fucked up anyway!"

Paul felt his judgment forming. Harlan Reilly seemed to be a shallow soul who was rapidly moving on from the first family he had created. A burden to him now, they represented his failures.

He felt a rise of anger. Nina wasn't a failure. She'd had her problems, but she was trying to train herself for a career and be a good mother, and he thought she was succeeding.

"My son in the hospital. Who's ever prepared for that?" Harlan patted his pockets, searching for something. Cigarettes? Gum? A heart?

"Here's what worries me." Harlan's mouth twisted

nervously. "People will assume I'm involved. It's always the husband or, um—ex, right?"

Interesting immediate reaction. "Was it you?"

"No." Harlan leaned against a tree.

"You knew Richard Filsen?"

Harlan sighed, shaking his head. "I hate this by-gone garbage. I knew of him, but never met him. Nina saw him for a while years ago."

"How does that explain why you hired the private investigator four years ago?" Paul should thank Armano for digging that from Mrs. Reilly's old paid-bills files. Armano was proving himself to be a real obsessive for detail work, a good thing, because Paul hated it.

"Oh, shit, you found out about that." Reilly dug holes in the green with his cleats. "The investigator came right after Nina had Bob."

Paul didn't say anything, just stood comfortably, arms folded, alert, letting the sea breeze ruffle his hair. Reilly was about to say something that was costing him some pain.

"Once I got the report, I hit the roof. I disliked the man. I disapproved. I couldn't believe Nina could fall for someone so—fake. Well, Ginny was there, quiet, taking it all in."

"How did she react?"

"She seemed okay. But apparently, one of her criticisms of me was true: I'm an insensitive clod. A few days later, she revealed that she had gone to Richard Filsen's office and made him an offer."

"What kind of offer?"

"She paid him to leave Nina alone. Nina didn't want

to have anything to do with him at that point. The payment—she never asked me. She shouldn't have done that. I was appalled. I wouldn't have paid that creep anything. I'd have just knocked his block off. We argued about it pretty intensely. Well, you were just asking about it. She ended up in the ER. We separated soon after."

"What were your objections?"

"Listen, guys like him never go away. He had boatloads of gambling debt, people after him. He'd got in too deep with Nina. He didn't want a son. Money—that's another story. That he wanted. Ginny and I weren't getting along by then. She didn't trust my advice."

"She went in by herself?"

Reilly nodded. "After that, Filsen told Ginny she had a deal, that he'd stay out of Nina's life."

"Did he?"

"Yes, until recently."

"How much did Ginny pay him?"

"Thirty thousand dollars."

"Where did she get that kind of money?"

"She had some money of her own that her sister, Helen, left her. She used that. All of it. That was why she was so goddamn poor when we separated. She spent it on that fool."

"Have you had any direct dealings with Richard Filsen?"

Harlan squinted. He turned back to face Paul. "Once. Last week. Tuesday before Thanksgiving, Ginny called me, all worked up. Matt let it slip that Filsen had been harassing Nina, threatening her and Bob. Ginny said she was going over there again. She would confront him." He sighed. "Well, guess what? I'm not a monster. I mean, this wasn't her kind of confrontation, but it sure was mine. So she made me promise, and I went to see him, over at his plush office in Seaside."

"When was this?"

"Tuesday afternoon, a little after lunch."

"What happened?"

"I told him to cease and desist or I'd cut his balls off." Harlan laughed mirthlessly. "Makes me look good now, huh? Just a father trying to protect his little girl. Whoever did it used a gun, right? Not a machete?"

"What did he say?"

"That piece of crap. He said I wouldn't want Nina to know about Ginny's little transaction of a few years ago. That might harm their relationship, right?"

"Would it have?"

"Do you know my daughter?"

"As a matter of fact, we are friends."

"Boyfriend?"

"Friends."

"Well, when you get to know her better, you'll realize she likes to control her own fate. She doesn't like anyone butting into her business. She doesn't even take advice well. That makes her wonderful in my book, but really tough to help."

"I can see how that would be so."

"So telling her about Ginny's and my invasion of her privacy would have incensed her and caused a rift. For Ginny, at this time, with all her health issues and family issues, it might have been fatal."

"What did he say when you got there?"

"He asked how much more we'd be willing to fork over to keep him quiet. He kind of laughed. I don't know how serious he was. I told him we'd see him in court, that taking a bribe to stay away from his own baby wasn't going to sit well with the judge."

"And he said . . . ?"

"'Bring the whole family along, pal.' Then he recommended lawyers Nina ought to use at the custody hearing. Chuckled. What an asshole."

"Then what?"

"Nothing. I left. I didn't go back to kill him, either."

"Did you tell Ginny what happened?"

"She insisted on every detail."

"Hmm. Let's talk more about that. Were either of you prepared to have this all come out at a custody hearing?"

"Hell, no! Nina can't know. She blames me for the divorce. She damn near hates me now. If she realizes how her mother and I interfered with her and Filsen— she'd never talk to me again. And she would see Ginny's role as a complete betrayal. Buying off the boyfriend. And it didn't work anyway. It would have been horrible for both of them."

"Nina's going to hear about this, you know. You can't hide it anymore. This man was murdered. Everything will come out."

"Maybe you can figure out how to put a good spin on this when you tell her all about it. You're gonna tell her, aren't you?"

"Why don't you tell her?"

"Huh?"

"Why not act like a father and go to her house, see how she's doing? Bring her some supper. Sit down and tell her what you and Ginny did?"

Harlan shook his head.

"Why not?"

"I just can't stand the thought."

"She just lost her mother. She needs you."

Harlan expelled a sigh. "I'm an expert at not helping her the right way."

"Well, in any case we need you to come into the station to make a statement."

Harlan got an appointment card with the supervisor's name and number. "I'm not hiding anything," he said, taking the card. "But I offer you this—don't even think about my son. He's sick, not violent."

They climbed the last hill to the clubhouse, spotting Angie on a deck overlooking the course sipping her Pepsi.

Seeing his wife, Harlan upped his pace like a kid spotting a video arcade. Just before they went into the restaurant, he said quickly, "I called Ginny a few days before she died. We talked about reducing the spousal support payments," he added, heading for the door, back straight, not looking at Paul.

Paul thought Harlan looked good for both murders, at least on the outside. However, his forthrightness about what had happened with Richard Filsen rang true.

Now, Ginny's involvement with Filsen—that definitely might lead in another direction. Paul made a note to check Harlan's alibis but had a feeling they might just hang together. "You talked about giving Ginny less money, okay. So how'd she take that?"

"Hung up on me. She knew she would lose in court. All I had to do was talk to the judge about supporting my new family. You really think he'd make me continue to support her forever?"

"She stayed home to raise your kids for decades, didn't she?"

"Oh, man." Harlan shook his head. "I wish I could show you how much I loved her when we met, and while we were having those two crazy kids. How pretty she was. How she made me laugh. But our relationship eroded. Things didn't work. She didn't like the way I handled the kids. She hated my messes, hated my successes because they took time away from her.

"Sometimes—I'm confessing here—I almost believed she made herself sick in retaliation for my leaving her."

Justification for bad behavior: Paul felt familiar with the concept.

Harlan waved. "Angie's waiting." They arrived at the bar. Angie had moved inside and sat at a table where the wide windows overlooked the steady beating of white surf. Even here in the warm bar with the windows closed they could hear the distant roar, evidence of a storm far out at sea.

"Life goes on or you die," Harlan said, dismissing his first love with those brutal words, moving toward his young wife. He touched her with lips to cheek. She shone in response.

Paul watched them curiously. He hadn't seen a happy couple for a while. Angie turned her head as his lips touched her cheek, and he met her lips with his. They hugged.

She was going to have a baby. They didn't give a shit about anything or anybody else.

He changed his earlier assessment. Harlan was not shallow but was happier than he deserved. The thought hit Paul like a mallet on a gong: as of today, he was no longer hitched. Laura was no longer his wife.

He looked at his hand, the slight crease at the bottom of his finger where he had worn the band. How long would it take the sun to restore this protected skin to its glorious tan?

On the trip back down the darkening Holman Highway, blinded by headlights, he drew a mental picture of Nina in this family. She played sane, he figured. The rest played eccentric.

The separation certainly cast Nina and Matt's father neatly as the villain in this piece. It went deeper. Paul had a feeling that the separation of the parents in this family had somehow led to all of it, all this pain and heartache. And if it hadn't directly led to these murders, it had poisoned the air somehow, poisoned things for Ginny, and then all of them.

Miffed at the feeling that he had missed something in the interview, Paul went over his mental notes, finding nothing new.

When he got back to the station, depressed, thinking about divorce in general, he called Jack. Good ol' Jack. They'd go out and get drunk and talk about the old days.

He got a recording. He didn't leave a message.

CHAPTER
36

EL ENCINAL CEMETERY IN MONTEREY ON A STORMY day conjured up one word, Nina thought, *bleak*. She had no trouble locating her mother's grave site. The mahogany casket sat above a deep hole in the ground, covered with flowers, surrounded by damp green grass, accompanied by a howling wind. A hearse had parked nearby on the narrow road, discreet and ominous.

She held Bob's hand tightly. Bewildered, he kept asking if Grandma was in the box. She shouldn't have brought him, perhaps. But she had decided earlier that day that Bob should be a witness to this, discover the passing away that occurs as part of the great cycle, have a vague childhood memory of the good-bye when he grew up.

Ginny Reilly had insisted on no formal service in her will. Here stood her friends and family, without the benefit of any spiritual tradition, no minister, rabbi, or priest. Shouldn't someone say something?

Nina couldn't. Her heart had turned to lead. She couldn't trust herself not to shout something angry into the wind. This was no soft death, the one she would have wished for her mother.

Harlan Reilly shivered, his arm around his wife.

Two gravediggers in dirty overalls stood with their shovels at a respectful distance, huddling against the cold. Friends and family, including Jack, Klaus, Remy, her mom's card group, and a few older women friends, stood with long faces beside the casket, black umbrellas above their heads, swathed in black coats, holding flowers for Ginny. Harlan, almost hiding behind Angie, held an ostentatious bouquet of gardenias.

Did he remember Ginny's wedding bouquet had been gardenias?

Vague recollection might have inspired him, but he didn't take the time to think why, Nina decided. She remembered her father kissing her mother under the mistletoe at one of his office Christmas parties way back when.

She should cry, but anger was what she felt as she looked around at the mourners. None of them should be here. They had all been injured. They had all gone over some sort of cliff.

She missed Matt. In lockup, detoxing, he could not make it to his own beloved mother's burial.

Buffeted by the wind, some umbrellas turning inside out, the mourners strewed flowers over Ginny's casket, piling them on when it was already covered. Nina approached the grave. She had bought pink carnations, her mom's favorite but not hers, unhappy that the hothouse flowers didn't hold a scent, unhappy even more that her brother was not beside her where he belonged.

Water leaked over the edge of her shoes, cold and alienating as dead lizards. She paused, looking down at the raindrop-tipped grass, feeling leaky herself, unable to face these other nice people who had cared enough about Ginny to show up on such a miserable day.

Jack took her arm. He walked her the rest of the way.

She laid the carnations over her mother's brass-detailed casket. She looked toward the gravediggers, shovels at the ready. "I'm going to stay here while they bury her. At least at first." Jack wore a pained expression. "Go on. I'm going to talk to her while this is happening. Could you take Bob and meet me at my house?"

"Sure, but—she's not here, Nina."

"Oh, yes, she is," Nina said fiercely. She stood silently, accepting a few more hugs, patting people, letting them fade away as time passed, until only she and the cemetery workers remained. Somewhere a funeral lunch would be happening, with a lot of food. She just couldn't go. Her mother's friends had told her it would be a celebration of Ginny's life.

Celebration of life? What illusions people could invent for themselves. This was death, deep and profound and inexplicable, as powerful as life. Better to stand forlorn and let it whirl around her now, than to fight or suppress it.

They waited for her sign, then used a winch to lower the casket into the waiting hole in the ground as the drizzle polished its fittings for the last time. She wanted to lie down on the wet grass next to the hole as the dirt began to fall on her mother, lie down close by to be with her. She took down the umbrella and let the rain touch her.

Still no tears. She let the sky cry for her.

The next Monday morning, as a dank winter fog swirled outside the picture window of the courthouse hallway, Jack met Remy for coffee.

Jack had just finished a sentencing hearing on the client who had molested a fourteen-year-old. He had told the judge that the young man was a case of arrested development, an alcoholic who had only one thing going for him: he could hold down a job as a cook if the judge released him from custody to live with his father. The judge knew and Jack knew that the Monterey County jails were overflowing anyway, and the California Supreme Court was about to issue another order that the jail population be reduced.

Lucky for Jack, it was the client's first offense of any kind. Released on probation, he showed no emotion and did not thank Jack. He would later, when it hit him that he was free.

Remy came in at the tail end of the proceedings to invite Jack for coffee. They took the elevator down to the depths of the building where a tiny lunchroom smelling of doughnuts and soggy tuna-fish sandwiches had been created out of an old storeroom. Undersized tables crowded against each other. A boy and a girl held hands, their baby snoozing in a bassinet against the wall.

They sat in back and talked in low voices. "So sad about Nina's mother," said Jack.

"She was a complicated person," Remy said. "I saw her a week or so ago, and even though she was failing, she had strong survival instincts. She must have been very lovely once," Remy said dreamily. "I wonder . . ."

"Don't tell me you question whether Dr. Wu put those needles in her?"

"No, no. I wonder how things would have gone if she hadn't needed the amputation."

"My gut says there's a connection between the two killings," Jack said, squeaking his Styrofoam cup against the tabletop.

"Besides Nina?" Remy asked. "Her lover and her mother died. She had cause to kill her lover, that's for sure."

"Wrong track, Remy. Don't be ridiculous."

"Oh?" Remy frowned.

"Sorry. You're not ridiculous."

"Maybe we should look closer at her brother, Matt, who's on drugs, who hated seeing his mother suffering, who must have hated the man threatening his sister and his mother?"

Jack said, "Put it like that and I get worried the kid could have done it."

"He wasn't at the funeral."

"He's busy detoxing."

"I'm glad to hear that, if he didn't do it." Remy leaned close to Jack, close enough so that he could smell her perfume. "I heard from the governor's office," she almost whispered.

"Christ! You didn't tell me right away?"

Remy drew back, and Jack knew immediately he had made another major error. He hid his feelings, trying to feel good about the news for her sake. "You got it!" He stuffed congratulations into the comment.

Remy's smile, tremulous and triumphant at the same time, told all. Jack got up and came around the table to hug her. She bent like a willow in his arms. When he let go, she had tears in her eyes.

"It's all I ever wished for."

"When do you go up?"

"Pretty quickly. I'm leaving the firm on December fourteenth; I'll be inducted at the first of the year. I already asked Judge Sturdy to swear me in."

"You deserve this." Jack gave her a broad, only slightly phony smile.

"I'll have to load work on you, Jack. Klaus can't take it, and Lou only knows his way around tax court."

"We'll work things out."

"At least you won't get stuck with the Reilly case."

Jack went over to the counter to refill their cups. In the corner, talking so quietly to each other, they were as isolated as if they were in a high-walled booth. Remy's pale skin seemed to glow above the soft blue suit and the pearls. She wore $200 pumps. Jack had heard her once instructing Nina about the importance of wearing the most expensive formal high heels she could find. Something about being at eye level with the guys. Nina drank it in, but still wore her worn black boots under her jeans, Jack had noticed.

"I feel closer to you than I have in a while."

She touched his hand.

"You seeing anyone else?" It just slipped out. He hadn't known he'd say it. He cursed himself, then relaxed, because he needed to know.

She didn't answer, just squeezed tighter.

"Rick Halpern?"

"You assume I slept with him to drum up support? He has four children and goes to confession every month at his church. Give me a break!"

"You're not around for me anymore. I call you, I get your answering machine. You don't have time for me at work. I guess I want to know—how do things change now that the judge campaign is over?"

"You didn't waste a minute reviving the old complaints, did you?" She pulled her hand away. "It just doesn't compute with you, does it? This is about me, not you." She seemed to soften a little as she looked at him. "We never made any commitments to each other, Jack."

"You slept with Halpern." Jack paused, succumbing to the wave of despair, drowning. She had slept with a married Catholic with four kids. "Don't bother lying." He knew she didn't love Halpern, either—she had done it out of ambition. He should get up and leave. If only mad love worked that way. Even so, he looked straight at Remy's hard core, and the live, warm current between them began to cool at that instant.

"If so—hey, if I stay away from other men, will you stay away from Nina?"

"What?" He felt stripped. "We're friends, for chrissake! She just lost her mother and needed a warm shoulder. I work with her. Jesus."

"You were next to her at the funeral."

"I represented the firm, like you. She's a friend."

"She has a crush on you. She stops into your office constantly. Lately you stop into hers. You're letting your emotions get the best of you, as usual. Or your physical urges?" Remy asked. "Are you falling in love with her?"

He considered the statement. "Not at all, honey," he said quietly. "It is you I love."

"You don't act like it."

"It's you I want," Jack said, feeling something frightening approaching. He wanted to stave it off but his mind blanked. "You're hurting me, though."

"Oh, right, you're just a victim. You know, Jack, this is just too complicated." Remy rose to her feet, swinging her purse over her shoulder in one smooth movement. Straightening her shoulders, she walked away, graceful and self-possessed as a dancer onstage, threading her way through the other tables to the hallway exit.

Jack stared after her for a long time. The tumult in his head paralyzed his body. He hated himself for not living up to her, for not being able to handle her, for being so goddamned confused about what was going on. Sitting in that grim, little basement room, breaking the Styrofoam cups into a thousand white bits, he suddenly pictured Nina beside her mother's grave, fragile, unfathomable. Damn pretty, but—

But Remy—unique. Pale. White and pink in bed. Shimmering. He had time to fix everything with her. All she needed was a little convincing.

CHAPTER
37

"HERE WE GO, RIGHT INTO A LOW-RENT English TV sci-fi show, *Dr. Wu*," Armano said as Paul and he climbed the steps to the acupuncturist's home, which turned out to be a Spanish-style mansion, spanking new, with a red-tiled roof, bowed extrusions, and pristine landscaping, located up a private road on a hillside in Carmel. "A show made with two sets max and special effects like on the old *Star Trek* shows."

Today, Monday, made a week since Virginia Reilly had died, and eleven days since Richard Filsen's murder. They had little to go on besides the motives and suspects, which were ubiquitous. Forensics in both cases had yielded almost nothing—the killer or killers had either been professional or entirely lucky.

Albert Wu greeted them at the door, escorting them into an atrium drooping with tropical foliage. No visible heating system explained why it was at least fifteen degrees warmer there than outdoors. The two detectives sat gingerly on wicker chairs.

"Here we are again," Wu said.

"And here you are again, popping up in a second murder investigation," Paul answered.

Wu crossed his legs, hooking his fingers around his knee, looking as prosperous and well kept as his surroundings.

He wore a suede jacket over suit pants, the knot of a blue tie peeking out. He shook his head and said the whole thing was shocking.

Paul took him back to the Virginia Reilly malpractice claim, as Wu picked a few yellowing leaves off the old dwarf lemon tree beside him. "As I told you before, she had no proof of any wrongdoing on my part. I did nothing incorrect. From the very beginning, this whole matter was merely a nuisance. Mr. Filsen was adamant that we not offer any settlement, however, not even a nuisance settlement. I would have gone all the way to a trial if necessary. It has been quite distressing." Wu crumbled his cache of leaves into a brass urn.

"Aw," Armano said. "But now there will be no trial. There is no more nuisance."

"Once again, these insinuations," Wu said without rancor, apparently having risen above them into serenity and peace again, not a problem in the world.

"So was she just trying to make a buck, do you think?" Paul asked.

"Perhaps. But sick people often have serious underlying psychological problems. They think, 'Why did this injury, this illness, happen to me?' They build a theory to explain logically what can never be explained. They look for someone to blame. We have already talked about this, when I came to see you regarding Mr. Filsen."

Wu continued in his reassuring voice, "I understand, since I haven't read of any arrests in this case, that you must consider if I might be the perpetrator, as I had some involvement with both Mrs. Reilly and Mr. Filsen. I consulted my appointment book before you came, and while I was alone in the early morning of the day Mr. Filsen was killed, I was seeing patients at the time Mrs. Reilly was—passed away. Here." Wu handed Armano several copies from some sort of log.

"We'll take the originals, please," Armano said, waving away the copies. The acupuncturist went out and returned with a black leather planner. He went to the middle and, consulting his copies, tore out a few pages and handed these to Armano.

"We'd like to see the whole book," Paul said. "Put things in context."

"Sorry. Patient confidentiality. Those are the only references to Mrs. Reilly and to my activities at the time of her death. I have added the phone numbers of the two patients I was helping at that time. I have spoken to each of them and they are willing to talk to you."

"And we should just take your word that there are no other references to Mrs. Reilly?"

"Or serve a subpoena *duces tecum*."

"Well, listen to you. You sure have that lawyer lingo down. We might do just that," Armano said.

"I will be here." Wu gave Armano a benign look. Armano glowered back. Wu lowered his eyes to his watch, the face of which twinkled with tiny diamonds. He sighed. "I am cooperating. I am sorry about all this. I am sorry these two people couldn't prepare for their deaths properly, prepare their families, consider what comes next. The last moments of life are most precious of all. That is when we truly begin to understand our situation."

Paul ignored this. "Have you given us all records of your conversations with Mr. Filsen in these papers?"

"I did not keep notes of such conversations."

"How about appointments with him?"

"I did not record my appointments with him. I only met with him twice. The last occasion was unfortunately the day before he died. He came to my office during lunch and told me that he was informally working with the lady attorney on the other side to conclude the matter without any financial outlay on my part other than his attorneys' fees."

"How long did the conversation last?" Paul continued.

Wu got up. "About as long as this one. Look, I have proved I could not have harmed Mrs. Reilly. My receptionist will confirm that for you. I had no dealings with Mrs. Reilly directly. And now, sorry, I must return to my office. My patients await."

"Not for long," Paul grunted.

The acupuncturist stared at the two detectives. Then he sat back down.

Armano said, "Nice certificates on the wall in your

office. We checked 'em out. You're not a certified acupuncturist or a certified anything. My information is
that you will be shut down tomorrow," he continued,
oblivious to Paul. "DA's office always has a little lag
time. Fair warning. Oh, and, Doc?"

Wu turned reptilian eyes on Armano.

"We'll be back with that subpoena tomorrow."

Nina took off her sweater and turned the key in the ignition, alternately cursing and praying as she tried to
get the MG going. She cranked the motor three or four
times until the weak chugging convinced her the car
would not rally. Bob, sitting in back in the car seat,
threw toys to amuse himself while she cursed silently.
Just about when she gave up, he hit her on the side of
the head with his tiny, green metal Porsche.

"Ow!"

"Sorry, Mommy."

"Are you mad? Did you hit me on purpose?"

"Your head was there." Bob blinked innocent eyes
her way into the rearview mirror.

Getting out of the car, she called a law school study-
group friend, who came to pick Bob up. "In Vermont,
we'd heat the spark plugs in the oven, and everything
worked just fine."

"They didn't explode?"

"Nah. But that won't work here."

Nina called a garage and waited for a truck for
forty-five minutes. While she waited, she found herself
remembering how her mom made pancakes on Sunday,
oatmeal on Monday, and how she, Nina, liked the oat-

meal with brown sugar and Matt loved the pancakes smothered in maple syrup. After the jump start, it was all she could manage just to park and go up the stairs to the Pohlmann firm offices.

Klaus saw her first. He bustled around making sure she got fresh coffee. "Do you need time off? You have it."

"No. I have school and I have this job. I need both." And I need to know who killed my mother, she added silently.

"Good, because we need you here." Klaus clasped her hand warmly, departing only after she took her first sip. She sat down at her desk and began to sort through the mail.

Remy had been at the office for hours already. She had a weeklong trial starting this morning. Nina reread deposition transcripts, hurrying to get through all of them before Remy had to go, making notes to prepare her. Several cups of coffee made her stomach cramp.

She brought her notes in to Remy.

"You okay?" Remy asked, eyes glued to a doctor's deposition. She was in full trial regalia, black wool suit and white blouse, pearls and four-inch black pumps with some sort of intricate texturing. Nina looked at the shoes with envy. Remy got up and gave Nina a brief hug. "Are you sure you ought to be here? And I say that even though we need you badly."

"I'd rather be here than sitting on the couch at home. We've got ten depos in this case, right?"

"If you don't count Harrison. The architect."

"Oh, yeah. Useless number eleven."

Remy dug around on her desk and found one thick

file. She loaded files into her rolling briefcase. "I hate carrying all this garbage," she mumbled, almost to herself, and started to dig around in a credenza behind her desk. "Where is it!"

"Let me help you. What are you missing?"

"My notes on Judge Rios," Remy replied, turning smoothly in her chair, attacking a file-cabinet drawer.

"He's the judge?"

"You know him?"

"I only know that Jack says he's a pussycat. He gets along fine with him."

"Jack," said Remy, "gets along fine with everybody, doesn't he?"

"Well, I—anyway, I'll help you find—"

"Never mind. I'll call Jack. He has a copy." Remy picked up her phone and began to punch in the numbers. She waved Nina out. Nina left the office, thinking that while Remy was finally beginning to show the occasional sign of wear, she would never change. Unless she was looking right at you, you didn't exist, and yet she was the best advocate you could get to fight your legal battles. But then Remy had another attribute of a good lawyer: she was careful only to pursue cases that were strong in the first place.

Nina stood at a machine running copies, wishing she had talked some more to Remy about her mother's lawsuit while she had Remy's attention. Not that Remy would have had much to say in the minutes before a trial, and not that Remy would ever admit that she had decided based on things other than the merits of the case.

Maybe there would be a closing memo in her mother's case file that would explain things, and she wouldn't have to bother Remy. Seemed like a good place to start her own private investigation.

Remy was sitting in a chair by the front door in the outer office, flipping through files in her briefcase, checking for something else at the last minute. Lou and Griffin, the temp, stood beside her. Nina knew from the looks on their faces they would not welcome an interruption, so she asked Astrid, who was at the front desk, where to find her mother's file.

"Everything's in order," Astrid huffed with unusual vehemence. Remy must have been on her case about something. Everybody's case, it looked like.

Nina poked through Astrid's file cabinet. Finding nothing, she went back to her office, but veered into Remy's office and took a look around the credenza full of current cases behind Remy's desk, looking for her mother's name. Again, she found nothing. What chaos. How did Remy find anything? she wondered, sliding doors over the mess. Out of time, she went back to the distraction of work.

CHAPTER
38

Jack invited Nina to lunch. She called Bob's preschool and told them to go ahead and let him nap there after eating. She had class tonight, a law school teacher who counted off failure to dot *i*'s on the blue books among other things. "We're not *doctors* here, you know," she would say. "Somebody somewhere is going to have to read what you write. Be precise, people." With laptops starting to appear in the classroom, that teacher would soon have to find something new to criticize.

Nina had problems in the class that went way beyond neat handwriting. For the first two months her eyes glazed and she began to think about all the places she hadn't yet visited in the world every time she picked up her Advanced Civil Procedure text. Plodding through the pages of each chapter with grim determination, she operated at half speed and about one-quarter comprehension. But nuts-and-bolts subjects such as this made for good law practice. She had to learn this stuff. She had joined a new study group recently, and some of the other students were excited enough to pique her interest in the subject, so it looked as if she was going to be able to stave off the escapism until next term, when she would have a new subject: Corporations. Bylaws, articles of incorporation, directorships, stockholders' suits, mergers and acquisitions, ratification—had she really told Paul she might become a corporate lawyer?

Jack met her at the Hog's Breath Inn. Close by, not always quick on service, it was always lively. She and Jack ordered sandwiches. Nina bit into hers with approving noises. Jack tried his and smiled. "It's nice to eat with a woman who enjoys her food. How are you?"

"Can't remember when I last ate. I'm starving. Thanks for getting me over here. I probably would have skipped another meal, gotten crankier and crankier, gone to class tonight and told off Professor Meacham."

"With precision, I hope."

"You know her? She's so stiff, you could use her to prop up a wall."

"I dated her."

"Sorry," Nina said, wondering, did he ever prop up a wall with her? To her horror, she began to cry noisily.

"Me, too." He wiped her face with his handkerchief. "But not half as sorry as you seem to be."

She laughed through her tears, took a long gulp of iced tea, and told Jack about Matt. "Our dad's paying for rehab. It's expensive, and since Dad's embarking on a new family, I'm guessing he'll resent it."

"How does Matt get along with him?"

"I hope he and Dad can make peace someday." At Jack's look, she said, "Our mother's illness affected Matt. He leaned on her a lot, and when she got sick, he started going downhill, too. It's weird. I don't quite understand what has happened to my family."

Jack put money on the table and stood up. They walked out the front door together and stood on the sidewalk, jostled by strollers. "Come with me?"

Nina began to protest, but he had her arm and was pulling her briskly along. They walked downhill toward the beach. He sat her down on a rock and didn't say a word for several minutes.

"You did invite me to lunch," Nina said. "It has just struck me that this might not be all about me and my family."

"I just wanted to talk and I thought of you."

"Here I am."

"It seems unfair of me to lay my troubles on you—you've suffered a huge loss."

"Come on. You're good to me. Let me reciprocate for a change. Now, tell me what's up."

"I'm thinking of quitting law."

"No!"

"True." He held up a hand. "I don't know if I like practicing law anymore, it's been so long since I did anything that really meant something to me. There's something about the sheer amount of human misery that I deal with every day that makes me feel like I'm back in school playing football. Playing to win. I used to practice every day, dumb things like running in and out of tires."

He moved closer to her on the rock, but didn't touch her. "I was an awkward kid and not naturally graceful, but I loved the game so I got good through sheer hard work. The rest of the world is pretty lazy. You can excel if you work just a little harder. Anyway, I played for four years in high school. Then I quit.

"I quit because I didn't have fun anymore. I'd seen most of my teammates injured, legs broken, herniated disks, dislocated shoulders. I threw my shoulder out and continued to play loaded on painkillers. Coach didn't care." Jack sounded dreamy. "Coach just wanted to win." He turned toward her. "It's just like that here. Like I'm loaded on painkillers. It's natural to turn off your normal reaction to all the misery you see and experience, because then you work better.

"Our fearless leader, Klaus? Well, he's got Coach beat by a mile. He's a thousand times more subtle. He's got us out there twisting our ankles on tires, and we do it for him so he'll pat us on the back. Klaus backs winners, like Remy." He turned to face Nina. "I really want to help you and Matt, if I can, okay? Beyond that, I need a life, and I'm not sure it's possible in this profession. Maybe I'll just hang out around the ocean at Big Sur, hike, scratch my poison-oak rash, and forget this whole thing."

"You've lost heart," Nina said. "Did you just lose a case, by any chance?"

"Yes, but—"

"I saw you like this after the Vasconcellos appeal was dismissed."

"This isn't about a case." He turned abruptly and started walking up the hill.

She caught up with him, took his arm. "Things aren't going well with Remy?"

"I wouldn't throw away a career because of a bad love affair. That would be beyond stupid."

Nina bit her tongue. All she could think in the spasm of selfish joy that followed was, Jack's free. His drawn face showed the extent of his suffering, and she cautioned herself. He needed a kind listener, not a friend with an agenda.

"You've lost heart," Nina repeated. The words seemed to strike Jack this time. He let out a mirthless chuckle. "Okay. I've lost heart in every damn thing."

"Good time not to make career changes."

"Can I crash my car then?" They walked back up the hill, and Jack let it out, and Nina listened.

Nina spent another night lying on her back looking at the shadows her night-light cast on the walls. In the next room, Bob, wearing footie pajamas, snored the way kids do, softly. Her brain moved into a new gear, as if the initial shock of her mother's death had worn off and she could think again. She thought, how had this happened to her mother and why? Who could have done this to her mother? What could be more cruel than a life obliterated at the bottom of a cliff? Ginny had been so frail, so ill! Jesus, Mary, and Joseph! Nina sat up in bed. She pulled a pad of paper and a Sharpie into her lap and made notes. "Think like a lawyer!" Professor Meacham seemed to say loudly, interrupting the turmoil in her mind.

First of all, admit her mother, like Nina, had an obdurate streak. Work from there.

• • •

Years ago, they had plans to go to Hawaii for Christmas. Harlan had objected. He had too much work. Ginny peacefully acquiesced to his arguments, bought tickets, packed his bag, and put him on the plane with the family before he had a chance to say boo. As a teenager, Nina had run into that sweet deceit more than once. Her mother didn't argue. She won battles, sometimes in an underhanded way. Yet, she had lost this final war and she was dead. Who was her enemy?

Paul had let Nina read Dr. Wu's statement in the police reports. At lunch Jack had told her Wu was unlicensed, about to be shut down, and likely, prosecuted. Wu talked about the Buddha, and at the same time he hurt people who came to him, trusting and sick. He did it all for money.

Could the acupuncturist have done this over money? She didn't know enough yet. But she knew he had a motive.

She wanted it to be Wu because he was guilty of terrible things. He was a vicious man who preyed on weak people, a liar, a man who would go to great lengths to avoid damage to his reputation. Richard had been his lawyer. Her mother wanted to sue him. The case had to be the connection between the two deaths.

She doodled a cross and a Buddha figure. Made a connecting line and thought some more.

Then she thought of her father, Harlan. She recalled dramatic scenes between her parents, memorable, awful moments that were an indelible part of every childhood. Her father had loved her mother once. But he was like another man now, one he called "new" in the old sense of the word, not necessarily improved. And violence had been there. And money was a real issue there. He cared too much about money. She knew it was wrong to hold it against him; he was no hypocrite and this was something to admire in him. The thought that her father might be involved in some way shook her. Even though she would never forgive Harlan for hurting her mother, she couldn't help loving him.

And what about Richard? Was anyone sad for him? Bob no longer had a father. The results of the paternity tests had still not come in, and she couldn't help feeling relieved that Richard was dead, out of the picture. If he had lived, could he have taken Bob? His death—ah, might as well admit it—had been a relief.

No, she couldn't let herself think that about Bob's father.

She decided to call Richard's associate, Perry Tompkins, in the morning. Time to get the custody case dismissed.

She went to the kitchen with its awful overhead light. Two in the morning, when all insights became suspect. She popped a diet orange drink, turned off the light, and walked to her room.

Jack believed people were capable of anything. Could he possibly suspect she was involved? Was there any possibility for Eros in this Thanatos-ridden spinning globe that housed them all briefly?

Two a.m. thoughts for sure.

Paul thought she knew something. She had sensed

it immediately in the way he had maintained a clinical distance since the deaths.

Did she know something? Every once in a while she had the feeling if she could just close her eyes and for once see nothing, just darkness, an answer would leap at her. Let a thought come, don't force it. She thought about how Paul had talked, how he had regarded her, and the picture of him merged with the confusion in her mind, ending with an image of herself in the stormy waves off Asilomar Point, swimming furiously, heading straight out to sea, toward a blurry figure on the horizon, dry, serene, gloating.

CHAPTER
39

A T SEVEN THIRTY IN THE MORNING, THE SKY LIT A pale gray, Paul drank a second double espresso Nina had made for him. He stretched out his legs and sighed.

"You look tired," she said. He looked the way she felt.

"I want to ask you something about Matt. Matt told us that he came to meet you at Bob's nursery school one afternoon in September and witnessed an altercation between you and your ex."

"Richard?"

"He says he was ready to jump right in if the guy ever really hurt you, but that he decided then he would just bide his time."

"Matt was watching from the bushes?"

"That's what he told me."

Nina let out a short laugh. "He loved spying on me

when we were little. But, Paul, don't imagine he has anything to do with Richard's murder. He doesn't."

"We have to look into it. It's not impossible, though I hate saying this to you. Maybe he wanted to protect you and Bob from Filsen?"

"He has a good heart, but he's young and screwed up at the moment. He couldn't protect a fly."

"He also told us that your mother seemed not averse to the idea of a merciful death, one that she would decide on for herself. Did she ever imply that?"

"Well, yes, but—my mother did not kill herself. I will never believe that."

"Maybe . . . she asked for help? Maybe Matt wanted to help her in the only way he knew how."

"By pushing her off a cliff, forcing her to drop groceries and grab a knife? I know you have to examine all the possibilities, but surely not to the point of absurdity?"

"Maybe they planned it together."

"Maybe you are way off course. Don't even suggest that my little brother killed our mother or I'll lose all respect for you. She did everything for him, sacrificed her time and money, placed utter faith in him. He loved her. He would never, ever, harm her."

Paul directed his hazel eyes into Nina's brown ones. "Tell me more about you and Filsen. Did you and Matt ever discuss Filsen?"

"No."

"What about you and your mother?"

She pulled her sweater tightly around herself and frowned.

"Did you?"

"She wouldn't have said anything to Matt."

"When did you tell her?"

"I never confided much in my mother, especially lately, with her feeling so rotten all the time."

"Uh-huh."

"But after Richard cornered me at Bob's preschool and Perry served me with papers about custody and visitation, we had a birthday party for Matt at my mom's house. That's when I told her what happened. That Richard wanted a DNA test, joint custody, and visitation at the very least."

"What did your mother say?"

"She said forget he ever had anything to do with our lives and especially with Bob's. That Richard didn't have a hope of winning a custody battle. To concentrate on the future. That I was a good mother."

"Did she talk about the malpractice claim?"

"She hoped the malpractice case would bring in some money to help me and Matt. She didn't want to be a burden. But it wasn't all about money. Once she realized what Dr. Wu did to her, I think she saw this as a matter of principle."

"Were you a witness to the argument between your parents that landed your mother in the hospital some years ago?"

Nina looked down. "You know about that?" she said in a low voice. "No. I was at school. My father told me about it, about how he and my mother had a bad fight. Mom threw a pan at Dad, in self-defense probably. Dad hauled off and hit her and cracked her jaw. Then Matt came in and helped Mom. The police came and charged my mother with assault, can you believe it? Dad was charged, too. Everything was dropped eventually. Oh, no. This just can't be. Now you're accusing my *father* of killing my *mother*?"

Nina was still breathing hard. "My father would never kill my mother. My brother would never do such a thing either. I'm not sure I can stand to talk with you anymore right now, Paul."

"It's my—"

"I suppose in your professional capacity you have to consider whether I did it, killed Richard at least. And my only alibi is a four-year-old boy."

"Did you kill him, Nina?"

Nina's jaw dropped.

"Did you? You have a very strong motive. Tell me if you did and I will help you with all this. I mean it, Nina, tell me right now."

"No!"

"I didn't think so."

Nina collected herself. "Really? You really don't suspect me?"

"Guess I know a few things about you. You know how to be patient. You aren't the impulsive type."

Nina stretched her arms above her head, intertwined her fingers. Paul couldn't help admiring the result. "You're wrong. I'm just as impulsive as Matt. But I'm willing to accept that you have a hunch."

"I don't believe in hunches, just facts. Besides, I'm quite sure you would not hurt your mother, and I think these two deaths are connected."

She ran her fingers through her hair. "Anyway. What did you want to know?"

"Your assessment of your mother's claim against the acupuncturist."

"All right. I thought at first she had a strong case. Clear-cut right and wrong, that she would have all kinds of sympathy, too, perfect material for a jury trial if it came to that. And with Remy trying the case, well, I just think when Wu took the stand, he would have looked absolutely guilty as hell. He *was* guilty as hell. Of something." Nina twisted the fringed end of her sweater. "But Remy realized we had a problem with the facts. We had no proof that Mom had been treated with acupuncture, no receipts, nothing. The punctures—they would have been so tiny, and Mom had the—the infection. They had a witness who would call Mom a liar."

"You can't pursue this thing legally now?"

"No. We can't get damages for my mom's pain and suffering, and she was the main witness. For lots of legal reasons, a death of a party brings an end to a malpractice matter. I hope you're looking hard at Dr. Wu. I keep thinking he's the only person I can imagine who might hate my mother. Maybe he hated his lawyer, too, who knows? I'm doing a little digging myself."

"Stay out of this investigation, Nina."

"Paul, let me tell you something. You lack bedside manners. You could help people relax and be more—I don't know, chat a little first, loosen them up, then sound casual when you ask the honking questions."

"What makes you such an expert on police interrogation techniques?" He was smiling. He had a good smile, full-out, crinkly at the eyes. But he was hard to read.

And now Jack was free.

"I took a class last spring on Trial Psychology. How to approach witnesses at trial, for instance."

"You find me stiff? Ha-ha, no pun intended."

"Well, I know you a little, Paul. Your normal manner would work better."

"Thanks. I'll take that suggestion to heart."

"Seriously?"

"Meantime, where were you November twenty-sixth? Let's go over it again."

Nina hesitated. "Typical. Monday. I stayed home with Bob in the morning. I had a test that night and needed to study. I wasn't at work that afternoon. I went to the law library at the courthouse on Aguajito. The clerk wasn't around. I didn't see anybody I knew." She gave him the details and he marked them down, but she knew her movements couldn't be verified. She had no alibi for the day her mother had died.

"Think back to Thanksgiving Day, November twenty-second," Paul said, "that morning."

The morning Richard had been shot. "Slept until Bob woke me up, hungry, around seven a.m. I called Matt. Prepared a couple of vegetable dishes. Got ready to go. From five o'clock on, Bob and I spent the day at Mom's. We helped with dinner. Matt called me right before I left my house."

"Was Matt at your mother's when you arrived?"

"Not till—"

"Go on."

"He came not long after us. I'm not sure what time. Not long."

"It would help if you knew what time Matt arrived."

"I don't remember." Nina jumped up. "Sorry, I'm out of time. The day beginneth."

Nina changed out of her sweat suit and into clean cotton pants. She filled Bob's backpack with lunch, a blanket, and a bear. She pulled him away from the television and washed the cereal off his face. She put dishes into the dishwasher and considered starting a load of laundry, deciding it would have to wait one more day. After dropping Bob off at preschool, she drove to work.

Her desk, usually buried under piles, sat empty, accusing. She buzzed Jack, who did not answer, then stopped by Remy's office. Remy stood in front of a case full of books searching for something, mumbling something. Nina waited for her to finish.

"You talk to yourself, too?"

Remy turned and saw Nina. With a small smile, she closed a book. "I think out loud. The trial yesterday got continued to next March. Typical."

"Do you have work for me, Remy? I know you're trying to wrap up a lot of cases."

"I sure do. I'm going to dump most of my cases on Jack, but you can help by organizing some of these files. I'm desperate for breathing space. After I clean up here I take off for Hawaii for a couple of weeks, right after the Christmas party."

"I'm going to miss you. I've learned an awful lot from you."

Remy said, "Remember, four-inch heels are a girl's best friend. You'll be seeing me in court, Nina. I know you're going to make it."

Nina had a new realization. Not having Remy around anymore would spell major changes to the firm. With Klaus getting on, Jack threatening to quit, and Remy leaving, who exactly did that leave? Louis, Nina, and the secretaries. The office would have to be reconstituted. Life is flux, the old Greek philosopher had said. But how much flux could she stand?

"Hey, here's a mystery," Remy called out a moment later. Nina stuck her head back through the door. "I reviewed the Davidson Marital Settlement Agreement. Some of the attachments are missing." She handed the file to Nina. "See if you can track down the rest of the dissolution papers."

Nina located them buried on Jack's desk with a note from Remy asking him to take a look at them. When Nina finished her required hours for the day, she started typing a draft for schoolwork onto the computer. She ran out of time before finishing, so she saved the file and grabbed her purse. Jack came in before she left, leaving files with handwritten instructions neatly stacked on her desk. She saw him swing into Remy's office and heard his casual invitation to dinner. She couldn't hear Remy's reply. When she left, she heard a door slam in Remy's office.

Unfair of her, but she hoped it was Remy slamming it in Jack's face.

CHAPTER
40

WILLS AND ESTATES, THE OLD-TIMERS STILL called it, a deadly subject for law students, the lame joke about deadliness being only an introduction for the most settled, the most precedent-laden, most sedentary subject in law school. Nina knew that in the ancient past of fifty years ago, women law professors were caged in this back-office legal specialty, drafting wills and trusts, never seeing daylight from solstice to solstice. They coddled the elderly and soothed the distraught families when the loved one passed away, leaving the money to the wrong person or charity or to the cat.

The paperwork was detail-oriented, the payment preset, and the opportunity to make new law almost nonexistent.

Residual resentment still kept many women lawyers from going into this specialty. You might as well be a mummy, preserved in aspic or whatever the Egyptian priests had used.

Nina had no intention of enjoying this class, but Tom Cerruti, a lawyer in his forties who maintained an intriguing Italian stubble, had also been thinking about these things. He had announced during the first class in September that estate planning could be sexy—which had gotten him a big laugh from the fifty exhausted students taking his night class—and he had set out to prove it with the cases he chose for the class to study.

He practiced law and ran marathons. He flew down to Rio every February for Carnaval. He liked fly-fishing in Oregon and was a fervent surfer. Every woman in the class had looked at him at least once as a potential lover, but he never dated students. He was a wise man as well as an entertainer.

Tonight the class was discussing the case of the pretermitted heir—the biological child who wasn't mentioned in the will of a wealthy woman named Florence Connaught, who had passed away in Florida in 1980.

Nina, sitting toward the back, doodled into her notebook. Crosses. Ocean waves. Wiped-out surfers.

A sad attack. They came two or three times a day.

She was floating like flotsam in the flux, and her friend Lacey was sitting right beside her, worrying about her.

Maybe a leave of absence would have been better. She couldn't concentrate tonight, even with the professor's slide show and his jokes and Lacey's concerned looks and hand pats.

"Talk about a dysfunctional family," Cerruti said.

"Look at this guy. Meet Herb Connaught." A huge, goofy fellow in a wifebeater, at a barbecue, appeared on the screen. "Herb was born stupid, shallow, and in need of lots of chemicals. He put his parents through quite a few challenges: the DUI on his sixteenth birthday in the car his father had given him that day, the cocaine bust, the marriage to a woman twice his age.

"Herb never cottoned to the idea of working for a living. He knew his parents were well-off and he expected to be supported for the rest of his life. His father went along with that, and many were the excuses he dreamed up—Herb was dyslexic, he had attention deficit disorder, he couldn't handle stress—for many years Herb's father kept Herb's shrinks in fine brandy.

"Then easygoing Mr. Connaught passed on, and Herb and his mother took a look at each other. Florence pursed her lips—here's a photo of her—and said, 'Herbie, get a job, because I'll have a new husband in six months.'

"And lo and behold, she did marry a man, who soon after was diagnosed with a fast-developing case of muscular dystrophy. He became wheelchairbound within a year. The year after that, Mrs. Connaught caught a cold that turned into pneumonia and she also passed away."

Professor Cerruti snapped his fingers. "Like that, Herb, age thirty-three, was an orphan. He was making porn films out of a cheap apartment in Hollywood and owed a lot of money to several dangerous creditors. He had not had any contact with his scandalized mother for two years.

"At the funeral, Herb and his mother's husband had an altercation over the burial arrangements. There was some pushing and shoving—funerals are not always entirely sane events.

"A week later, Florence's most recent will was filed with the probate court by her second husband." A slide of the will went up. Wow! It was handwritten! Nina had never seen a handwritten will before. "She left everything to her husband. And lo and behold again, there was no mention of Herb in the will. Herb was prominent only by his absence."

The class laughed appreciatively.

"So Herb went to a probate lawyer. And what advice did he receive? Ms. Reilly?"

Bad luck! Lacey's concerned eyes said. But Nina had read the case.

"First, the lawyer confirmed that the will omitted Herb entirely," she said.

"A faithful reflection of his mother's mind, no doubt."

Laughter.

"But that wasn't the first thing he confirmed, was it, Ms. Reilly?"

"Well, he confirmed that the will was entirely handwritten."

Cerruti nodded and said, "Yes, it's a strange and archaic thing, but in California you can still write out a legal will entirely in your own handwriting, leave it unwitnessed, leave out all sorts of boilerplate, and it's valid. It's called a holographic will, and all you need to do is state your intention to dispose of your estate, say where you want it to go, date it, and sign it. No need for Dewey Cheatham and Howe in there, right?"

"Wrong," said Nina. The professor gave her a nod.

"Well, Ms. Reilly?"

"Since she had no legal advice, she didn't know about the doctrine of the pretermitted heir."

"Who would?" said Cerruti. "Originally, the idea was to take care of heirs who were accidentally omitted from the will, especially illegitimate children, but soon enough it applied to heirs the decedent might have wanted to omit and failed to mention. So put it in a nutshell for us, please, Ms. Reilly. What happened to Herb after his mother ignored him in her will?"

"He was awarded half his mother's estate at the succeeding trial. The probate court followed the well-established rule that, in the absence of a specific statement in the will that Florence wanted Herb to take nothing from her estate, Herb would receive what he would have received if Florence had made no will at all."

"But how could that be?" Cerruti said in mock horror. "She had told both her husband and Herb that she didn't want Herb to inherit anything."

"The language specifically omitting Herb had to be in the will, and nothing she said outside the writing of the will could be considered."

"But it was only a technicality! We knew what her intentions were!"

"I guess that's why people who love technicalities go into probate law," Nina said.

Cerruti smiled. "Yes, those pesky technicalities.

Listen up, class, because I'm now going to tell you the secret of practicing law successfully. It's this: Never, never forget the technicalities. When you take a new case, check the other side's compliance with the technicalities first. Always start there. A case you can't win may become an easy win because a crucial boring detail was overlooked.

"Now here's a slide from one of Herb's movies. He used up his inheritance making several porn classics." The class stiffened.

On the screen a grotesquely enlarged, jointed portion of the human body suddenly appeared. Impossible to tell which part. The students craned their necks to make it out.

After a minute, Cerruti said, "Actually, that's my elbow. Sorry, best I could do."

Nina's cell phone rang at the break. "I was wondering how you're doing," Jack said. "Made it to class?"

"Yes, but I think I'll leave early. I just feel—I don't know—"

"I'm still at the office."

"At nine o'clock? What have you got tomorrow?"

"A preliminary hearing that's gonna blow up if I don't put a lot of work in tonight."

"Can I stop by?"

"Stop by the office? Sure, you need to talk?"

"It's not that. I have a bad feeling, Jack. That Wu is going to get away with what he did to my mother."

Jack said in a soothing tone, "We don't know what happened yet, Nina."

"And we never will. I'm so angry all of a sudden, Jack. First I just felt sad. Now—" She felt herself choking up.

"Come on by. I should be up to par for the prelim by the time you get here."

The downstairs offices were dark, but Jack's light was on. Nina dragged herself up the front steps and he let her in. He had a concerned expression. "You don't look good," he said. They went into Jack's office and sat down across from each other in his client chairs. Jack didn't represent his best self either in sweatpants and a gray T-shirt, almost half of it wet.

"Sweat," he admitted, smiling, noticing her reaction. "Disgusting, isn't it? I lifted weights tonight at the gym, then came straight here feeling buff and strong and ready to beat all bastards with a tire iron. It's all about balance, right?"

"I wouldn't know. My balance is so far off right now I feel like I'm about to hit the sidewalk."

"That's natural."

"I don't get it, Jack. Why would Dr. Wu kill my mother, if her case against him was no good? He had to keep a low profile. All he's gotten out of these murders is bad publicity—he closed his office today, before the state regulators closed it down for him. What are the police missing? My prof tonight was talking about paying attention to the details. I'm gonna work on this myself, Jack. Nail him."

"How?"

"Start by going through the file. Look for some small detail that would explain all this. All my medical research is in there, notes from Remy's interview with my mother, Mom's journal, the claim letter, any correspondence with Richard—"

"Sure, take a look at it." Jack looked at her. "What, you're gonna do this now? It's late. You have to be exhausted."

"It's amazing what a double espresso at six p.m. can do."

Jack ran fingers through his hair. "Go home, look at it tomorrow."

"I have no time tomorrow. Bob's with the babysitter for another couple of hours tonight. I'm going to find out why Wu did this. I thought solving murders was all forensics and police procedure, Jack, but this is about why. This is about motive."

He leaned over and rubbed her jeans-covered knee, an unexpected gesture that felt natural. He got up from his chair with a peculiar look on his face and put out his hands and took hers and drew her up so they were standing facing each other. His arms went around her and he gave her a long, tight hug. "Sorry about everything, honey," he said.

She took a huge breath and let it go, relaxing her body for the first time since her mother's death. What a relief, being hugged like this. She could feel his warm core, as if a little sun burned in there.

He released her.

"Thanks," she said. "You know I have a crush on you."

"This isn't about a crush. It's about you being too lonely, with too many cares right now. Please go home."

"Will you come home with me tonight? Stay?" Nina cursed the smallness of her voice, how fragile she sounded. She heard that midnight-dreamy flaw rising up in her, the one that fell back on men, back on sex, for comfort. But there he stood, so male, so stable, so damned attractive. She imagined herself inhaling him, taking him in. She imagined herself taken care of.

"Oh, Nina—"

"You asked what I needed." She heard how she sounded, husky, shaky, even lustful.

He looked at her for what seemed like a long time. "I can arrange a potluck, a babysitter, a driver. But, honey, I'm not over Remy."

She hit the chair behind her, on wheels, which skidded across the floor as she walked away.

In her office across the hall, she got her computer going, then slammed the keys until she heard the door closing behind Jack.

She indulged herself in naming him awful things, the least of which were idiot and dork.

Later, she was alone in the Pohlmann office. She went back to Astrid's file cabinet in the reception area, turned on all the lights, and hunted for the file.

CHAPTER
41

NINA DID NOT FIND THE VIRGINIA REILLY FILE among Remy's files, which were admirably thin, like Remy. As she had said she would, Remy had pared things down to the basics. Nina also found nothing about the case in Astrid's main file system, and by then she had two paper cuts, both painful.

Okay, they had closed the file. That meant she had to go up to the attic.

Up there, thick, dusty, decrepit dead files reposed. To access them, you had to lower a stairway, climb through a trapdoor, and not be severely allergic to dust mites.

Nina took a flashlight along, although, as she remembered, a single lightbulb dangled up there, illuminating the files almost no one ever touched. You had to keep them forever, as the rules of the state Bar regarding the number of years they had to be maintained seemed to change every year.

The ladder staircase came down creakily and seemed sturdy enough.

She had just made herself into a complete fool, even though Jack would forgive her. She loathed herself, not for wanting him, but for coming out with it and getting shot down. She did not have a hard shell. No, she had a thin one, sensitive to touch, easy to break.

Damn!

So she said, then stepped onto the rough floorboards of the attic.

Although the space below always seemed crowded, the attic stretched unimpeded throughout the whole building, with shelves stuffed with yellow folders that seemed to take all the air out of the place. The low ceiling added to her discomfort. Many boxes full of files were directly in front of her, set on the floor by someone reaching up from the staircase who hadn't bothered to take a step up there. Loose files were piled on top of the file cases.

Who puts this stuff up here? The perp was probably Astrid, solid-seeming, on board. Maybe this represented the place where Astrid played out her small resentments, filing *A*'s beside *D*'s without apparent reason, or maybe she planted files from the seventies close by those of the eighties. Maybe Astrid enjoyed imagining the descendants of the current staff flummoxed, because who wouldn't be, given this chaos.

Nina dug in, grim.

No file, at least she couldn't find it under all the

obvious initial letters. She sneezed and decided to pack it in.

At the top of the staircase, she hesitated. She heard something. A creaking, rattling, as in a horror movie—something there behind her—

She stopped breathing. Before she had time to assimilate that somebody else was in the attic, she found herself falling, falling—

She landed hard at the bottom of the staircase, confused. She looked up and saw nothing, no one. Blood trickled down one corner of her head. She looked at it on her hand, bright red, nasty.

Like a white cloud over a black night sky, a shadow shifted above her.

Dazed, not thinking, she grabbed the rope that pulled up the staircase and pulled hard. Up it went. Bang! It closed up in the ceiling.

She ran.

Holding a hand over the bleeding place on her head, she ran out the front door, found her way down the bumpy cement steps, and stumbled toward the gas station on the corner.

In a pocket, she found money. She inserted coins into a telephone, dialing 911.

"Spell your name and give me your location," the dispatcher told her.

A patrol car arrived within three minutes. Nina talked rapidly as she led two patrol officers back to the office, letting them in. They insisted she wait outside.

Using the same pay phone she had used to call

emergency, she called Harlan Reilly. "I have a babysitter for only fifteen more minutes."

"Huh?" he said thickly, sounding half-asleep.

"Dad, can you please take care of Bob for me for a few minutes? I won't be long. I need your help." She told him in a few words what had happened.

Red lights on the top of the official vehicles whirled. Sirens blared irritatingly, like a flock of dueling birds. Nina pondered whether the people of Carmel got more attention than the people of Monterey because they were richer, then felt guilty for her suspicion, because she needed the police right that second. She needed them to check out the office and who might still lurk in the attic.

Not too many minutes later, after one of the officers tried to convince her to go the ER and she refused, she got her answer.

"Nobody up there," a guy about her age, late twenties, said.

"I pushed the stairs up. Whoever did this has to be up there!"

"There's a fail-safe mechanism, miss."

"What?"

"Yep. So no one gets locked in the attic. A lever up there. So people won't accidentally get locked in."

"So they got away."

"Not in the building anymore. Yep."

"Mr. Pohlmann doesn't answer his phone."

"We'll go over there and tell him. He's on Peter Pan Road in the Highlands, right?"

After the police cars left and the young policeman

had satisfied himself with her statement, Nina found her car and headed home.

Her head had begun to hurt. Her elbow hurt. Driving home, she felt that now familiar fury. Who?

She turned the radio off, following the familiar foggy highway from Carmel to Pacific Grove. Down there somewhere was the vast, dark ocean, but the mist floated in her headlights and she had to slow down. She was starting to feel the bruise on her hip. Her wrist was sore. At least the bleeding on her forehead had stopped.

She found it difficult not to break down now. Her mind replayed the moment when she had tried to turn and been pushed.

Wu! He was small but strong-looking.

She steeled herself. She had to evaluate a case now with objectivity, seeking facts. Okay, he must have followed her to the office, waited for Jack to leave, sneaked in through the unlocked door, then saw the staircase and heard her rummaging around up there.

Incredible! He had tried to kill her.

She gave in to a moment of self-pity. She had no one to call. Her mother, Matt—she had to stay away from Jack, it wasn't fair to him. She had nobody watching her back.

Her father had probably rolled over and snored himself back to the golf-course dream. But the babysitter wouldn't have left Bob alone.

Pulling up to Aunt Helen's run-down house, the ocean soft in the distance, she saw Harlan's newest red Audi, trim and confidence-inducing.

She didn't have to unlock the door. Angie flung it

open. "Oh, Nina," she murmured warmly, embracing her. "Poor thing."

Nina wanted to shake her off, but an odd thing happened. She felt herself melting into Angie's firm arms. Her heart steadied. Her breathing normalized. Hugs again. Good medicine. She felt Angie's baby bump against her own stomach. She was going to have a sibling. She and Angie would be linked forever.

"Bob's asleep."

"He's—?"

"Fine!" Angie steered her into the living room, which was uncharacteristically lit with candles. A merry fire burned like Christmas in the usually cold hearth.

Angie took Nina's coat. "You okay?" She touched the place on Nina's head that had sprouted a bruise. "Harlan's so worried. He said you sounded really upset."

Nina pushed her hand back gently. "Beat-up. Just need to sit down."

"Okay." Angie stepped into the kitchen. "Ready?"

"Yup," Harlan's voice said.

Moments later, he appeared with a huge bowl full of soup, what he used to call accident soup, a mixture of vegetables and cabbage they all loved, including Ginny.

The small dining table held lit candles and a fresh tablecloth.

"Oh," Nina said, overcome. She picked a seat, suddenly ravenous.

"You sounded so upset, honey," her dad said, ladling soup into a bowl in front of her.

"I'm fine."

"Sure you are. I'm staying tonight, Nina-pinto. Got my favorite pillow all ready on the couch. I'll make breakfast for you and Bob tomorrow."

He put a spoon down next to her bowl. "Don't forget how we handle it in this family. We're resilient. We don't let the bastards get us down and we kick back. The best defense is a good offense."

"That's what you always said."

"And I'm always right." Her dad patted her on the shoulder while she thought about kicking, what that entailed, how to do it, and how glad she was he had come to stay with her tonight.

The next morning at breakfast, he told her what her mother had done. Thirty thousand dollars, Aunt Helen's bequest to Ginny, given to Richard Filsen so that Nina and Bob could live peacefully.

Then she cried, but her dad was there, and Bob was there, like rocks in this stream of change.

CHAPTER
42

NINA SAT AT HER DESK TUNING OUT THE OFFICE din, leafing through the police and autopsy reports on her mother's death. Paul had made her copies at her request, not without a look of disquiet and an attempt to dissuade her. She had a right to see all of this, though, and he knew it.

She had a nasty scrape on her elbow and a headache and a strong desire to do something about that. As soon as she had come in, there had been an emergency meeting in Klaus's office about the intruder in the attic. Everyone but Remy, who had court, was there. Lou said, "Shit, Nina, what were you doing up there?"

"Looking for my mother's legal file. I looked again half an hour ago when I came in. It's not there."

"It was there but now it's not there?"

"No. I never found it. I called Remy at court about

it. She says that's where it should be, since she had closed the matter."

"But then—" Lou turned to Klaus. "We seem to be involved in a double-murder investigation." He pointedly did not look at Nina. He didn't like trouble, and she had brought in a typhoonful of it. "The Filsen shooter could have been the one up there."

"I was followed up there," Nina said. "By a very dangerous person. I think it was Albert Wu, though I can't prove it."

Klaus said, "You must be very careful, Miss Reilly. I am worried about your safety."

Jack said, "Whoever that was, I am going to personally bust their ass into a thousand pieces."

Lou said, "Our premises liability insurance will cover whatever medical expenses you may have, Nina. Even though this happened after hours and had nothing to do with office business."

"I'm fine," Nina said. They all went back to work.

Reading about her own mother's autopsy would not be easy. That no longer mattered. Still, her eyes roaming down the pages, she found herself entering an odd state of mind. She was entering her mother's body. It didn't exactly hurt. She felt horror, but from a distance.

Whether she would sleep tonight, that was the question.

No fingerprints had been found at the scene, on the body, or on her mother's purse. The police had not yet located the car used in the commission of the crime. The description by eyewitnesses had been too vague. These witnesses also failed to identify from NCIC photographs who had pushed her mother.

The medical examiner's report contained details of Mrs. Reilly's breakfast along with a litany of breaks and abrasions and crushings to her body. Her injuries appeared consistent with a fall. But of the injuries, none could be assigned to a push. On the television police shows the detective always found some suspicious bit of information from the autopsy to pursue. Nina found nothing.

Her mother's kidneys had been failing. Nina hadn't known that. Her mother's heart had been affected by her illness, too. Nina wondered how much her mother had known about her illness. Very likely, she had protected Nina and Matt from her darkest worries.

The medical examiner concluded that Virginia Reilly had died of multiple traumas consistent with the fall. She had hit the rock face of the cliff on her way down.

The file held shocking photos, which Nina instantly turned facedown on the desk.

The rest of the report consisted of details, but Nina read every word several times, compelling her mind to take it in.

Flipping through a few stapled pages describing her mother's purse contents, she saw the Pohlmann firm's letterhead on a copy of a letter from Remy dated the Friday before her mother's death. "This confirms our conversation that this office will be unable to pursue the above-entitled matter . . ." Remy had referred Virginia Reilly to three local firms who handled medical-malpractice cases.

A flash of memory: her mother young and healthy. She would stand in the doorway of Nina's room in the morning and sing her awake, making up silly songs. Even a sullen teenager didn't have the heart to yell at her, even on Saturday mornings.

Nina also read the report of Officer Howard Hirsch, a sixteen-year veteran of the California Highway Patrol, reluctantly provided by Paul. A specialist in vehicular accidents, his territory included the Highway 1 stretch around Pfeiffer Park, Nepenthe, and all of Big Sur.

Hirsch told it like a story.

He had received a call at 4:22 from Dispatch on November 26, telling him that a woman had gone over the Bixby Creek Bridge lookout. Upon arrival at the scene, he called for backup and paramedics.

He had observed the body hundreds of feet below on the rocks under cliffs near Bixby Creek Bridge. He couldn't get down immediately. Because the only trail follows Bixby Creek and is miles long, Officer Eli Vogel climbed down with him on a rope belay, which took a long time. They did not request helicopter backup.

They found Virginia Reilly lying facedown between the rocks, curled up, body parts oddly twisted. Nina knew that had to do with her mother's medical condition. Hirsch mentioned blood around the head. He speculated that she had lived for a few moments after the fall, only long enough to change her body position.

Nina put the report down, went into the hall, found the coffee machine, and poured her fifth cup of the day.

Considering the lack of a vehicle parked nearby, along with the 911 call, which certainly suggested that

Virginia Reilly had been pushed, Officer Hirsch had decided to treat the death as suspicious. He called in the Monterey Sheriff's Investigations Division, staked the crime scene, and taped off the overlook up on the cliffs.

He expressed concern that someone else might have gone along for the ride, but further search of the scene yielded no other body. The victim died at low tide and the rocks directly below the cliff were not usually covered by water. He concluded that if the witness was right, and somebody really was there with the victim, he would have had to commit the homicide, get in a car, and drive north toward Carmel or south toward Los Angeles. There was one other route out, the old winding road that led across the Lucia range east and inland right beyond the pullout. Inquiries in a fifty-mile range on these three roads had yielded no new information.

Officer Hirsch felt that it was significant that Nina's mother had been murdered in broad daylight. He wrote, "This individual apparently waited until he or she thought there was no traffic on Highway 1 approaching or leaving the Bixby Creek Bridge, but that's roughly a mile and a half of well-traveled road, and there could have been several eyewitnesses. A risky and public thing to do, this may reveal something about the character of the perpetrator." His comment left Nina wondering. The killer must have been desperate, a gambler. What had her poor mother done that had driven someone to desperation?

The report continued, "As it turned out, the witness's Ferrari vehicle, which was said to be an exceptionally quiet car by another witness, should have been out of eyesight. The witness happened to be looking in his rearview mirror and saw what he described in his statement: two people, one pushing the other backward. A big, white, American car. Nothing else."

The police departments of the towns of Carmel, Monterey, and Big Sur, the County Park Ranger Department, the State Highway Patrol's office, and the district attorney's office had made other efforts to locate the car. They checked with cab, limo, and rental-car companies, but found nothing. None of the victim's friends or family admitted they drove her there. If she hitchhiked, the only other possibility, no one had come forward with information about it.

Nina thought. The car was key. Her mother seemed to have driven down the coast with her killer.

Police interviews with neighbors had yielded nothing. Most had worked all day on Monday. Many had also spent Thanksgiving weekend visiting distant family or just getting away. Uniformly, they expressed their sadness about Virginia Reilly's death but offered no useful information.

Closing the folder, Nina shut her eyes and put her head down on the desk.

At five she went to visit Matt at the rehabilitation facility located near Veteran's Park, a hilly, quiet neighborhood of Monterey. The setting sun shot lines of orange through the sky. The place looked like a large home, set well back, with Monterey pines and grass, windows lit already. But there were bars on the windows and a security check to go through before she could meet with

Matt, who appeared in the new jeans she had bought for him. He looked tired and moved slowly.

She jumped up and gave him a hug, feeling his flimsiness. His bones felt as brittle as a convalescent's. Letting him go, looking into his blue eyes, she hoped he was healing.

His eyes reddened and tears ran down his face. "Stupid, stupid, stupid," he said, hanging his head. "I'm fine. Off everything but the prescriptions. They slow me down. I'm sleeping better." He cried again.

"You'll feel better every day."

"The worst is the first forty-eight hours. They kept me sleeping a lot at the hospital. But the nightmares, Nina—the nightmares—I have to tell you something about Mom."

"I'm here." Nina watched his wringing hands and dreaded what he might say. "Go ahead, Matt."

"I hit her. You know, the time she had to go to the hospital? I did it, not Dad. He covered for me. Some friends—ah, not friends, I don't know what the hell they were—they gave me PCP or maybe something else. I don't really know what they gave me. I was out of my mind, Sis, please believe me. I didn't know what I was doing. Dad came in and took it all in and I just ran out the door, just ran. Dad took Mom to the hospital and talked to the police. He lied. He said he hit Mom."

Nina shook her head. "You're dreaming, little bro. Dad told me so himself. He felt very guilty about it. You're medicated right now. Confused."

"My head's clearer than it has been in a couple of years. I hurt our Mom. Me." He touched his heart.

"Matt Reilly, your loser brother who totally hates himself."

"Mom would have told me—"

"She would never. You would have hated me. She didn't want that, so that whole incident became a secret. Everyone protected you. They didn't want you to know the truth about me."

"But—Dad—he was arrested!"

"I expected the police. They never came. So I took some more drugs and forgot the whole thing on days when I could afford to."

Nina was quiet for a minute. She withdrew her hand from Matt's. Then she said an a whisper, "You're out of control, Matty."

"I'm a crack addict. That's right. I get paranoid, Nina. I don't even remember all that has been going on. I can't believe I kept that job at the liquor store so long. The owner's a recovering addict. Maybe he thought I'd get straight someday. For sure he has covered my ass many times." The hand-wringing escalated, and his eyes dulled and looked haunted.

Nina considered leaving to think things over. Instead, she screwed up her courage. "Matt, did you take Mom down to Big Sur . . . you know . . . the day she died?"

"Oh, please don't think I killed Mom. Please don't think that."

She gulped. "Did you?"

"I hit her once years ago and I can't forget about it. I never would have hurt her again. No. No. No."

"She would have gone with you. You were so

messed up, isn't it possible you just don't remember, or—"

Matt shook his head. "No."

"I'm not trying to make you think anything that isn't true."

"You think I wouldn't remember?" His voice rose. He jumped up and paced around the table. "You want to believe I killed Mom?"

"Sit down!" Nina commanded. She spoke close to Matt's ear. "You don't remember anything about that?"

"No! Jesus! No! I loved her!"

"Okay. Okay."

"You have another visitor, Mr. Reilly," said an attendant, followed closely by Zinnia, who had dressed herself up in dirty white jeans. Her long black hair hadn't been combed in a while, and crawled around her face like spiders.

"How you doing?" she asked Nina, who folded her arms and waited for Matt to speak.

"What are you doing here?" Matt asked.

"I need you to take care of your end. You promised me last week."

"You'll get your money."

"I borrow, too. I owe people. They aren't as nice as I am, do you understand that? Now, from what I understand, you're better fixed than you were."

"What?" Nina said.

"I heard your mom died." Zinnia turned to look at Nina. "Sorry for your trouble."

"Get out of here or I'll have you arrested!" Nina said.

"How you going to do that? You know nothing about me except that I keep your brother happy."

"I'll pay you back when I can," Matt said. "You need to go, Zinny."

"When?" She waved at the flat-white walls. "How long you stuck here for? Because they're going to do more than kick my ass, y'know! They'll hurt me."

"You're a drug dealer. That much I know," Nina said.

"Oh, prove it, paralegal." Zinnia kicked a chair, which scooted across the floor.

"You're my drug dealer," Matt said. "Now she knows for sure. And I'll tell anyone who asks, including a judge."

"What crap. No judge in his right mind will believe an addict. So shut the fuck up and pay me, Matty," Zinnia said, turning her back on them.

"They're teaching you something in those group sessions," Nina said as they watched Zinnia beelining for the exit.

"Nobody gets off the hook. Nobody," Zinnia muttered.

CHAPTER
43

Nina drove Bob to his preschool, clutching him in a warm good-bye hug before he jumped out of the MG. She watched him scamper up the stairs.

She had now lived one-half of a life and had viewed her mother's final half. That made a life in its entirety, fragments strung together really, discontinuous when you stepped back and took a good look. A new life had begun with this small wild animal. She saw herself in him as well as her mother.

She wondered if Matt would ever have children, ever be healthy and happy enough to sustain a serious love relationship.

On the way to her mother's house, she stopped in to buy coffee at the bookstore café. The woman behind the counter greeted her, brought her cup, and left her alone. A neighbor had been browsing the philosophy section nearby. He told her how sorry he was about her mother and offered to help her clear things out of the house. She declined his kind offer but felt cheered.

Leaving the car parked near Lighthouse Road, she walked to her mother's. She wanted to walk. She would fetch the car later when the time came to load it. A soft sea breeze scooted up the street, and the sky had turned a thrilling clarified blue. Like everything else on the Central California coast, the climate in winter was mellowed by the presence of the ocean. The temperature seldom dropped below forty degrees on the Monterey Peninsula, although it could feel colder because of the moisture in the air or wind. She jaywalked easily across a no-longer-busy road, stepping through piles of mildewing leaves at the curb.

Yellow-flowered breakfast dishes still cluttered the sink. She began by washing them.

In the old rolltop desk, her mother had kept orderly files for bills and records. Her mother had told her there was a "small" insurance policy, which lay under the photo. This policy, along with the sale of the cottage, would in fact amount to about $200,000 for each of them after paying a Realtor and taxes.

Nina sat back in the chair. She could quit working and devote her nonschool time to Bob if she wanted to, she thought, staggered. She looked at young Ginny in the photo and said, "Oh, Mom." Then she sat on the couch and thought some more about it. This money would make her life so much easier, but—

Like the tail of a scorpion, this windfall would sting

Matt. Paul, who no doubt had a copy, would wonder if Matt had known about it. Had he mentioned it to Zinnia one weak night? Nina hadn't known the amount and assumed Matt had not. But then there was also the cottage, free and clear and now to be sold. Paul must realize Matt had a financial motive to kill his mother, along with all the other crazy stuff.

Well, Zinnia had a financial motive. Nina didn't even know the girl's last name. She wondered about this person who had invaded their lives, who didn't bother to hide her own desperation.

Harlan's windfall, the disappearance of his spousal support obligation, would also suggest a motive to Paul. For about half a second she entertained the possibility that her father or brother had murdered her mother.

Of course not. But if, Nina said to herself, breathless at the thought, if—that would be the end of me. I would never recover.

Heart as heavy as an anvil, she put the policy into a manila envelope in her bag, which already held her copy of the will. Her mother's will left everything to her and Matt, share and share alike. Very simple, very clear. Not like Professor Cerruti's will case.

She remembered the pretermitted heir discussion in class. Let's see, if a will made no specific mention of a child—meant to protect after-born children—

Wait. Maybe Bob was a pretermitted heir, if Richard had a will and had left him out! She really had to talk to Perry Tompkins, take him out to lunch or something.

A desk-sized appointment book, left over from busier times, lay open on the desk. Marks here and there noted times for doctors, dentists, and lately the lawyers. A note taped to the front indicated that the police had copied this book and had taken last year's.

Nina checked the days right before her mother died, finding only that her mother had refilled a prescription, called several repair places about her car, met with Remy, and noted names of several lawyers she planned to call on Monday, the day she died. Nina flipped back to the page for Matt's birthday, where Ginny had noted the birthday party and drawn a happy face. Nina slammed the book shut.

She located empty boxes in the shed and filled several with papers from the desk, all the old letters and mementos of her and Matt as children. Her mother had never packed them away. She must have taken them out to look at once in a while. Piling picture albums into a box, Nina knew she would not be able to look at them for a long time. Clothes, shoes, and personal items she packed quickly in plastic bags for donation. She kept the pearl earrings for herself and a few rings with real stones.

Matt might like something. An auction agency would be hosting an "estate sale" this weekend to clear out the antique furniture. "All my junk," her mother had called it.

Nina carried the boxes out to the front lawn, walked to her car, drove it to the house, and stuffed it full. With the top down it held rather more than she had expected. She locked the house behind her and took a long look at the rattan chair and flowered cushion dusted with dead leaves and blossoms on the front porch. She would remember the smell of the house for the next half of her life, drifts of baked ham, old papers, sachet, and all the rest.

CHAPTER
44

JACK STOPPED BY THAT EVENING LOADED DOWN WITH food. A disheveled, surprised Nina answered the door. Bob stood silently in the middle of a pile of rough, dirt-encrusted wooden stakes on the living-room rug, his face splotched with anger and distress. Nina had just come upon this scene after putting the vacuum away and just opened her mouth to give Bob some harsh words.

"Hey, little rascal," said Jack. "I've got a bag of stuff in the car I could use some help with." He offered Nina a warm smile, walked the little boy out to the car, and handed him a small plastic bag.

When they got to the kitchen, Jack turned on some music and helped Bob unload and name the items as they came out of the bag. Nina disappeared into the back of the house, but she could still hear the talking in the kitchen. "Mom's pretty mad, huh?" Jack was suggesting mildly.

Bob said in his tiny voice, "I can fix it." It broke her heart and the irritation went out of her.

Nina returned, composed now. She knelt by Bob and touched his shoulder. "I told you to leave those stakes where the builder put them. Remember?" He nodded. "He measured everything very carefully, and now he will have to do it all over again. That takes up his time and costs me money. So you behaved badly, didn't you?" He moved his head, yes, again chewing on the inside of his cheek. Nina stood up and touched his hair. "You are a good boy, Bob, and that's why it surprises me when you misbehave. Will you try harder to listen to what I say?"

Her son released a sigh. "I'll put them back." He grabbed the wood and ran out the front door, slamming the screen with a bang.

Nina winced.

"You have the one-minute scold routine down," remarked Jack, handing Nina a can of beer. "I heard there was a party here and decided to crash."

"I'm so glad to see you." She smiled slightly at him. "I do believe the party just started."

"Bearing up all right? I can't stop worrying about you. No sign of Peeping Toms? No bumps in the night?"

Nina had put on a long, purple sweater that stopped above her thighs, which were covered in black tights. Her brown hair lay in waves on her shoulders, fluffed with a brush and otherwise left to fend for itself.

She shook her head, saw him looking at her, and looked down. "I'm influenced by teenaged babysitters. I love the way they dress."

"You look great," he said. "Always. Wearing what-ever."

Bob came back in, his hands and knees black from his digging. Nina pulled him to her and smoothed his wild dark hair, then took him off for a wash. When she came back, while they were fixing dinner, she told Jack about the insurance policy. "That was a major sur-prise."

"I'm glad for you and Matt. Glad to hear it." Nina saw him bite his lip, deciding not to say any more. She knew he was thinking about Ginny and a motive for murder. If he had said anything further at all, she might have gotten angry. He didn't. Instead he grew a little in her estimation.

Jack wore a black T-shirt with a LED ZEP logo. His arms were as solid as pistons from bench-pressing and freckled all the way down. Nina thought he had wanted to hug her as she let him in, but he was her boss. She was also afraid she might respond too warmly. She ex-perienced a little thrill as he brushed by her.

He had dropped by as if they had a date, or as if he were her brother who came by all the time, or as if—why had he come? To be supportive? Collegiality, friendship, love even, all lay on a spectrum. He proba-bly couldn't explain what he felt right now either. Maybe he had come because *he* was the lonely one.

They ate garlicky scampi that Jack sautéed, but-tered French bread, red lettuce and avocado with home-made salad dressing. They also scarfed down bakery chocolate cake, then she bathed and put the protesting Bob to bed. Nina and Jack finished the beer.

They sat on the rotten porch steps and listened to the white noise of the surf a few blocks away.

Nina picked up a hammer lying on the porch and whacked hard at an invisible nail. The moon rose over the gables of the house next door, and they heard the honking of geese the neighbors kept behind a fence. In the midst of the upheaval and worry, she felt very aware of his comforting physical presence.

Jack had put his arm around her waist as they sat. His fingers now stroked her hip. Nina edged away.

"Jack?"

He looked at her and took a deep breath, smiling as if he were drinking her in.

"Still going to quit law?" she said.

"Why are you going into it?"

"Oh, I figured out that the world runs on law. I still believe that. Law is slow, and sometimes biased, but it's a check on wrongdoing from the White House on down to credit ratings and improper late fees and bad tickets and all the other indignities of daily life. I mean, well, I always felt a little unsafe on this earth, Jack. I knew I'd be on my own a lot from an early age. I wanted to understand the machine and be able to manipulate it to protect myself and my family. This kind of knowledge really is power."

"Ah, all this female empowerment. A few years ago, I might have said, what about a husband? Historically, they have performed some of those—"

"I don't know if I'll ever get married, Jack. My parents' breakup was so bitter it destroyed all the good memories from earlier, everything they built."

"What about Klaus and Elise? They've been together for fortysome years, I believe."

Nina waved a hand. "We don't even know if they're married."

"Were you in love with Filsen?"

"God knows why I picked him. Because he was the brightly colored bird in the next tree? Noisy. Convenient. Attractive."

"What was he like?"

She sighed. "A hypocrite, but I didn't see that. I never heard anyone talk more about honesty who could tell more lies. But, at least in the beginning, I had no idea he was lying. He told me bald-faced stinkers: he wanted everything I wanted, it seemed. I think he lied to himself all day long; that made him believable. I was gullible."

"At what? Twenty-three? You're not supposed to be a hardened cynic at that age. In fact, it's probably better to go through life believing what people tell you."

"I was a hick."

"How'd you get over him?"

Aha, Nina thought, this is definitely about Remy. She thought for a second, then said, "I ran away and stayed up at Tahoe for a few weeks. That's another bad experience I'll spare you from hearing about, but I thought for a short period that I was in love with another man."

"Where's he?"

"Long, long gone."

"Okay."

"Anyway, after my fling with Richard was over, I

found out I was pregnant. I never considered not keeping the baby, and I never considered getting back with Richard, who was seeing other women."

"Isn't it strange," Jack ruminated, "how when you feel close to somebody, you have this pigheaded perception that they feel close to you?"

She smiled. "I came home from work one day and found green leaves on the front path. He had gotten mad because I was late and hacked up all my houseplants. Little green corpses everywhere, I suppose that was the symbology. I wasn't frightened. I'd say I felt liberated. That was it, that and the obligatory dinner date where I officially told him it was time to go our separate ways."

"Did you see him after that?"

"No. Not until he came around that one day. And you know the rest." Jack didn't know the rest, he didn't know that her mother had spent her inheritance on ensuring Richard would stay away. That was none of Jack's business, that was family business.

"What about the custody case?" he was saying.

"I'm taking Perry Tompkins out to the Firehouse Restaurant and getting all that cleared up tomorrow. But—I suppose we'll have some confirmation in the next few days, since the paternity testing has already been done." Again, she didn't mention the possibility that Richard's estate might go to Bob and—it's all too complicated! she cried to herself.

Her face must have looked blasted with misery at that moment. Jack reached over to hug her. She hugged him back. Then, sniffing her neck, he moved toward her mouth for a kiss.

She stood up, pulling away before they connected. "You're still with Remy."

"Not with her. I still have feelings for her, yes. But you are such a sweet sight, Nina, with that porch light behind you, and all that hair shining like a halo." He also stood. "I guess I should go. I told Paul I might stop by on my way down the coast to my place."

She watched him drive away, wiping her wet lips with her hand. Such a good man, Jack. Loyal, honorable, no hypocrite.

Jeez, she really, really liked him.

Paul had moved to a condo in Carmel. The units, most with picture-window views of the Pacific, were two-story town houses with small lawns and flower boxes around the doorways. Paul's held roses of an indeterminate color in the gloom. His outdoor light was out. Jack could hear the distant barking of seals through a cool fog. He knocked, but no one answered. He tried the door, and to his utter surprise, it opened. How unlike Paul.

A familiar smell he couldn't place filled the air. He walked through the dimly lit living room, intending to tap on the bedroom door and let Paul know he was there. Maybe Paul would get up and talk, because Jack felt like talking. He thought he could talk all night—and do some drinking, too—and plan another climb.

At the door of Paul's room he heard a low female moan. Transfixed, all he could think was, if he tiptoed, could he get out without being noticed? The last thing he wanted was to spend the evening chatting up one of Paul's new friends. He tiptoed back toward the door.

Paul must have heard him as he made his way back into the living room, because he was on Jack Doberman-style. "Don't move," he snapped, pointing a police-issue revolver from the hallway before Jack could fade out. It was disconcerting, the way Paul moved so rapidly, held the gun with two hands. Jack wasn't about to move, wasn't about to permit his heart to make a single loud beat.

But then Jack's attention sprang from Paul's palm-tree designer shorts and Paul, who now stood there quietly, gun at his side. The woman who had moaned had run to the door of the bedroom.

Jack looked behind Paul at the pale face and golden hair of Remy, wearing a tan sheet that sure as hell didn't look like her usual streetwear. She opened her mouth as if to speak, but nothing came out. Paul's face had turned sheepish and he was trying to work up a speech, too, but Jack didn't feel like hearing it.

That's right, yeah, he thought as he stumbled back toward the door without a word. That was what he had smelled. Her perfume. Joy, by Jean Patou. His last gift to her.

CHAPTER
45

"COULD I TALK TO YOU ALONE FOR JUST A COUple of minutes, Dad?" Nina had planned to stop by Harlan's office at lunchtime on Thursday, but they told her he would not be in until two. When she arrived at the house, Harlan and Angie were in the middle of a tiff. She heard everything through the front door. Her father bellowed once, Angie replied reasonably, then quiet resumed. Nina gave them a moment and knocked. They came to the door together. Angie, now serene and looking happy, had linked her arm into Harlan's.

They talked for a few minutes, and Angie excused herself.

"You've met your match, Dad," Nina said, entering the house. She located a place on the couch not too thick with pillows and sat down.

"You got that right." Harlan sat down in the well-worn La-Z-Boy she remembered from the house she had grown up in. He had noted her somber manner and seemed a little nervous.

"I need to talk to you about that time Mom got hit and had to go to the hospital."

"Okay, then. All the family secrets coming out I guess."

Nina hated how nice he looked sitting there, how caring. She steeled herself. "Matt says you never touched Mom. He hit her."

Her father frowned. "Matt's a junkie." His big, handsome face wrinkled. He looked too old to be Angie's husband, too old to be Nina's vigorous, fun-loving father.

Nina chose her words carefully, examining his broad face. "You say he lied. Why would he?"

Harlan shifted. His shoulders fell. "Honey, you have a right to the truth."

"I do."

"I came into the kitchen just as Matt hit her. She fell against the stove and got hurt. He hit her, slapped her really. What bad luck it all turned out so bad."

"Why lie to me? Why?"

Her father sighed. "We saw you as the tough one, Nina, the one that would survive all the mistakes we made and come out smelling sweet." He smiled. "And you have, doll. But Matt was born with a chip on his shoulder. He held the opinion that the world owed him everything just for being his handsome, charming self. Your mother encouraged that. Maybe I sabotaged him, too. I don't know.

"Truth is, he was fragile, young when your mother and I started having problems, still at home. So, when this happened, your mother and I felt he needed our protection. We wanted him in treatment, not in jail. Give him a chance to redeem his life, somehow." He brushed dust off the coffee table with his hand. "Do you understand how many regrets parents have? You're a mother now."

Nina got up and stood beside her father. She put a hand on his shoulder, and he put his hand over hers. "I hated you."

"Yeah."

Their eyes met. Hers lowered. "So, I went to see him. He looks better than he has in years. He seems to have come back to us, Dad. He was tearful, too, but it was normal crying—you know? He has been prescribed a medication for a mood disorder, a drug to stabilize his moods. He says at first he was groggy, but his body is adjusting. He also claims they have a great cook there, can you believe it?"

"He hates anything gooey."

"He's so picky. I think they must go heavy on the desserts or the boxed mac and cheese."

"He loves chocolate." Harlan sighed.

"Yep." They sat surrounded by old ghosts.

"Did you ask him—" Harlan tried to form the words to finish his thought, but he couldn't do it.

"He swears he never touched Mom. He would never have hurt her again."

"Do you believe him?"

Nina struggled. "Yes and no. Sometimes, late at

night, I suspect he's been so nuts he might believe her death would be a mercy."

"For that reason only." Harlan nodded sadly.

"Then I wonder, if not Matt, who?"

Harlan was apparently following his own train of thought. He wandered into the kitchen and talked to her over the bar, putting dishes into the dishwasher. "When I left your mother, it wasn't so obvious to me how hard it was going to be on you and Matt. I never cheated on her, never wanted to hurt her. Yes, money made us fight, but that was just a kind of last gasp for our marriage. We would have worked that out eventually. When I left, I was thinking about my own life, how to salvage it. I wasn't in love with her anymore. And then I fell in love with Angie. Life's complicated. I never expected that."

"Well, don't worry about Matt. He's in good hands. They pay attention to him and disregard his mind games."

For a quiet minute, they both thought their separate thoughts.

"Dad? I have to ask."

"I didn't kill anybody, sweetheart," he said, looking right at her.

Angie arrived and planted a hand on Harlan's shoulder. "Am I interrupting?"

"No, I've got to go." Kissing both the women, Harlan grabbed a briefcase and headed out the door.

Angie and Nina looked after him.

"He's impossible," Nina said.

"Oh, no." Angie picked up fingernail polish from

the kitchen table. "He's a fusser. He worries about you, your brother, me, and our baby too much."

"He's happy in this new life. You must be a good influence."

"I am," said Angie matter-of-factly. She daubed pink on her index fingernail. "He does a good job on me, too." Nina watched her apply polish quickly to her left hand, then her right. She wiggled her fingers in the air to dry them. "I feel ugly. So fat."

"Oh, Angie. You're perfect. Pregnancy suits you."

Angie's skin was like a soft peach, smooth as an infant's. She was wearing her hair now in a soft, natural style and had stopped dyeing it. Her dress swelled softly under her breasts, and she kept touching herself, as if to make sure it was really true, there was indeed a baby growing.

"He tries to make me believe that, too." She looked at Nina. "You free for dinner, by any chance? On me? At the Tradewinds? I'd love to chat with you some more."

"That would be nice, sometime. Not tonight."

"Soon, then. I want to run some baby names by you."

Perry Tompkins looked harrowed. Nina was halfway through her iced tea before he appeared at her table at the busy restaurant with its brick walls.

"Oh, hello. Thanks for coming."

"Hello." He sat down opposite her. Just sat. Sober, there wasn't much of a there there. She hadn't seen him except professionally until the recent debacle at the

Hog's Breath bar. She wasn't going to refer to that stupid trick he had pulled if he didn't, and she sincerely hoped he had blacked it out of his mind.

She gave him her full attention. He had attended the Santa Clara School of Law. He didn't inspire gossip at the law dinners because he never attended. He had been too busy keeping Richard's firm going, she supposed, and he had always seemed shy by nature. Today he wore suit pants and a pale blue shirt, no tie. He had the softness of a guy who spends too much time in front of a computer, and a hairline heading north. His eyes snapped with intelligence behind the specs, though. He was not stupid.

They ordered. Perry had begun looking around as if expecting gunmen to burst in with AK-47s.

"I don't have much time," he said. "You can imagine. The clients. The custody case. It's dismissed. Here." He handed her some file-stamped court pleadings.

Nina took the papers. Joy filled her, and sorrow. "Thank you. That was prompt."

"Just clearing the decks."

"What about the DNA results?"

Perry shrugged. "You'll get the results directly from the lab, and I'll toss whatever comes my way."

"Not so fast."

Perry's eyes opened wider, and for the first time he appeared to be paying attention.

"Did Richard leave a will?" Nina raised a hand. "I have a very good reason for asking. My son."

"Your—" The color drained from his face as the full implications of that sank in.

"Exactly," Nina said.

"But—but—Richard has never been legally established to be the father. He never will be, unless—"

"Unless I have reason to make a claim on Richard's estate. As Bob's guardian. Will there be a probate of Richard's estate, Perry?"

"I—I—"

"Was there a will?" The food came, but neither of them picked up a fork. Perry seemed to have sunk deep into himself.

"Okay. Yes. There was. I'm the executor. He left the firm to me, lock, stock, barrel. It was the right thing to do, I had a big hand in building the firm; it's more or less my life. He left all his other possessions to his grandmother, his only other—"

"Did he specifically disinherit Bob?" The question hung there while Perry struggled to take it all in. Nina, too, was making some mental readjustments. She knew how Richard had treated this guy, and she was starting to wonder what Richard's law office might be worth.

"But this is—I never thought—"

"Can't blame you for overlooking this, my friend," Nina said. "Did the will mention Bob?"

"No. Doctrine of the—"

"Pretermitted heir. That old, old saw. Still has life in the courts though. Still happens now and then."

Perry stared at his plate. "The fucking pretermitted heir. What do you know. This is all so fucked up I just feel like—I wish—" He pushed the plate back. "Let me extrapolate. You're going to go after my law firm."

"It isn't yours yet," Nina reminded him. He was

looking away again, having some sort of titanic struggle within himself. She almost felt like apologizing. His oversight, though; he had the same information she had, and he hadn't thought it through as she had.

"Fucking fool," he muttered.

"I beg your pardon?"

"Sorry. I was referring to Richard."

"I'm with you there."

"He fucked up every single thing he touched."

"Right on." She gave in. After all, she had only had a couple of months with Richard. Perry had had years. "Sorry." It was an acknowledgment that they had things in common.

Perry began to weep. "He was a fucking black-mailer. Did his best to fuck up all my hard work, bring it all down. Ah, fucking hell."

"Really? Who was he blackmailing?" Nina asked quickly.

"I have to go now." Perry pushed his chair back and rushed out.

CHAPTER
46

"WHATEVER YOU DO," SAID JACK, TOSSING the *Monterey Herald* on Astrid's desk, "don't fall off that chair." Astrid stood unsteadily on her swivel, attaching sprigs of mistletoe to a chandelier hanging in the office reception area. Nina, observing from a file cabinet nearby, felt cheered by his presence.

Spotting her, he said, "Nina Reilly. Just the woman I need."

She felt a smile, then went on down the hall and into his office. He sat at his desk casting a brief look at his callbacks.

"What's up?" she asked.

"How are you doing?"

"Getting along."

"Matt?"

She thought about the normal responses, how he

was doing fine, making progress, and said, "I'm scared for him. Our dad has agreed to pay for further treatment. We'll put him into a private facility. Full-out rehab." She sighed.

"Good. What else can you do?"

"I don't know, kiss the boo-boo, make him all better?"

"I don't have any siblings. I only have Paul, a former best friend I can't trust. Ha-ha."

"Well, then you know exactly how it is having my brother." They both laughed one of those laughs that didn't extend to their eyes.

Later that afternoon, Astrid and Griffin tried to get Nina involved in preparations for the next evening's Christmas party. They played madrigals on the sound system and played with the decorations while four clients waited, exhibiting varying degrees of impatience.

Nina pled work, closing the door on her office. She knew everyone wanted to cheer her up. She appreciated their effort. Christmas without her mother would not be merry. Songs and decorations, however well-intentioned, could never extinguish her grief. If only she could skip to January.

On the other hand, she was on a new trail. She had been thinking a lot about Perry.

At about 4 p.m., Astrid came into her office to gossip. Nina poured her a cup of coffee.

"I have such a thing for Griffin," Astrid said. "He's

only twenty-five, but what's ten years if you keep in shape like me?"

"Sure." Nina had so much work to finish, and so much prep for her class that night, she didn't have time for this. Still, she appreciated Astrid's effort to keep things normal, so she listened for fifteen minutes while Astrid weighed the relative virtues of her imaginary relationship.

When Astrid finally left, Nina picked up the phone to call her father, then set it down again. She had told Angie about the office Christmas party at lunch. Angie said she would try to convince Harlan they should come, but she couldn't promise he would. "If I don't force him out, he stays home," she had said.

Angie was part of Nina's family now. Nina was almost ready to grow up and accept it.

Jack came in a few minutes later, a little the worse for wear after court. He said, "Guess who I saw over at Muni Court this morning on his way to the sheriff's office?"

"Who?"

"Dr. Albert Wu, that's who. Paul says he's being re-interviewed. They seem to feel they have a lot of circumstantial evidence pointing to him in both of the murders. Some shit is hitting the fan in Paul's office. I think they feel somewhat battered by the newspapers. They'd like to make the arrest. The prosecutor's office hasn't come out and openly criticized their handling of the case, but that's hanging in the wind. I plan to drop by the DA's office this afternoon and talk to them."

"They have proof Wu killed my mother?"

Jack shrugged. "They didn't say that, no. They managed to locate Wu's accountant. She told them about another client who had threatened a lawsuit a few years ago. He's dead now, too. But she swears it was all settled with a big under-the-table payoff from Wu. She insists that Dr. Wu is not capable of that level of violence."

"Maybe it wasn't Wu."

Jack came closer. "Yeah? You have some thoughts?"

"I'm thinking about Perry Tompkins a lot, Jack. He told me Richard was running the firm into the ground with his unsavory practices. Said he was a blackmailer. You don't know him very well, do you? He's not much of a socializer. Jack, he's taking over Richard's law practice."

Jack took a moment to reflect on this.

Nina said, "When I think I was sitting opposite him yesterday, and he might be the person who killed my mother and tried to harm me, I feel very odd, you know, Jack? I'm not afraid of him though. I'm just not."

"Well, now," Jack said. "But Wu's so perfect."

"Do they have hard evidence? Witnesses? Have they linked him to the gun that was found at Filsen's? Or to the white car that drove my mother—"

"They haven't traced the gun or the car. But you used to be able to buy handguns in California at flea markets in Salinas. Anybody can get an unregistered gun. And how many white cars are there in this state? They're still looking. Wu knows how to shoot. Turns out he hunts."

"I called Paul," Nina said. "Told him about Perry. Asked him to find out who Richard was blackmailing."

"Wow. Perry Tompkins? He's, like, hardly alive."

Remy came in for a moment to put some papers on Nina's desk. She looked coolly at the two of them, then gave Nina a stack of paperwork. "If you have any questions about this, call me. Astrid has my number in Hawaii, and of course after that, I'll be back in town."

Jack had moved away from Nina when Remy came in. He stood patiently to one side of Nina's desk.

As he started to leave, Remy tilted her head toward him. "Come see me when you have a second." She picked up a photo on Nina's desk. "How's your little boy getting along?" Nina nodded. Remy examined the picture. "He looks so much like you."

"Thanks, I think."

"Defiant. Jack's told me a few things." Remy smiled and left.

The air flattened. Nina replaced the photograph of her son Remy had left lying on the desk. She wondered if Jack noticed how much quieter the room seemed without Remy in it. She wondered when Jack had told Remy her history. She felt a tiny pain in her heart, which she set aside. This wasn't a question of competition between her and Remy. This was a question about her and Jack. And she would try to trust Jack because Jack was not Richard. Jack was a good guy.

When Jack arrived in Remy's office, she gave him papers on some cases he was taking over for her. Boxes of files were stacked in all four corners in preparation for her move. She talked breathlessly and brushed a tendril of hair out of her face. She would be gone soon. The place would not be the same. Jack suddenly realized she had never seen things between them the way he did, as a relationship with a future.

He was smarting, but resolved to be polite. They were in the office talking business. He would be professional.

"I hear they are moving in on Dr. Wu. I talked to the DA's office this morning. I'm glad they figured out who's responsible," she said, sipping black coffee. "What do you think about all this?"

"I think you have a hell of a nerve looking me in the eye."

Remy had the grace to look away.

"I'm a lot better guy than that cheesy slimebag I used to call my buddy."

"Stop, please. This isn't the—"

"How could you?" Jack said, hearing his voice rise like Joan Crawford's in a forties movie.

"Shut up," Remy hissed. "The clients will hear you."

"Think I care? I don't care. Now there's a truth. I don't care anymore, Remy. We're through."

"No kidding."

Remy hadn't even blinked at his outburst. Jack remembered where he was, took hold of his shrieking heart, and muffled it.

"Any more thoughts about getting out of the business?" Remy was asking calmly.

Did this follow from the preceding conversation? Was she hoping he would leave town? So cold, this thought. Jack didn't answer.

"I know I've said some things in the past that maybe made you feel that I don't entirely—" She stopped. "Let me start again. I think your clients are lucky to get you. I hope you decide to stick it out."

"You're the one bowing out right now."

"Not exactly," she bristled. "As attorneys, we play judge in secret. I'm just coming out of the closet."

"Oh, please."

"In my heart of hearts, I never doubted I would get here. Although back in Chicago, at the DA's office, I did something." Remy paused. "I let a guy go to jail who wasn't guilty. I just let the jury decide even though I was pretty sure he was innocent. He killed himself in jail. His family got him a pardon after his death.

"They let me leave quietly out of respect for all the honest years I put in, I guess. I told them about it when I went up to Sacramento. I just couldn't let the past hang over me like that, nagging me forever. And look what happened. They loved me for my truthfulness. Confession's not good for the soul, it's good for the reputation!"

"You made a judgment call that went sour, so forgive yourself," Jack told her.

"That's a very generous thing for you to say under the circumstances."

Remy colored the air with her mood, swiveling around in her chair, a blur of life. In the past, when Jack ran into an old girlfriend somewhere, he always wondered what in the world had attracted him in the first place, but Remy continued to pull. Her happiness reddened her cheeks. Her thinness—boniness he had called it—made her eyes large and important. They continued to invite him back into her world. How could he not admire the power she wielded?

Remy stopped swiveling in her chair and looked at Jack. "I want to tell you about Paul."

"Totally unnecessary. I already know the snake."

"I asked him to come to Sacramento with me. I was mad at you and he was curious about me, maybe jealous of you."

"I don't want to hear this."

She lifted her hand. "You should know what happened. I don't take it seriously and he certainly doesn't. See, Jack, I don't intend to marry anybody. I like my life the way it is. Nothing I said made you believe it. I guess I thought this would."

"Can I help you plow through any of this stuff?" Jack asked when it was clear she had finished.

Remy grabbed his eyes, then said, "Thanks, but Astrid promised to help me put everything in order before I move. She understands these files better than I do, and Nina's helping. Oh, Jack, before you leave, here's something I want to give you." She handed him a small photograph framed in sleek modern silver. He tucked it into his pocket, still looking at her.

What did you say to a woman you'd loved, fought with, slept with, included for a short while, however incompetently, in your dream? He walked to the doorway with his eyebrows furrowed. "Buy you a hot dog for lunch sometime?" She said yes, then added, laughing, so long as he didn't insist she eat it.

• • •

Dr. Wu's office was locked and the CLOSED sign gave a phone number. Nina called it.

"Hello?"

"This is Nina Reilly," she said.

Silence.

"I'd like to talk with you."

"Sorry, that's impossible."

"Not really, not when it's about blackmail. Richard Filsen blackmailing you, to be specific."

After a moment, Dr. Wu said in a tired voice, "I did not kill your mother. I would like to say that to you."

"I appreciate that statement. But that is not why I called. I need to know how much you paid Mr. Filsen. I don't care why he was blackmailing you."

"And why do you need to know that? Why should I tell you anything? I am about to be arrested for killing two people, and all I ever did was try to help. You have been part of the lynch mob. Why should I talk to you?"

"It might help you. And how can it harm you? Did you make some sort of cash payout to Mr. Filsen?"

"I must again ask, why do you want to know? You aren't asking to help me, I'm sure of that."

"My son is one of Mr. Filsen's heirs."

Wu began to laugh. He had a rich laugh, but it went on a little too long.

"Sure," he said. "Why not? Your son's father extorted twenty thousand dollars from me. In cash."

"Did Mr. Tompkins know about it?"

"Who?"

"His associate. Perry Tompkins."

"I don't know. No one has returned the money to me."

Perry must know about the money, Nina thought, or maybe Richard hid it, or put it in his personal account?

"Thank you, Dr. Wu."

"Do you believe me? That I did not kill your mother? I am not capable of such a thing."

"Do you admit you inserted needles into her fingertips, knowing she was a Raynaud's patient?"

Silence. Nina hung up, thought a moment, called Paul and left a message.

CHAPTER
47

As OFTEN HAPPENED WITH OFFICE HOLIDAY parties, half of the office looked forward to the interruption in the usual drudgery. The other half looked forward to leaving early.

Two weeks before Christmas every ornamental plant and tree in or outside twinkled with tiny golden lights. A pine-bough wreath graced the door. In the garden, small, round tables covered with red cloths were decorated with candlelight and served by a special bar set up outside. Several of the secretaries had stayed straight through dinner. The champagne flowed, the hors d'oeuvres were hot. The conference room, decked with miniature Christmas trees and candelabra, sparkled with Elise's crystal glassware and Bavarian china. A mist had flowed in from the sea, but no one seemed bothered.

Louis liked to network at parties. Nina, in her best

black silk shirt, wearing earrings that mimicked Christmas-tree bulbs, watched him schmoozing the politicians and business bigwigs in hope that some of their business might rub off on him.

But Remy was the star. Everyone wanted to get a last casual visit with the soon-to-be judge. Everyone had this last chance perhaps to cement their relationship before they might feel a need to call upon it for something.

Remy provided a contrast to the group that surrounded her. She wore tight black leggings with high heels and a belted, low-cut, red satin shirt that stopped in the middle of her thighs, with gleaming rubies on her ears. It was a daring outfit, as though she knew those legs would be hidden for the rest of her career under a black robe and wanted this chance to show them off for the last time. All around her, men in gray pinstripes deferred to her and chatted her up.

Nina drank some champagne. She sat in a hard chair, a chair that made other people ignore her, treat her as furniture, not engage her. She didn't feel like being engaged, and the oak made her feel slightly punished, like someone who should not thoroughly enjoy the occasion. Perfect, because she couldn't.

Elise sat beside her husband on a burgundy leather couch in his office holding the world at bay with clouds of smoke she blew to fend off interlopers. Nina watched as Klaus extricated himself from his wife's protection to wander off and join a rowdy group laughing too loud near the fireplace, where he was warmly welcomed. Although the details were not public, everyone knew that he had a bug. Old friends fussed over him, embraced him, reminisced.

Sipping her drink, Nina hoped to leave early. Saying good-bye to Bob that night as he lay in his bed begging for a story had been harder than usual. Lacking the proper spirit, she was determined to low-profile herself through salutations and depart.

She had spoken to Jack and the others, marveled at Remy's getup, and was considering whether she could leave without being missed when the Carmel mayor arrived with four or five cronies. He had no trouble subduing the noise as he recalled past moments in Klaus's heyday, putting his arm around the old man's shoulder and, at the last, encircling Remy in his warm approval.

Jack put a hand on the back of Nina's chair, ignoring the forbidden zone she thought she had established. "Did you see him giving Remy the eye when he came in?" Nina shook her head, drank. "In all the time I've known her, I've never seen her dressed like that. Maybe she thinks now that she's on top she doesn't have to follow the usual rules."

"Admit she looks cute," Nina teased him halfheartedly. She focused on the mayor. "Why is it that politicians turn everything into a speech?" she griped, wanting to go home. Jack steered her over to the food table and helped her from the china serving dishes to slab pâtés, breads, and sweets, all of which went onto a paper plate modeled after popular French hand-painted dishes.

As she ate, she wondered. This was home to him, the dark woods and leather smells mingled with bright talk and laughter. Did he feel the old life here drawing to an end? With Remy leaving and Klaus, at least for the moment, laid low, Jack remained the bulwark. That must bother him. He had always represented one pole, the idealistic and often impractical role. Louis represented another, cold professionalism. Would they ever reproduce that rich nuance of discussion Klaus and Remy took with them? Would this firm ever again feel as full-bodied?

Rick Halpern and Barry Tzanck stood beside Remy now, lifting their glasses in a toast. She had her head low and her mouth in a half smile. She harbored no regrets, that Nina did not doubt, watching Jack's eyes riveting on Remy.

Paul arrived late. He found Jack and Nina and raised his hand to wipe a smear of pâté from her cheek. He said hello briefly, then grabbed Nina for a surprise kiss, whispering, "Merry Christmas," and biting her ear before heading off toward Remy. Nina, who felt as red-hot as the cherry tart she had been nibbling, fought an idiotic impulse to march after him and demand more kissing. "Hnf," she said, noticing belatedly how annoyed Jack appeared.

"And yet you like the guy."

They watched as Paul kissed several women on the cheek, squeezing waists, making his way toward Remy.

"I'm not the only one," Nina said. "Not that I care."

"At the risk of sounding obvious," Jack said, "you have to be careful around Paul. I say that even though I hate the guy."

Nina nodded, feeling Jack's eyes studying her.

• • •

By ten o'clock, people had begun to leave, first the well-wishers who had come for the single contact with Remy or Klaus. They left satisfied. Then the mayor left along with all the judges. A rock band began to play and people started to dance.

Jack wandered off for a drink. Nina stood alone in a corner by the file cabinets, waiting for the editor of the *Carmel Pine Cone,* who had promised some time ago to bring her another drink. She saw Klaus wave a radiant, smiling Remy into his office. He shut the door behind them.

Nina went over to Jack, who seemed to be shouting at Paul. The two men had squared off. She couldn't hear what they were saying. Paul listened while Jack spoke, his thin lips tight. Jack made a point, and she liked the way his hairy wrist and big hand swooped through the air as he advanced his thesis. He was too theoretical, she thought, or maybe she herself had suppressed that impractical quality since Bob was born. Maybe she didn't like others enjoying the luxury. Apparently, Paul didn't either.

"Bullshit," she heard him say. "C'mon, Jack. Let's save this discussion. This is a party."

Away from the band, they picked at the food table while almost everyone else was dancing in the courtyard, these two good-looking men, Jack with his thick, long hair and his brown sweater embroidered in reindeer, and Paul tall and angular as a Bergman actor. Before Nina could respond to the way Paul put his arm around her as she approached, and as she read Jack's reaction and got ready for an explosion between Jack and Paul that would blow the party to smithereens, they all heard Klaus's door open. They turned as a unit and watched his grizzled head appear as he moved into the hallway, looking very sick. Remy was right behind him.

Elise rushed forward. Klaus allowed himself to slump a little on her strong shoulders. "We're going home now," Elise said, steering her husband through the crowd. They moved smoothly through the ranks of partygoers, Elise fending off well-wishers. She and Klaus disappeared into the white Jaguar out on the driveway in front of the office.

Remy also passed them, taking their hands firmly, holding Paul's and Jack's at the same time until Jack pulled his away. "Take care, Jack," she whispered to him. She kissed him. "Don't forget you loved me once. Or even twice." She smiled a wicked smile.

"Good night, Detective van Wagoner," she said to Paul with a wave. He reddened at this casual treatment.

To Nina, she blew a kiss.

Nina said it for the three of them as Remy walked away from them: "It's hitting Klaus hard, Remy's going. He looked like this was the end of the world."

"'A woman from nowhere comes and burns you like wax,'" said Jack, watching Remy leave. "To quote Jeffers."

Paul said, "Got to get back to the station. I'm filling in tonight. The holidays are our busiest season. Merry Christmas, Nina, Jack. I hope a better year is ahead for all of us." His little speech didn't stop the ugly flush that had risen up his neck when Remy left.

"Thanks, Paul," Nina said, grateful that even if Paul was pissed off, he had given her something to look at other than Jack, hangdog, staring after another woman. When Paul left and Jack had some time to recover himself, she said, "I wanted to leave early, and here I am, one of those guests who stays and stays."

"Let's make the most of it. Dance?" They went outside and danced on the cold, moonlit flagstones until the band started to pack up their gear. "I'll get our coats," offered Jack. He left her alone to wonder if he expected to come home with her.

Astrid bumbled over, draped over Griffin. "Hey, Nina," she articulated carefully. "Amazing Nina. You do it all, the mom, the worker, the student. How you doing?"

"Muddling along."

"You're so brave."

"Thanks, Astrid."

"Okay, well," she said, wobbling. "Bye for tonight. Happy hols and all. We do seem to see each other on hols, don't we? Remember Halloween?" Astrid fingered Griffin's ear. "Secretly skilled, I plied my needle and thread for her."

"I do." Nina smiled. "You were typing up that paperwork in a horrible rush but managed to make a four-year-old a very happy pirate—"

And, as if a well had turned upside down on her, Nina suddenly felt drowned. "Astrid, that paperwork you were finishing the day of Bob's party. Where would I find it?"

Astrid shrugged, then gave Griffin a sloppy kiss.

"In the dead files, I guess, up in the attic? Or possibly—I saw some copies of paperwork about your mom when I took the waste can out back yesterday. Just copies, I'm sure," she said, recovering herself just enough to realize how rude she sounded.

Jack returned with their coats. Nina took hers gratefully.

"Can I offer you a ride?"

"Thanks, Jack, not tonight."

He frowned. "Did I say something? Drink too much? Act like an ass?"

"No, no, you're perfect. Now go home." She nudged him with her hip, and to her surprise, he loped off toward his car without protest.

Probably tired, she decided, heading out into the fog.

Planted behind the small office building, behind a latched hatch intended to keep the raccoons at bay, the Dumpster sat, as usual not latched, overstuffed, damp.

Nina decided to make piles: to dump; not to dump without examination; and to definitely save.

A half hour or so later, all the lights went out in the building. Sopping wet but indifferent, she had three huge piles to look at with the small flash she kept on her key ring. An overhang on the back edge of the building left a dry spot where she sat examining any bags that looked promising.

Another half hour passed before she found it.

The letter to Wu. Neatly stuck into a fresh manila folder, creased, dripping, and greasy.

Nina tossed the rest of the bags back into the

Dumpster, then walked quickly to her car, puzzling over the papers. Reading brought it all back in a flood, her mother, her mother's sickness, her mother's pain. She stopped under a streetlight to read again and felt a different rush entirely, this time a rush of apprehension and horror. It was all right there at the top of the letter.

CHAPTER
48

PAUL LEFT THE PARTY EARLY NOT BECAUSE HE HAD to work, but because he found himself holding a drink to his lips, smelling the sweetness of bourbon, touching the icy sweat on the glass. If he drank that, he'd keep on and on and make a complete asshole out of himself among the wrong people.

He climbed into his Jeep, parked just outside in a convenient spot. A ticket flapped like a sick sparrow on the windshield.

So no more climbing with Jack. He would never get over that little scene at the condo. So much for all those years of friendship.

All worth the loss, so long as he had her. He wanted, really wanted, to get drunk and wild and violent and then to go find her. He was more secure about his appeal than just about any other guy he knew, but with her there was no security for anyone. She was an existential abyss; yeah, you could never know anything. The way she acted—aloof, this icy intellectuality—her delicate, slender body—this insanity in bed, this complete abandonment where all kinds of things happened, from sobbing to the heat, heat like only a woman who was so pent-up the explosion was imminent could have—

He called her. He got her machine. He left her a message, asking her—telling her—to call him.

He knew a lively bar on Ocean Avenue. The Enea brothers had once owned it. Who knew who owned the place now. Inside, the lineup at the bar was laughing and loud and having a good time. He had that bourbon after all. Then he had a brandy. Ordered another one. Now he was grinning, too, but it wasn't a happy grin. He wanted to take one of those women away from her partner and lean her against the bar and paw her like a fucking mountain lion. A couple of them were receiving his vibes, too, casting glances, as drunk as he was getting.

He had reached danger territory.

He couldn't stop the thoughts, the blood thrashing in his veins. Wounded by Laura, he had limped from one trap into another. She was bleeding him like a medieval doctor. He wrote her off in his mind; then he resigned himself to being her slave. Would she be home by now?

He went to his car, breathing the night air deeply as if it could pierce the wadding of his mind. The cop part of his mind estimated he was at .16, double the legal alcohol limit. He could lose his job. He took it slow, but not too slow, and concentrated hard through eyes that weren't working quite right.

As he drove along the beach drive toward Remy's place, he went over the apology he would make. He would tell her he was sorry about being such an asshole at the party, because he had been. He had seen her there in the middle of all those men, charged up, empowered by their groveling, and it had made him crazy, a small word for those feelings, that machine-gun fury. Flirts, kisses—regret nothing, eh, Remy?

So many women were like that these days, jealous of their prerogatives, fierce defenders of their independence. It didn't mean they wanted to be alone. What they wanted was to hate the guy afterward. But meantime, they still wanted it, all of it. That was his real fear. He knew her almighty pride—pride or arrogance or insecurity, what did it matter?—might not allow her to forgive him.

Tough. She didn't have to forgive him, she just had to have sex with him. That would not be a problem, if he could get close to her.

It all had begun so casually, with the unexpected invitation to ride along with her to Sacramento, light and free, almost a joke on Jack, but not quite, because his own attraction, the post-Laura emptiness, made him agree. That night, when she whispered a few words and gave him her back, pushing her skirt up over her nakedness—the jungle of her bed and cries in the darkness catapulted him into a new phase, a fierce one, numb to blows and friendship. She wound around him, into him.

Another night, later, walking to his car at dawn, banished from the flurry of white sheets and that smell that made him want to eat her alive, he began to recognize the immensity of his error. Look at the way he had treated his oldest friend like shit over her. How about considering his incipient attraction to Nina? Look at the garble he had made of his cases, due to her distraction. He barely cared about his work anymore. He was the rogue elephant tromping through the forests, destroying small villages without thought.

Over the knowledge that he should not be involved with her, his deepest worry imposed itself: he didn't like the way Remy had said good-bye to him earlier. He knew what she wanted from him—absolute loyalty. She needed to command him, like everyone else. He'd balked.

And now she seemed to be blowing him off. But he was going to bring her back into himself. Cage her. Make her shut up.

One day Remy described to him a time in court when the opposing counsel had bested her on a simple point of law. She would never forget the public humiliation, she told him, emphasizing the word *public*, her eyes like bullets. He had seen her like that again tonight.

He was not invited to her home. He was about to break their tacit rule. Yeah. Fine.

She better be alone.

CHAPTER
49

NINA LEFT THE OFFICE FAST. RUNNING TO HER CAR, she unlocked it with fumbling fingers and flew down the road, questions popping like blood vessels in her brain. The car heat kicked in, but she didn't stop shivering for the few blocks it took to reach Scenic Drive and Remy's house. She parked on the ocean side of the street, deserted at this hour, under a white streetlight that neatly mimicked the moon hovering above.

She knocked. After a long time the porch light came on. The door opened, and Remy stood before her, backlit, wearing white now, a silk nightgown with ruffles and tie and God knew what else, all a mystery to Nina, who wore tank tops and bikini panties to bed. Remy's legs were lean and her knees had just the right bony look. It occurred to Nina, as she greeted Remy and walked into her living room, that a man might be expected. But they seemed to be alone.

"Sit down." Remy's voice was soft. Nina heard her own breath coming out in rough gasps. "Can I get you something?" Now Remy openly studied Nina, languorous hand touching one hip.

"I found my mother's file. You shouldn't have thrown it away. We have rules about that."

Remy looked down at her pink toenails. When she looked up again, Nina saw a face flash she'd never seen before, hard and skeletal, then the old Remy, slightly interested looking, returned. "We have rules, you're right about that. You were hunting for that? Why?"

"Something was wrong."

"You couldn't leave it alone. I know that feeling." Remy was nodding. "So?"

"I want you to get dressed and come with me to talk to Paul."

"About what?"

"About the date on the claim letter."

"What about it?"

"How stupid do you think I am?"

"Oh, I don't think you're stupid. In fact, I should congratulate you. You're a bulldog."

"You're a murderer. You—you killed my mother. Do you—"

"Don't go all emotional on me, please. Let's talk this through. Sit down. Let me explain."

Thrown off by Remy's calm, Nina tried to ignore the acid rising in her mouth. "Astrid typed that letter the day I was making Bob's costume on Halloween, which was past the ninety-day deadline for a claim letter. You committed malpractice. You were in Sacramento when it should have gone out." They stood in Remy's house at the foot of a wide oak stairway, next to glass shelves full of translucent, vividly hued objects. Nina couldn't believe how warm Remy kept her house. She felt circles of sweat pooling under her arms. "It never got sent."

"Richard knew," Nina went on. "Of course he knew it was late, he would have been watching for it, counting down the hours until the ninety-day time limit for a claim letter went by."

Remy said, "I gave it to Astrid in time. That love-crazed fool. I couldn't even fire her ass without drawing attention to myself. She put it at the bottom of her stack and didn't give it to me to sign until it was too late."

"It was your responsibility," Nina said.

Remy gave a little shake of her head. "Precisely."

"You should have shredded the original after you killed Richard and—and—"

"I should have. But Astrid does the shredding. How odd it would look, me working away at the shredding machine behind her desk. I could have gone in after hours, but—made a mistake there. Didn't expect a Dumpster diver. Come on. I'd like to try to make you understand. I know you have—had—a good opinion of me."

Remy paused, her long white arm rummaging in a drawer. Nina had time to wipe her forehead with her fingers, amazed at the effort needed to mount the dark steps her mind was climbing.

"Maybe I should apologize. Would that help?"

"No," Nina said, looking at the nickel-plated Colt

in Remy's hand, then at Remy's face, which glowed like a death mask in a cave, quite elegant if you were a ghoul.

"Just found it and came running over here to tell me to turn myself in? Wanted to give me a chance to be classy about it?"

"Jack knows," Nina said through dry lips.

"Liar, liar, pants on fire," Remy said, smiling. "He's got more experience than you. He wouldn't have let you come here at all. Why didn't your mother listen to me? She wanted a referral to another lawyer, who would certainly spot my error. And then she would have sued me for legal malpractice. I couldn't take that chance, Nina. It would have meant the end to my hopes for a judgeship." She gestured. "Sit down. Listen to me."

"Put the gun down and we'll talk."

"Sit or I'll shoot you now."

Nina sat. Fright hammered a hole in her chest. Remy wanted her dead. She held a gun. She might shoot any second—

Remy looked at her for what seemed like a long time. "You're a woman. You know what it's like. But you grew up here, didn't you, in one of the most desirable, privileged places to live on earth.

"I came from nothing. My parents were both addicts. I took care of them, then I proved myself in law school every day by being more intelligent, more diligent, more competent, more. Now you give me these looks, like I'm nothing all of a sudden? You condescend? You're a single mom, struggling. Oh, everyone thinks you are so special. You're so tough. Well, your ass belongs in the trash heap and I plan to put it there. I am much more important than you, Nina."

Nina started to speak but Remy waved the gun almost playfully, closing one eye, aiming at Nina's head.

"I had some problems in Chicago. I moved here, and for the first time everything that I was working for, everything that I was or ever wanted heaped itself on my plate. Klaus hired me, liked me, even respected me. He was my father. Jack, well I wanted him to want me and he did. And then Paul. Did he ever sleep with you? I loved having him and having Jack. For a while, both of them."

Nina couldn't remove her eyes from the steady white hand holding the gun. Remy would shoot her, probably soon. She tensed, readying herself to make a rush for it. If she got a chance.

The corners of Remy's mouth rose. "Here in California, there was this pretense that women got to play by the same rules as the men, which I bought until I realized that it was the same old same old. So I learned the local moves. I faked my way in. I played and won a few times. I developed a taste for blood sports." Remy laughed a little. "It wasn't just a job. Think what I was accomplishing. This was not your new kitchen stove—this was something for all of us. I never doubted there would be sacrifices. For you, you idiot. Every woman judge is a miracle. I'm not talking about traffic cases either. Superior Court. Then the Court of Appeals. I could go all the way. It's where the power is, Nina." Remy's mood seemed to change and she said almost pleadingly, "I wanted you to strive for it like I have. Forgive me for doing something necessary. Your mother didn't have long."

"Here's what we're going to do," Nina said, trying hard to keep her voice from shaking. "Get you a great criminal-defense lawyer. You had a breakdown, that's what happened."

Remy put a finger to her lips and seemed to be considering this. Then she said in a reasonable tone, "Think like a lawyer, Nina. You know how hard it is to win with an insanity defense. They'd put me in an institution at best. I'd rather die, myself. What use would all my effort be?"

"Let me help you."

"I killed your mother. And you want to help me. Sure. Why did you do this to yourself? Why? I liked you. My God, I'm going to have to figure out how to get rid of you now without implicating myself. How could you set yourself up for this? Damn you!"

When Nina stood up, her mouth open, Remy reached to the lamp table with the hand that was not holding the gun, picked up a copy of *Witkin's California Evidence* and swung it like a sword, cutting edge out, with both hands, into Nina's skull. Nina's eyes closed, and she fell hard against one arm of the chair before reaching the floor. "Besides the built-in disadvantage of being female, besides being so fucking small, you're slow, Nina." The words faded as she crashed. "That's why you would never have made it as a lawyer. You have to think on your feet."

CHAPTER
50

WELL, EITHER NINA DIDN'T LIKE HIM, WHICH
he did not accept, or she had some mysterious
business that didn't involve him, Jack thought,
feeling the effects of an evening of the Sangiovese wine.

After stopping at a bar and visiting with some
people he knew, he decided to buzz by Remy's place on
his way home, hoping not to have to face any more unpleasant surprises in that department. But he needed to
know if Paul's car was outside.

When he pulled up to Remy's gray and burgundy-
trimmed house on Scenic Drive, he spotted Nina's MG
and Remy's Acura, but no lights were on in the front
room. The women must be sitting in the dark. Mysterious. Remy's house had a wall of glass looking over the
ocean, which she covered with blinds at night. Any light
behind them would easily be visible for miles on a clear
night at sea, hence, no light.

What the hell? Remy and Nina having a chat late at night, post-party? He found it hard to picture, but then again, Remy had been Nina's mentor and was leaving. Maybe she had a few more words of wisdom to impart.

He walked up to the door. He knocked. No answer. He walked back toward the side yard, but couldn't get in through the locked gate. He could see clearly enough into the front by bending his head down to peek through the slatted blinds. Nobody inside.

He walked back toward his car, which he had parked on the ocean side of the street. He started to put the key in his locked door, glancing out toward the water at the silver stream of moonlight. He would sit here, he decided, and listen to music. Watching for them both, for Remy, for Nina. But it was late, and the music and rhythmic pounding made him sigh, yawn, and finally slide down into his seat to doze.

Nina woke up propped by the front door. She tried not to moan. Where was Remy? There was no sign of her. The house was quiet. Her legs seemed to be working. She pulled herself quietly to her feet and opened the door. She had to get to her car, go to the police. The churning wind off the ocean cut her to her bones. With the occasional headlights, small pools of gold below the streetlights, and this moon, she would be as visible as any star in a spotlight. Moving uncertainly across a driveway, she stepped slowly, and then started running.

Another hard whack to her head sent her reeling. Remy had swooped out of a dark alley from the home next door. She pushed Nina's face down on the grass, jabbing her knee into Nina's back. She wound her sash around Nina's hands. The moon disappeared behind a flowering cloud. There was a moment of silence between waves when the wind halted. Nina cried out.

"Shut up!" Remy hissed, pressing her knee harder into Nina's back.

"She wouldn't have sued you. She wouldn't have because I wouldn't have let her—bad law. She might not win a legal malpractice case—"

"—if the underlying cause of action was no good," Remy finished. "Don't tell me the law. But she wouldn't have listened to you. She didn't listen to me when I explained. She would have found a lawyer slavering for a crack at me, at my assets and reputation."

A second passed, and another sound came, that of a large vehicle lumbering along the ocean road. "And now we need to shut you up. Don't want to disturb the neighbors." Remy hammered a fist into Nina's back for emphasis.

A truck, moving slowly along the opposite side of the winding road, made its way past the women on the sidewalk. Another car racketed by, and another. Nina, her arms breaking and her mind thick, wondered what they could be doing out at this hour. The moon reappeared. The stark outline of houses and cars in complete relief inspired her to scan the street for a light, for another soul, but it was too late for the locals. They were all sleeping; the crashing of the surf just across the street had drowned out the sounds of her struggle.

At that moment, she thought she spotted Jack's car down the street, but she could see no one in it.

Remy saw her looking that way and said, "They're never really around when you need them, are they?" Her hands held Nina's arms in a steel lock.

"Richard tried to—" Nina repeated.

"Offered to work with me on that. He wanted money and my favors and client referrals and a free ride for the rest of his life. He wanted to own me. Nobody owns me. I did you a favor there." As Remy spoke, she pushed Nina closer to the edge of the sidewalk. Nina saw why. A white limousine sped toward them, barely making the curves. Remy untied the scarf. Nina straightened her arms, throwing her hands down, trying to shake Remy off, but Remy held her. She twisted madly, but Remy did not let go.

Another second and the limo, accelerating into a curve from the far side of the street, hurtled toward them. "Bye-bye," whispered Remy, kicking the back of Nina's knees and shoving her into the street.

Nina jumped into the push and heard with surprise a second later the crash that should have killed her. She cried out as a thousand whips slit through her back. She was down, thrashing through the branches of a tree the limo had destroyed instead, pulling herself up in time to watch the truant limo back up into the street and wobble away without even a wave.

She got up and stood, not very steadily. Still here, she thought. She felt possessed by a massive calm. It was an anger she felt, but so deep it was neither hot nor cold; it was a force, a purpose, not to be denied.

She moved back toward Remy's house, unstoppable. Remy wasn't getting away. Her mother was with her. Nina felt like the Angel of Death.

The door flew open. Remy was holding a pair of jeans. She took a second to review the situation, flattened Nina like a linebacker, and breezed down the beach stairs and onto a slippery, low rock pier that extended into the surf in front of her house.

Nina crossed the street to the hillside, saw Remy on the rocks below, and went there.

She reached the pier, made of riprap that some engineer must have thought would look natural, not much use in high tide. Remy stood on a rock, poised to leap toward the sandy shoreline along the surf. Nina put her hand up to call, she didn't know what, when, without warning, out of the blackness of the ocean a hooded rogue wave broke and rushed across the low pier and knocked Remy down.

For a moment there was only surf. When it receded, Remy was no longer on the pier.

Nina stared dumbfounded at the ocean, which had intervened so unexpectedly. She scanned the waves for a head, anything, but a momentary gloom made it impossible to see. Suddenly, as if in reply to her whispered messages, the moon obliged, coming out from hiding to shine on a rough ocean. There, between pointed stars of small whitecaps, out beyond the rocks, a head bobbed. Remy had been swept—or maybe just jumped—into the water.

"Help! Help!" Nina called out to the deserted night. The surf acted like white noise, covering her cries. She slipped and slid as far out on the pier as she could, to the last barnacles, spotted Remy's head again beyond the first set of breakers, spread her arms like a butterfly, and belly flopped into a wave.

CHAPTER
51

T HE SURF CAUGHT NINA AND SLAMMED HER around. Her heart seemed to have temporarily stopped. There was no pain, just the awesome shock. She knew this cold, had surfed in it, but seldom without a wet suit. Fifty-two degrees on average. Survival time limited. She had five or ten minutes before she would need to save herself.

Her fingers froze into paws, good for dog-paddling and little else. She thrashed through the water. And found the hair.

But it was all she could do to hang on to it. Remy seemed beyond struggling. Her eyes were closed. The ocean dragged at them, the rip current urging them farther out to sea. A wave crashed over them; then the backwash, as it receded, pulled the body in her arms away. Flailing around in the inky pool, tangling with the kelp, Nina made her fingers search. After a moment that seemed like an eternity, she caught hold of sodden clothing, rose to the surface to breathe, and pulled the wet head out of the water for a second.

Remy thrust her arm up, balled her fist, and socked Nina hard. A rolling ten-footer caught and lifted them both. Propelled forward, rolling like a rock downhill, Nina stumbled out onto the beach and began to run up and down looking for Remy. For a long time she saw nothing. Someone was shouting far away.

Nina, the wind flapping her wet shirt, caught sight of Remy three or four hundred feet out. She ran back into the sea, puffs of white clouds against a starry night making it all look lustrous, unreal.

This time, she remembered to dive under the waves, get out past the breakers, where she could float for a moment while she froze to death. She lay on her back, arms and legs cramping. No sign of Remy. Nina was still too close in.

Picking up the same rip, she rode it like a sports car on a smooth road straight out to sea this time. The salt in her wounds felt excruciating, her limbs moving like a broken machine, her eyes stinging.

You're not gonna get away and die, she kept repeating to herself.

Looming before her, she saw Remy's uncanny white face circling around and around out there.

Nina called all her swimming experience into play. She counted her strokes, concentrating on making each one count, moving quickly across the waves with her powerful arms, resting her hurt shoulder when she could, oblivious to her own pain. She swam parallel to the rip now, getting back in control. Reaching a spot in front of Remy, Nina slid through the waves once more toward the hair tangled and glowing in the dark.

In a moment, she had her fingers ensnared in Remy's hair. In her fatigue she pushed Remy underwater for a second. This galvanized the other woman, who came up sputtering and swinging. Nina tried to remember how to knock out drowning people so they could be towed to shore. She had the training, she just couldn't get her thoughts together anymore. She took an awkward poke at Remy's jaw. She connected with nothing and noticed with detachment and shock that Remy was laughing through her frozen mouth.

"Trying to save me?" Remy coughed through the water. She tried to get her hands around Nina's neck, but Nina was stronger and fought her off. "Then we'll go—together."

"No!" Nina spat out water. "Stop! We're both going to die out here!" She tried again to get a tow hold, but Remy was scratching her now, in the face, on the arms, anyplace she could touch. A wave broke over them both, but Nina held on to the drifting white nightie.

Remy put her arm on top of Nina's head and pushed her under with amazing strength. "You first!" Nina swallowed a mouthful of water, then pushed her way up from under the other woman's hand. It was incredibly difficult to exert pressure of any kind when they were practically weightless. She pulled herself up by grabbing Remy's shoulders, climbing her.

Remy sank, and when she bobbed up again, her

face twisted with wrath. Treading water in a moment of sudden calm, the two exhausted women faced each other. "Give up?" Remy taunted, and the skull reappeared in her face, stark bone above lips frozen into a grin. She vomited out a spurt of water, hurled her long arms out toward Nina, but too late. Nina was faster in the water, more assured than on land. She swam swiftly out of reach.

When she turned around, Remy was gone. Nina swam in a frenzied line back and forth along the shore searching.

Nothing. Dark water pulling her down. She was so tired. Easier to let go.

CHAPTER
52

NINA FELT STRONG ARMS PULLING HER IN. SHE muttered and kicked at them. "Remy's out there. I won't go in without her, goddamn it. She's not allowed to die—"

Jack was fresh and strong. He caught her up and pulled her to the shore.

Pulling her arms up and turning her on her side, he tried to make her comfortable for the next few seconds while she coughed and spit up water. He grabbed his jacket where he had left it on the sand and covered her with it. Nina was starting to black out and barely felt Jack yanking at seaweed tangled in her hair. Cursing, he let go and stood up.

"Remy!" he shouted toward the ocean, his voice a piteously small squawk in the roar of wind and surf. He walked to the edge of the water, waded in until the water was waist deep, calling again in all directions, but no head appeared, no hand. The waves continued to crash and the sky continued its glorious light show.

Nina was sitting up, rigid with shock. Her eyes too scanned the horizon. When Jack tried to help her off the beach, she shouted and raged incoherently. He pulled her up the stairs to the road. Stuffing her into the backseat of his car, he found a beach blanket in his trunk and tucked it around her. A hand was beating on the window.

He rolled his window down. "Jesus, Paul. Remy's still out there somewhere! Do something!" Paul took one look at Nina, nodded, and ran to the beach.

Jack turned on the heater in his car and began to drive toward the hospital.

"Jack, take me home," Nina said. She sat up and grabbed him by the hair, repeating, "Take . . . me home," through clenched teeth.

"I'll take you to my place, honey, it's closer, and we'll figure it out from there," she heard him say, and then she lapsed into shivering that reminded her of childbirth, a natural force completely beyond her.

Five minutes later they arrived in the Highlands. In the dark backseat, her head lolling against the upholstery, her face puffed purple, Nina looked like a drowning victim. Jack didn't want to wake her up. He debated again turning toward the hospital. She hadn't been unconscious in the water, but he knew she was in danger. He tried to pick her up, but she cried out in some pain, so he half woke her. Then he saw the welts on her body, the fresh blood in her hair, the wounds that seeped. They lumbered up the porch steps. Wet, cold, and curs-

ing, he said, "Where are the goddamned keys!" He located them in the planter.

Once inside the empty cabin, he wrapped Nina in a
dry blanket while he called the Coast Guard rescue
number, then turned up the thermostat and lit a fire. He
put a kettle on the stove to heat. Nina was lying on the
couch with a sleeping bag over her, shivering violently,
and Jack remembered reading that shivering was a good
sign. He woke Nina again nevertheless to satisfy himself that she was still alive and marched her into his bedroom. Her clothes seemed soldered to her body. He
peeled as much away as he could, lifting first her legs off
the bed to pull off the pants, then supporting her back
with one arm, tugging at the shirt. "What the hell's happened here?" he mumbled as he worked on her. The
seaweed had dried in her hair. He left it.

Tucking her under a thick comforter, piling a few
extra blankets on top for good measure, he put in a call
to his own doctor, whose service assured him he would
call back right away. "Emergency. Urgent," he told
them, trying to find the right words. "Life-and-death."
He stripped off his own wet clothes and pulled on his
sweats, shivering quite a bit himself, though he wasn't
feeling cold. Adrenaline still surged through him.

He brewed some tea. When he returned to the bedroom, he found her standing beside the bed, rummaging in a dresser drawer. "Get back in that bed," he
commanded. "Either you stay right here or I shackle
you to the bed."

Her teeth chattered uncontrollably. "Don't leave,
Jack. Don't leave yet."

He held her head against his sweatshirt until she was quieter. "Can you talk? What happened?"

"She tried to kill me." Nina sputtered out a few more words.

"Because she missed a deadline? A stupid, shitty mistake she made? She killed two people and attacked you? No, no."

"Yes." Nina closed her eyes.

Paul arrived a few minutes later. "The Coast Guard told me you called from here." He wanted to see Nina. When he saw her sound asleep on the bed sprinkled with sand and seaweed, face puffy with bruises and cuts, he yanked Jack out of the room.

"We couldn't find Remy. The rescue boats arrived with searchlights." Paul spoke like a man without feeling, but his hands were shaking too much to hold his cup. He put it down. Jack watched his old friend's face crumble. "We got there too late."

"Listen, Paul. Nina just told me the most incredible story—"

When Jack's doctor showed up, Jack left Paul in the living room, his head in his hands.

The doctor woke Nina. Plucking her eyelids, probing with tiny lights and forcing her to answer questions to which she replied dully, he said, "You should have taken her straight to the hospital."

He explained that she was in shock with a dangerously low body temperature. She needed fluids intravenously. She needed to be warmed slowly, in a place where they were equipped to deal with hypothermia.

Would she die without that treatment? Jack asked. The doctor, exasperated, said, "Maybe." So they waited for an ambulance.

The paramedics lifted Nina expertly onto the gurney and wheeled her out. She stopped them, motioning to Jack and Paul, saying so softly, as if talking to herself, that they leaned in to hear, "Richard tried to blackmail her. He's the only other person who saw the paperwork except Astrid—she doesn't read what she types." Nina clutched at Jack.

"Ninety days. She missed the deadline."

CHAPTER
53

REMY HID UNDERWATER FOR AS LONG AS JACK AND Nina were still in sight, coming up quickly just to gulp breaths of air. When they finally left the beach, she crawled out of the water, creeping up the edge of the beach in case anyone was watching. But she found herself bloated with salt water and colder than she had ever been, sluggish, shivering uncontrollably, and knew she was very ill.

She lay for quite a while on the hillside behind a small pine tree trying to gather her strength, but the rest seemed to have the opposite effect, leaving her enervated, barely able to move. The cold air swirled around her as she shook out of control on the rocks for a long time, then made her way up the hill to the street. She wished she had time to change her clothes, but she couldn't take the risk. She had to leave right now. This was a time for intense self-discipline. She spotted Paul's car parked by her house, but he was down on the beach, she could see him like a moving pin dot.

Her keys were gone, lost in that wild battle with Nina. She was exhausted and slow, searching underneath her car for the extra key. She hadn't had time to throw her suitcase in before Nina surprised her, but she always kept a day bag with spare clothes in the trunk, and cash and a credit card in her glove compartment.

Her body shook so she could hardly stand. With great difficulty she opened her car door. Once inside, she took her time pulling out onto the street, not wanting to draw attention to herself from the beach below. Some people down there were looking for her body. She would have laughed if she could, but she was concentrating on her clumsy fingers, trying to steer.

Flipping a lever, feeling the blast of cold air, she remembered that the heater had broken again. Another challenge to surmount, that was all. Confidence was everything. If she wasn't so numb, so clumsy, so slow— the police weren't even following her yet. She thought she had at least an hour to get somewhere before an all-points went out on her car. Monterey Airport wasn't likely to have flights out at this hour; anyway it was too small, much too dangerous. San Francisco would be better, more anonymous, but that might mean another hour on the road and she didn't think she had that kind of time.

She settled on San Jose International Airport, turning onto Highway 68 east, watching nervously for cruisers. None appeared.

The shaking had slowed into occasional wracking spasms, and she felt sleepy. She couldn't afford to stop and find something dry to put on. She willed herself to stay awake, turning on the radio, listening for news. Nobody mentioned her. After she got onto Highway 101, she headed north, driving easily up the hills, past the Red Barn flea market, like a movie set in the night. She had stopped feeling cold at all now, but her hands kept slipping off the wheel and her eyes weren't focusing well on the speedometer.

Mustn't get pulled over for speeding—as the car mounted the last hill before the descent into Gilroy, it choked once and went dead. The stupid thing was out of fucking gas.

She pulled to the side of the road. Before she had time to think what to do, she saw the Highway Patrol cruiser in her rearview mirror. She leaped from the car, taking just enough time to slam the door behind her. She ran, cutting her bare feet on rocks, until she found cover behind a stand of eucalyptus trees. The patrol car pulled up behind her car and parked.

She watched from far away as the officer called in her license number. She heard him talking on his car phone, reading it out loud, waiting for them to tell him he should find her. She dragged herself as far as she could up the hillside toward the piles of granite that would hide her better. Finding a dark hole between two icy boulders, she crawled inside, wishing for the first time not to be so thin, so dangerously numb.

"I'm afraid," she thought, experiencing the darkness around her, the small alien noises of the night. She wasn't shivering at all anymore, though she seemed to feel a distant aching all over.

She looked up. No stars, clouds over her eyes. She was not the type to give up. She would hide until the policeman left and make a new start. She was good at that. She tried to lean forward to see around the rocks to the road below, but discovered she couldn't. She commanded and her body refused. With amazement she recognized that she would not be able to leave this hole, that her only hope was to call for help. Her mind, now loose, slow, failed her. It began knitting colorful webs around pictures of her life in Chicago and California.

She played with the pictures, amused herself with changing the colors and images, thought once of Klaus—something nice for the old man—stopped fighting.

And let the sleepy cold and dark carry her home.

EPILOGUE

Three weeks later

AFTER WIPING PEANUT BUTTER FROM HANDS that had amused themselves all the way from preschool smearing the inside window of her car, Nina extricated Bob from his car seat. He had had even more fun making this process as difficult as possible, holding his arms tightly against his chest, laughing, refusing to budge once she had him unshackled. Finally, firmly, she picked him up and set him down. He ran screaming around the front lawn. She loaded his backpack onto her shoulder. Dragging herself to the mailbox, she collected envelopes.

Matt stood on the porch, watching, then took pity on her. "At least it's Friday," he said, removing the backpack slung on her other shoulder. Inside Aunt Helen's cottage, a fire crackled. Matt's boots dried on the hearth, stinking like cabbage. His college-application notes lay piled on the coffee table and he hadn't got to the dishes.

Nina felt as warm as the orange logs in the hearth at these sights of normal life. She hung Bob's pack on a peg by the door after peeking inside to make sure nothing would rot there overnight.

Matt was back with Bob and her, clean and detoxed, helping as much as he could. She smiled at him and collapsed onto the couch.

"What can I get you?" Matt asked.

"White wine, a half bottle in the fridge. Majorly large serving."

"You're not nervous I'll suck it down and substitute lemon-flavored water?" Matt asked from the kitchen.

She heard liquid glugging into a glass. "Should I be?"

He sighed. "Call me responsible. Yes, I'm reliable."

She leaned back, closing her eyes. When she opened them again, her wine awaited, poured into an actual wineglass. She sat up and took a sip. Matt knelt by the hearth, poking at the logs, adding to them, apparently hoping to create a raging bonfire in Aunt Helen's big old fireplace.

Her face flushing in the heat, Nina stretched. She used a fingernail to peel open the mail. She slit open the phone bill, the utilities bill, the newspaper bill, the water bill, and made a neat stack to be dealt with when she felt financially sturdy some fine future day. Eventually, after discarding the junk onto the floor, which

Matt confiscated for the bonfire he was nursing, she came upon a white envelope addressed in Jack's handwriting.

She opened it. Inside, on a kiddie valentine, a boy in overalls presented a girl in a pink dress with a flower. "To my funny valentine, Nina," Jack wrote. "Love forever from your Jack."

He was in San Francisco this week, interviewing with some firms for a job.

"Why, Jack?" she had asked him when he'd first broached the subject of leaving the firm. "I thought you loved it here. I never pictured you leaving."

"Lots of people to help, Nina, even in the city. It's a great opportunity. I feel obligated."

"Dreamer."

"And you love that about me. Come along for the ride?"

"You know I can't."

"Not yet?" he had asked, hopeful.

She remembered smiling.

She closed the note. Her mother's problems, Remy, all this turmoil, all had conspired to bring her to her own career decision. She had decided to go into criminal law. Like Jack, she felt obligated.

She flipped open another envelope. "Uh-oh."

Matt looked up.

"Paperwork from the County of Monterey." Nina held up a thin sheet against the fire, as if she could see through the paper. "It's the DNA test results." Matt came over to stand beside her while she read the contents of the notification and read them again. "What the—oh, no. Someone screwed up big-time. This is impossible."

"Let me have that." Matt took the paper from her hand.

Nina rubbed her mouth, then grabbed her glass, downing its contents in a couple of gulps. She coughed, then jumped up and paced the room.

"Don't you worry, Nina. There's an explanation."

"This is impossible," she repeated.

"Or—now don't jump on me, Nina. Is this impossible? Maybe you made a mistake?"

She leaned into the fire, watched it flick, felt her heart flickering. "Oh, my God."

"Ah," Matt said. "You are human. Just as I suspected."

A laugh rose and grew inside Nina until she could no longer contain it. She felt tears, relief, fear for the future. Holding her stomach, she asked, "Where's Bob?"

"Comfy in his room, playing his keyboard."

"Ha-ha—Matt—oh, oh—"

"What? What, Nina?"

"Richard's not Bob's father!"

"So they say. But—"

"Oh, I just can't—this is too much—"

"The tests are right, aren't they, Nina? It's not impossible at all. Bob doesn't have any Filsen DNA in him, does he?"

"So it—ha-ha—seems!"

"So who is Bob's father?"

"I'm so happy it's not Richard! I never saw him in

Bob, but I thought that was because—oh, this sounds terrible, but it is absolutely true. I never wanted to see him in my son."

"Nina—" Matt paused. "Do you now know for sure who Bob's father is?"

She slapped his arm. "Of course I know."

"Hey, I'm just asking."

"I can't think about what this means right now! I can only celebrate. Isn't that awful?"

"You're evading."

"No. I just have to think."

Matt stirred the fire. "Okay, so now what?"

"No idea." Nina tossed down a handful of peanuts from a bowl. "Excuse me, Matt. I'm going to have a shower, then hug Bob till he screams for mercy. Then I am going into my room to laugh. And cry. Then I'll be really hungry for dinner."

"I'm making quiche, okay?" Matt said.

"You know how to make quiche?"

"Well, as a way to cope with the shakes and the shivers and the sweats, we had various life lessons. This one took. I mean, it's not so hard: frozen crust, eggs, milk, and whatever the heck else spices you can find."

"You found actual useful food in my fridge?"

"Leftover sausage. Leftover chicken. Leftover spinach. Chunks of cheddar and Havarti cheese. I bet you throw this stuff out, mostly."

"Yeah."

"Well, not tonight." Matt moved toward the kitchen, then stopped in the doorway, silhouetted, still heartbreakingly young and so vulnerable. "I'm feeling pretty good. Guess what. I met someone."

Nina thought about what that might mean. "Another recovering addict?"

"No. She's a social worker named Andrea. Funny, huh? I think I'm in love."

She hugged him. "I'm so glad for you."

Moving into the hallway, Nina listened to Bob's dissonant music. She heard Matt clanking around in the kitchen, finding lids, chopping on the wooden board. In the backyard, the sun turned vague as the evening fog drifted in.

Her mother's favorite chair sat out on the front porch, rocking slightly in the coastal wind. Nina gave herself a minute to sit out there on the porch step, feel the coolness, remembering. Early budding crocuses reminded her that spring was not so far away. Winter in California could end in a blink.

Spring, season of new starts.

Jack came up the walk.

Her heart lurched, watching him approach. She wanted to be in love, but she could settle for this good, warm man for now. Didn't she deserve that much?

But she had made mistakes. Shouldn't she avoid mistakes?

She doubted that she could. As her mother had said numerous times when she was young, before she got sick, and as Nina herself had repeated in her mind, if it's not terrifying, it's no fun.

Jack took her in his arms, and they watched together as the sun set in a riot of rose over the Pacific.

Matt, with a delicacy she didn't know he had, left with Bob as soon as they all finished eating.

Still holding each other, Nina and Jack staggered off together to her soft bed, the one she cried in and loved in and one day many years from now would probably die in.

ACKNOWLEDGMENTS

OUR GRATEFUL THANKS TO THE PEOPLE AT Pocket Books/Simon and Schuster who worked with us on this book: Louise Burke, our dedicated publisher; Carolyn Reidy, CEO and advisor; Dahlia Adler; Steve Boldt, meticulous copy editor; Lisa Litwack, art director in charge of the smashing jacket art, and above all, Maggie Crawford, who edited the manuscript with an unerring eye.

At Lowenstein-Yost Associates Inc., we want to thank Nancy Yost, as always, a powerhouse and rock all in one; her indispensible assistant, Natanya Wheeler; and Zoe Fishman, their foreign rights associate, who has been a vocal supporter.

Nita Piper, our dedicated assistant, has helped us with the business side and been a great friend, too.

Andrew Fuller, Steve Parker, and Joseph Ferguson all made valuable suggestions that helped the manuscript, as well as offered encouragement that was much appreciated.

Mary would like further to acknowledge the following people: Brad Snedecor, Doyle Maness, Bill and Ruth Dawson, Pat Spindt, and Jim Nicholas, for their unfailing humor, suggestions, and support; Pell Osborn and Joanna Tamer, who read the book way back when, and took it seriously.

Pam would also like to express appreciation to Michael Fuller, Bruce Engelhardt, Caroleena Epstein, Cindy Chen, Elizabeth Vieira Pittenger, Harry Berger, the folks at Poetry Santa Cruz, and her friends and colleagues at tcp.com, who have been so generous with their time and talent.

And a tip of the hat to Kanani Cherry, who kindly made a charitable donation in order to have her name in our book.

Pocket Books proudly presents

DREAMS OF THE DEAD

Perri O'Shaughnessy

Coming soon in hardcover
from Pocket Books

Please turn the page for
a preview of Perri O'Shaughnessy's
thrilling new Nina Reilly novel . . .

PROLOGUE

AFTER I TAPE UP HER MOUTH AND DRAG HER toward the car, I wonder what she'll be thinking soon, dying in the grave I've prepared for her.

She struggles hard. I have to hit her again, which makes her bleed and makes me angry. I stuff her into the trunk of her rental car. In spite of her injuries, she continues to fight me. I can hear her trying to speak, although what comes out is as potent as the murmur of a drowning kitten.

Closing the lid on her wide, screaming eyes, I indulge in the worry that has kept me awake countless nights. I wonder what the dead dream.

I find the keys on the passenger side of the car. She left them in her bag, readily accessible, along with tissues, a small flashlight, lipsticks. I insert the car key into the ignition, and the white, innocuous rental car that looks like a thousand other rental cars starts up eagerly.

I drive the speed limit in town. A few cops patrol now and then, with not much to do in this prosperous town except to nab out-of-town speeders.

Not more than a mile from the middle of town, I turn toward the steepest pass in Tahoe. Once I drove it in snow without chains and almost died. You drive straight into a whiteness as definite as death, hoping that vague gray stripe in the road ahead of you will lead somewhere safe. You skid, you correct, you recognize a higher power.

Death.

I hear her beating her feet—fists? against the car. There's nobody else around to hear. A weeknight in Tahoe, early spring, easy definition: black, empty. On this highway, a few cars straggle back toward Reno after a day of skiing, rude, in a hurry. They are familiar with this road and don't take kindly to strangers.

This night in early April, the stars hide behind cloud cover. The lake, a distant huge presence, behemoth and ancient, swishes in the distance, alongside the road here and there as I drive her to the spot I picked, not so very far away, up Mount Rose Highway, near but not one of the usual tourist haunts.

I don't go all the way up to the meadow. I stop at the turnout that shows the lake at its most beautiful, sprawled out, reflecting mercury-colored clouds.

On a typical day or evening, people come off the road here to take pictures of one of the world's most spectacular sites. At night, when the moon's full, they get their miniature cameras out and try to capture the whole thing in a click, a scene primordial in its effect and beyond capturing. The lake spreads like miasma; the stars shoot their light from millions of miles; the moon lords over it all, illuminating the landscape below like an ancient gaslight, only one that covers hundreds of miles.

I make sure nobody else is parked in this pullout. I wait for several minutes to see if anyone's tempted.

They are not. Fifteen minutes go by and not a single car stops.

I get out and open the trunk. She stares up at me. Her eyes are now almost entirely red.

She's heavier than she looks, but her grave is not far away.

I drag her through the mucky mud of spring, past stands of fir, down a slippery slope to the grave site. She protests, but the tape keeps her voice as small as any tiny animal in the woods. I can hear her, but the world cannot.

I had the hole ready, so the easy thing would be to tip her in without ceremony. However, I feel the moment deserves more. I untie the rope I had used to secure her hands behind her back, and the one that held her ankles together. That one was loose. She had been kicking, not using her hands, I decided, tucking the ropes into my pocket. The empty casket, a heavy oak top-of-the-line, awaits her, hungry.

I pull the tape off her mouth. "If you are as great as you are supposed to be, you won't be here when I return in twenty-four hours, at least, not as you are now, living and breathing. Sane. Soulful. No. That's all about to end. You'll be—what? Have you thought about what you'll be when you die? I think about it."

"Don't fuck with me! I'll get out and then I'll hunt you down! You'll find out what you'll be, you stupid—"

"Make your peace. Your destiny is most likely that you'll die in this grave. You'll die of asphyxiation, starvation, dehydration or exposure. This time of year, early spring, the cold's glacial, slow and inexorable. True, the frozen ground is getting softer. A few brave flowers have shot up, and you're brave, thinking you might live through this. But when you know history, as I do, you know nobody survives being buried alive. It's not possible."

I won't repeat what she said then. Who could blame her for being angry?

"Along with an air hose that will probably only prolong your suffering, I did provide you with some wrappings, just to keep things sporting."

I pull wool blankets that I bought at the charity shop in South Lake Tahoe around her. Untraceable, just in case, but warm for the moment.

I tip her into the casket. She fights me, but I manage to lay her out. I make sure she's tucked in, and check my special touches to make sure they are in place.

"You know, the dead live on for a thousand years, if you count the cells and the organic detritus and miasma from which we all came and all return. You will dream of things for a thousand years."

"I'll dream of you dead!" she said, just before I fasten the lid carefully over the coffin.

I don't have a shovel, so the burial takes a long time.

CHAPTER

1

SANDY WHITEFEATHER WALKED INTO THE INNER office and sat down in one of the orange client chairs wearing her usual expression of firm dignity. Nina, on the phone with a probation officer who was preparing a sentencing report for one of her criminal defense clients, raised her eyebrows, but Sandy's expression did not alter.

The secretary and lone staffer in the Law Offices of Nina Reilly, which consisted solely of the offices of Nina and Sandy, Sandy did not like the client chairs and ordinarily stood at Nina's desk, so either she was tired or some cataclysm was afoot. By eight a.m. Sandy was usually well into her fourth cup of coffee, so she wasn't tired.

"Call you back later. Sorry, gotta go," Nina told the officer and hung up. "So?"

"Scumbags have been sitting in these chairs for four

years now," Sandy observed. She wore a belt with small silver conchas and brown leather-worked cowboy boots under a longish skirt. A member of the Washoe tribe, Sandy had lately gone country-western in her dress, and the appearance of a snorting stallion in the hall to take her home some night would not surprise Nina.

"They do the job." Nina got up, spun one, and tried not to notice the ugly brown stain decorating its back.

"We need new chairs. Comfortable. Leather so they clean easier."

"That's low on the expense list right now," Nina said. She indicated the files and phone messages stacked neatly on her desk. "Today, we work on generating cash, not spending it. As I recall, you told me on Friday that we are low on the accounts receivable front. Not that we shouldn't be, considering that nobody in town seems to have a dime to litigate these days."

"Fine if you like cooties."

Exasperated, Nina said, "We can steam-clean the chair seats. Do we need to have this conversation right now? Is that why you came in? I have stuff to do."

"I saw brown leather chairs at Jay's Furniture down in Reno this weekend. Four hundred apiece, but your clients can rest their heads and they won't have to put their arms on this cold chrome."

"No money for that right now."

"How about if you could make five thousand bucks in ten minutes?"

Nina waited, but Sandy sat, arms crossed, enigmatic. Unable to stand it any longer, Nina asked, "New client?"

"Someone we know. Waiting outside."

"Who?"

"Philip Strong."

"Strong?" Nina felt a nasty stirring in her gut. For two years, she had tried to put that name out of her mind.

"Yep. Jim Strong's father."

"Oh, no. That's all over. What could his father want?"

"I thought it was over, too. Maybe something new?"

"That's impossible. What did he tell you?"

"He's willing to pay a big retainer for whatever problem he has."

"Philip Strong's waiting in our outer office?"

"Just marched in. Says it's urgent."

Nina looked out the window that showed her a sliver of the lake.

"I don't want to see him, Sandy."

"You should."

She heard herself, voice higher-pitched than usual, like a little girl, scared. "I don't want to."

"Listen. You have an appointment with Burglar Boy in twenty minutes. Just hear Philip out and I'll scoot him away when you are done."

"No, Sandy. Send him upstairs to John Dominguez."

Sandy shook her head. "He says he needs to consult with you. You and nobody else."

"Did he tell you why he came here?"

"No details, but I'm thinking it's about the ski resort he owns."

Paradise Ski Resort. Nina remembered the intimate family lodge up there, the roaring fires, handsome people pulling off their rigid boots, scarfing down hot chocolate, beers, and champagne, singing loudly, throwing arms around each other before they eventually ventured out into the night heading for cars, rented condos, or a long night gambling.

Straddling the border between Nevada and California, a neighbor to Heavenly, Paradise had the reputation of being a hidden gem at Lake Tahoe. Those in the know realized the lifts cost less, the lodge had delicious food, and the lines were short, and the runs rivaled world-class Heavenly in their variety.

"I don't know why, but the phrase 'deep pockets' popped up in my mind the minute I saw him," Sandy said. "You should fit him in."

Nina leaned back in her chair. The sharp sunlight of Lake Tahoe in January lanced through the window. Only a few miles to the east in Nevada, down the Sierra massif, a huge desert lay and sent its sun to reign most of the year. Outside in the well-plowed street, Hummers and other giant SUVs tankered by, as though the price of gas had never been close to five bucks a gallon. Nina mentally put up her palm, saying *no, no, no.* "Get rid of him."

"Forget the chairs. Forget next month's rent. You need to control whatever is going on."

"I never want to hear Jim Strong's name again."

Sandy nodded. "Neither does Philip, I'm thinking. Look, he's one of the few people in this town with any money." Sandy scratched at the metal arms of the chair, then leaned forward to see the result of her handiwork. "But more important, it struck me that you need to know what's going on here even if we don't accept him as a client."

Nina grappled with that thought. "Nothing to do with that family will be good for me."

"'Cuz if it's about his son, it's gonna affect you. You might get lassoed into his stuff sideways if you're not careful. At least find out what's going on."

"I don't want to talk to him. Make an excuse and get rid of him. Now."

For the moment defeated, at the outer door Sandy turned once more to Nina, her eyebrow cocked into a final question mark.

"No," Nina said. The door closed, and Nina jumped up and went to the window to look at the old snow walls along the boulevard, dingy and diminished as April approached the Sierra.

Philip's son was named Jim Strong. No one had ever hurt her, hated her, or scared her like he had. The fact that he had been her client made the situation worse a hundred-fold. And there was much more that she hated thinking about, memories she'd obliterated.

In the outer office, loud voices were raised. Nina recalled Philip Strong as a quiet man, and Sandy never raised her voice, so why all the shouting? A crash made her rush to the door.

Sandy had hold of the back of Strong's parka and was pushing him out the door. Strong had grabbed the jambs, preventing her from getting him out, yelling something about not going.

"Sandy, let go! Everybody calm down."

Sandy let go. "He really wants to talk to you." She adjusted her belt and pulled on her skirt. He pulled a hand through his thinning hair. Then they both looked at Nina.

"You want to see me?"

"That's right." Strong righted himself and said, "Sorry, Sandy."

"*Hnf.*" Sandy went to her desk and plopped down to a ringing phone. While she answered it and Philip Strong tucked his shirt back into his pants, Nina took a good look at him.

Dark hair that once curled around the bottom half of his skull had changed to wispy white since she last saw him. He had lost weight in two years. He must be about sixty by now. The hair might have thinned, but the ski tan remained. He wore a red parka and jeans that accentuated his lean legs.

"It's about Paradise," he said.

"Isn't everything, ultimately?" Nina smiled.

"Ha," he said.

She crossed the room and shook his hand. "Philip, thank you for thinking of me, but your family and I have a history, a troubled one. I don't think I'm the right person to help you, no matter what is going on."

"I have news, Nina. It's killing my family. It might well kill you, too." His face held a suffering, blasted look. Nina steeled herself for what he was about to say. She always tried immediately to consider the most catastrophic possibility in any situation, but she couldn't have prepared herself for what came next through his clenched jaw.

"Jim's alive, Nina. My son's alive."

Don't miss these riveting thrillers from Pocket Books!

Joy Fielding

CHARLEY'S WEB

An ambitious South Florida journalist is in a heart-pounding race to save her children and herself from a killer's deadly designs.

Robert K. Tanenbaum

ESCAPE

District Attorney Butch Karp takes on a controversial defense in the courtroom, as a deadly terrorist plot unfolds in the heart of Manhattan.

Robert Ferrigno

SINS OF THE ASSASSIN

Radical forces battle for control of a nuke-ravaged nation…the land once known as America.

Bob Reiss

BLACK MONDAY

A worldwide epidemic—affecting not humans, but oil—causes civilization to descend into chaos.

John Connolly

THE REAPERS

A chain of killings is obscurely linked over a long passage of years, and it is time for the blood debts to be settled.

Available wherever books are sold or at www.simonandschuster.com

20474

Nonstop thrills
from
Pocket Books.

STEPHEN HUNTER
The 47th Samurai

An avenging hero on a quest for blood uncovers
a dark and dangerous underworld—where
breaking the rules could cost him his life.

JONATHAN NASAW
When She Was Bad

Love, madness, and murder merge when a
twisted duo embarks on a killing spree.

MATTHEW REILLY
The Six Sacred Stones

A deadly ancient mystery threatens the earth.
Can a team of heroes solve the puzzle, or will
this mission be their last?

Available wherever books are sold or at
www.simonandschuster.com

19585